Sinner

SHERIDAN ANNE

A DARK SECRET SOCIETY REVERSE HAREM

Sheridan Anne

Sinner: Empire (Book 3)

First Published in 2023

Anne, Sheridan
Sinner: Empire #3

Cover Design: Sheridan Anne
Photographer: Tatyaby
Editing: Fox Proof Editing
Formatting: Sheridan Anne

To bad bitches . . .

Uhhhmmmmm . . . don't really know what to say.

If you think you fit the description then cheers to you!

Also, nice tits!

CHAPTER 1

Cross

The echo of the explosion rings in my ears as I brace my hands against the metal beam pinning me to the ground and crushing my fucking chest. Clenching my jaw, I suck in a sharp breath through my teeth and take in the rubble of the ballroom scattered around me.

"Fuck," I grunt, pushing it up just enough to take a deeper breath, only my lungs fill with the thick smoke flooding the room. If it weren't for the plume of smoke billowing from the small window Oakley disappeared through, we'd all be fucking dead by now.

Sawyer kicks the splintered remains of the wooden door off him and rubs at the blood cascading down the side of his face from a deep gash in his head. He's woozy, and if he doesn't control the bleeding soon, he'll pass out. Then it's only a question if he'll die from the blood loss or smoke inhalation.

Rubble falls from the ceiling above, raining down around us as I hear Zade's pained grunts from beneath the window. The metal beam blocks my view of him, and I have no choice but to believe he's alright. Dalton though, I've got no fucking idea.

Sawyer starts coughing around the thick smoke, and I flick my gaze back to him, watching as his head falls against the charred wall with heavy eyes.

"Yo, Sawyer," I spit through my clenched jaw, demanding his attention while Zade attempts to pull himself together, cursing and grunting as he takes note of his injuries. "Get up, man. You need to control that bleeding or you're no good to any of us."

His eyes open a little wider, trying to focus on the sound of my voice and peer through the smoke before finally taking me in. "Ahh, fuck," he mutters, trying to find purchase against the wall to pull himself to his feet.

Sawyer stumbles across the small room, putting pressure on the gash in his head as he flicks his gaze toward Zade, checking the fucker is alive. Continuing toward me, he tears off what's left of his suit jacket, balls it up, and presses it against his head, hissing in pain.

"You good?" he grunts, moving in beside me. His gaze shifts over the metal beam, trying to assess the situation, as Zade grips the windowsill above his head and uses it to haul himself to his feet. His sharp stare quickly scans the room as the terrified screams of our people come from deeper within the ballroom.

I shake my head, the smoke really starting to fuck with me. "Nah, man," I say, blowing out my cheeks as I strain under the weight of the beam, not able to hold it off my chest for much longer.

Zade steps in beside Sawyer and they grasp the metal beam. "On three," Zade says as Sawyer nods. They each let out a breath, knowing this is going to fucking suck for all of us. Then not wasting a fucking second, Zade starts his countdown. "One, two, three."

They heave against the metal beam as I push up against it, desperately trying to lift it enough to get my ass out from under this bitch. My muscles strain under the weight, the veins protruding from my arms.

"Ahh, fuck," Sawyer grunts, spitting the words through a clenched jaw as the beam finally begins to lift. We keep pushing until the beam is finally off my chest enough for me to take a full, smoke-filled breath.

The tainted oxygen pulses through my veins, and I pull myself out from under the beam, my feet barely clearing it before it tumbles out of Zade and Sawyer's hands.

"Fucking hell," Sawyer mutters, collapsing against the wall as Zade moves in beside him, grabbing the discarded suit jacket and pressing it to Sawyer's head, using the arms to wrap it around him like a bandage.

Zade looks at me, his gaze sailing over my body as I try to get to my feet, my head woozy from hitting the ground. "Dalton?" he asks over the deafening sound of the fire out in the ballroom.

I shake my head and search the room, peering through the thick smoke. "He's gotta be here somewhere." I start moving around, holding my jacket to my face and trying to filter out the smoke, knowing damn well that this is only the beginning.

Trying to think back to the moments before the explosion, I remember racing through the back of the kitchen, storming after Zade, unsure if I was trying to stop him from going after Oakley or if I was trying to get her myself.

Sawyer was just in front of me and Dalton was behind. I was so focused on the small window Oakley was pulling herself through, so focused on the agony of her betrayal that I don't even recall if Dalton made it into the room before the blast.

My heart races, the adrenaline pumping heavily through my veins as I make my way around the room, moving shit out of the way and checking for Dalton as dread fills me. Being in that room offered us an extra level of safety from the blast, but if Dalton was still out in the kitchen . . . fuck.

"He's not here," I say, limping toward the door as I lift my hand to my neck, unconsciously feeling for Venom. Before a new panic sets in, I remember she's safe in her enclosure, locked securely in the penthouse of the DeVil hotel.

"Fuck," Zade says, moving in behind me and following me out of the room. "We need to find him and get out of here. Every fucking second that passes, Oakley only gets further away."

"What?" Sawyer grunts. "After all of this, you're still gonna go after her? Just give her the fucking night to breathe. Where the hell can she go anyway? Besides, my sister is still in there somewhere. My mom, everyone we fucking know. We're not leaving until I know they're safe."

Zade clenches his jaw but wisely keeps his mouth shut, and despite how much I want to go after Oakley, this is where we need to be. Empire is burning around us, and now more than ever, it's important for Zade to stand up and show his people that he can rise to the occasion. What better time to prove your worth than in the face of a tragedy?

My eyes widen in horror as I move into the kitchen. Soot-covered bodies litter the floor, lying motionless in the rubble as flames quickly move in their direction. Knives protrude from the charred drywall after the blast sent them soaring across the kitchen like bullets.

The thick layer of broken porcelain crunches beneath my shoes as I search the kitchen, my gaze shifting over the faces of the bodies around me. I take another careful step, noticing the broken pipes shooting water over the sink, but as Zade curses and shoves past me, I freeze.

I follow his gaze across the kitchen and dart after him, finding Dalton slumped against the wall, a knife plunged deep into his thigh. "Fuck," Sawyer says, racing after us and trying to keep low to avoid the growing cloud of smoke over us.

Zade falls to his knees beside Dalton and shoves his fingers against his neck, searching for a pulse as Sawyer and I hold our breath, watching with wide eyes. The seconds seem to pass like lifetimes when Zade finally lets out a sigh of relief. "Fuck, he has a pulse," he says, choking on the smoke. "It's weak, but if we don't get him out of here soon, he'll be dead."

Thank fuck.

Moving in on Dalton's other side, I lean down and grab his bloodstained arm, pulling it over my shoulders as Zade does the same. Then being careful of the knife sticking out of his thigh, we lift him and turn to the exit, the room now fully engulfed in flames.

"Fuck," Sawyer grunts, his hand at his head, searching for a way out through the thick smoke and the eerie orange glow. He moves up ahead of us when a loud crash rumbles through the kitchen, the ceiling caving in over us. Sawyer backs up, barely making it through the debris without getting scorched alive. "Go back," he roars. "It's blocked. We can't get through."

FUCK.

Without hesitation, Zade and I whirl around and head back toward the room we just came out of, moving right up to the small window Oakley had barely managed to crawl through five minutes ago. Sawyer moves in next to Zade and takes Dalton's weight as Zade steps up to the window and grips the frame.

He pulls himself up, having to go at an angle to fit his shoulders through, and with a little wriggling, he pulls himself through the window and drops to the street on the other side, ready to catch Dalton.

Glancing at Sawyer, we try to figure out how the hell we're going to get Dalton through that fucking window, and I have to admit, this isn't exactly the first time we've had to shove an almost dead body through a small space while a building was ablaze at our backs.

Good times. I'm sure one day we might even laugh about this, but first, we need to make sure we survive this shit to be able to laugh about it later.

Not having the chance to really think this through, we reach down and grab him by the thighs, my hand on his back to steady him as we hoist him up. Hoping like fuck the hilt of the knife doesn't catch on the window frame and tear his thigh into ribbons, we painstakingly feed his head through the window before finally getting his big fucking shoulders through.

Then with my hand shoved halfway up his fucking ass, I shove hard and get the rest of his torso through. His arms fall out the other side, and I feel Zade balance him, ready to catch him when he falls through. Sawyer adjusts Dalton's body, keeping the knife safe, and with one more shove, Dalton falls out to the street.

With Sawyer still losing blood, I stand in close as he grips the window frame and hoists himself out just in case he needs me, and as the heat in the room gets almost too much to bear, I almost push the fucker out, quickly running out of time. The second I hear Sawyer's feet hit the ground, I follow suit, my lungs screaming for fresh air.

The frame is hot under my hands, but I withstand the pain as I pull myself through, twisting my shoulders as I feed my body through the small hole. Once I'm on the other side, I hastily spin around and throw myself to the ground, finding Zade hovering over Dalton as Sawyer takes off up the street, most likely to find another entrance into the building to make sure Cara and his mom are alright.

Dalton is laid out on the sidewalk with Zade's hand clutched around the hilt of the knife. Without hesitation, I tear off my suit jacket and grip the bottom of my shirt, tearing it into strips to use as a bandage. Zade clenches his jaw, not enjoying inflicting pain on any of us, but he'll do whatever the fuck he has to do to care for the people he loves. "Good thing he's out cold," Zade grunts, his fist tightening around the knife before quickly yanking it out.

"AHH FUCK," Dalton roars, his eyes springing open.

Well, shit. Perhaps he wasn't as passed out as we thought.

Blood quickly seeps from the wound as I drop down beside Dalton and tightly wrap the makeshift bandage around his thigh, trying to control the bleeding, but it's clear that the knife didn't hit an artery. Hell, it's gonna take a shitload more than just an explosion to take one of us out.

"Fucking hell," Dalton grunts, dragging his hand over his face as he peers up at the burning building. Zade slips his arm around Dalton's back, not giving him even a second to ease into the pain, but we don't have time. If Sawyer doesn't play this right, he'll end up killing himself searching for Cara in there.

We take off after Sawyer, and I don't miss the way Zade's sharp gaze looks up and down the street for Oakley, despite knowing damn well that she's long gone. Though I commend her efforts to get away and hope like fuck she can somehow survive this, she should know better. There's nowhere she can go where Zade DeVil won't find her.

Fuck, just the thought of it darkens my soul. There's not a single part of me that doesn't belong to Oakley Quinn, and it kills me that this is what she's being reduced to—a fucking power play in Empire's wicked games.

I hope she fucking runs to the end of the world and doesn't dare look back. At least for ten more days and then after that . . . I don't know. She can't come back here. Once word of her lineage gets around, that she, a woman, is the real blood heir, she will be slaughtered like cattle. There's no surviving this. The threat she holds to the many who want to take Zade's place is unfathomable.

Even with us at her back, even if Zade forfeits his claim to rule, Oakley will never be free.

Turning the corner, I quickly take in the chaos before me.

The road outside the main entrance of the ballroom is flooded with people, each one of them in a different state of shock. People are bleeding, screaming, crying, and fretting. Ambulances wail in the distance, but there's no way in hell this city has enough to cater to all the injuries here tonight.

I spot a few of The Circle members racing around and caring for the wounded, and despite looking haggard and dirty, they appear just fine. We get deeper into the fray when I pull Dalton's arm off from around my neck. "Stay out here and help where you can. I'm going after Sawyer."

He nods, and as I spare a glance toward Zade, I see him scanning the faces of the crowd, desperation flashing in his eyes. "She's not here," I spit through a clenched jaw, demanding his attention. "She's gone. Get it through your fucking head. Tonight, you help your people. Lead them. Prove to them that you have what it takes to stand in your father's shoes and be their hope, be everything your father wasn't. Then tomorrow when the ash has settled, we get our girl."

His stare hardens, and I know exactly what's going through his head. He doesn't give a shit about being these people's hope or putting on a fucking show for them. He doesn't care about leading them or claiming the fucking power, he only wants Oakley. And fuck, I know the feeling.

Knowing he will do what's right, I turn away and race back through the main entrance, back into the flames, and come to a stop, looking over the disheveled ballroom, the beauty that once was now nothing but horror in the wake of the explosion.

Blood soaks the dance floor, and I take in the many dead bodies—bodies of our people, *Zade's* people, who he has to protect. Without a single doubt in my mind, I know that we will find the asshole responsible for this and make them pay for the lives they've taken tonight.

With the thick smoke billowing toward me, desperate to escape out into the night, I duck my head and race down into the ballroom, my gaze shooting left and right, desperately seeking out Sawyer. People are scattered everywhere, the smoke making it almost impossible to see.

"HELP!" The raw desperation and terror in the woman's voice brings me to a stop. Glancing down through the thick smoke, I find a woman stuck beneath a table and immediately recognize her as one of my mom's best friends. Then despite knowing I need to find Cara, I stop, grip the edge of the table, and pull it off her.

My gaze trails over her, and it's clear she's got a broken leg, and judging by the blood matting in the back of her head, I'd say one hell of a nasty concussion. Not wanting to leave her here to die, I swoop down and pull her into my arms, her ballgown making it difficult to carry her. She cries out as the movement jostles her injuries, but I don't have time to pull back and take it easy. The longer we're both stuck in the thick smoke, the worse it's going to get.

With the woman gathered in my arms, I race back to the main entrance to call for help. I don't take notice of who I'm handing her off to, but with my arms free, I circle back around to keep searching.

I don't waste a second, breathing in the fresh air before diving back into the ballroom, squeezing past the bodies trying to get out. My sharp gaze scans the room before finally finding Sawyer hovering over his mother, and I hurry in to help, assessing what's going on. She's got a piece of glass protruding from her chest, and from what I can tell, it's probably wedged down between her ribs. It's clear why Sawyer hasn't already taken her outside. If he moves her, if that glass has pierced through her lung, he could kill her.

Moving in beside him, I see the sheer panic in his eyes. "Come on," I tell him, watching her shallow breaths, the smoke inhalation quickly claiming her. "We'll lift her together. We need to get her out of here."

"No," he says. "Go and find Cara. I've got help coming."

"You sure?"

"Yes," he booms. "Go."

Racing back toward the storeroom we were in before Oakley took off, the same room where I first touched her, I find rubble and debris banked up in front of the room. I quickly search around, my gut telling me she's inside, but if I'm wrong . . . If I spend the time trying to get in there only to find she's already gone, I could be condemning us both to death.

Fuck.

I try to go over everything I know about Cara to figure out her way of thinking.

We were only gone from that room for a few seconds. Everything was heated, and Sawyer and Zade were in each other's faces. Cara was frustrated and scared after being initiated into The Circle and more than ready to make Zade bleed, but then Oakley left and so did we, leaving her behind.

She'd been locked up by Zade for a few days after finding out that she was responsible for giving up Oakley's location to our enemies, but at the same time, she's very clearly in love with him too. If she was going to run, this would have been her only chance, but now being part of The Circle, she might have thought that this closed the gap between them. She's not just Sawyer's twin sister anymore, she has power of her own.

The question is—did she run or did she stay?

Fuck. I've never liked her. I've gone out of my way not to have known anything about her, but if she's anything like her brother, she would have stayed to face the music in an attempt to get what she wanted. And with that, I start grabbing the debris and throwing it out of the way, taking slow breaths and trying to preserve what little oxygen I can get.

Making it halfway through the debris and getting closer to the door, I start calling out, hoping like fuck she's actually in there. "CARA?" I yell over the sound of the roaring flames. "CARA, ARE YOU IN THERE?"

"Cross?" she says from the other side of the door. "Cross, is that you? Fuck. Get me out of here. I can't—I can't breathe."

Fuck.

"I'm coming," I call back. "Move away from the door."

With that, I move faster, heaving planks of wood and charred bits of rubble out of the way before finally getting close enough to reach the door. "Hurry," Cara says, choking on the smoke as I hear her falling against the wall. "I can't—I don't—"

Fuck. Fuck. Fuck.

My hand curls around the handle, but it doesn't budge, so I shove my shoulder into it, only getting a slight flex. Then as the struggle for oxygen becomes all too fucking real, I shove my shoulder into the door one more time, giving it everything I've got left and finally unjamming it.

The door swings open, and I storm into the room, finding Cara slumped against the wall, struggling to cling to consciousness, and I curse before scooping her right into my arms.

She clings to me, locking her arms around my neck as I double back, racing for the exit with my lungs screaming for mercy. I glance back toward where Sawyer and his mom were, relieved to find them gone, knowing without a doubt that Sawyer wouldn't have left unless she was safe.

Then breaking out into the night, both Cara and I suck in a deep breath of clean air as I crumble to my knees, both of us falling onto the asphalt as others hurry in around us, checking we're alright.

Sawyer barges through the crowd to get to his sister, and with that, I shakily get back to my feet. With Zade stepping back into my side, we head straight back in, determined to save as many of our people as possible.

CHAPTER 2

Oakley

Tears stream down my face as I run for my life, one foot slamming down on the asphalt after the other. I should be happy, I should be rejoicing that they're dead, and yet, my heart is breaking.

Dalton. Sawyer. Easton . . . Even Zade.

Over the past few weeks, I've come to know them, some I've even come to love, but despite how I feel or how they *felt,* they were still going to use me in their twisted game and offer my heart as a sacrifice to Empire. They were going to kill me, even if it meant tearing out their own hearts in the process.

There was no loyalty there. Did my love mean nothing?

All I know is there's no way they could have survived an explosion like that.

One minute I was running, my heels breaking as I fell from the window. Zade's voice screaming my name was echoing down the street, the horror and rage in his tone making me want to double back and fall into his arms. With no regard for my own life, I wanted to submit to his evil will and give him everything he's ever wanted . . . and then, BOOM!

I've never felt anything like it. The way the blast lifted me off the ground and threw me across the street, the debris shooting through the air, and the undeniable heat at my back. It was terrifying, yet to think the boys were in that . . . fuck.

There's no way they survived a blast like that, nobody could have, right? But if they did, if some kind of angelic force field shone down on them and spared their lives, then shit. I don't know what's worse, being slaughtered by Zade's hand or spending an eternity craving the man I have to run from.

Empire is crumbling, burning up in flames, and being reduced to nothing but ashes, but despite Zade and the boys being dead, I have to run. This could be my only chance at freedom, my only shot at saving myself. Once the flames have settled, what remains of Empire will regroup, and when they do, they'll be coming for blood.

But one thing is for sure, I'll be long gone when they do.

Only, there's one thing I need to do first.

Heavy sobs tear from the back of my throat as the tears spring from my eyes, staining my cheeks and dropping to my destroyed gown. I should be relieved that they're dead, yet every single part of me screams to run back to them, screams to save them.

God, it hurts so bad.

The idea of never seeing Dalton again, never hearing those filthy words falling from his mouth. Never getting to taste those lips or feel my heart race when he walks into the room. I can't fathom a life without him. I know I didn't know him long, but for the past few weeks, he was my salvation, he was my hope that I could make it out of this alive.

Not anymore.

Sawyer and I were only just beginning. He'd been going through a lot with his father's execution and learning about his sister's betrayal, and while he kept me at arm's length, I felt those barriers starting to break between us, and I know without a doubt that I was starting to fall for him.

Easton though, there was something exotic and dangerous about him. His silence was the biggest turn-on I'd ever experienced, but it had nothing on that deadly stare of his. The way his gaze would leave me breathless is something I will never forget, and every day of the rest of my life, I will crave that kind of intensity. He was different from anyone I've ever known, and I hate that he's gone. Just like Sawyer, the walls were starting to crumble, and the more time I spent with Easton, the clearer it became—he owned a piece of my heart.

Once all the dust settles and it's safe, I'm going to have to get back to Zade's penthouse at some point. I don't know much about snakes, but I can't leave Venom alone. She will grieve Easton just as much as I will, if not more. Their bond was unbreakable.

I have mixed feelings about Zade. Nobody has ever confused me the way he did. The push and pull between us was exhausting. One minute he was telling me how he would plunge his hand into my chest and tear my heart right out of my body for his sick ritual, and the next, he was holding me while I slept, keeping me safer than I'd ever been in his warm arms. Half of me despised him, while the other half was quickly falling for the devil.

It's for the best. With the boys out of the picture, I can move on from this. I can get out of here, find somewhere safe to go, somewhere I can try to have some kind of semblance of a life. Perhaps make a new name to be able to finish school and get a job while flying under the radar. Maybe I might even find it in me to love again. Though, how will anything ever compare to what I had with the boys?

Wiping the tears off my face, I force myself to breathe through the sobs, desperately trying to regain control of myself. The boys might be dead, but that doesn't mean my fight is over yet. It's only just beginning. I can't fall apart yet.

My aching feet slam against the asphalt in my broken heels, but I don't dare stop. My chest heaves, desperately sucking in the smoke-filled air, refusing to look back at the raging fire behind me.

I only have a short window before Empire starts to regroup, and I need to be long gone before that happens. Or hell, maybe I shouldn't. I am the heir of Empire, *the real blood heir,* right after my father.

With Zade now out of the way, we could rise up and claim what is rightfully ours. I don't really know the man my father is after being apart from him for so long, but from those few short hours talking with him down in Empire's cells, I know the idea will spark something in him. But at the same time, he would want me to flee. He always told me to run. Run as far as I could and never look back.

Ironic, seeing as though that's exactly what I'm doing right now. Only I'm not running away from Empire, I'm running right into the heart of it.

My chest heaves, quickly running out of breath as my muscles scream for sweet relief, but I don't dare stop until I'm cowering at the opening of the old train tunnels, sirens blaring through the city. My heart races, though I can't tell if it's fear from even thinking about doing this or the marathon I just ran through the city.

Fuck, this really is stupid. The last time I voluntarily walked through the doors of Empire, I ran into Nikolai Thorne and was almost slaughtered in the creepy murder dungeon. If it hadn't been for Zade . . . shit. I don't even want to think about it.

But this is too important.

I vowed that I would save my father, no matter what it took. He's been rotting in Empire's cells for over twelve long years, and today, while Empire burns to ashes around me, he will get his freedom.

Swallowing over the lump in my throat, I will myself to calm down, my heavy panting sounding like some kind of stalker hiding in a woman's closet. Then putting one foot in front of the other, I slip into the darkness of the old train tunnels, knowing I could be potentially handing myself over.

With every step I take, I try to remember what I know of the inside of this shitshow. The blueprints I found in Zade's office would have been helpful if I knew what the fuck I was looking at. It was impossible to decipher between the old tunnels that lead down to the cells and the new modernized areas with the fancy Italian marble and conference rooms.

I've got nothing but my memory to go on.

The only question is how the hell am I supposed to get through the main door and the security checks within? Last time I needed a key, one that I certainly didn't have, and yet somehow Nikolai knew I was here the whole time. Perhaps there are sensors or something along the tunnel, alerting Empire when people are approaching. I wouldn't put it past them. It's not the most fucked-up thing they have ever done. In fact, it's kinda smart when you consider everything they have to protect.

Quickly hurrying down the long tunnel, it becomes startlingly clear just how out of shape I am. Not even the intense dicking I've been getting on the regular is enough to boost my cardio. Though, I'm sure it certainly helps. After all, I just made it halfway through the city and haven't collapsed yet. But knowing my luck, I'm sure it'll happen at the most inconvenient time.

My gaze remains locked on the tunnel walls, trying to find Empire's secret door, and just when I think I've gone too far, I find it, just as imposing and intimidating as ever.

I swallow hard, nerves pulsing through my veins.

How the hell am I supposed to get inside and through security?

Shit. I think the bigger question is how much am I willing to risk to save my father?

Hoping like fuck I was right about the security sensors, I pound against the big door, and the echo of my fists makes my skin crawl. It's pitch-black down here, almost impossible to see another foot in front of me. Anybody could be hiding in here and I'd never know. That thought alone has me pounding harder until finally, I hear that same little click of the lock I'd heard when Nikolai Thorne stood on the other side.

Fear pulses through my veins, and I take a hasty step back, my hands shaking with unease. I watch as the door pushes open and there, hidden within the darkness is a man I've never seen before. He's older, maybe in his fifties, and he looks tired, almost as though he'd been woken and forced to watch while everyone else ran to the rescue after the explosion.

He looks at me, his gaze narrowed, clearly able to tell I don't belong, but from the ripped gown, tears staining my face, and the cuts and bruises decorating my skin, it's clear I've come directly from the ball. "Who are you?" he demands, not ready to shrug me off just yet.

"My name is Oakley Quinn. I am the granddaughter of Julius DeVil—the true blood heir of Empire," I say, watching as his eyes widen, "and I know who's responsible for the explosion at Cara Thorne's initiation ball."

The man gapes at me, not knowing what to say or even think, and I cross my hands over my chest, raising my chin and silently demanding respect. "What are you waiting for? Let me in. I need to speak with whoever is in charge. Zade DeVil is dead, and there's no knowing just how many of The Circle are rotting in hell right beside him."

"I, umm . . . Yes. Of course," he says, nodding. "Right this way, Miss . . .?"

"Quinn," I say firmly.

"Quinn," he repeats, ushering me through the big door and pulling it closed behind me with a heavy bang. "That's not a name I recognize."

"No, it wouldn't be," I say. "Lawson DeVil went to great lengths to hide it as did his son, but I won't be hidden a moment longer. Now, please, show me to whoever is in charge."

He nods again, and seeing the suspicion in his eyes, it's clear he thinks I'm full of shit. Like he said, my name is not one widely known around here, nor do I really want it to be, but this guy doesn't need to know that. He only needs to know enough to entice him to open the door.

"Zade DeVil is dead, you say?" he questions as he steps into the wall and lowers his face toward the retinal scanner to unlock the security gate.

"That's correct."

"What a shame," he mutters, stepping into the gate and opening it wide, the heavy clanging booming down the long tunnel ahead. "He would have made a great leader."

An ache settles into the pit of my stomach as I force a smile across my face. The idea of Zade never getting to achieve his dreams and dying like that tears at my chest. God, I wish I could have been strong enough to give him what he wanted, but I'm not ready to give up yet. I'm too young to die for someone else's dream. "I'm sure he would have."

The man steps through the gate, his suspicious stare still heavily trained on mine. "Right this way," he murmurs, ushering me through the gate.

I walk ahead, and as I pass him, I can almost feel the wheels turning in his mind as he puts everything together like a puzzle. It's the same look Nikolai had when he realized exactly what was at stake, and assuming this guy believes I am who I say I am, he knows that taking me out will leave the throne open for the taking.

It's anyone's game then.

Not liking the thought of having this strange man at my back, I move to the side and wait for him to pass, watching him like a fucking hawk. "So," he throws over his shoulder, his hand hovering too close to the gun at his hip. "You're Julius DeVil's granddaughter? I wasn't aware Lawson had a second child."

"He didn't."

The man stops and spins on me. "That makes no sense, girl," he roars, spittle hitting my face as his hand rests against his gun. "Who are you really?"

"I am who I say I am—the real blood heir of Empire," I tell him. "Julius DeVil was my grandfather. I am the daughter of his only biological son, Matthias Quinn. Lawson DeVil might have been raised as Julius' son, but he was a fraud. He did not possess the blood. My father was the result of an affair and ruthlessly shoved aside like some kind of stain on the family name."

"You lie," he spits. "Julius DeVil had one son, one legitimate son, and that was Lawson DeVil."

I arch a brow in challenge. "Are you sure about that?"

The man clenches his jaw, and deciding he's had enough, he storms into me, his hands gripping my shoulders as he slams me up against the cold wall of the tunnel. "How dare you come into our holy grounds and speak ill of Julius DeVil. He was a saint among mere mortals, and you dare have the audacity to try and muddy his great legacy. I will not tolerate such blasphemy."

Ahh, shit.

This isn't exactly how I planned this to go.

The man whips me around, slamming my face against the wall as he wrangles my wrists behind my back. "You assholes are all the same," I seethe. "You say you're loyal to the blood, yet when a blood heir is standing right in front of you, your only thoughts are of how you could use this to benefit yourself."

"I am loyal to the blood," he spits in my ear. "That is exactly why I cannot allow an imposter like you to try and come in here, in the wake of a tragedy and try to claim it for your own. If Zade DeVil is truly dead, then a war is brewing, and I cannot allow such filth like yourself to come in here and try to take advantage of us during this time of mourning."

With that, he pulls me away from the wall and starts pushing me ahead of him. "Where are you taking me?" I rush out, trying to fight against his hold.

"To the cells," he rumbles. "Where you will remain until we can figure this mess out."

To the cells, huh? Seems like this asshole is going to hand-deliver me exactly where I want to go.

"NO," I scream. "I AM THE BLOOD HEIR. UNHAND ME, RIGHT NOW."

We break out through the tunnel and into the deserted bar that usually looks like some kind of gentleman's club, and I can only assume it's all hands on deck at the ball. There's not a soul in sight, and I quickly realize that this might be my one and only shot.

"Look around you, girl. You can scream all you want but nobody is coming to save you."

Clenching my jaw, I take this fight into my own hands. I shove my ass back into him, nailing him right in the dick. The asshole doubles over, groaning in pain as he loosens his grip on my wrists just enough for me to pull free. Then without a moment of hesitation, I dart across to the bar and curl my fingers around the neck of a whiskey bottle, spinning back around and grinning wide at the asshole who thought he could put his hands on me.

Then, holding the bottle in both hands like a Louisville Slugger, I rear back and swing with everything I'm worth. His eyes widen in horror, but it's too fucking late to even blink. The thick glass bottle slams across his temple, the momentum knocking him right off his feet. He drops to the ground like a sack of shit, and I move in closer, peering down at him and hoping like fuck I didn't just kill him.

I've been down that road before, and while it was necessary at the moment, it wasn't exactly my finest hour.

After confirming he's still breathing and just knocked out, I grab his ankle and heave, pulling him around the corner of the bar, just in case someone decides to walk through here before I get the chance to free my father. He's a heavy fucker, but I eventually get him out of sight, then knowing he's going to wake at some point, I turn on my heel and get my ass down to the cells.

CHAPTER 3

Oakley

The tunnels are just as daunting as I remember, long and winding with every footstep echoing off the cold walls around me. I've been down here three times now, and I haven't enjoyed a single one of them, and something tells me this time is going to be no different.

A chill sails down my spine, infecting every cell in my body, and my only saving grace is that Harrison, the cell guard, had an unfortunate incident with Zade's gun, and I doubt with everything that's been going on, they've had a chance to replace him. Or hell, they probably aren't even aware he's dead yet.

Reaching the security gate, I grip onto it, trying to figure out how to bust this fucker down, when it moves under the pressure of my hands. My brows furrow as my eyes widen, and I push a little harder, sucking in a breath as I realize it's been left unlocked.

Not wanting to wait around to figure out why, I push it open just enough to slip through, all too aware of just how loud this fucker can be when the old hinges are pushed to their limits.

Hurrying down the old metal stairs and to the cells, I try to ignore the images that assault my memory—the man the boys killed when they broke me out of here, the blood splattering over my body when Zade shot Harrison, the fear during the darkness and silence of the night.

I wasn't built for this world, and yet here I am trying to break my father out of prison.

Maybe I'm exactly what this world is all about.

Finding the row of cells my father and I were locked in, I slow my pace and creep down them, peering into all the cells on my left, knowing my father was along here somewhere. The whole thing was a rush of mixed emotions. I have no recollection of just how far down his cell was, but after coming to the end and finding nothing, my heart races.

He's not here.

I quickly turn on my heel and look around. Could I be in the wrong place? The wrong row of cells? No, definitely not. I know I'm fuzzy on the details, but there are only so many wrong turns I could have made and I'm certain I'm in the right place.

I double back, looking again, taking my time and really peering into the cells, searching in the shadows just in case I missed something.

"Dad?" I whisper through the darkness, my voice sailing right up the long, chilling corridor. "Dad? Where are you? It's me."

I get nothing. Dead silence.

Where the fuck is he? Did they take him somewhere?

All of the cells are neatly put together, the beds made with empty shelves, yet one cell has me stopping. The sheets are crumpled as though someone spent hours on end lying in them. There's a single picture of a woman who looks like an older version of me, and a tray with food scraps at the end of the bed.

This has got to be my father's cell. So where the hell is he?

Stepping right up to the bars, I peer in, shaking my head as I try to piece it all together when the security gate at the top of the stairs squeals through the cells. My heart thunders in my chest and I go to run when the voices sail down the long corridor.

There's got to be at least three of them, all men, and moving way too fast to make any kind of getaway.

Out of time, I step back into the cell that used to be mine and hide in the shadows as I peer out into the hallway, the sound of footsteps sending a raw fear pulsing heavily through my veins.

"Find her," one of the men rumbles, something eerily familiar about his tone.

"Of course, sir," a different voice responds. "You have my word, she won't escape us again."

The first guy scoffs, now so much closer. "She has evaded your every attempt," he says. "However, with Zade DeVil out of the way, that shouldn't be quite so challenging for you."

The men all but storm down the cells, and as they get closer, I shrink back into the shadows, my heart pounding. They come to a stop outside my father's cell, and I inch back to get a better view, finding all three of them in suits, each looking disheveled and bloodied as though they'd been victim to the explosion at the ball.

Their backs are to me, but it's clear their suits are expensive, exactly what one would expect from the men of Empire. That ball was like a fucking men's fashion magazine, and while the women looked incredible, it was nothing compared to the men. Especially *my* men.

They hover in front of my father's cell, and the longer they remain there, the more my brows furrow. What the hell are they doing?

The man in the middle pulls off his suit jacket and hands it to the man on his left before stepping right into my father's cell. He starts unclipping his cufflinks before unbuttoning his shirt, and as he slowly turns to face his men, I suck in a breath, my heart lurching in my chest.

The man making demands for these strange men to find me, the ones who have been making attempts on my life . . . is my father.

Sickening betrayal claws at my chest, and I slap my hand over my mouth to keep from crying out in brutal agony. All I can do is watch. Watch as he undresses and hands the pieces of his suit to his men, watch as he pulls on his ragged clothes from his cell, watch as he messes up his hair and rubs dirt over his face, playing the part of the perfect prisoner.

But he's anything but.

Matthias Quinn is a liar. Just like everyone else in this fucked-up world.

He's been playing us all. Who knows how long he's been able to slip in and out of these cells. When I went out to dinner a few nights ago, he was able to get a note to me, telling me to run. Hell, he demanded I run. He wanted me to be safe, but this . . . is he truly behind all of this? Is he the one who's been ordering all of these attacks on me, trying to end my life?

No, it couldn't be. There has to be some kind of explanation for this.

His men pull his cell closed, and I watch as the one on the right pulls a key from his pocket and locks him inside. "Don't fuck this up," my father says, a chilling demand in his tone. "She's going to be running. Scared. She's not to slip away, you hear me? The game has changed. With Zade out of the picture, this is my time to rise. Do not fail me. Bring my heir to me and use whatever force necessary."

Fuck.

Use whatever force necessary.

"Yes, sir," the two loyal followers say in unison before double-checking that everything is as it should be and slipping away into the darkness.

I've been such a fool. Twelve years I spent missing this man, wishing he was here to love me like a father should, to tell me everything was going to be okay and mend the ache in the pit of my stomach. If I knew this was the man I was mourning . . . I never would have wished him back. I would have allowed the hot pits of hell to consume him.

I watch my father for a moment, watch how he so casually drops back onto his unmade bed, propping his arm behind his head as though he doesn't have a single care in the world, as though he didn't just give an order for his men to grab his daughter with any force necessary.

My whole life has been a lie.

I should have known. My father has the blood of Empire pulsing through his veins. He's a callous, cruel man just like his father was, just like Lawson was. Is this what I'm going to become? So hungry for power that I would risk my only child's life?

Fuck. I don't want anything to do with this world.

I need to get out of here. It was a mistake coming back.

Remaining in the shadows until I know my father's henchmen are gone, I finally find the courage to step out of my hiding spot and watch as my father's head snaps up.

His eyes widen, but he doesn't take his stare off me, watching as I step out of my cell and put myself right in front of him. He gets up from his bed and moves right in front of me, knowing damn well I just heard everything, and fuck me, he doesn't even try to deny it or come up with some bullshit excuse.

"Oakley," he says, keeping his chin held high as if he has something to be proud of. "What are you doing here?"

I laugh, embarrassed by my own foolishness. "I suppose that doesn't matter anymore," I tell him, willing myself not to break. "You're not going to get away with this."

"Oh, my sweet girl," he says. "My how you've grown. You're the perfect heir. So strong. It's a shame my great Empire will never see you as anything more than a weak woman. You would have ruled Empire flawlessly."

"I'm never going to rule Empire," I tell him. "I'll burn it down before it ever comes to that, you and every other power-hungry asshole along with it."

"I believe that's what you want, and if you put your heart to it, I know you will succeed. You are my daughter after all. My flesh and blood. But you will never get that far, Oakley. I won't allow it. I have worked too hard for this. I can feel it. We're almost there, right at the finish line. Empire is mine to take back, the way it should have always been before Lawson DeVil stole it out from beneath me. You'll see, my sweet girl. I'm going to rule this great Empire, and there's not a thing you can do to stand in my way. Hear my warning, Oakley. There's nothing I won't do to keep from getting what is rightfully mine, even if it means ending your precious life."

I laugh, backing away from his cell and watching as he grips the bars tighter. "You're a joke, Father," I tell him. "Zade and the boys might not be here to save me anymore, but look at you. You're a joke. Trying to play me and Empire as fools. But locked here in your little cell, waiting for your henchmen to come and free you, you're a sitting duck, and the second that the news of Zade's death begins to spread, it will be war. It would be a shame if the people of Empire learned of your existence. I wonder just how quickly someone will come and put a bullet between your eyes, wanting to claim leadership for themselves?"

My father clenches his jaw, seeing just how easily I can fight fire with fire, and when he doesn't respond, I go on. "I can't fault you, Father. Trying to claim Empire is a good plan, but it's flawed, and unfortunately for you, you've gone and pissed me off, and there's no telling what I might do with my newfound freedom. Hell, I might even take Empire as my own just to watch it burn."

"Oakley," he warns. "Don't do anything stupid. I won't hesitate to end you."

"I'd like to see you try," I say, a smirk kicking up the corner of my lips. "Like you said, I've evaded every single one of your henchmen's attempts on my life, all while being locked up myself. Haven't you figured it out yet? No matter how hard you try or how many times you wish to fool me, you can't touch me. You're a disappointment, Father. Nothing at all like the great man I always imagined you would be."

And with that, I give him a fake smile before turning on my heel and making a break for it, more than ready to get out of here.

"OAKLEY," he roars at my back, the loud clanging of the bars echoing up the hall, but I don't dare turn back, the betrayal, heartache, and grief clawing at my chest, threatening to destroy me.

I force the tears away as I race up the rickety old stairs and back into the tunnel, passing through the open security gate and hoping like fuck nobody decides now is the time to check on the prisoners.

My aching feet slam against the cold, dirty ground, echoing right up the long tunnel. It must have been at least an hour since the explosion, and soon enough, Empire is going to regroup. Hell, there's a good chance they already have and I'm about to bust out into a room full of assholes who want me dead.

Fuck, what was I thinking coming here?

After everything I've been through with Zade and the boys, I should have learned by now that I can't trust anyone in this world. Yet

I blindly trusted my father, blindly believed that he wanted what was best for me, wanted me safe, but he's just as bad as the rest of them, if not worse.

Reaching the top of the tunnel, I slow my pace and peek out into the main bar. There are a few men in suits who look as though they might have been in the explosion. Their backs are to me, far across the bar, and from what I can tell, I don't think they've noticed the body I left behind the bar.

My gaze shifts to the exit as the men talk among themselves, whispering as though trying to put some kind of fucked-up plan together, probably trying to figure out who's dead and where that leaves them in Empire's hierarchy.

It's only a short dash to the exit tunnel, and I hold my breath. The consequences of being caught right now are not something I want to deal with. The last guy might not have known who I am, but something tells me these guys know exactly what's been going down.

Knowing the longer I wait, the closer I am to being caught, I slip out into the bar, my hands shaking as I try not to allow my father's betrayal to break me now. There will be time to process and crumble about that later, right now, I need to grab this shit by the balls and make it my bitch.

I creep across the bar, tiptoeing and hoping like fuck I don't get caught. Sweat forms on my forehead, and every step I take has me feeling as though I could pass out. I keep my eyes locked on the men, and thankfully, they're so deep in their conversation, they don't seem to notice a damn thing.

Finally reaching the exit tunnel, I let out a shaky breath and collapse against the wall, needing just a moment to gather myself before taking off like a fucking bat out of hell. I'm so fucking close. All I need to do is get through this tunnel and out the gate and I'm home free.

The tunnel seems to go on forever when I finally reach the first security gate and start to panic before realizing I don't need a key or passcode to get out. Relief pounds through my veins, and without wasting a single second, I pull the gate open and fly through before finding the heavy door that leads right out into the old train tunnel.

There's an old brass key that remains in the back of the door, and after twisting it to unlock the big fucker, I find myself curling my fingers around the brass key and pulling it free from the lock. Never knowing when something like this might be useful, I slip it down the front of my ruined gown and into my bra. Then with both hands, I grip the heavy door and pull it open, having to use every last ounce of strength I possess.

Stepping out into the old train tunnel, I almost expect to be grabbed. My luck hasn't exactly been great when it comes to trying to evade the assholes of Empire, but as I peer through the long tunnel, I find myself completely alone—not even a hint of goosebumps or hair rising on the back of my neck.

Then letting out a heavy breath, I go to make my way out of the tunnel, facing the way I came before I think better of it and turn in the opposite direction. There's no telling how deep this tunnel goes or what kind of monsters could be hidden within it. All I know is that at some point, the masses are going to turn up here, and when they do, there's only one direction they'll be coming from, and I'll be damn sure that I won't be there when that happens.

Without another moment of hesitation, I take off at a sprint, racing deeper into the old train tunnel and hoping like fuck I haven't just made a terrible mistake.

CHAPTER 4

Oakley

I've been running for what feels like an hour when I finally get just a hint of hope, hearing the subtle sounds of traffic on the street. My feet are blistered and aching, but I don't dare stop, determined to see this through.

My chest heaves, and after another ten minutes of torture, I finally see the opening of the old tunnel. There's a wicked chill in the air, and as I creep closer toward the opening and peer out into the world beyond, it's clear that I'm not in Faders Bay anymore, and that thought alone is exactly what I need to push me on and give me just a ray of hope that I might survive this.

I slow as I step out of the tunnel, desperately searching the rundown town. It must be at least two in the morning, and despite the odd car speeding by every now and then, it's practically a ghost town.

I stick to the shadows and keep away from the main roads, slipping up and down back alleys as I try to find some kind of salvation. Finally, I see the one thing I've been looking for—a rundown motel with the word vacancy flashing in the window.

Tears spring to my eyes, and I dart across the street, my heart pounding in my chest. I'm so close.

I all but fall through the door, startling the night shift attendant sitting behind the counter, watching videos on his phone. The room smells of mold, musk, and the scent of a man who doesn't wash often enough, but I try to push it aside as I race toward him. "Please," I cry, stumbling right into the reception desk and locking my gaze on his. "Please, you need to help me. I need a room."

His filthy gaze sails up and down my body, taking in the expensive torn gown, and I watch as he makes some kind of bullshit judgment about me. The asshole narrows his gaze, hunger flashing in his eyes. "I've got a room, but it'll cost you."

My heart sinks. "I haven't got any money."

The attendant stands and rubs his cock through the front of his pants, making my skin crawl. "Good thing I'm not looking for money."

Oh, fuck no.

After dealing with more than my fair share of assholes in Missouri, long before I came to Faders Bay, I force a fake smile across my face and prepare to show this asshole who the fuck he's dealing with. I slowly walk around the reception desk and let a sparkle hit my eye, lighting up my whole face. "You want me on my knees, huh?" I ask, walking over to him, and watching how he watches me. I trail my fingers over his desk until I stand right in front of him before moving my hand to his chest and slowly brushing down to his dick. I grip him hard through his pants and watch as his whole body jolts. "You want to know how fucking good it'll feel to have your cock slamming into the back of my throat, or would you prefer to spread me wide open and take my little cunt?"

His hand drops to my waist, squeezing tight. "All of it, baby. If you want one of my rooms, you're gonna pay the price."

Releasing his cock, I hold his gaze as I grip his belt buckle and start undoing it. "Then what the fuck are you waiting for?" I question, opening his pants just enough to see the top of his pathetic cock. Then lifting my blistered foot, I kick his desk chair, rolling it back against the wall. "Take your fucking cock out and sit."

The asshole looks at me as though he can barely believe what's happening, and without hesitation, he turns his back and makes his way to his chair. He adjusts his pants, opening them just enough to pull his stumpy cock out, and as he settles back into the desk chair and fists his dick, I scan over the desk, finding exactly what I'm looking for.

Slipping the paper knife into my hand, I turn and fix this moron with a sultry smile as I stride toward him, rocking my hips the way that used to drive Dalton wild with hunger. His fist tightens on his cock, and I almost throw up at the bead of moisture already pooling at the tip.

Why the hell was this so hot when it was one of my boys but so fucking disgusting with this guy?

Grabbing the armrests of the office chair, I drag him toward me before straddling his lap. "You hungry for me?" I murmur, reaching up and fisting my hand into his hair, before tearing his head right back and not allowing him even an inch to move, showing him a dominance that I can guarantee he's never experienced before. "Answer me," I growl. "How fucking hungry are you? How much do you want my sweet little cunt."

"Fucking starving, bitch. Take my cock."

My gaze drops to his pathetic dick, my stomach clenching with disgust, then leaning over him as if preparing to take him, my hand whips up to his exposed throat, the paper knife digging into his flesh. "Oh, I'll fucking take it, alright," I tell him, watching as his eyes widen with fear. "Tell me, how much do you think it'll bleed when I cut it off? Should I leave the balls or take them too? I mean, I don't think you'll need them if there's no dick there, but honestly, I feel for you, a life without being able to come ever again. Fuck. I'd kill myself."

"You're a fucking crazy bitch," he panics.

"Yeah," I laugh, pressing a little harder on the paper knife and watching as a bead of blood sails down the thick column of his throat. "I am a crazy bitch—a crazy bitch who's had a really fucked-up night, but you know what? I'd rather be crazy than a sick fuck like you."

He clenches his jaw, and I continue, letting him see the desperation in my gaze, silently telling him just how far I'm willing to take this. "Do you think you'll bleed out and die before I can even find my room key?" I ask, channeling my inner Harley Quinn.

"Fuck, okay," he rushes out. "Just have the fucking room."

I smile sweetly. "That's what I thought."

And with that, I climb off his lap and keep an eye on him as I riffle through the desk drawer and pull out a roll of masking tape. I toss it into his lap, clipping him right on the tip of his dick and getting the sweetest satisfaction out of it. "Tape yourself to the chair," I tell him, watching as he quickly gets to work, knowing damn well he's only going to be able to complete half the job.

Satisfied he's staying put for now, I start searching the desk. "Room key?"

"Second drawer."

Pulling it open, I find the keys scattered through the drawer and curl my fingers around one with a green tag for room four. "Where's four?" I ask, looking back to find one of his wrists bound before quickly stepping back and quickly taping the other.

"Top floor. Go right at the top of the stairs."

I give him a beaming, innocent smile and make sure to take the paper knife with me. "Wonderful." I get halfway around the desk when I double back and keep searching the cupboards and drawers until finding a small first aid kit and smiling to myself. I grab it and walk back to the door and shove it open. Then standing half in and half out of the motel reception, I look back at my new friend. "You don't even want to know what will happen to you if you even attempt to come near my room while I sleep. Understood?"

"Yeah, yeah. Whatever, you crazy bitch. Just get out of here."

With that, I step out into the cold night, my feet bleeding and sore as I glance around the motel, searching for my room. Then with the paper knife and key tucked firmly in my hand, I dash up the stairs and turn to the right before finally coming to a stop in front of room four.

I quickly unlock the door and barge through to the small room, instantly getting hit with a damp mold stench and groan, but hell, I'll deal with a foul smell over being slaughtered by the men of Empire. Locking and bolting the door behind me, I switch on the lights and turn to take in the small room.

It's exactly what I expect—a piece of shit, but it'll have to do. Hell, I've definitely stayed in worse places.

Getting straight to work, I dart across the room and grab the set of drawers before inching the heavy piece of furniture across the room, certain the sound of it dragging across the floor would be waking up my new neighbors.

Once the heavy chest of drawers is blocking the door, I check that the windows are locked and pull the blinds closed, not feeling great about them. All it would take is a quick fist through the flimsy glass and I'd be dead, but what other options do I have?

Certain I'm as safe as I could possibly be, I grab the small first aid kit and make my way into the dirty bathroom, my face scrunching with disgust. I fight my gag reflexes, wanting to empty my stomach just to get the taste of dirt and mildew from my mouth.

The small bathroom is dingy and grimy with bright white ceramic tiles on the floor and dull brown walls covered in nicks and smudges. It's disgusting and reminds me of something you find at a truck stop that's generally been destroyed by oversized men who probably shouldn't have had that last bite of Mexican food before hitting the road.

Trying to ignore it all, I strip out of my torn gown and toss it out of the bathroom, not risking dropping it on the filthy tiles. I pad across the small space and reach into the shower before turning on the tap and waiting as the water warms, then the second the bathroom starts filling with steam, I step into the water and let it cascade over my body.

I close my eyes, tipping my head back, and for the first time since the explosion, I feel at ease. Grabbing the motel soap, I scrub the dirt and ash from my body, and as I get down to my feet and really take in the extent of my injuries, I crumble, falling into a ball on the shower floor.

Sobs tear from the back of my throat, and I sit in the shower until the water runs cold, tears streaming down my face.

The boys are gone and my father . . . fuck.

In one single night, everything I knew was wiped away, and now I'm more alone than ever. Don't get me wrong, I would have killed to be able to get away from the guys like this, to be able to secure my freedom, but I would have never wished them dead, no matter how much I might have said otherwise.

Dalton. Sawyer. Easton. Zade.

They were bigger than life, and just like that . . . they're gone.

I know I barely knew them for long, but the short, intense time we had together was enough for them to each leave a mark on my heart. God, I hated them most of the time, but even on my darkest days, they gave me something to live for, something to crave and dream of. Hell, that even includes Zade.

I despised that man. He was ruthless, callous, and cruel, yet there was a vulnerability about him as though he was screaming for someone to save him, begging for a freedom of his own, a freedom that being the head of such an insane society would never allow.

Zade challenged me in a way I wasn't prepared for, and he dared me to fight him at every chance I got. He wanted me to be strong, wanted me to fight for my life and prove to him that the blood in my veins made me worthy of being the true heir, even if I didn't grow up in his world. And in turn, it was that fight that forced me to become a stronger version of myself, not some weak girl who would fall apart at the drop of a hat—Hell, fall apart like I'm doing right now.

If Zade could see me now, he'd be so disappointed watching me crumble to pieces on the floor of a dirty motel shower, but then he'd be the very first to drag me into his bed and hold me until I was strong enough to fight another day.

There's no denying it, Zade DeVil was one hell of a complicated man, and I think I'm only just realizing how addicted I'd become to his wicked ways.

With the shower running cold, I pull myself to my feet and hastily shut off the water. No amount of scrubbing will make me feel clean tonight. Finding a towel, I wrap it around my freezing body before drying my hair and trudging back out to the bedroom, having no choice but to put my destroyed gown back on.

Then with the paper knife, the main key for the heavy door of Empire, and my room key right here beside me, I crawl into the shitty excuse of a bed and close my eyes before allowing the exhaustion of today to claim me.

CHAPTER 5

Zade

"Where the hell is the girl?" Hartley Scott demands, trying to sound as though he actually has a set of balls as we stand in a closed meeting, the twelve members of The Circle somehow all alive and well after tonight's explosion at Cara's initiation ball.

"What's it to you?" I throw back at Hartley, wishing I could put a fucking blade right through the center of his spine and watch him crumble. "Oakley Quinn is of no concern to you. She's my sacrifice."

Hartley scoffs and steps toward me, getting too fucking close for his own good, especially tonight when Oakley is gone, and I have no fucking idea how to get her back. She's disappeared off the face of the fucking earth, and there's not a goddamn thing I can do about it until this bullshit meeting is done.

"Witnesses place Oakley Quinn fleeing the scene following the explosion. Her presence is required for questioning," he spits. "If that bitch had something to do with taking all of those lives, then she will be executed without hesitation, your ritual be damned."

My hand shoots out, locking around Hartley's throat as I slam him up against the wall of the conference room, Cara's shocked gasp the only noise in the big room. "If you even think about touching a fucking hair on her head, you'll be the one who finds himself in a shallow fucking grave," I growl, leaning in closer and lowering my tone. "Don't think for one fucking second that I have forgotten your connection to my mother. Your crimes and betrayal against this institution should have you locked in a prison cell. If it weren't for the requirement of needing a full circle for my ritual, you'd already be dead."

Hartley swallows hard, and I feel the movement beneath my palm when Cara steps into my side, her hand on my arm, forcing me back. "Let him go," she says. "This isn't helping anything."

I reluctantly release Hartley and step back, needing my fucking space, when Cara turns to Hartley. "You're full of shit if you think Oakley had anything to do with the explosion. She would prefer to sacrifice her own life than be responsible for killing so many others, and the fact that you're trying to push this narrative that Oakley did it is ridiculous. Every last person in this room can see it's nothing but a power play on your part, wanting to take her out before Zade can complete his ritual."

Ira Abrahms nods from across the room. "The girl has a point,

Scott."

I scoff. "Less than twelve fucking hours ago, you stood in Cara's initiation and claimed she wasn't fit to stand as a member of The Circle, and now you have her back?"

"I do not change my mind," he spits, unable to keep from hovering his hand over the bullet wound at his shoulder. "Cara Thorne is not fit to stand at the head of our organization. She is a weak woman who has not been trained for this position. She's still a child, however, that does not mean I cannot agree with her logic. Hartley Scott has been a thorn in my side for far too long, and it is clear that his attempts to see Oakley Quinn executed before the ritual is nothing but a play for power."

"Whether you think my intentions are pure or not, the fact of the matter still stands—Oakley Quinn has escaped Zade's hold. She knows too much of our world and is a danger to our very existence. She needs to be brought in immediately."

"Remember your place," I spit. "You do not make the orders around here."

"And you do?" he throws back at me. "As far as I am concerned, you are nothing but a child playing dress up. You are incapable of completing your ritual and will never be my leader. And with Oakley now missing, that is becoming even more clear. Forfeit your position at the head of Empire, Zade. Admit that the great DeVil legacy ceased to exist when you slaughtered your father in cold blood."

"You're fucking brave when you think you have protection at your back," I tell him. "But look around you. There's nobody in your corner, nobody fighting to see you succeed. Whether I ascend Empire's throne or not, you will still fail, and when your *protection* no longer needs you, you'll be discarded like the trash you are."

Hartley narrows his gaze, not fucking man enough to admit he knows what the fuck I'm talking about in front of the other Circle members.

Cara groans and gives me a blank stare. "Are we done with the pissing contest yet? My mom is in the hospital, and I want to get this shit over and done with so I can go sit with her, seeing as though you bastards killed her husband and she has no one else."

Guilt soars through my chest despite Cara's exaggeration. Sawyer's mom is loved by many around here. Nikolai was part of The Circle for decades, meaning his wife was all but royalty in the Empire social circles. There's no way that woman is sitting alone in a hospital room and Cara knows it. Though, she won't expect her son to visit any time soon. Despite his need to check on his mom, Sawyer, Dalton, and Cross aren't going anywhere until we've secured Oakley and I have her back in the safety of my home.

Letting out a breath, I step back and address the room. "Tonight's explosion was a tragedy that has rocked our whole world, a tragedy that we will get to the bottom of. Mark my words, we will find who was responsible for this, and they will be punished accordingly."

Every head in the room nods, and I continue. "As it was so bluntly pointed out, Oakley Quinn is out of my possession. She is on the run and I will be putting all of my energy into securing her before the ritual. There are only nine days remaining and I intend to make every second count. With that in mind, I will not be hanging around to hold your hands through this tragedy. It is time for you all to step up and be the hope our people need right now."

Again, they nod, ready to take on any task in the wake of the explosion. "Cara," I say, turning to meet her eye, hoping like fuck she has the balls to take this bullshit by the horns and make it her bitch. "You are in charge of the proceedings from here. I want a head count and list of every person who perished in the explosion. I want you to personally reach out to every family and offer our condolences and let them know we are working tirelessly to find the person or organization responsible for this. Following that, you will organize with each of the families how they wish to proceed with their burial. All expenses will be paid for, and if they wish, Empire can hold a mass burial."

Cara's mouth drops, realizing the magnitude of her job, and the fact that she's going to have to try to coordinate the other Circle members while dealing with their bullshit, but I've known Cara for a long fucking time. Despite her recent betrayals against me and Oakley, out of everyone in this room, I trust her the most.

Then before she gets a chance to ask a single fucking question, I excuse myself, having much more pressing things to deal with, like getting Oakley back into the safety of my home.

I can't blame her for running. Hell, I'm fucking proud of her for having what it took to actually evade me, but fuck, it really messes with my plans.

Storming out the door, I make my way down the hall to find the boys and see what progress they've made when I hear someone running up behind me.

"Zade," Cara calls out.

For fuck's sake.

"What?" I spit, not even close to having forgiven her. "I don't have time."

"I know, I just . . . are you in love with her?"

"What?" I grunt, whipping around to face her. "What the fuck are you talking about?"

"Oakley," she says, a strange mix of sadness and jealousy flashing in her familiar eyes. "You and I, we've been, you know, fooling around for years, and you've never once gone hard for me the way you do with her. She sleeps in your fucking bed, Zade. I've never been allowed to do that, not even close."

"You don't know what you're talking about."

"You're in love with her."

I shake my head. "She's my sacrifice, that's it," I tell her, hating that I'm even having this conversation. "Besides, if she was more, that's none of your fucking concern. You and I have never been anything more than convenience. I'm not in love with you, Cara. I can barely tolerate you."

Her face falls, and I resist the urge to roll my eyes.

"I don't have time for your fucking feelings, Cara, and honestly, neither do you. You're not some spoiled rich girl anymore. You're the twelfth member of The Circle who has direct orders from her future leader. So either go get it done, or I'll find someone else more qualified. But if you don't, you can go back to being a prisoner in my home.

Don't think for even a moment that just because you stand in The Circle means that your betrayals against me have been forgotten. I'm giving you a fucking chance, Cara. Don't waste it."

She swallows hard and her gaze drops before pressing her lips into a tight line. "I get it," she murmurs. "I'll have a list of our dead by morning."

I nod, and with that, I turn on my heel and storm down the hall, my only focus getting Oakley back.

I weave through hallways and take stairs two at a time, making my way deeper through Empire's underground system until finally barging through to one of our many control rooms. Sawyer, Dalton, and Cross have hacked into the city's surveillance system to search for any sign of our girl. "What have you got?"

"Not much," Cross says, bringing up Empire's private footage and moving back from the screen to show me. "She was here shortly after the explosion. Cameras clocked her entering the tunnel from the north side. She was met at the door by James Langford and they seemed to have talked for a moment before she was brought in."

Cross fast forwards, and I watch as James ushers Oakley through the tunnels. There's a moment where James shoves her against the wall, and my hands ball into fists at my side, desperately wishing I knew what the fuck that was about. "What was she doing here?"

"I'll give you one guess," Cross mutters, the footage speeding by as we watch James lead her through the main bar, only for Oakley to knock the bastard out and take off at a sprint.

Dalton laughs, peering over to Cross's screen. "Fuck, that gets me hard every time I watch it," he says, adjusting his cock in his pants before focusing his attention on his own screen. But he's not fucking wrong. There's something so erotic about seeing Oakley fired up like this. Hell, it's part of the reason I like getting under her skin so much. She's fucking lethal when she's mad, and it gets me worked up like no other woman has before.

It's a real fucking shame I have to take her life. I would have enjoyed keeping her around.

Cross slows the footage, and I watch as Oakley takes off toward the cells, unease pulsing through my veins, knowing exactly what she wanted down in those fucking cells. "Fuck," I grunt, clenching my jaw. I should have fucking known this is what she was planning, after all, she told me multiple times just how far she'd go to save herself and her father. "Where'd they go?"

Cross shakes his head. "See, that's the thing," he mutters. "*They* didn't go anywhere."

"What?"

He skips forward an hour and my brows furrow, watching as Oakley races back up the long tunnel, tears streaming down her face, that familiar crease between her brows telling me something went down in those cells. "Why would she leave without him?" I wonder. "She would have taken our lives just to save that bastard."

"Something happened down in those cells," Sawyer mutters from across the room. "Look at her face. The last time she looked like that—"

"Was when she knew what I really wanted with her."

Cross nods. "Yep."

"Fuck." I drag my hands down my face and begin pacing behind the row of computers. "Where did she go after that?"

"That's what we're working on," Cross says, exiting out of Empire's private surveillance and opening the live surveillance, courtesy of the city. "We have her leaving here, only she doesn't head back to Faders Bay. She never exited the tunnel from the north side."

"Shit."

"My thoughts exactly," he says. "We've got her stumbling out of the south end an hour later, but she goes dark after that."

"An hour?" I ask, my brows arched. "That tunnel is nearly five miles long."

Dalton nods, looking impressed. "Nobody can claim that girl isn't amazing."

Sawyer rolls his eyes. "It's the adrenaline. She's fighting for her fucking life," he mutters. "She would have run all night if she had to."

Glancing back at Cross, I hope he's got some good news for me. "Tell me you've got something after that."

He shakes his head. "Nothing, but she couldn't have got much further than that, not after everything else that went down tonight. We've been scanning the streets, 24/7 diners, everywhere, but this isn't Faders Bay, man. Our resources are limited, and this town isn't exactly throwing cash toward their surveillance."

"Fuck."

"She'll show up eventually," Dalton says, sounding fucking sick to his stomach at the idea of Oakley being lost out there, on the run from him. "She has to."

Letting out a heavy breath, I stop pacing and grip the back of Cross's chair, hanging my head as I try to figure out where the hell to go from here. "Keep searching the surveillance," I tell Cross before glancing up at Dalton and Sawyer. "I want you two out on the fucking street. Search back alleys, dive bars, the fucking gas station bathrooms. Everywhere."

Sawyer and Dalton nod in unison, getting to their feet, ready to spend the night searching the streets despite the hell we've already been through tonight. "And you?" Cross asks, glancing up at me from his screen.

"I'm going to find out what the fuck went down in those cells."

Without another word, the boys take off, and I file out behind them, frustration burning through my veins. When Oakley's name was first given to me, the boys and I went out of our way to take every form of identification from her, her bank cards, passport, driver's license, and while they sure as fuck helped to keep her hidden with us, it's working against us now. We could have tracked her through purchases or been notified if she tried to fly her sweet ass out of here, but we've got nothing. The only way of tracking her now is by trying to get inside her mind and figuring out her game plan. It's not exactly new territory for us, we've tracked many ghosts through the country, but Oakley is different. I made a point of not letting her in, and now I wished I'd taken the time to let her inside my head and figure out what makes her tick. She would have been so easy to read.

The ball is in her court now.

Oakley has spent the past month and a half learning everything she can about us, and while she doesn't possess the skill that comes with years of training, she has an edge that concerns me. She knows we're coming for her, knows we won't stop looking for her, and it's only a matter of time before she fucks up. She's already deep in the boys' heads, she knows them, knows how they think, how they feel, and what's more, she knows they're no longer able to take a fucking shot if need be.

They will lay down their lives for her, and that scares the fucking shit out of me.

Sawyer and Dalton take off toward the exit while I step in the opposite direction, leading me down toward the cells. The long tunnel is like a breath of fresh air, giving me a moment to calm myself. It's almost comical. When I brought Oakley down here with me, she was fretting, the long tunnels sending chills down her spine as she remembered her own experiences being locked in the cold cells, but for me, it's peaceful. The darkness is where I excel. People always fear what they might come across in the darkness, they fear the unknown, but I am that unknown. I am the Boogeyman hiding in the closet, the darkness under the bed.

Pausing at the end of the tunnel, I find the last security gate left open, and unease rocks through my veins. That's not right. Even with Harrison out for the count, there should be someone standing guard.

Pushing through, I head down the stairs and turn to the right before making my way down the long, chilling hallway. Cells line either side, and I don't stop, able to smell the slightest hint of Oakley's perfume still lingering in the air.

Making my way almost to the end, I come to a stop right outside Matthias's cell to find him lying back in his bed, his hands propped behind his head.

Upon seeing me, he flies to his feet, already on the defense. "Well, this is shaping up to be one hell of an interesting night."

"Cut the bullshit, Matthias," I growl, watching as his eyes widen, realizing I've known exactly who he is this entire time. "Where is she?"

His gaze narrows. "You lost her."

"Where is she?" I demand. "I know she came down here, and I know she left without your bitch-ass which could only mean you fucked up."

His gaze tightens, and I watch as fury flashes in his eyes. "You don't know what the fuck you're talking about."

"You betrayed her trust," I say, not missing a damn thing. "She came down here to free you, and you broke her. You shattered any hope she had of surviving this. All she wanted, more than saving her own damn life, was to save you, and you let her down, just like you did twelve years ago when you left her to fend for herself."

"Watch yourself, Zade," he spits, laughter brimming in his eyes. "You have nine days to get her back and perform your ritual, and things aren't looking great for you. But don't worry, I have my men out searching for her as we speak, and they'll be sure to dispose of her just right. After all, we wouldn't want Empire falling into the hands of a fraud, would we? Especially when the true blood heir has been here, lying in wait this whole time."

I scoff, my hand shooting through the bars so fast, he doesn't see it coming. I clutch the front of his dirty shirt and pull him hard against the bars. "Let me make myself clear," I growl. "If you touch her or even look at her wrong, I will happily put a bullet between your eyes."

"Fucking do it, Zade," he spits.

"Oh, I would, and I would enjoy every fucking second of it, but why do it when I could offer Oakley the chance to do it herself? After all, she's giving her life for me, so why not allow her the chance to take yours in the process."

Matthias scoffs. "She would never. She's too weak."

"You underestimate her," I tell him, releasing my hold and shoving him back. "She's going to surprise you, and by then, it'll be too fucking late for you."

Then with that, I turn on my heel and storm back up the long hallway, knowing without a doubt that Matthias Quinn doesn't have the answers I'm looking for.

CHAPTER 6

Oakley

The early morning sun creates a slight glow through my darkened room, and I pull myself out of bed, rubbing at my sore, tired eyes. It must only be five in the morning. I've slept for barely an hour, but I can't stay here much longer. I need to be as far from this place as possible.

My feet ache with every step I take across the small room, but it's got nothing on the dull ache residing in my chest.

After quickly using the bathroom and trying to brush my teeth with my finger, I spare a glance in the mirror and hate the stranger staring back at me. This isn't where I hoped my life would take me. I was supposed to be enjoying college life, working for rent in Danny's shitty dive bar, and making memories.

Empire was never a part of my plan.

Using up precious minutes I don't have, I haul the big set of drawers away from the door and slip out into the dewy morning, not nearly as refreshed as I'd hoped. But an hour of sleep is better than no sleep at all.

There are only twenty minutes or so until the sun will be in full force, and I need to be off the streets before then. I can't risk being out in the open. Empire will be on the hunt by now, and I can only assume there were cameras in the old train tunnel to tell them exactly where I ran to. Hell, I'm lucky to still be alive now, but if I don't get a move on, the luck will quickly burn out.

Peering around the shitty motel, I take in the shadow, making sure I'm not being watched when I slip down the stairs and dash across the lot to the main office. Barging through the door, I find the horny asshole from last night, sleeping in his desk chair, his wrists still bound to the armrests and his limp dick hanging out.

His eyes spring open at the sound of me storming into the room, and seeing me, he tries to scurry away, pushing back and rolling the chair right into the back wall. "Chill out," I grunt, not in the mood to deal with his shit as I make my way around his desk to the computer. "I'm not gonna hurt you, not unless you try to do something stupid."

Moving the computer mouse, the screen comes to life, and I search for the quickest way out of here when I realize that if I want to get out of the state, I'm going to have to backtrack back into Faders Bay to get a train out of here.

Fuck. The biggest question is where the fuck am I going to go.

After quickly searching the train schedule, I come up with a plan, which is probably just as stupid as going back to Faders Bay in the first place. Then turning back to the motel attendant, I give him a beaming smile. "Where's your phone?"

"Seriously? After all of this, you're gonna steal my shit as well?"

"Well, I was just going to order an Uber, but that's not a bad idea. I'm gonna need your wallet too."

"Fuck."

He lets out a sigh, and ten minutes later, I walk out of the motel with all of his cash, his hoodie, and an Uber waiting right at the doorstep. The need to double back for the phone pulses through my veins, but knowing my luck, Empire will find out about it and use it to find my stupid ass.

Getting into the back of the Uber, I scooch down in my seat, keeping hidden from the outside world as my stomach turns with the thought of heading back into Faders Bay. I could have caught a million different buses, taking much longer to get anywhere and being exposed while waiting at bus stops, but taking a train will get me where I'm going in no time. Kind of.

It'll still take a few hours of traveling, but once I get where I'm going, I can take a break, regroup, and come up with a game plan. Until then, my heart won't stop racing.

The Uber driver tries to chat, but after quickly realizing there's no use, he gives up. As we fly back into Faders Bay, passing through the early-morning city filled with runners and cyclists, I start to feel sick.

We pass straight by the DeVil hotel, and I can't help but gaze up at the penthouse, so many fucked-up memories there, but also, some really good ones too. This isn't right. The boys shouldn't have died like that, and just thinking about it now is making it hard to breathe.

I needed to get away from them, but not like this. I'd give anything to know they were still breathing, still searching every corner of this fucked-up world for me, knowing their hearts still beat for me.

I can't accept that they're not here. It hurts too much.

The driver takes us right across town, past Danny's bar and what used to be my home, until finally pulling up at the train station, and without a second of hesitation, I bust out of the car and straight into the station, keeping my head down in case there are any cameras in here.

Hurrying up to the attendant, I get my ticket and spend the next twenty minutes pacing the terminal, hoping like fuck the train comes on time. My gaze remains locked on the doors as the fear of being caught almost cripples me.

When the train finally arrives, I hastily rush onto the car and find the furthest seat. Pulling the hoodie right over my head, I settle in for the long haul with my gaze locked out the window, hoping like fuck nobody comes for me.

My knee bounces, and the few minutes before the train leaves the station are some of the worst moments of my life, but the second the doors close and the train takes off, I can finally breathe.

It's a long, six-hour train ride back to Missouri, and I spend every minute of it wishing I could be anywhere but here, but honestly, I don't know where the hell I could possibly go. Missouri is my home.

It's where I grew up after my father was captured by Empire. It's where I went to school and learned what kind of person I am. Though, who could have known that I still had so much more to learn about myself.

The woman I thought to be my aunt was an imposter placed in my life by Empire, but at least she gave me a loving home. She kept me safe and warm and ensured I had the best life I could possibly have, and with any luck, she'll be able to give me some sort of guidance on how to survive this.

The long six-hour train ride seems to last a lifetime, and when we finally arrive at my stop, I almost expect Empire's henchmen to be waiting at the door for me. Hell, maybe even my father's. I wouldn't put it past the old bastard to jump me the second I feel as though I've found freedom. After all, he gave his men the order—*any force necessary.*

Fuck, it's been hours since hearing those words fall from his mouth, and I still can't seem to process the magnitude of his betrayal. All these years I have imagined the man my father could have been, imagined the life we could have had together, all the things he would have taught me, and now that little girl who lives within my heart is shattered.

I think it was Zade who told me I couldn't trust anybody in this world, and I never understood quite how literal he was being until last night. I knew Zade would betray me, and I knew that even after falling for them, the boys would too, but my father? I've never been so blindsided in my life.

As the doors open and people start stepping off the train, I take my time trying to blend in with the crowd. I feel as though I should be running or seeking shelter. I'm too exposed out here, but then, nobody knows I'm here. How could they?

Making my way off the platform, I search for a way to get back to my aunt's place. I don't exactly have that pervert's phone to order an Uber again, and a taxi . . . Wait, do taxis even exist anymore?

I suppose I'm taking the bus.

Crossing to the bus shelters, I look through the schedules posted and try to figure out which bus I need to be on. Twenty minutes later, I'm sitting at the very back of the bus, my whole body shaking with unease.

It's a good forty-five-minute bus ride back to my non-aunt's town, and after getting off at my stop, I'm left to walk through the streets until finally making it back to the only place I've ever truly called home.

Tears well in my eyes as I look up at the familiar home. It's not much, but for a long time, it was all I ever had, and that means the world to me. Aunt Liv's car isn't here, so I can only assume she's out for the day, and despite needing to see her face, it's probably for the best. I need some time to gather my thoughts and clean up. Hell, maybe even find some clothes that aren't torn to shreds and fit me properly.

Making my way toward the door, I stop by the third garden gnome on the left and tilt his hat back to find the spare key, smiling at how normal and familiar this feels. It's almost as though I can pretend none of the bullshit ever happened and everything is back to how it used to be. But then, denying the boys ever happened only makes my chest ache that much more.

After quickly unlocking the door, I glance up and down the street, double-checking that I haven't been followed before slipping inside and locking the door behind me. I run around the house, pulling all the blinds closed before finally collapsing on the couch.

My stomach growls with hunger, but I don't dare move, needing a moment to take it all in. Not a thing has changed, yet it feels so different now. Maybe *I'm* what's changed.

The exhaustion quickly catches up with me, and before even taking a minute to shower and clean myself up, I scoot down on the couch and press my head against the familiar cushion, quickly losing my battle with consciousness.

It's well past nightfall when I wake to a dark home, rubbing my hand over my sore, tired eyes before pushing up on the couch. I can't help but quickly scan the room, making sure I'm still alone, and it's clear Aunt Liv hasn't made it home just yet, but she was always a busy woman, in and out. I never could nail down her crazy schedule.

Getting up from the couch, I risk a peek out the window, inching the blind aside to peer up and down the street before moving into the kitchen and looking out into the yard. Then deciding it's safe enough, I finally allow myself the chance to feel human again.

Making my way down to my old bedroom, a small smile pulls at the corner of my lips, finding it just how I left it, clean clothes and all. Don't get me wrong, these aren't exactly my favorite clothes out of my collection. All of that stuff was taken with me to Faders Bay, but it'll have to do for now.

After grabbing a pair of workout leggings, clean underwear, and a tank, I make my way down the hall before stopping at the linen cupboard and taking a towel. Moving into the bathroom, I can't help but lock the door behind me before finally facing the mirror and peeling off the motel attendant's hoodie and my destroyed gown—a gown I first thought was absolutely breathtaking, only now it's nothing but a reminder of the hell I've been through over the past twenty-four hours.

My gaze sails over my naked body, taking in the subtle bruising and scrapes along my skin. Hell, I don't even try to look down at my feet, knowing exactly what I'll find there. There's still a massive gash across the front of my chest from Zade's brilliant idea of taking me into that shitty old warehouse with a bunch of assassins, not to mention the lingering dark red scarring on my arm from the Ghost's bullet.

This world has turned me into the worst kind of piece of art. I was a blank canvas before learning of Empire, and now I'm covered in horrendous memories, ones I'll have to live with for the rest of my life.

Unable to take it a second longer, I reach into the shower and turn on the water, elation booming through my chest at the amazing water pressure.

I don't hesitate, stepping into the shower and finally making myself feel somewhat human. I mostly cleaned up last night, but there's nothing quite like the familiarity of your own shower. I scrub my hair before moving onto my body and going as far as to run a razor over my legs.

Feeling like a whole new person, I step out of the shower and wrap my towel around me before perching my ass on the edge of the bathtub and rubbing lotion into my sore, aching body, being extra careful with the blisters on my feet.

After getting dressed and fixing up my hair, I trudge into the kitchen, my stomach demanding to be fed, but the cupboards and fridge are empty. Hell, it looks as though Aunt Liv hasn't been living here in weeks, and I suppose if she was placed in my life by Empire, then perhaps there's no need for her to be here anymore.

The thought has sadness creeping into my chest, and I push it to the back of my mind before climbing up onto the counter and searching the highest shelves, finding Liv's collection of old vases. Then reaching for the red one, I pull it down and smile, finding our old cash stash.

There's only a couple hundred dollars, but it's enough to get me started and fed for the next few days.

Grabbing a pair of shoes and a hoodie, I head out, making sure to lock up behind me before making my way down to the grocery store, my hunger pushing me faster and faster. I try to keep in the shadows and hide my face, only in the fluorescent lights of the grocery store, it's not as easy as it sounds.

I pick up a few things while picking at a bag of grapes along the way, and just as I go to line up at the cash register, a familiar voice sounds behind me. "Well, fuck. I'd recognize that ass anywhere."

Ahh shit.

Chills sail down my spine, and I clench my jaw, turning around to find one of my many high school boyfriends, Dylan Delgardo. He was a fucking pig, and from the sound of it, he still is. I don't know what the fuck I was thinking apart from the fact that he was hot. Though, it seems the past few years haven't been kind. There's something darker about him, something wicked, and I don't like it.

"Dylan," I say, trying to keep the bite out of my tone.

His gaze sails up and down my body, not that he sees much as it's mostly hidden beneath my hoodie. "Oakley fucking Quinn," he purrs. "I always wondered how you turned out."

"Funny," I mutter. "I've not once wondered about you."

"Come on, baby. There's no need to be like that," he says, inching toward me. "What are you doing tonight? You were such a whore for me in high school. Fancy taking another ride for old time's sake."

I scoff, my brow arching in disgust. "Weren't you in prison?"

"Got out last month."

"Oh, cool," I murmur, wondering where the hell these Empire assassins are when you need them. "What were you in for again?"

Dylan's gaze narrows. "That's none of your fucking business."

"Just what I thought," I scoff. "Look, thanks for the invitation, but I'll pass."

"What?" he grunts. "So you think you're better than me now?"

"Open your eyes, Dylan. I am better than you," I tell him. "You were a low life in high school, barely scraping by, and now look at you—standing in my personal space, trying to get me to fuck you for old time's sake. What the hell is wrong with you? If you can't get laid by picking women up the normal way, then pay for it, but leave me the fuck alone. I've got more important things to worry about than having to ohh and ahh at all the right times while you flail around on top of me with no idea how to satisfy a woman. Tell me, did you ever figure out where the clit is?"

"Listen here you little—"

"Next," the lady at the cash register calls out.

I beam up at Dylan. "It's been such a pleasure," I tell him. "I really wish I could stay and talk, but I must be going. Let's hope you can make it through the next few years without getting your bitch-ass locked up again."

Without another word, I step up to the cash register and put my groceries on the conveyor belt while watching Dylan from the corner of my eye. "Are you okay?" the woman behind the counter asks, keeping her voice low. "That asshole has been lingering around here for the past few weeks. Gives me the creeps."

"Yeah," I say with a dismissive scoff before grabbing a candy bar and placing it down on the conveyor belt, a treat for the walk home to applaud myself for an escape well done . . . kind of. "I'm fine. He's child's play compared to the assholes I've been dealing with."

"Okay," she says. "But if you want security to walk you to your car, just let me know."

I give her a tight smile, hoping I don't look like a bitch, but after the past twenty-four hours, my resting bitch face has become the norm. "Thanks," I tell her. "But I'll be alright."

She finishes ringing up my groceries, and with two heavy bags in each hand, I make my trek out of the store, desperate to get home, feed myself, and then figure out what the hell I'm going to do from here.

As much as I might want to, I can't stay here. This will be one of the first places Empire checks, and I need to be long gone before they do. I have a few friends here who would let me crash with them, but I can't possibly bring this bullshit to their door. That wouldn't be fair. I think it's time to admit that I'm more alone than I've ever been before.

Letting out a sigh, I push the thoughts aside and focus on getting home. It's only a short fifteen-minute walk, but with these heavy bags, it almost feels like a lifetime.

Just like on my way out, I keep myself glued to the shadows as I slink through the streets, going out of my way to take the back streets rather than make myself vulnerable on the main roads.

When a tingle sails down my spine, I slow my steps, my gaze traveling up and down the deserted street. I thought sticking to the shadows would keep me safe and concealed, but creeping around dark corners poses another risk I didn't think about before. There's no winning here.

Not able to see anything, I keep myself moving, determined to get out of here, when I hear the rustling of fallen leaves behind me. My head whips around, and again, I see nothing but the deserted street I've just walked.

My heart races as my palms grow sweaty, realizing this is it. Empire has found me already, and now they're lying in wait, needing me to get off the streets before they make their attack, but like fuck I'll be making it that easy for them.

Turning the corner onto my street, I peer up ahead, seeing my home, but I don't dare risk taking off toward it. Instead, I slip into the yard of the corner block, slinking across the lawn like some kind of jungle cat before hiding around the side of the house and silently lowering my groceries to the ground.

Reaching behind me, I slip my hand into the small pocket at the back of my workout leggings, slowly unzipping it and reaching in until my fingers close around the handle of the paper knife.

I peer out from around the corner, knowing in my gut that someone is there.

A moment passes, and just when I think I'm hearing things, that I'm going crazy with paranoia and that it's safe to step out and continue home, a hand clamps over my mouth from behind, and a body presses firmly against my back.

I go to scream, but the big hand muffles the sound as I'm dragged back, and my fear hits an all-time high. I didn't come all this way, suffer through kidnapping, imprisonment, and gunshot wounds just to be taken out now. If I'm going to survive this, I need to fight, and I need to do it now.

Clutching the paper knife tighter in my hand, I ram my elbow back into the asshole's stomach, and as the familiar *oomph* sounds through the yard, anger explodes through my chest. Tearing out of his arms, I whip around to find Dylan Fucking Delgardo.

"Fuck," Dylan spits.

Knowing there's only going to be a second before he recovers and comes at me again, I spring into action, reaching up and gripping the back of his head before slamming it down against my knee. Pain rocks through my knee but every second is worth it to hear the sweet sound of his nose shattering into a million pieces.

Blood spurts across the lawn as Dylan roars in agony and falls back against the side of the house. "FUCK. You broke my fucking nose, you little bitch," he grunts before reaching for me, his eyes flashing with wicked plans. "Now you're really gonna fucking pay for it."

Not daring to back down, I shove right into him, pressing the paper knife against his throat and watching as he stumbles back against the wall again with nowhere to go. "Touch me one more fucking time and see what happens, you sick pervert," I growl, leaning into him as his eyes widen with fear.

"You won't fucking do it," he says before spitting a mouthful of blood at me.

I clench my jaw. Maybe the sixteen-year-old girl he used to know might not have done it, but the woman I am now is someone who's learning just how far she'd go to protect herself . . . and fuck. I think the boys were also learning that lesson right along with me.

Not wanting to prove him right, I pull my hand back, and just as his eyes flash with relief, I barrel toward him, the paper knife sinking deep into his chest. His eyes widen, his gaze dropping to my hand as he screams in agony.

I shove a little harder, sinking the blunt blade deeper as I smile up at the asshole. "Fuck, I love it when assholes like you underestimate me. It always makes for such a lovely teaching opportunity, don't you think?"

And with that, I yank hard on the paper knife, tearing it out of the wound before tossing it into the grass. Sparing only a single moment, I watch Dylan fall to the ground, blood coating the front of his dirty shirt. Then determined to get my ass back home, I scoop up my groceries and run, hoping like fuck that I've left Dylan Delgardo for dead.

CHAPTER 7

Sawyer

First my father, then Cara, and now Oakley. Something has got to give.

Sure, life as a member of Empire was never going to be straightforward, it was destined to come with a lineup of bullshit, but this is too fucking much. I can't take it anymore. The idea that Oakley is out there somewhere and I can't find her . . . fuck. It's doing my head in.

I need to know that she's alright.

Empire is hunting her, and I'll be damned if we don't get to her first.

She's been gone nearly thirty-six hours, leaving only eight days until the sacrifice, and it makes me feel sick. A part of me wants her to get away, but the other part wants her here with me. But bringing her home means certain death, and I couldn't live with myself if I stood by and watched as Zade tore her heart right out of her chest.

What the fuck is wrong with me? I know better than to fall in love with someone like that, but Zade insisted on bringing her into our lives, and fuck, Oakley Quinn is not a woman who can be resisted.

Wait. Love? Am I really in love with her? Truth be told, I have no fucking idea. I know Dalton is, and Cross, he's well on his way there, but me? I'm not sure. I've never loved anyone apart from my family before. I've never cared enough to want them in my life, but Oakley dug her claws into me and demanded I be hers.

Whatever this is, whatever I feel for her, it's more than real, and it's fucking with my head.

Why can't this be easy? It was supposed to be easy. We were going to watch her from afar, keep her safe from Empire, and then on the sixtieth night, we would have taken her, and Zade would have performed his ritual without a single one of us bothered. And now? Fuck. I want to slit Zade's throat for even considering going through with this, but he is our leader, and it's been instilled in me my whole life that I will follow his rule. My loyalty belongs to him, no matter how fucked up that might be.

Zade DeVil has been one of my best friends since I was a kid, and I can't fucking understand how he could stab me in the back this way. The night my father attacked Oakley, Zade could have turned his back and handled it quietly. Instead, he locked my father in the cells and brought his betrayal to The Circle, forcing my father into a trial that was a guaranteed execution.

I thought that was as bad as it was going to get, and when my family was scrambling to rebuild, Zade went and put another nail in his coffin by naming my twin sister as my father's heir, forcing her to take his place within The Circle—a place not meant for a woman. She'll be torn to shreds by The Circle, and now it's not just Oakley's back I need to watch, but Cara's as well.

Don't get me wrong, I sure as fuck didn't want to inherit my father's position in The Circle, but I'd take it a million times over if it meant saving Cara from it. Hell, no matter how much I despised the idea of it, I grew up understanding that was my fate. Come hell or high water, I was going to sit as a member of The Circle. There was never even a question of which twin the position belonged to.

On top of everything, now with Oakley gone, I feel as though I'm spiraling. My world is closing in on me, and I don't know what to do. I have to find her, have to bring her home.

I sit in Zade's penthouse, computers and equipment spread from one end of the dining table to the other as the boys and I scour every inch of the earth trying to find her. I feel as though we're getting closer. We know she took off through the tunnels, and after searching through the next town, we found a run-down motel with a half-naked moron strapped to his own fucking chair and could only assume Oakley had been there.

From there, the corner store across the street has surveillance of Oakley getting into a car, and that's as far as we've gotten. Where that car went? I've got no fucking idea.

A mug is placed down beside me, and I glance up to find my sister. She's been working tirelessly since the explosion, trying to collate names and organize a mass ceremony. She says she's trying to prove that she's capable of doing this, but I know her better than anyone—she's doing it to keep busy and avoid the other Circle members. Hell, I wouldn't be surprised if she's even going so hard to try and win Zade's approval.

"Find anything yet?" she questions, pressing her lips into a hard line.

"Would I still be sitting here if I had?" I snap.

"Jesus Christ, Sawyer," she grunts. "Don't come at me with your bullshit. I was just checking in."

"I don't need you checking in, Cara," I tell her. "Don't think I've forgotten how you were giving up her location to Hartley Scott. All those attacks were on you, and had she not been so fucking terrified of being here, maybe she wouldn't have taken off like she did."

"Please," Cara scoffs, crossing her arms over her chest and rolling her eyes. "She was terrified because Zade was only days away from slaughtering her. It's got nothing to do with me. I was only trying to protect you."

"I don't need protection. I can look after myself," I spit, getting to my feet. "You should have come to me."

"Lay off, Sawyer. I get that you're pissed off about the whole situation and worried that she's out there alone, but that doesn't give you the right to treat me like shit. You've been ignoring me for days and I'm over it. Yes, okay? You're right. I should have come to you with everything, but I didn't because I thought I was doing the right thing. How long are you going to hold that against me?"

"As long as it takes."

Cara narrows her gaze at me, watching me all too closely. "You're in love with her, too. Aren't you?"

My head snaps up. "What?"

"I don't get it," she says. "Does she have a magical pussy or something? Why has she got all of you by the fucking balls?"

"You don't know what you're talking about."

"I know you're all letting yourself fall for a dead bitch," she grumbles, inching away from me. "Tell me, how does it work? Is there a schedule? You each get to fuck her on alternating nights, or do you just go at it all together?"

"I swear to God, Cara. If you weren't my sister—"

"What?" she cuts me off. "What the fuck would you do about it?"

My fist slams down on the dining table, and I fix her with a lethal stare, letting her see the fire burning in my eyes. "You'd already be fucking dead," I roar. "How the hell can't you see that? This isn't a fucking game. This is Empire. Dad's not here to protect you anymore. If you fuck up, there are real consequences, and you are pushing the fucking limits. I'm trying to protect you, Cara, but you're making it too fucking hard."

"I don't need your—"

"Don't even finish that sentence," I spit. "If it weren't for me, Zade would have slit your throat the second he found out you betrayed him."

Cara shakes her head. "No, he wouldn't do that to me. Me and him . . . I mean something to him."

"If you really think that, you're more fucked in the head than I ever imagined. Zade's been using you for years because you're an easy screw and kept your mouth shut about it. He's not in love with you, Cara. Wrap your head around that."

"You don't know what you're talking about."

"Right."

"As soon as Oakley is gone, everything is going to go back to normal. You'll see," she tells me, turning away, tears brimming in her eyes. "He just needs to fuck her out of his system, and when he steps up and completes his ritual, he'll be under pressure to marry and produce an heir, and then he'll come right back to me."

Cross scoffs, walking past the dining table. "You think he's going to settle for you?"

Fuck.

Cross and Cara have never liked each other, and while he's right, he could have said it with a little more tact. Though, I suppose there's never been anything subtle about Cross. It just irks me. Despite how frustrated I am with her right now, she's still my twin sister.

Cara's face falls, and I let out a heavy sigh, not having time to deal with her hurt feelings, when Zade calls out from his office. "Yo, I think I've got something."

Dalton flies up off the couch as I push my chair back and step out from behind the dining table. We all race to Zade's office and hover behind his desk, looking at footage of Oakley slipping onto a train in the Faders Bay station.

"Fuck," Dalton rushes out. "She was back in Faders Bay? Right under our fucking noses."

Zade nods. "Yep. I've got her Uber going right past the fucking hotel."

"Shit," Cross grunts. "Do we know which train she was on?"

"That's what I'm trying to work out," Zade says.

"What's the time stamp on that?" I question, pulling out my phone, more than ready to search up the train schedule.

Zade fast-forwards the footage before pausing right as the train departs. "6:15 departure," he tells me.

Searching through the schedule, I find the right train and let out a heavy sigh, realizing this isn't a local train, this one goes right across the fucking country. "Shit," I mutter, searching through the list of possible stops and trying to figure out which one she would have taken.

"What is it?" Dalton rushes out.

"She's out of state."

Zade flies to his feet and starts pacing, his hands balling into fists before coming to peer over my shoulder. "Where the fuck is she?"

Helplessness begins washing over me as I scroll through the long list of stops, not finding a damn thing until I look a little further and see the train entering Missouri. "No fucking way," I breathe, my heart beginning to race, feeling one step closer to my girl. "She went home."

"What?" Cross grunts across the office. "What do you mean she went home?"

"To Missouri," I tell him. "The train goes straight through her hometown."

Dalton rushes over and plucks the phone out of my hand. "Bullshit," he says, looking at the list of stops as Zade drops back into his desk chair and starts hacking into the surveillance footage from the Missouri train station. "What time would she have gotten there?" he questions, a moment later.

"Ummm, a little after midday," I say, double checking the schedule.

Zade hacks into the network with ease and scrolls a while before hitting play on the footage of the train's arrival at the station. He slows it right down as we all hover over his shoulder, watching the screen and hoping like fuck we find her.

Minutes tick by as we watch the people step off the train, and then just when I think we've missed her, the blonde goddess steps off the train with her head down. "There," Dalton rushes out before I get the chance. "I'd recognize that sweet ass anywhere."

"Good," Zade says, standing. "Let's go."

"Hate to break the news," Cross says. "Missouri is at least a twelve-hour drive. She's already been there since midday. She'll likely be gone before we get there."

Zade shakes his head. "If she knows what's good for her, she'll still be there," he rumbles before glancing up, his lips pressed into a hard line. "We're taking the jet."

CHAPTER 8

Oakley

Reaching up to the top of my old closet, I grab my suitcase and pull it down, having to quickly dart out of the way before being squished by the damn thing. I open it on the floor and get busy throwing everything I can into it while trying to come up with a plan to save my ass.

I've already been here too long, and it won't take a genius to realize that I might have gone home. It's only a matter of time before someone comes here searching for me, and I sure as hell don't want to be here when that happens.

Grabbing handfuls of tops and hoodies, I dump them into the suitcase before reaching for my pants drawer. I'm just about finished packing my underwear and shoes when I hear the familiar creak of the front door.

My heart races, and I fly to my feet, my whole body shaking. I quickly peer around my room, searching for something to use as a weapon when a voice rings through the silence. "Hello?" Aunt Liv's hesitant tone questions from out in the living room. "Is somebody here?"

I let out a heavy breath, relief surging through my veins. "Aunt Liv?" I call out, racing to my bedroom door and peering out into the hallway. "Is that you?"

"Oakley?" she responds.

Thank fuck.

I rush out of my bedroom, down the hall, and out into the living room. Aunt Liv gapes at me, and I can't stop the tears before they're streaming down my face. I crash into her, and she wraps me in her arms, her handbag falling off her arm and spilling across the floor in the process.

Liv holds me tight, gently rocking me like she used to when I was a kid, as I cry into her shoulder. "Oh, my sweet girl," she coos, her hand gently roaming up and down my back.

"I . . . I . . . "

"Shhhh," she soothes. "You're safe with me."

I pull back, wiping my eyes, hating being so vulnerable when she always taught me to be strong. "I know everything," I tell her. "I know all about the Empire and what horrid things they do and how you're not really my aunt."

Liv's eyes widen, pain deep in her gaze. "Oh, Oakley, honey. I'm so sorry. That must have been so hard to hear, but if you know anything about the Empire, then you know that I was only following orders. Your father . . . from what I know, he wasn't a great man, and all those years ago when I was assigned your case, all I was told is that a little girl really needed my help, and I was more than happy to provide you with a safe and loving home. I never could have imagined how deeply I would love you, Oakley. We might have come together as strangers, but don't mistake my feelings for you. I love you as though you were my own child."

She grips my hands and gives a gentle squeeze, and I let out a breath, knowing all too well what would have happened if she had stood against the Empire's wishes. She made the most of a fucked-up situation. I should be grateful for how she raised me. She really did offer me a safe and loving home.

Pulling my hand free, I wipe my eyes on the back of my hand, feeling as though I'm going to break. "You should have told me," I whisper. "How could you let me go back to Faders Bay when all of that was waiting for me?"

"You have no idea how many times I wished to tell you everything," she says, tears brimming in her familiar eyes. "But surely you must know that if I had known what was waiting for you there, I never would have let you go. Please, sweetheart. You must know that I would never intentionally let you walk into danger like that."

I nod and let out a breath, having no reason to doubt her. You know, apart from my entire childhood being a lie, she's always had my back. She was the one to hold me after my first heartbreak and teach me how to use a tampon. We may not share the same blood, but she's still my only family . . . and after learning who my father really is, I can honestly say that Aunt Liv is the *only* real family I have.

"You're right. I'm sorry," I say, dropping to collect all the things from her spilled handbag as Liv hastily stoops down with me, trying to grab everything. "I've been questioning everything. The people I thought I could trust turned out to be the ones I needed to fear the most, and I feel so lost. I don't know where to—"

I stop, my gaze shifting down as my hand closes around a familiar card—the black Empire calling card. The same one the assassins use before a hit.

My brows furrow, and I glance up at Liv. "Why . . . Why do you have this?"

Panic flares in her eyes, and I watch as she tries to come up with a good explanation for this. "I . . . I found it on the door as I came in. I thought maybe it was for me, but when I realized you were here . . ."

She lets her thoughts trail off, and I shake my head, not liking the hesitation in her eyes. There's no pin hole, nothing sticky on the back, no evidence at all that it had been stuck anywhere. In fact, this one looks new. "You're lying," I challenge, keeping my gaze locked on hers as I stand. "It wasn't on the door, Liv."

I swallow hard, nervousness pounding through my veins as I hope to God that this isn't what I think it is, that she wasn't coming to deliver that herself.

Liv straightens and holds my stare, unease flashing in her eyes. "You can trust me, Oakley," she says, hesitation in her tone as she creeps toward me. "I wouldn't hurt you."

"You had Empire's calling card," I say, inching away from her, my heart pounding.

"I . . . I told you. It was on the door. You're not safe here. I was coming to tell you."

I shake my head, not believing her for one second. After all, she's always been one of them, always at their beck and call. When they told her to look after an orphaned child for thirteen long years, she was their yes-man, jumping right into action. Her loyalty is to them, not me—just like the boys.

"No," I say, backing up faster, watching as her hand slips behind her, the same way Zade's used to whenever he was reaching for his gun. "I don't believe you."

"Oakley," she warns, watching me like a target and slowly stalking me down the hallway. "Don't do anything stupid. I'm here to help you."

"How did you know I was here?" I ask, my voice wavering as my hands begin to shake.

Liv doesn't respond, and I watch as her hand begins to move out from behind her back. My gaze drops, waiting to see what's going to happen, hoping I'm just being paranoid, but the second her lips twist into a wicked smirk, I know I need to get out of here.

Liv's other hand lifts to her ear, and she presses something as she holds my stare. "I've been made," she says into some kind of earpiece. "GO. GO. GO."

Fuck.

My eyes widen, horror blasting through my chest, and I barely get a chance to turn on my heel and run before she aims her gun at my back. I race down the hall, my feet pounding against the old floorboards as terror and betrayal cripple me.

BANG!

"Shit," I scream, feeling the whiz of the bullet as it sails straight past my head. I grip my door frame, using it to propel myself into my room faster, and I hastily grab the door and slam it behind me, quickly locking it and moving away in case she shoots right through it.

Holy fuck. What the hell is happening right now? I knew Empire would eventually track me down, but never in my wildest dreams did I think Liv would betray me like this.

"Come out, Oakley," Liv says from the opposite side of my door as I scramble through my room, desperately searching for the kitchen knife I stashed in here earlier. "We have the whole house surrounded and orders to bring you in dead or alive. I don't want to shoot you, but I will."

No, no, no, no. This isn't happening.

Liv is supposed to be family. But then, so was my father.

"Screw you, Liv," I yell through the locked door. "And for the record, your meatloaf tasted like feet. It can rot in hell with you."

"Don't be like that, O," she says, gripping the handle and rattling the locked door with the force of a cargo train.

Someone appears in my bedroom window and my brain turns to mush, having no idea what to do or how to save myself. Liv said the house was surrounded, and I can guarantee these assholes had similar training to what the guys had. They're probably all trained killers and I'm just . . . me.

Fuck. Fuck. Fuck. What do I do?

Trying to channel my inner Dalton with his fucked-up little craving for violence, I race across my room, scrambling through the shit on my bedside table before finally curling my fingers around the handle of the serrated bread knife. It's not the best kind of knife for the job. I would have preferred one of those heavy-duty butcher knives, but this will have to do.

Hurrying across the room, I flatten myself against the wall right beside the window, listening to the sickening sound of the guy breaking the glass and reaching in. The blinds are blocking his view, but with one quick, sharp yank, he tears the blinds right out of the frame.

They clatter to the ground, and I suck in a breath, my whole body shaking. Then, not being able to see me from his position outside the window, the guy begins climbing into my room. Without a moment of hesitation, I lash out with an ugly roar, my serrated knife sinking deep into his throat.

I yank it out, and blood spurts across the room, drenching me as I scream in horror, but if it's his life or mine, I choose mine every damn time.

He grips his throat in a feeble attempt to stop the bleeding, but judging by his gurgling and choking noises, there's no coming back from this. He's fucked.

Not having it in me to wait around to watch him die, I grab his big body and haul him the rest of the way through the window before quickly patting him down and stealing his gun. I'm terrified of what I might find outside this window, but I can't stay here. Not now. I'm a sitting duck.

Keeping the gun firmly in my hand, I climb out of my bedroom window just as three gunshots sound through the house, wood splintering from my bedroom door.

BANG!

BANG!

BANG!

My eyes snap back across my room, realizing that Liv is trying to either break the door down or shoot through the lock. My time is running out. Scrambling the rest of the way out of the window, I hastily look left and right, trying to figure out a plan. When I see a body sprinting around the side of the house, I scream and hold up the gun without thinking, firing off three shots of my own.

BANG!

BANG!

BANG!

He goes down, gripping his shoulder, and I scream some more, my body violently shaking. Then despite being down with blood pouring from his shoulder, he still reaches for his gun. My eyes widen in horror, and I whip around, breaking into a sprint. I have no idea where the hell I'm going to go. But I have to get out of here.

BANG!

BANG!

The bullets whiz past my head as I race around the property, running straight to the boundary line and throwing myself at the fence between the houses. Gripping hold of the top, my feet scramble against the side of the wooden fence, trying to find purchase to help launch me up and over the top.

"OAKLEY," I hear Liv screaming at my back. "DON'T BE FUCKING STUPID. YOU CAN'T OUTRUN THIS."

Not knowing if she has seen where I've gone, I keep quiet as I finally get to the top of the fence and pull myself over into the neighbor's yard. I drop to the ground, my knees buckling beneath me as I land.

The neighbor's dog, Rocky, rushes into me, his tongue already on my face, and if it weren't for all the treats and scratches I used to slip him, he'd probably be in attack mode by now.

Shakily getting to my feet, Rocky jumps up against me, knocking me back, and I shove him off me as I race across the lawn. "Not now, Rock," I spit through my teeth before running right around to the side gate.

He barks at me, his deep tone probably giving me away, but when someone follows me over the fence and drops down into Rocky's yard, the dog reassesses the situation, quickly realizing that I'm in trouble. He turns on the Empire henchman, giving me the chance I need to turn my back and unlatch the side gate, and like the brave warrior Rocky has always been, he makes my attacker his bitch.

Finally getting through the gate, I make a point to close it behind me, hoping like fuck the gate latched properly. Then without another moment of hesitation, my feet slam against the hard earth, propelling me down the street.

I keep to the shadows, racing down streets I used to walk nearly every day of my life. "OAKLEY," I hear from behind me, far back down the street.

Liv.

My heart thunders erratically, but she sounds too far away, like she's searching for me, probably assuming I'm hiding out in one of these surrounding properties. The girl she raised wasn't exactly a law-abiding citizen, but she was honest and a little timid, and Liv has no idea I'd be brave enough to make a run for it. But these past few months with Zade and the boys have changed me. I'm not that little girl who's going to sit around and become a victim of somebody else's wicked games. I'm in survival mode, and I don't plan on giving up any time soon.

If she wants me, she's going to have to put in the effort, and unfortunately for Liv, it's not going to be easy.

Needing to find somewhere to go, I head for the city, patting my pocket to be sure the old brass key to Empire is still right where I left it. The nightlife here is insane, and the streets will remain busy right into the night, making it easier to blend in and hide, but I don't know how well I could possibly blend in when I'm running around barefoot and covered in blood.

I run for almost an hour, making my way into the city before slowing to a walk when I reach the busy streets, not wanting to draw any unwanted attention to myself. Then seeing the mall up ahead, I hurry toward it before slipping inside and finding the bathroom.

I clean myself up the best I can before searching for some discreet five-finger discounts, needing a pair of shoes and something substantial to eat to keep me going through the night. I find a jacket and yank off the tags as I walk around. It's not exactly jacket weather, but who knows how cold it might get through the night, and for the first time in my life, I might be spending a night on the streets.

By the time I exit the mall, my heart has calmed enough to try and put some kind of plan together. Judging by the rush of people walking through the streets and the increased traffic, I can only assume business hours are over and everyone is trying to get home.

People bump and shove against me as I try to make my way through the crowd, and not knowing where I'm trying to go, I step to the side of the walkway before falling into a back alley. It's dark down here, but I welcome it, and instead of staying near the opening of the alley, I follow it right to the end. Confident that I have a few different escape options if I need to make a break for it, I lean back against the wall and slide down until my ass is on the dirty ground.

My gaze remains locked on the street, watching the traffic fly by, completely oblivious to the fresh hell tormenting my mind.

I killed someone. Again. And two others are seriously injured.

This world has turned me into something I don't recognize, and I don't know whether it makes me feel strong or weak, but what I do know is that I don't like it.

Tears fill my eyes, and the longer I sit here and torment myself with the horrid memories, the harder the tears fall. I bury my face in my hands as the hours tick by, and before I know it, the street is pitch black and the passing cars have slowed to one every few minutes.

A chill fills the air, and I snuggle into the jacket, my eyes growing heavy. This isn't exactly the best place to stay the night, but it's going to have to do. I'm concealed by shadows, so anyone walking by won't easily see me, but that doesn't make this situation any better.

Bringing my knees up, I brace my arms against them and drop my face, trying to find just a little bit of comfort on the cold ground. Then just as my eyes close and I'm fading out of consciousness, a deep, raspy tone startles me awake. "Come on, Lamb. Let's go home."

CHAPTER 9

Oakley

My head snaps up, my eyes already filling with tears as I see Zade standing before me, and for a moment, I wonder if I'm seeing a ghost. He's covered in cuts and bruises, and his dark eyes look haunted. Yet as he stands here looking down at me, they're also filled with relief.

How can he be here? I thought he . . .

Zade lifts his wrist to his face and presses a small button on his watch. "I've got her," he says, keeping his stare locked on mine. Then before I get a chance to even question how he's here, he bends down and scoops me into his warm arms, holding me close to his chest, and I hold him with everything I have left.

He turns and starts making his way out of the dark alley, and all

I can do is breathe him in, the tears still streaming down my face. Locking my arms around his neck, I hold on as tight as possible, my heart racing with . . . I don't even know. Fear? Relief? It's impossible to tell. I know Zade will keep me safe. He'll have my back and look out for me, but at the end of the day, he's the one who's going to kill me.

Burying my face into his shoulder, I wipe my eyes against his shirt. "How are you here? I thought you died in the explosion. I—"

"What? You think a little blast like that is going to take me out?" he rumbles, his deep tone vibrating right through his chest. "Maybe you've forgotten who I am."

I shake my head, glancing up and meeting his heavy stare. "Not possible," I whisper before swallowing hard, my heart thundering with unease. "If you survived, then—"

Zade nods before cutting me off. "They're alright," he tells me, stepping out of the dark alley and into the street. "All of them, but fuck, Lamb. They're pissed you ran."

Relief slams through my chest, and for the first time in the past few days, I feel as though I can finally breathe. I was so torn up and filled with pain and grief when I thought I lost them, and all this time, they were right there, searching for me, needing me to come home.

My head falls back against Zade's chest, my eyes closing as relief and exhaustion begin weighing down on me. I don't even care if they're angry with me, nothing else matters as long as they're all alive. "I did what I had to do," I tell him, my fingers knotting into the hair at the back of his neck. "And if the roles were reversed, you would have done it too."

"I know," he says. "I get it, and I'm proud of you for fighting, but the only difference is if the roles were reversed, I wouldn't have been captured in the first place."

My fingers unknot from his hair, and I pull my arms away, rolling my eyes. "Wow. I'm glad to see the explosion didn't manage to knock back your ego."

"Just stating facts, Lamb."

I push against his chest, wanting him to put me down before I remember how much I hate his stupid ass, but he only holds me tighter, refusing to let me go. "Stop calling me that."

"FIREFLY?"

My head snaps up at the familiar deep tone that comes booming from down the street, and the tears return, finding Dalton racing toward us. I suck in a breath, somehow clambering out of Zade's arms until my feet are slamming against the pavement.

My heart thunders in my chest as I run toward him, not able to get to him fast enough.

He runs right into me, our bodies slamming together as I jump right up into his arms, my legs locking around his waist. He holds me against him as his lips crush down on mine. I sink into him, tasting my tears in our kiss as his hands roam over my back and into my hair.

Dalton kisses me deeply, and I never want to leave the security of his warm arms. He keeps walking us back to Zade, not once pulling away from me until my back is pressed against the door of a black SUV. We come up for air and he drops his forehead against mine. "Fuck, Firefly. You scared me."

"I thought I was never going to see you again," I tell him as he strokes his thumbs across my cheeks, wiping the tears away. "That explosion! I thought—"

"I'm fine," he murmurs, holding my face.

Zade scoffs and my brows furrow. "You're not fine, man."

I stare at Dalton in horror, searching his eyes as unease pulses through my veins. "What does he mean? What happened? Are you okay?"

"It's nothing," Dalton says, his tone soothing. "Zade's overreacting. It's not like I got shot or anything. Just a small stab wound. Nothing a few stitches couldn't handle."

"What?" I shriek, shoving him back a step. "You have a stab wound and you let me jump all over you? What the hell is wrong with you? What were you thinking?"

Dalton rushes back into me, his hands gripping my waist as his face drops to the curve of my neck, his lips brushing over my sensitive skin. "I was thinking if I didn't get my hands on my girl, I was going to fucking die," he breathes, sending shivers sailing across my skin. He pulls back just enough to meet my eyes and stares heavily into them. "Now, please. Can we take you home?"

Pressing my lips into a hard line, I finally nod, and Zade lets out a heavy breath, stepping up to the back door and opening it wide. "Get in," he mutters, his gaze dropping to Dalton's hands on my waist, jealousy flashing in his eyes before he lifts them back to mine. "We have to go find Sawyer and Cross first."

My eyes widen as I move toward him, excitement drumming

through my veins. "They're here too?"

Dalton steps into my back, his hand falling back to my waist. "Would they be anywhere else?"

A small flush spreads across my face, and I instantly hate myself for how good that makes me feel. I love these guys. We definitely started off with a rocky relationship, but over the past few months we've worked through that, and I've gotten to know the broody men they are inside, but that doesn't change the fact that their loyalty belongs to Zade and the ritual. Maybe not Dalton though. He's been fighting this since the second he realized how much he loved me, desperately trying to find a way to save me.

Needing to see the boys with my own two eyes, I go to move into the car when I pull back and step closer to Zade, my hand resting against his wide chest. Lifting my chin, I look up into those troubled eyes and force a small smile across my lips. "I know you're only here because of the ritual, but thank you for coming," I whisper, not having the strength to explain why I've needed them so much, especially after running and thinking I had what it took to do this on my own.

Pushing up on my toes, I press a small kiss to his lips, and his hands fall to my waist, holding me there and refusing to let me go. He meets my stare, those dark eyes expressing everything he's always refused to say out loud. "Yes, I need you for the ritual, but that's not why I'm here, and don't pretend like you don't know that."

I swallow hard and shake my head, my heart pounding. "You can't say those things to me, Zade," I beg, needing to put space between us. "I told you not to let me fall in love with you."

I hold his stare and there's not an ounce of regret in his eyes, and seeing this isn't going anywhere good, Dalton's hand returns to my back. "Come on. I'm ready to get you home," he says, pushing me into the car.

Stealing my gaze away from Zade's, I go willingly into the backseat, and Dalton comes in behind me as Zade walks around to the driver's seat. Dalton pulls me right into his lap, and I barely even notice when Zade hits the gas.

Dalton's hands rest on my hips as we fly across the city. "You need to tell me more about this stab wound," I demand, meeting his intense stare.

"And you need to tell me why the fuck you thought it was a good idea to run from us. Haven't you learned anything?"

I shake my head and narrow my gaze, not giving up with this. "Stab wound, Dalton."

Zade mutters from the driver's seat. "You're sitting on it."

My eyes widen in horror, and I scramble off Dalton's lap, hoping like fuck I didn't just make it worse. Glancing up at him, I reach for his belt. "I need to see. Take your pants off."

"Chill the fuck out, Firefly," he says. "The only way you're getting my pants off is if you're about to suck my cock, and while I'd love to sit back and watch how deep you can take me, now's not the time. I'm fine. Cross stitched me up. It's barely a scratch."

Rolling my eyes, I settle into my seat and wrap my arms over my chest, satisfied with his answer . . . for now, at least. "For what it's worth, I would have still sucked your cock, but joke's on you because now I'm not sucking anything."

Dalton scoffs, his eyes sparkling with the challenge as his hand skims up my thigh. "We'll see about that."

A smile pulls at the corners of my mouth, and I press my lips into a hard line, trying to hide my amusement. Hell, just the thought of getting my hands on the big, pierced cock has me all hot and bothered.

"You're really not hurting?" I ask in a small voice as we sail through the city.

"The only thing that's been hurting me is the fact we couldn't locate you for two fucking days," he tells me, reaching across and cupping the side of my face, forcing me to meet his stare. "Don't fucking run from me again, Firefly. I can't handle it."

"I had to," I whisper, knowing that he knows and understands why I did it, but I suppose just because someone understands something doesn't mean they have to like it. "I have no hope here with you guys. Zade is still going to go ahead with the ritual. Whether I run or not, I'm still going to die, but out here on my own . . . I would have had a say in how I went. Kinda. I would have eventually been killed out here, but it would have been done with me fighting right to the end, which I can accept. But I refuse to die for someone else's gain. Especially in such a brutal way."

"I get it," he tells me. "But give me a fucking chance, Oakley. I'm going to find a way to save you. I promise you that. I'm not going to let you die."

Scooching over, I move in right next to him and take his face in my hands, holding him close. "I know you want to save me, and I believe that you're going to try everything in your power to do so, but don't make me promises you can't keep. You and I both know Zade isn't going to let me go. I'm dying in seven days, Dalton. Let's just make the best of it."

Zade thankfully remains silent from the front of the car as Dalton pulls me back onto his lap and wraps me in his arms. "Wow, your lack of faith in me really makes me feel like the fucking man," he teases.

"Sorry," I laugh. "I do have faith in you, and it's because of that I know just how hard you're going to fight for me, but I'm also a realist, and you and I both know that the only way I'm getting out of this thing alive is if Zade magically changes his mind."

Dalton lets out a heavy breath and drops his forehead to mine, not bothering to respond because honestly, what could he possibly say to that? He knows I'm right, and he's not about to start lying to me now.

Zade slows the SUV and pulls off to the side of the road, and before I even get a chance to look up, the back door flies open and I see Sawyer and Easton staring back at me with stupid grins across each of their faces. "Well fuck," Sawyer says. "There's a sight for sore eyes."

He clambers into the SUV beside me and Dalton, leaving Easton to take the front, and before Sawyer's even settled in beside us, his hands are already on my waist, hauling me onto his lap. "You've got no fucking idea how happy I am to see you," he says, giving me the first real smile I've seen on his face since before his father's execution.

I grin back at him, my hand snaking around the back of his neck, and before I even get the chance to respond, he pulls me in hard against him, crushing his lips to mine in a bruising kiss.

I sink into him, taking everything I can get as I hear the sound of Easton getting in and closing the door behind him. Zade hits the gas and the momentum has me rocking harder into Sawyer, but he holds me tight, not daring to let me go.

I grind down against him, coaxing a long groan from his throat, and just when I'm ready to heat this up, an arm locks around my waist, pulling me away. I squeal as Easton hauls me across the SUV, and I expect him to pull me right through to the front beside Zade, only he's cramped in beside Dalton, the three guys squished in the back, leaving me nowhere but their laps to sit on.

Easton doesn't give in until I'm straddled over him, those stormy dark eyes locked on mine. "You really fucked me up there, Pretty," he says, his words like a knife straight through the chest.

"Try being on the other side of that," I tell him, my hand cradling the side of his face. "You guys have been fucking me up since the day Empire gave you my name."

He nods, accepting it for what it is—fact.

His fingers trail up my body, his heavy gaze following the movement before coming back to meet my stare. "You good?" he questions. "I saw the mess you left behind at your aunt's place."

My eyes widen, and I tense on his lap. "You saw that?" I ask, my heart kicking up a notch.

"Mmhmm," he says as I feel Zade's laser-sharp stare on me through the rearview mirror. Easton pulls me in, his lips brushing gently over mine. "It wasn't smart coming back here."

"I know that now," I tell him. "I thought I could come here and re-group, try to figure out a plan and check in with Liv, but turns out she's the one who gave me away. She's been working with Empire this whole time. I was an idiot for thinking I could trust her."

"You're not an idiot," Sawyer says, reaching over Dalton to take my hand. "An idiot couldn't cause the kind of hell you caused back there. You did what you had to do and got out of there before they had a chance to retaliate."

Dalton scoffs. "Retaliate? The guy was fucking dead. He couldn't retaliate even if he wanted to."

Sawyer rolls his eyes. "You know what I meant," he says, probably referring to Liv and anyone else who was there.

Needing to change the topic, I glance back at Easton. "So what now?"

"First, you're gonna kiss me like you fucking mean it, and then we're taking you back to Faders Bay where we can watch over you properly."

"You mean, keep me safe until Zade can kill me himself?"

"Something like that," Easton says, not bothering to sugarcoat it. He lets out a heavy breath before focusing his stare right on my eyes. He pauses a moment as if trying to gather his thoughts before finally letting me have it. "Don't get me wrong, Pretty. I know why you ran, and I accept that, but fuck. I'm so fucking angry with you. When you ran, you weren't just running from Zade. You ran from me, and I don't fucking like it. It kills me that I couldn't keep you safe, and because I wasn't there to have your back, you were almost killed by the very people we've been trying to protect you from."

"Surely you must know that I wasn't intentionally running from you. I was doing what I had to do to save myself. You guys might be trying to save me from Empire, but they're not the only ones I need saving from," I tell him. "But you don't have to worry anymore. I'm not going anywhere. Forty-eight hours out here on my own was enough to learn that I'm not strong enough to survive this by myself."

Easton shakes his head. "You are, Oakley," he says. "We followed you this whole time, tracking your movements and watching you through CCTV, and the way you've survived has only proven just how strong you are. You did what you had to do to get this far—"

Anything else he was going to say is cut off when an alarm sounds through Zade's phone. All eyes turn to him, and I watch as he unlocks his phone and looks down at the screen. "Fuck," he spits a moment later. "The jet has been compromised."

"What? What do you mean jet?" I ask.

"We weren't about to drive twelve hours across the country only to get here too late," Dalton tells me, his hand on my thigh. "We took one of Empire's jets, and clearly the risk paid off. We got you back in one piece."

"But, how do you know the jet has been compromised? What's happening?"

Zade reaches back, handing me his phone, and I look down at the screen, watching a live feed of men storming through a jet and planting explosives. I suck in a gasp, horror resting in my chest. "How did they find it?"

"All of Empire's jets have tracking systems," Zade tells me. "It's just a question of whether they're smart enough to hack into it or not. Either way, you might as well get comfortable. We're in for the long haul now."

Well, shit. A twelve-hour drive across the country, stuck in the back with these three guys. I wonder what we could possibly do to pass the time.

Turning back to Easton, a smile pulls at the corner of my lips, and within seconds, the same, devilish smile tears across his face. He knows exactly what's about to go down.

CHAPTER 10

Oakley

We've barely hit the highway when my lips lock onto Easton's and his arms wrap around my body, holding me so damn close I can barely breathe. I kiss him with everything I've got, letting the fear, grief, and pain of the last few days seep out of my body, leaving me with nothing but pure passion and desperation.

It's only been two days since the explosion, but so much has happened since then, and I feel as though a whole lifetime has passed.

Feeling him harden beneath me, I grind down against him, groaning with pleasure before tipping my head back. His lips trail down to the base of my throat, and my eyes roll in the back of my head, loving the way he works his tongue over my skin.

Feeling Dalton's wanting gaze on my face, I turn to take him in, loving the heated desire in his eyes. I can't help but reach out and pull him toward me. He leans in, and without skipping a beat, his lips come down on mine, claiming me.

Easton's hands roam over my body, slipping beneath the waistband of my pants and pushing down to my ass. He grabs ahold, squeezing tight, so I press back against him, wanting more, and he doesn't disappoint.

My pussy clenches, and I hastily reach down between us, working his belt buckle and freeing that undeniably thick cock. He's already hard and ready to go, but that doesn't mean I'm not going to take my time warming him up before pushing him right to the edge.

My hand closes around him, my thumb and fingers not even close to being able to touch, and I watch the way his eyes become hooded with desire as I work him just the way he likes it. My thumb roams over his tip before trailing all the way back down, and he groans, his body tensing beneath me.

Easton has never been the type to take without warming me up first, and he can barely wait before his hand is freed from my pants and he grips my waist, pulling me up just enough to pull my pants down my legs, taking my underwear along with them. He settles me back on his lap, his fingers reaching between my legs and brushing over my clit, making my whole body jolt with pleasure.

He does it again and this time, he doesn't dare stop.

Dalton adjusts himself beside us, and instead of making him suffer, I reach down and free him too, and the second my fingers are wrapped around that pierced monster cock, he leans back in, claiming my lips once again.

I grind against Easton, needing more, and reading my body so perfectly, he pushes two thick fingers deep inside my pussy, keeping his thumb on my clit, driving me wild with need. His fingers pulse inside me, and I tip my head back, the pleasure almost too much to bear.

"Fuck, I need you now," I tell him.

A deep growl tears from the back of his throat, and the second I push higher on my knees, he adjusts his cock beneath me and loses his pants. Then as I lower myself back down, I take him deep, my pussy clenching around his delicious size.

"Fuuuuuck," he groans, his eyes fluttering as I take all of him. Keeping one hand on Dalton's cock, I grip Easton's shoulder with the other and pause, getting used to the way my walls stretch around him. Then when he lifts his hand and brushes the backs of his knuckles down my face, I almost come right then and there. "Dance for me, Pretty."

Goddamn. Yes, Sir.

His hand drops to my thigh, his fingers roaming over the small cross he branded on my skin, and it sends a thrill shooting right through me. Gripping his shoulders tighter, I start to move, dancing for my man, and when he grips my tank and pulls it right over my head to expose my body, I've never felt so free.

Dalton inches in, his big hand closing around mine on his cock, both of us working him together, and when he can't take it a second longer, he nods to Easton. "Turn her around," he rumbles. "I need to taste her."

My brow arches, not understanding how this is possibly going to work in such a small space, but if he has a plan, I'm good to go with it.

Without hesitation, Easton flips me around until I'm facing the back of the driver's seat. Zade's intense, desire-filled stare finds me in the rearview mirror, and my skin prickles as his eyes drop to my tits, taking in the way they gently bounce with my movements.

With my pussy now on display, my cunt so perfectly taking Easton from beneath me, Dalton reaches over, his fingers rolling over my clit. The pleasure blasts through my body, and I lean back against Easton's chest, his arm wrapping around my body and gripping my tit.

Dalton plays, his fingers exploring and dipping lower to where Easton's cock is buried deep inside me, and he doesn't hold back, pushing them inside me and feeling the way I bounce on top of Easton. "That's right, Firefly," Dalton murmurs. "Show him how fucking good you give it."

There's no denying that Easton knows damn well just how good I give it, but who am I to correct him when I appreciate his approval so much?

He draws his fingers out of me before lifting them to my mouth and trailing my wetness over my lips. "See how fucking sweet you taste, baby?" he murmurs, watching the way my tongue greedily pokes out and takes everything he's offering.

Hunger blasts through his stare, and knowing how hot it gets him, I hold his stare and push him a little further. "More."

Dalton growls deep in his chest before forcing his fingers inside my mouth, and I take it eagerly, sucking the taste of my pussy off him, and before I get a chance to swallow, he grips the back of my neck and kisses me deeply, his tongue sweeping into my mouth and tasting me.

Without skipping a beat, Dalton moves in front of me before dropping down between me and the back of Zade's chair, barely fitting, but fuck, do I love a man on his knees. The tight space forces Easton's knees wider, which pushes mine even farther apart, and I sink deeper onto Easton's cock.

"Fuck," Easton mutters in my ear, his grip tightening on my tit, but I barely notice it when Dalton's mouth closes over my clit, his tongue flicking right over the tight bud. I cry out, my hand knotting into the back of his hair and holding him there.

"Hold her still, brother," Dalton murmurs, the intense hunger in his tone making my eyes roll in the back of my head.

Easton is more than happy to oblige as his hand releases my tit and locks tighter around my waist, holding me up just a little so that he can fuck me from below, his cock moving up and down, massaging my walls with every delicious thrust. Dalton groans with approval, his tongue working my clit, and I don't miss the way he travels down to my cunt, more than happy to let Easton in on the fun.

Zade's gaze flicks between me and the road, and his attention is more than enough to push me to the edge, but I'm not quite there yet. After all, there's one more heated gaze locked on my body across the backseat, and it would be a tragedy if he missed out on the sweetest reunion I've ever had.

My gaze travels up and down Sawyer's body, watching the way he rests back in his seat, his beautiful, angry cock already gripped in his strong fist. You can call me a greedy whore if you must, but goddamn, I have to have it.

"Hey," I murmur, letting Sawyer hear the intent in my tone. His heated stare instantly lifts from my body, meeting mine as my tongue roams over my bottom lip, drawing him in with my gaze alone. "What are you waiting for? I'm still hungry."

He doesn't wait a damn second, moving across the backseat, losing his pants in the process. "I thought you'd never fucking ask," he mutters, his fingers gently gripping my chin.

"Then stop making me wait."

"Fuck me," he murmurs, moving in nice and close, one knee braced against the backseat as his hand moves around the back of my neck, pulling me toward him. I open my mouth, my tongue poking out and lapping up the small bead of moisture pooling at the top of his cock before opening wider and taking him right to the back of my throat.

Dalton works his way back up to my clit, closing his mouth over me and gently sucking, his tongue flicking at the same time. I groan around Sawyer's cock, my pussy clenching over Easton as he pushes up into me again.

It's too much. Too fucking good. I can't take it all, but I will. I need it more than ever before.

Easton's lips drop to the base of my neck, working his tongue over my sensitive skin, and my body jolts with a bolt of electricity straight to my core.

"Mmmm," Dalton murmurs between my legs. "She's close."

Hell yeah, I am.

They don't stop, giving me everything they've got as I work Sawyer's cock, feeling him right in the back of my throat and pushing past my boundaries as my tongue works over him, moving over his tip before taking him deep again. His hand clenches in my hair, and as Easton's fingers dig into me, I realize just how fucking close he is.

"Fuck, Pretty," he murmurs against my skin, his tone sending shivers sailing across my body.

He slams up into me one more time, and as Dalton's tongue flicks over my clit, I come hard, my orgasm shooting through me like an explosion as my gaze locks onto Zade's once again. Easton comes with me, shooting his hot cum deep inside of me, but neither Dalton nor Easton dare stop, working me as my high tears through my body.

I clench my eyes, gripping the base of Sawyer's cock, and just as I start coming down, Sawyer's hand tightens again, holding me still as he comes right along with us. I gulp him down, taking every fucking drop he has to offer, and the second he pulls free, he drops back into the seat, his chest heaving as he watches me in awe.

I make a show of licking my lips as I settle into Easton's lap, all of us out of breath, apart from Dalton, who pulls himself off the floor of the car and back into the middle space, his gaze locked on mine. "Oh, baby. That was only a warm-up," he says, locking his arm around my waist and pulling me off Easton's cock before lowering me to his lap and filling me right back up with his.

After coming so intensely, I take my time with him, rocking my hips as I lock my lips on his, both of our bodies slowly moving together until I'm coming once again. Dalton reaches his high right along with me, and not a second later, I'm collapsing against his chest, my head lowering to his shoulder as I catch my breath.

"If you're done spreading your DNA through the car," Zade mutters. "I have a few questions for you."

I scoff and pull back, meeting Dalton's gaze. "Is it just me or does Bossman sound jealous?"

"Oh yeah," Sawyer laughs. "Offer to suck his cock. It might take the edge off. Otherwise, the next eight hours are going to pass very slowly."

I laugh and swivel on Dalton's lap, reaching down and searching for my clothes on the floor. Then not having enough space to get dressed, I climb my naked ass through to the front seat and drop down, making myself comfortable before pulling my clothes back on. "I mean, Sawyer's right," I say to Zade, knowing damn well he's not about to take the bait. "If you need a little something, just say the word. I'm more than happy to give you what you need, but be warned, it'll cost you."

Zade scoffs. "And fuck your already cream-filled pussy? I'll pass."

I laugh and smirk at him. "Speaking of that. I'm going to need a bathroom break," I tell him. "Otherwise this really is going to be a long drive home. I mean, don't get me wrong, being filled to the brim with your friends' cum is sexy as hell and gets me off harder than anything else ever could, but there comes a point when it's not warm anymore and it just kinda feels gooey and starts spreading between my legs, you know?"

Zade glares at me. "We're not stopping."

"Then I'm not answering your bullshit questions."

He clenches his jaw, gripping tighter onto the steering wheel until his knuckles turn white. "Fuck, it's been so peaceful not having you fighting me at every turn these past few days."

"Shut up," I scoff, rolling my eyes and seeing right through him. "You love it and you can't even deny it. I see it in your eyes every damn time. The question is, how are you going to live with yourself once you've killed me and all of that juicy goodness is gone?"

"You've got to stop thinking of it as me killing you. It's a sacrifice. I'm *sacrificing* you."

I gape at him. "A sacrifice is something you give up willingly, usually for those you love, and I'm not sure if you've been paying attention, but you can't give up something that isn't yours to give away. You might be happy to slaughter me for your own gain, and it might be seen as a sacrifice in your eyes, but I'm not giving myself up for anybody. It's cold-blooded murder, Zade. You're not sacrificing me, you're killing me for a step up in the world."

He narrows his gaze at me, and a moment passes before he reaches to my side of the car and opens the console in front of my knees. He digs around for a moment before pulling out a napkin and tossing it into my lap. "I'm not stopping," he tells me, his attention focused on the road. "That's the best you're gonna get. Take it or leave it."

Fuck.

I glare at the asshole in the driver's seat, never wanting to suffocate him with a pillow more in my life. "Remind me why the hell I was so torn up about the idea of you being dead because I suddenly can't seem to remember."

"What wouldn't you be torn up over?" he questions, refusing to look at me, though I see the glimmer sparkling in his eyes. "I'm a fucking catch."

"Is that what you call it?" I ask. "Funny. I have a different name for it."

Zade doesn't respond, and realizing just how serious he is about not stopping, I let out a heavy breath and clutch onto my pathetic little napkin before shoving it down my pants and doing my best to clean myself up. Though let's face it, I'm going to need one hell of a shower when we get back to Zade's penthouse.

The boys do what they can to smother their laughs, and once I'm done, I yank the cum-filled napkin out of my pants and fix Zade with a beaming smile. I hold my hand out to him, the napkin in the palm of my hand. "Be a dear and dispose of this for me."

Dalton howls with laughter, no longer capable of holding it back, and in a split moment, Zade's ferocious glare snaps to mine. His hand crashes into the back of mine, propelling the used napkin up into the air and sailing in the perfect arc right into Dalton's face.

Dalton gasps in horror, groaning in disgust though I don't know what his problem is—half of that is his. Then, forcing a fake smile across his face, Zade looks back at me. "Satisfied?"

"Asshole," I mutter.

Dalton scoffs. "Careful, bro," he warns Zade. "Keep fucking with me like that and I'll shove this napkin so far down your throat you'll be tasting me for weeks."

Zade glares at Dalton through the rearview mirror as I settle into my seat, crossing my arms over my chest and turning my body toward the window in the hopes of blocking Bossman out, but something tells me evading his questions isn't going to be that easy.

We drive in silence for an hour, and before I know it, the guys are asleep in the backseat, the three of them squished together like sardines. My head falls against the window, and realizing just how long this drive is going to be, I close my eyes and try to sleep, but as soon as the darkness seeps in, the memory of the serrated knife plunging into that man's throat flashes through my mind.

"Why'd you leave him behind?" Zade questions, his deep tone filling the car.

My brows furrow, and I lift my head off the window to meet his eyes. "What are you talking about?"

"Your father," he explains. "All you've wanted to do since you found out he was alive was save him, and you had the perfect opportunity. You were right there in those cells, so what happened? Why would you turn your back on him like that?"

My gaze falls away, and I turn back to the window, watching the other cars' headlights pass us by. I've gone out of my way over the past few weeks to hide my father from Zade, and now . . . I no longer know what side I'm on. "He's not the man I thought he was," I tell him. "He's been lying to me this whole time."

"What do you mean?"

Letting out a shaky breath, I turn back to him and hate the concern I see in his eyes. He shouldn't care about me like this. It's not fair. "When I got down there, his cell was empty."

Zade shakes his head. "No, that's not possible."

"I was about to leave when I heard people coming. There were three of them in dirty suits, like they'd just been at Cara's initiation ball and narrowly escaped the blast. One of them was my father, so I hid while they talked."

"And?" he prompts.

"And he's a bigger asshole than you are," I say bluntly. "He thought you were dead and was saying how his plan is finally in motion, and it became pretty freaking clear that his men were responsible for the attacks."

"No, my mother is responsible for that."

I shake my head. "Maybe they both have their own agendas," I tell him with a shrug of my shoulders, not really understanding. "He was ordering his men to find me, and when they said they wouldn't let him down, he scoffed at them and commented how I'd already evaded them before. He's planning something."

Zade nods, going silent for a moment. "What does he want with you?"

"The same thing everyone does," I say with a heavy sigh. "He wants me dead so that when he can finally claim Empire, there's no one left to challenge him. He told his people to take me with any force necessary."

"Shit."

"Mmhmm," I murmur, pressing my lips into a hard line. "Liv pretty much said the same thing, that her orders were to take me dead or alive. It seems like every step I take, there's someone coming for my throat. I'll never be safe in this world."

Zade reaches across the center console and takes my hand, gently squeezing it while staring straight out the windshield as if pretending this isn't actually happening. "I'm not going to let anyone hurt you, Lamb. You're mine."

A perfectly round tear falls from my eyes, falling off my jaw and splashing against my chest as I turn back to him. A soft smile pulls at the corners of my lips, and what kills me is that I know how much he means it, every damn word. He'll never let anyone hurt me, never allow them to take me away and use me for their own sick plans . . . apart from his own.

Letting out a soft sigh, Zade holds my stare, and I know he sees the brokenness in my eyes. "If only you weren't the monster I needed protecting from," I tell him, and with that, I turn back to the window and get comfortable, willing myself to close out the pain and finally fall into a deep, dreamless sleep.

CHAPTER 11

Oakley

Soft jostling wakes me, and I open my eyes to find myself snuggled in Zade's bed, his warm arms wrapped around me. The early morning sun is streaming in through the window, and as I turn in his arms and take in his face, it's clear he's in a deep sleep. Hell, of all the nights I've slept here in his arms, I don't think I've ever seen him in a deep sleep. He's the sleep-with-one-eye-open kinda guy.

He must have driven right through the night, looking over the rest of us as we slept in the car. I have no recollection of waking up and making my way up into the penthouse, so I can only assume that Zade carried me up here and put me to bed.

My heart breaks for him. He's always the one to carry the burden on his shoulders—no matter how big that burden is. Any of the guys could have driven across the country through the night and they would have done it without question, and yet Zade didn't even ask.

Bringing my hand up, I gently lay it across his face, hating how deeply I'm falling for him. It's wrong. I shouldn't feel this way for him, yet every dark corner of my heart craves him, needs him, desires him. If anything, I should take this chance to reach across to his bedside table, take his dagger, and end this once and for all, but the reality of the matter is that I would rather give my life than see anything happen to him.

How fucked up is that?

Leaning in, I press a gentle kiss to his cheek before lifting his arm from around my waist and slipping out of bed. My feet hit the ground, and I pad across to the bathroom, desperate to finally shower and feel somewhat human after spending hours sitting in a dirty alley.

The water is like heaven on my face, and despite wanting to stand in here for the rest of my life, I make it quick, scrubbing the dirt from the bottom of my feet and washing the blood matted in my hair.

Stepping out of the shower, I quickly towel dry before finding my silk robe hanging on the back of the door. After pulling it on, I pad out into Zade's room to find my slippers. "Where are you going?" His deep tone sails across the room.

Glancing back at him from the door, I go to walk out before thinking better of it and making my way over to him, knowing if I were to walk out of here without a word, the big bastard would follow me right out and probably put a leash on me. Pressing my knee into the mattress, I lean over and drop a kiss to his forehead. "Coffee," I tell him, grabbing the blanket and pulling it up over his bare chest. "Go back to sleep."

Zade nods, and as I go to leave, he catches my hand, stopping me. I glance back, meeting his stare, and while not a single word is spoken, a million messages pass between us. I hold his stare a moment longer before pulling my hand free, determined not to get swept away by his wicked heart.

Stopping by the door on my way out, I grab my Sharpie and stare up at the tally marks on Zade's bedroom wall. Then letting out a heavy sigh, I get to work, filling in the days I've missed before adding one more for today.

Six days to go.

Six days before Zade DeVil tears my heart right out of my body.

I wonder how he's going to do it. Will it be quick and savage, trying to get it done as fast as possible, or will he take his time, trying to savor the moment? The Zade I met on day one wouldn't have cared. He would have thrown me down, lunged at me with a dagger, and enjoyed my terror-filled screams, but the Zade I've come to know . . . I'm not really sure anymore. He'll probably be gentle, try to make it hurt as little as possible. Maybe he will knock me out so I don't feel the pain.

He's worked for this his whole life, trained to be the best leader Empire could ever need, and there's no question about it, Zade will be an incredible leader. I've watched him slaughter men without a single care, but I don't know what kind of man will be left behind after he takes my life.

Risking looking back, I find Zade's stare locked on the wall as if counting every single one of the tally strokes I've drawn, each one of them like a knife right to his chest. Having no words to offer him, I walk out the door, not wanting to hear what he could possibly have to say about it.

The second I step out into the living room, Cara appears from the hallway, stopping awkwardly as we stare at each other, neither of us knowing where to go from here. "So, umm . . . You're back, huh?"

"Observant," I mutter, swallowing over the lump in my throat and continuing to the kitchen.

She glances away, and just when I think she's about to slink back to her room, she moves across the living room and plonks her ass on one of the stools beneath the kitchen island. "I, umm . . . I just wanted to say that everything that happened, you know, it wasn't personal. I was trying to save my brother."

I scoff, gaping at Cara as though she's lost her mind, and honestly, yeah . . . I think she has. "Not personal? Are you kidding me? Of course it was personal. I thought we were friends, Cara. You lied to me about who you are since the moment I got to Faders Bay, but then giving me up to Hartley Scott? How the hell can you sit here in front of me and act like it doesn't mean anything?"

"I was trying to save my brother," she throws back at me. "Maybe if you had siblings or a real family, you would understand."

"Oh, I understand," I tell her, grabbing a mug and turning back to fix her with a hard stare. "I understand you did everything you had to do to save his life. I get it, and I sure as hell would have done the same thing if I were in that position. But the difference between you and me is that the second he was safe, I would have done everything in my power to make it right. Instead, you allowed it to go on. You continued to give me up to Hartley, continued to betray your people."

She shakes her head. "You don't know me, Oakley. Don't start pretending like you have any idea how it was for me. I did what I had to do to keep my family safe."

"No, you did what you had to do to keep *you* safe," I tell her. "You're a coward, Cara."

Her gaze falls away. "I just . . . I wasn't coming here to start an argument with you. I feel like shit about everything and so I was trying to apologize."

"You were trying to clear your guilty conscience," I mutter. "And unfortunately for you, it's not my responsibility to bear the burden of your betrayal. I'll be dead in six days, and honestly, I don't give a shit if your conscience is cleared or not. If you want to make it up to me, then do that, but it's not going to happen by coming to me with bullshit excuses for what you did. Admit your errors and learn from them so you can become a better person."

"I'm trying," she tells me. "Ever since being initiated into The Circle and having nearly every member of Empire actively wanting me dead, it's starting to open my eyes to just how shitty this is. I really don't know how you do it. I know the guys want to find a way to save you, and that's great and all, but I understand why you ran. Hell, if I had half a brain, I would have run with you."

I shrug my shoulders. "I mean, you could have, but I would have been paranoid you'd give me up the whole time."

Cara scrunches her face with a cringe. "Yeah, I deserved that," she says as a small smile pulls at the corners of her lips. "Do you think you can find it within you to forgive me? I know I don't deserve it, but I swear, I have your back now. You can trust me."

Letting out a heavy sigh, I turn and find a second mug. "I don't know if I'll be able to forgive you," I tell her, being as honest as I can. "But considering I only have six days to live, what can it hurt to try? The last thing I want is to have to spend the last six days of my life living in misery. Despite everything going on around me, I want to enjoy what little time I have left, not lingering on the bullshit. Don't get me wrong, I'm really hurt and betrayed by what you did, but for Sawyer's sake, I want to find a way to move past that."

"Yeah?" she questions, hopeful.

"Yeah," I say, sliding a coffee across the counter to her. "Just don't fuck it up."

"Cross my heart and hope to die," she says with a beaming smile before realizing what she just said and cringing again. "Sorry, I umm . . . bad choice of words."

"Ya think?"

I watch Cara as she gets up with her coffee and moves through the penthouse to the dining table. She lets out a heavy sigh before putting her mug down and bracing her hands on the table, looking over the array of papers before her. My brows arch, never having seen such a mess of papers in my life, but the frustration in Cara's eyes tells me that whatever these papers are, they're important.

Striding across the penthouse, I make my way to her side before glancing over the table. "What's all of this?" I ask, picking up a list filled with names.

"These are all the dead from the explosion," she says. "Zade put me in charge of putting together a mass funeral for all of our dead, and every day new names keep being added."

"Shit," I say with a slight gasp, hating myself for not asking about this. How fucking self-centered could I have been? "They're still finding bodies?"

"No, Empire works fast. All the bodies were pulled out of the rubble that night, but many of them were left seriously injured," she says, picking up a slip of paper and showing it to me. "These are all the people who died in the hospital after the fact."

My gaze scans over the paper, horror blasting through my chest. There must be at least thirty names on this list. "What's the death toll so far?"

"Eighty-three," she murmurs, heaviness in her tone.

My eyes widen, my gaze snapping up to meet hers. "That many?"

"Yeah, it was terrible. I don't know how much you saw, but it was like nothing I've ever seen. The screaming . . . I'll never forget it."

"I mean, I know I'm not the best at this kind of stuff, but if you need any help with this . . ."

"Thanks," she says with a sad smile. "I appreciate that, but no. I need to do it myself. This happened during my initiation ball, and the task has been handed to me directly by the future leader of my people. It's my burden to bear and mine alone."

I nod, not wanting to argue. "No problem," I say, scanning over the images in the center of the table and seeing the remains of what was once an incredible ballroom, now covered in blood and rubble. "Do they know who is responsible for this?"

"Not as far as I'm aware," she tells me. "But there are plenty of theories going around, none of which seem to be plausible."

Damn. "And when they do figure it out?"

"They'll be punished to the full extent of our law," a deep tone says across the room.

I glance back to find Sawyer striding toward us, Venom curled around his wrist, and just when I go to ask why the hell he has her, Easton comes barging through the living room, tearing cushions off the couch and looking beneath them.

"Looking for something?" Sawyer questions, glaring at Easton, clearly not happy with whatever is going down right now.

Easton's head snaps up, and that dark, stormy gaze zones in on his precious snake. He lets out a breath of relief before crossing to Sawyer and taking Venom out of his hand. "Why the fuck do you have her?"

"I think the better question is why the fuck aren't you keeping a better eye on your snake? I woke up to her in my fucking bed," he says. "I thought it was Oakley's hand trailing down to my junk. Turns out it was your goddamn snake."

I laugh, walking across to Sawyer and pressing my hand to his bare chest, my fingers trailing down his abs. Pushing up onto my tiptoes, I press my lips to his. "Who would have known that snake was such a pervert?" I murmur as Easton puts Venom back in her enclosure. "But don't you worry, I can pick up where she left off."

"Suck his cock on your own time," Zade says, making his presence known across the room. "We're doing recon today. Go get dressed."

"Recon for what?" I ask, stepping out of Sawyer's arms before I get carried away.

"It's time for a family reunion," Zade says just as Dalton walks out of his room, dragging his hand over his face as though he only just woke up. "We're paying a visit to my mom."

Dalton sighs and spins on his heel, walking straight back into his room. "Ahh fuck," he mutters. "And here I thought I was gonna shoot some hoops and spend the day buried in my girl."

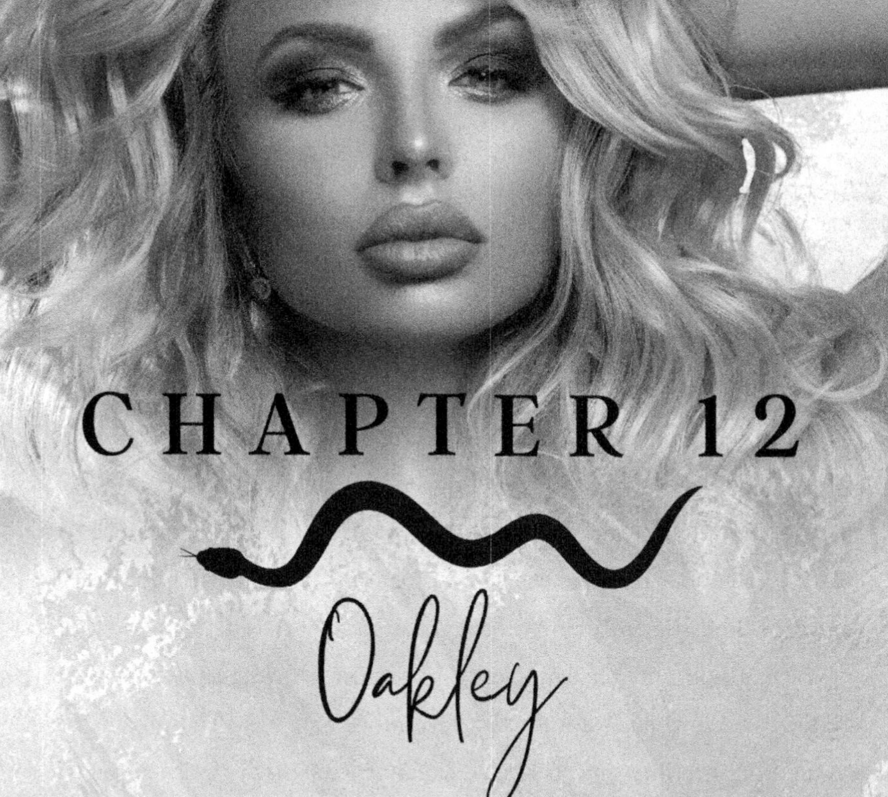

CHAPTER 12

Oakley

The drive across town and out into the countryside is silent. I sit squished between Sawyer and Dalton like the most delicious sandwich I've ever had, Dalton's hand on my thigh while Sawyer's arm is draped over my shoulder, pulling me into his side.

What should have been an almost three-hour drive is done in a little over two, and I do what I can to not shake my head at Zade's driving. There's no doubt about it, he's an amazing driver and can pull off maneuvers I could only dream about, but he also has a lead foot and doesn't understand the meaning of slowing down. Considering this is Zade DeVil, I wouldn't expect anything else.

The countryside is beautiful, and I stare at it all in wonder. I've always loved being a city girl and living close to anywhere that offers UberEats, but I can see the allure that living out here would have. The safety it could offer someone like me would be mind blowing. Hell, just the thought of being able to go to sleep at night without fearing for my life is reason enough to move out of the city. I could have a whole security system out here, live up on a big hill and be able to see someone coming from miles away. But then . . . UberEats definitely wouldn't deliver.

Zade approaches a huge estate, and he does his best to keep concealed, but in broad daylight in the countryside, that's not as easy as it sounds. There are no other cars around, not even parked outside the mansion, and it makes it just a little easier to breathe. Over the past few weeks, while I've learned I have more fight than flight instincts, jumping headfirst into a hostile situation really isn't my cup of tea, despite having the boys here to save my ass when everything inevitably goes wrong. Because let's face it, when has anything ever gone right around here?

Zade parks on the side of the property behind a row of bushes, and while we're concealed from the mansion, there's practically a big red arrow pointing us out to anyone driving past. All four of the guys look over the property, taking in every inch of it and searching for possible entry points and threats, and I do the same just to fit in, but honestly, I've got no fucking idea what I'm searching for.

"I don't think anyone is here," Sawyer muses, his gaze narrowed toward the mansion. "It's too quiet."

Easton shakes his head. "There's at least two guards patrolling the east end of the property," he says. "Another farther back in the bushes."

"Yes," Sawyer agrees. "I meant inside. I don't think Zade's mom or her team are here. There's no movement, no noise. It's too still."

"I agree," Zade says, his brows furrowed. "She's not here. We're too vulnerable out here. She would have attacked by now."

"She could be trying to lure us in," Dalton says. "Give us a false sense of security only to attack once we're behind enemy lines."

"Either way," Zade mutters, checking his gun. "We came here to do a job. Whether she's here or not, we go in. Gather what intel we can, find out what she wants, her goals, her team. I want to know what makes her tick."

"And her security?" Easton asks, not taking his eye off the two guards he pointed out on the east side of the property.

"If they pose a threat, take them out. Otherwise, let's not draw attention to ourselves. If they were any good, they would have already tried to take us out. They're just hired help, not sufficiently trained."

The boys nod, and with that, they make their break, pushing their doors wide and slipping out into the fresh air. "Uhhhh . . . What am I supposed to do?" I ask, seeking out Zade's stare. "And don't even think about telling me to sit here and look pretty. You know I'm only going to slip out and follow you."

Zade sighs and presses his lips into a hard line. "Fine," he mutters. "You're with me, but I swear to God, if you fuck this up or even breathe wrong, you're going to—"

"I'm going to what?" I challenge. "You'll punish me, kill me, make me regret it? You're already tearing my heart out of my chest. What more could you possibly do to me?"

Zade clenches his jaw, clearly frustrated. "If you're coming, then get a fucking move on. You're wasting my time."

Rolling my eyes, I scoot along the backseat, following Dalton out of the SUV until my feet finally hit the asphalt. Dalton steps into me, his hand sliding around my waist as he leans in and presses a kiss to my temple. "I know you can't fucking stand each other but do me a favor and don't do anything stupid," he insists. "I don't want to have to come and save your asses because you were both too stupid to keep your mouths shut for ten minutes."

I give him a tight smile, making a show of zipping my lips and locking it before throwing away the key.

Dalton rolls his eyes and fixes Zade with a heavy glare. "You've got my whole fucking world in your hands right now," he warns him. "If you fuck this up, I'm coming for you."

Zade doesn't respond, but honestly, we all know the likelihood of Zade fucking this up is zero to none. He isn't the kind of guy to fuck up. He's too calculated for that.

"Let's just get this done," Sawyer says. "I'm supposed to be having dinner with my mom tonight, and I don't want this taking any longer than necessary."

With that, the boys make a break for it, each of them taking off in different directions, and if it weren't for Zade's hand closing around my wrist and dragging me behind him, I probably would have been left in their dust.

After snaking our way through the trees, Zade and I emerge onto the manicured lawn like two moronic targets demanding attention. I try to keep myself hidden, hastily searching for the quickest route to the mansion, but Zade doesn't share the same urgency. He simply walks across the lawn as though taking a Sunday afternoon stroll through the park. Hell, if anyone really were inside this property, we would already have bullet holes right through the center of our skulls.

"What the fuck are you doing?" I hiss. "Hurry up. You're gonna get us caught."

"You really think I would let that happen?" he mutters.

"How the hell am I supposed to know?" I throw back at him. "It wouldn't be the most fucked-up thing you've done since meeting me. Hell, perhaps you have childhood abandonment issues and are hoping to use this as some way to gain mommy's approval."

"Fucking hell," he grunts to himself before lifting his gaze to mine. "You have some seriously fucked-up trust issues, you know that, right?"

"Ha," I scoff, amusement bursting through my chest. "I wonder how that happened."

Zade rolls his eyes and thankfully picks up his pace, moving around the side of the property before finally taking pity on me. "If there were someone inside, we would have been shot at the second we got out of the car. We're in the clear."

"How do you know that?"

He nods up ahead, and I follow his gaze to the camera pointed right at us. "From what I can tell, there's at least thirty surveillance cameras across the property. If my mother wanted us dead, it would have happened by now."

"So then . . . What does she want?"

"That's a good fucking question."

Reaching the mansion, Zade leads me to a side entrance, and just as he picks the lock, movement across the property catches my attention, and I whip around, preparing myself for the worst. A gasp tears from the back of my throat, and just as Zade jumps on the defense, ready to save my ass, I realize it's just Easton.

He moves across the property like a ninja, and Zade lets out a sigh, watching as he sneaks up behind one of the guards who Zade specifically said to leave be. "He can't fucking help himself," Zade mutters beside me as we watch Easton effortlessly snap the guard's neck. Zade meets my stare. "This is what happens when someone fucks with his head," he says accusingly. "He forgets where his loyalties lie."

"Good thing I'll be dead soon, huh?" I say, reaching past him and opening the door, ready to get this shit over and done with. "You can have your little henchmen back after that, though something tells me it's not going to be the same."

"What's that supposed to mean?" he questions as I step through the door, only to have him hold me back and go first with his gun drawn.

"You will always have their loyalty," I say. "That much is clear. You'll be their leader, but that's it. Because once you take me away from them, once you slaughter me for your own gain, they will never respect you. They'll live a life resenting you, and that friendship you've spent twenty-something years building will be gone. They'll see you as nothing but weak."

Zade shakes his head. "You don't know what you're talking about," he says, stepping into me, that big body of his crowding me. "You've known them for two seconds. I've known them their whole lives. We have a brotherhood, a bond that not even you or your tight little pussy can infiltrate."

"You see, that's just the thing," I tell him, lifting my chin and brushing my lips across his. "It seems this tight little pussy already has."

Zade clenches his jaw and hardens his stare before finally pulling away and stalking up the long hall. "Keep up," he throws over his shoulder as a stupid grin stretches across my lips. I've never been one to gloat when I'm right, but damn, right now, I want to scream it from the rooftops.

I think putting Zade DeVil in his place just became my favorite thing to do . . . right after fucking his friends, of course.

Moving through the mansion, it quickly becomes clear that we are alone here. There's not even a hint of life within these walls. The food in the kitchen looks old, and there's a light layer of dust building across the furniture.

We do a whole sweep of the property, and by the time we make our way back downstairs, we find the boys in the impressive home office, trying to seek out any secrets this home might be holding. "Looks like she left in a hurry," Easton says, his gaze shifting over her valuables that have been left behind.

"I'm not surprised," Zade says. "I would have taken off too. She was compromised the second I found her here."

My brows furrow as I glance out the window to the guard's body left on the lawn. "If she's not living here now, why keep guards here at all? It doesn't make sense."

"It's her way of keeping tabs and protecting herself," Easton says. "Those guards would have specific instructions to report any movement back to her. Meaning the second we left, she would have had a full report. She would know where you are, who you're with, and exactly how to get to you. And considering that Empire still thinks you're halfway across the country, that doesn't exactly benefit us."

My gaze shifts back to the dead guy. "Hence why you snapped his neck," I mutter, realizing that Zade was wrong again. Easton didn't betray his loyalties when he went against Zade's orders and killed the guy, he did it to protect me. Again.

We start looking closer, trying to figure out who Zade's mom really is. What her plans are and how she's intending to pull them off. The boys throw theories around the room as I shake my head, none of them really feeling right, but I suppose this is how they work through this shit and figure out the most plausible reason for any of this.

"What if this has been her plan all along?" Dalton questions, meeting Zade's stare across the room. "Right after your father's initiation. She went into hiding and had to give up her life for him to be able to stand at the head of Empire. What if she was doing all of this to steal the crown off his head, not expecting you to have stepped in and taken your father's life before she could."

Zade shakes his head. "It's possible she had planned to take him out, but I don't believe it was for the purpose of taking Empire for herself. There are too many people she would have to get through before she could claim the crown. She never could have pulled it off, and the people of Empire never would have accepted her as their new ruler."

My gaze shifts over the floor-to-ceiling bookshelf, taking in the little trinkets and book titles she felt were important enough to put on display, and as my gaze shifts over a photo frame, I find myself stopping and reaching for it.

My heart races, unease rocking through my chest as I swallow hard. "What if she's not the mastermind behind all of this?" I ask, having no idea how this photo even got here or why Zade's mom felt the need to put it on her bookshelf. "What if she's just another pawn in someone else's game?"

"What are you talking about?" Sawyer questions, my line of thought completely off from any of the theories they've been throwing around.

"No," Zade says. "When I followed Hartley Scott here, he answered to her. She's the one pulling the strings."

"I don't think so," I say, turning the picture around to show him. "She's not the mastermind, my father is."

All four of the guys stop what they're doing and take in the photo of my father and Aunt Liv embraced in each other's arms, looking happier than I've ever seen either of them to the point it makes my heart hurt. Liv looks young here, maybe in her mid-twenties, and the way my father is looking at her in this photo, I can only assume they were deeply in love.

"What the fuck?" Zade breathes, striding toward me and taking the frame out of my hands, his brows furrowed, confused and unsure.

"Yo," Dalton laughs. "Since when was your mom slumming it with Oakley's dad?"

"What?" I grunt, snatching the photo back. "That's not his mom. That's my Aunt Liv."

"Uhhh, I hate to break it to you, Firefly," Dalton says. "But that is definitely Zade's mom."

Horror fills my chest and my gaze locks onto Zade's, pieces of the puzzle starting to fall into place. My father was having an affair with Zade's mom, though from this photo, it's hard to pinpoint a time frame. All I know is that from the day I was born, I never had a mother in my life. My father never really talked about her, just said that she had died too young and that was it. But what if—no.

My eyes widen, panic tearing through my chest. "Oh, fuck no," I breathe, hoping like fuck that Zade and I don't share a parent. "Tell me we're not related."

Sawyer and Dalton howl with laughter as Zade just stares at me. "No," he says, shaking his head, though there's a hint of doubt creeping into his eyes that puts me on edge. "Nah, we couldn't be."

"How can you be so sure?" I demand, waving the picture around. "I never knew my mom and then after my father's imprisonment, I was sent to live with my 'aunt' who just happens to be your mother? Come on, Zade. I know you don't believe in coincidences."

"I don't but . . . there has to be some kind of explanation. If you were my—I would know."

I scoff, throwing my hands up as humiliation washes through me. "Great, I've been fantasizing about my brother."

"I'm not your fucking brother," Zade hisses. "My father was initiated as the head of Empire when I was nine, and up until then, my mom was there every fucking day. She was all I had. You're only four years younger than me. If she were pregnant, I would have known. She's not your mother."

"You're sure?"

Zade nods, and I see the relief flashing in his eyes, certain that our parents' affair was nothing more than two people screwing around, and who knows, this photo could have been taken years later, way after my father was locked up and she was in hiding. Maybe they could have found each other then. Who knows, maybe the whole thing is romantic. But then, maybe my father is the mastermind and she's his little puppeteer, pulling the strings for him while he rots away in Empire's prison, preparing everything for when the time comes for him to make his move. Now that sounds more likely, and as I look around at the guys, it's clear they're coming to the same conclusion.

"Alright," Zade finally says. "I think we got what we came for. Let's get out of here."

Easton nods and steps in beside me, his hand falling to my lower back and leading me out of the home office. "You good?" he murmurs.

I shrug my shoulders. "I don't know," I tell him honestly. "Every day something happens that fucks with my head just a little bit more. First, my father isn't who he says he is and wants to take over Empire, then he tells me he wants to take me out to ensure there are no heirs to claim his title, and now Zade's mom, who was supposed to be dead, is his secret mistress and running the show? I mean, when is this bullshit going to end? I feel like every person I know wants me dead for one reason or another."

Zade scoffs from in front of us. "You act as though taking your life is going to get me hard."

"Please," I mutter. "I've seen the way your eyes light up when you take someone's life. All of you. You fucking love it. It's like it gives you some kind of power rush. It's kinda fucked up if you ask me. You all need to be heavily medicated."

Dalton rolls his eyes. "If we find a way to save your ass, I promise, right after fucking you until you scream, I'll show you just how good taking a life can really be. The lives you've taken have been done out of necessity, out of fear and survival, but it doesn't always have to be like that. It can be calculated, like a game of cat and mouse, and it's one of the best thrills you'll ever experience. In that moment, when you feel that power pulsing through your veins and the life fading out of their eyes, you're a fucking god."

"Untouchable," Sawyer agrees as a shiver sails down my spine.

"Fuck me," I mutter to myself. "I've been so blinded by sensational dick, I failed to see just how messed up you assholes really are."

Easton grins down at me, letting me see the darkness flashing in his eyes. "And don't you forget it," he says, his hand dropping to my ass and giving a firm squeeze that has me ready to bend myself over the desk so he can have his wicked way with me.

Then before I get a chance to see this delicious fantasy through, I find myself back in the SUV and heading all the way home to Faders Bay, feeling as though we're only seeing the tip of the iceberg when it comes to my father. I don't know exactly what his plans are, but I know his endgame, and unfortunately for me, it's not going to end well.

CHAPTER 13

Dalton

The ball drops directly through the rooftop hoop of the DeVil Hotel, and I jog forward, catching it on the rebound before jumping high and shooting again, needing the calm that comes from being on the court. Only tonight, it's not working.

We're running out of time. I can't save her, and it's fucking killing me.

Making my way back up the court, I try to focus on the sound of the ball against the ground, the feel of the ball rebounding back up into my hands, the night breeze whipping across my face, but I can't. My every thought is of *her*.

I never thought it was possible to love somebody like this. She's my whole world. My heart beats for her, and I don't know how to make it stop. Zade warned me not to get too close, and now I'm ready to risk it all, ready to take her away from here. I would have done it already if it didn't mean landing us both with a death sentence and betraying the only family I've ever had. Sawyer and Cross though, I couldn't take her from them.

Getting her out of here is in her best interest, but I'm not blind, I know she loves them too, and I couldn't break her heart by forcing her to leave them. Hell, a part of me even wonders if she's in love with Zade too, but that couldn't be right. Sure, she might be attracted to him, but love? I don't think that's possible. As for Cross and Sawyer, while I can see how she loves them, I don't know if she's realized it yet. She has us all wrapped around her little finger, each one of us willing to risk it all just to save her . . . If only there were something we could do.

Whipping around, I jump high and shoot from far across the court, watching as the ball flies in a perfect arc and drops straight through the hoop. I wait for the rush and satisfaction to start pumping through my veins, but nothing comes, and I just stand there feeling deflated.

Fuck.

I needed that rush, needed the adrenaline to dull the coarse pain shooting through my chest, but I'm on my own tonight, and if I'm not going to get it from basketball, then I can only hope I can find it at the bottom of a bottle.

Leaving the ball slowly rolling across the rooftop, I turn on my heel and stalk back toward the elevator before heading back down to Zade's penthouse. The door opens and as it's quickly creeping toward the middle of the night, I expect to find everyone asleep, only that's the last thing I find.

Oakley sits in Sawyer's lap, her arm slung over his shoulder and her head resting against his chest as her feet rest on Cross' lap, the three of them looking miserable.

"There you are," Oakley murmurs through the quiet room, forcing an encouraging smile across her face, but there's no mistaking the tension in the room. Hell, it's so fucking thick, it's almost impossible to breathe. "I thought we were going to have to send a search party up to find you."

"What's going on?" I ask, striding across the living room and dropping down in the armchair, resting back against the cushion. "I thought you'd be in bed by now."

"Tried," she says with a soft shrug of her shoulders, her gaze settled on Venom in Cross' hand. "I just . . ."

"Too much on your mind?" I ask.

Oakley nods and rests her head back against Sawyer's chest, his hand gently roaming up and down her back as I meet Cross' stare, needing to know that she's alright, but he simply shakes his head, that one movement causing me more pain than any knife ever could.

"Wanna talk about it?" I murmur, meeting Oakley's stare across the living room.

"I do," she whispers, her gaze falling away. "But I don't know what else I can possibly say that I haven't already said. No matter how hard I try, or how far I run, I can't save myself, and I hate that I'm being so messed up about it tonight. We only have a few more days, and I've been trying to hold myself together so we can make the most of them, but it really fucking sucks. I'm terrified. I'm not ready to die."

Sawyer holds her tighter, and my fingers itch to tear her out of his arms and do it myself, but if she wanted to be in my arms right now, she would have gotten up and walked right into them.

"I fucking love you, Oakley. I'm not going to stop fighting for you, not for one fucking second," I tell her, holding her gaze. "I know you're scared. Fuck, Firefly, I'm fucking terrified too. The idea of letting you slip through my fingers kills me. I can't bear the thought of sending you in to be sacrificed and never being able to see you again. Hold you. Feel you. I can't—fuck. I can't picture a life where you don't exist."

Tears fall down her face, and she pushes off Sawyer and walks across the living room before climbing into my lap and straddling me, her arms locking around my neck as she clings onto me like a koala. "I don't want to leave you," she murmurs in my ear, her tears falling onto my shoulder. "But I'm losing hope. I can't save myself."

"I'll find a way," I promise her. "I'm not going to let this happen."

"Down in those cells," Sawyer says. "You asked for my word to save you. You cashed in your favors, and we're right there with you, Doll. I don't know how, but you have to keep faith that we will pull through for you. We'll figure out a way to save you that doesn't force a target on your back or Zade's."

She shakes her head. "Zade spent years going through the bylaws, trying to figure out a legal way to dethrone his father. If there were some way to save me, he would have already done it. I think it's time to face the music and admit that it's over. Without Zade on board, there's nothing we can do. I'm going to die in six days."

"Five," Cross mutters with a heavy breath. "It's after midnight."

Oakley's tears fall harder, and she holds onto me a little bit tighter. My hand roams up and down her back, desperately trying to figure out what the fuck I can do or say that could possibly make this better, but there's nothing—unless I can magically offer her freedom, but she and I both know I don't have the power to do that.

"What's the likelihood that you guys will hold Zade down while I kill him?" she says against my neck, her words muffled by my skin.

Cross chuckles to himself, knowing she doesn't really mean that, and Sawyer scoffs, probably actually considering the idea. The tension between Sawyer and Zade has only gotten worse, slowly building each day, and soon enough, they're going to break. But while Sawyer wants to hate him now, he could never hurt him . . . at least, not permanently.

"You don't mean that," I say, knowing just how uncomfortable she is with the idea of murder, even if it meant saving her own life. Hell, she did what she had to do in the past, but when there's also feelings involved, she wouldn't be able to do it. If she hurt Zade in any kind of way, she'd never be able to forgive herself.

"He has no problem doing it to me, so why shouldn't I hesitate doing it to him?"

"He cares, Pretty," Cross says, lifting his gaze from Venom to focus on our girl. "He cares so fucking much it's killing him. Can't you see that? I've known him since I was a kid. We've always been tight, and every time you even mention it, a piece of him dies. It's like a knife straight through his chest. This ritual is making him sick, Oakley. He never expected to care like this, he's always been a cruel and calculating motherfucker, but you . . . You're making him care for you. Surely you must know that he doesn't want to do this. You are so far under his skin, just like you are mine and the boys, and the idea of hurting you or never getting to hold you again is tearing him to pieces."

Oakley sinks against me, and I hate how down she is. She's always held her head high, and while she has always fought for what's right, she's never allowed herself to fall apart like this.

Silence fills the room, and just when I think she's falling asleep, her soft, wavering tone vibrates through her chest. "I don't know what to do."

"Honestly," I tell her, pulling her back just enough to meet her stare before pressing my fingers to her chin and forcing her to hold her head up high. "Allow him to fall in love with you. Let him see the real you, let him in, Oakley. He's halfway there, but he needs that push from you. Let him see what it means to really be in love with someone."

"How the hell is that supposed to help?"

"Because if he loved you like I do, truly fucking loved you, he'd forfeit his claim to Empire in order to save you, even if it meant sacrificing himself in the process."

Oakley presses her lips in a tight smile, and the sadness in her eyes eats me alive. "I understand where you're coming from, but I don't think Zade is capable of loving in that kind of way," she says, her hand cupping the side of my face. "He's broken. He's not like you."

"You're wrong," Sawyer says, getting up and making his way toward us. "He's broken, that's for sure. But he's not incapable of loving you.

If you were anyone else, then yeah, I'd say there is no hope, but you're the brightest fucking light I've ever seen. If anyone can make him lay down his weapons, it's you."

With that, Sawyer leans down and presses a gentle kiss to Oakley's lips, and watching the way she so openly craves us all has my cock hardening beneath her. Sawyer squeezes her shoulder and breaks their kiss, and after holding her gaze a second longer, he pulls away. "You know where to find me," he says before turning on his heel and making his way out of the room.

"I'm gonna crash too," Cross says, getting up and walking past us, stopping to drop a kiss to Oakley's temple before continuing through the living room to Venom's enclosure and putting her in. "You guys need anything while I'm up?"

I shake my head. "Nah, man. We're good."

Cross disappears a moment later, leaving me with my girl, and I grip her ass before lifting her into my arms and getting to my feet. "Come on," I tell her, needing to get up after that sweet ass of hers has been weighing down on the healing stab wound on my thigh. Honestly, it fucking hurts, but I'm not about to tell her that. "Let me take you to bed."

"No," she rushes out. "I don't want to—not with him. Not tonight."

"Good," I murmur. "Because it wasn't his bed I was planning on taking you to."

Oakley relaxes against me, and I walk us down the hall to my room, kicking the door open before striding in and laying her down on my bed. I move in beside her, pulling her into my arms and making sure the blanket is pulled right up to her chin. "You good, Firefly?"

"Not really," she admits, lifting her chin to meet my stare. "But I feel better with you. I always feel better with you."

My heart rattles in my chest, barely able to keep up. "Fuck, I love you so much."

Her eyes sparkle with happiness, and she quickly closes the gap, pressing her lips to mine with a lingering kiss, but the longer she kisses me, the harder it becomes to resist her. I lean into her, deepening the kiss, and she opens her mouth wider, her tongue warring with mine for dominance.

Her hand snakes up my body, hooking around the back of my neck as I cage her in my arms, rolling us until I'm hovering over her with that delicious thigh hooked high over my hip. I can't help but grind down against her, and that soft groan has my cock flinching in my pants.

Needing to touch her, I reach down between us and grip the hem of her tank before pulling it over her head, and she doesn't hesitate, grabbing the fabric at the back of my neck and yanking it off until I can finally feel her skin on mine. My hands roam over her body, greedily exploring every inch of her as I claim her with my kiss.

The hunger intensifies between us, and I break our kiss before working my lips to the base of her neck, loving her sharp inhale of breath quickly followed by a pleasured groan. She tilts her head, opening up for more as I reach down between us, freeing her of her sweatpants and grinning against her skin when I realize she didn't bother with underwear.

"Oh, God. Dalton. I need you," she pants, her fingers knotting into the back of my hair as her other hand dips down between the blankets and slips inside the waistband of my basketball shorts.

Her soft hand closes around the base of my cock, and my eyes flutter as she tightens her grip. "Fuck, Firefly," I grumble as her hand starts working up and down, her thumb roaming over my tip and teasing my piercing.

My fingers brush down her waist, and I smile against her skin as she sucks in a breath, always ticklish in that same spot, but I don't dare torture her with it. Instead, I trail them down over her hip and dip between her legs. She's so fucking ready, and the second my fingers skim over her clit, her whole body jolts beneath me. "Oh, God. Again."

"You like that, Firefly?" I murmur, pushing up on my elbow and watching her face as I do it again.

She cries out, her head tipping back as her grip tightens on my cock, holding me hostage. "Fuck, yes," she pants.

I apply more pressure, this time rolling my fingers over her clit in small circles before dipping down and pushing two thick fingers inside of her, feeling the way her walls clench around me. Oakley lifts her hips, begging me to take her deeper, so I do it again, repeating the same movements. Only this time, I keep my thumb circling her clit as I push my fingers deep inside of her.

Oakley's eyes roll in the back of her head as her fingers tighten in my hair. She pulls me back down to her, kissing me deeply as her hand pumps up and down my straining cock. "Don't make me wait," she breathes into my mouth. "I need to feel you stretching me."

Goddamn.

This woman knows exactly how to bring me to my knees.

I know she's expecting me to keep this simple, to pull back, spread those pretty thighs, and slam my cock deep inside her sweet cunt, but she deserves so much more. She deserves it just the way she likes it and more.

"Roll over, baby," I tell her. "Get on your knees and let me see that pretty cunt."

Oakley's eyes flutter, and a seductive grin settles over her lips just as I pull back and climb off my bed, dropping my shorts to the ground. I fist my cock, squeezing hard because fuck knows if I don't, I won't be able to make it through the next two seconds.

Oakley watches me as she rolls over, her greedy stare locked on the way I work my fist up and down my cock. "Mmmmmm," she groans, getting onto her knees and spreading them wide, dropping her chest right down to the mattress to put that sweet pussy on full display. "Is this how you like me?"

My tongue rolls over my bottom lip as my gaze trails over her, taking in her glistening cunt. My hand falls to her tight ass, cupping her cheek before lowering down between her legs and slowly pushing inside her entrance, and fuck, I can't look away.

The way my fingers come out glistening with her arousal. Goddamn.

I do it again, this time pushing a little deeper, listening to the way she moans with each thrust. Splitting my fingers, I roll them inside her, massaging her walls, and when she pushes back against my hand for more, I feel like a fucking king. "That's right, Firefly. Take it like a good girl."

"More," she groans into the mattress.

"You want it harder, baby? Deeper?"

"God, yes!"

I slam my fingers deep inside her cunt, and the sound of her gasp speaks right to my cock as I watch her hands ball into tight fists in my bed sheets, holding on for dear life. I do it again and again before the need to taste her becomes too much, and instead of climbing on the bed behind her, I grip her thigh and twist her around, lining that perfect pussy up with my cock.

She's spread open so wide, ready for me to take her, and I will, but first I need to feel her walls squeezing around my fingers, I need her on my tongue.

Dropping to my knees beside my bed, the excitement drums through my veins, and I breathe her in as I push my fingers back inside her, circling and teasing, exploring every inch of her. Then when she's desperate for more, I close my mouth over her clit and give her what she needs.

Oakley pushes back against me, and I flick my tongue over her clit, gently sucking and teasing as my fingers work her sweet cunt. "Oh fuck," she cries, making my grip tighten on my cock. "Dalton."

I don't dare stop, feeling the way her walls tighten around my fingers, knowing just how fucking close she is. I push her closer to the edge, desperate for the high that comes every time I watch her come, and she doesn't disappoint.

My tongue works up and down her pussy, teasing her clit as she comes hard, squeezing me so fucking tight. She cries out, panting and desperately trying to catch her breath as her high continues to build.

Not ready to feel her come down, I quickly stand and press my cock to her entrance, letting her feel my piercing against her sensitive skin. "You want my cock, Firefly?"

"God, yes," she pants, gripping the bedsheets and pushing back against me, and not wanting her high to fade, I slowly push inside her, stretching her convulsing walls and listening as she sucks in a slow, deep breath, her groan getting louder with every passing second.

She's squeezing me so fucking tight that I can already tell just how intense this is going to be for both of us.

I push all the way in before circling my hips and drawing back, my cock glistening with her arousal. My eyes roll with undeniable pleasure, and I drop my hand to my cock, my fingers soaking in her wetness before dragging them up to her ass. I gently press against her, and when she pushes back for more, I give her exactly what she wants, dipping my fingers inside.

Then, having her right where I want her, I fuck her how she deserves, claiming every inch of her body until she's screaming my name. I fuck her hard, her pussy shattering around me as my balls slam against her needy clit.

"Oh fuck," she pants, her knuckles turning white as she grips the sheets tighter. "It's too much."

"Hold onto it, baby," I say through a clenched jaw, my chest heaving as I watch the way her pussy stretches around my cock, fitting so fucking perfectly. My fingers pulse in her ass, taking her deeper as I feel my balls tightening, needing to explode with her.

I thrust into her again and hold it there, grinding against her, and as she cries out, her walls wildly convulse around me, squeezing me like a fucking vise. I come hard, shooting hot spurts of cum deep inside her sweet, pulsating cunt.

"Oh, God," she cries, reaching her absolute limit, her legs shaking as I grip her hips to keep from collapsing over her.

We each come down from our highs, both panting and exhausted, knowing damn well I found that release I was searching for on the roof. "You good, baby? That was intense."

"I . . ." she pants, "can't breathe."

I laugh and gently inch out of her, knowing she must be sore after allowing me to take her like that, and without skipping a beat, I reach down and scoop her into my arms before walking us into my bathroom.

Oakley wraps her arms and legs around me, holding on tight as I step into the shower and reluctantly letting go when I demand to take care of her. Soaping up a loofah, I slowly roam it over every inch of tantalizing skin on display. Oakley closes her eyes, allowing the warm water to wash over her body, and the moment we're done, I wrap her in a towel and walk her back out to my bed.

We don't bother getting dressed, and she curls into my chest the same way she was earlier, only now my fingers brush through her hair, knowing that this can't be the end for us. We've barely even begun, and

I haven't had the chance to give her the world or build a life together yet.

Exhaustion claims her, and she quickly falls into a deep, well-needed sleep when Zade steps into my doorway, his gaze sailing over Oakley, probably assuming I would have delivered her back to his bed tonight, but there's no fucking way. Not tonight. She's mine.

His gaze flicks between us, and I don't miss the flash of jealousy in his eyes, and I realize just how right Cross was earlier. He's already halfway there. It would only take the smallest push from Oakley to have him fall for her the same way we have, but the thought of having to share her more . . . fuck. I don't like it, but if it gives us the chance to hold onto her just that little bit longer then I'll take it.

That doesn't change the fact that I'm not willing to give her up tonight.

As if sensing my desperate need to cling to her, Zade simply nods before sparing one last lingering glance at Oakley's face and walking away. With that, I pull her closer to my chest, fearing the day she slips between my fingers.

CHAPTER 14

Zade

"You ready?" I say to Cara, grabbing my keys off the kitchen counter and glancing back at Cross and Oakley, hating the thought of leaving her, but she's in good hands. Despite how the boys feel about her, I know this is exactly where she'll be when I get back.

Cara swallows hard and glances at her brother, the nerves clear in her eyes. "Does it really matter if I'm ready or not?" she questions, grabbing her handbag and looping it over her shoulder, not that she'll be needing it where we're going.

"I suppose not," I say, making my move toward my private elevator with Cara heavy on my heels.

"Yo," Sawyer says from across my penthouse. I turn back to find his cautious stare locked on me, unease flashing in his eyes. "I'm trusting you man. If anything happens to her, if those fuckers even try to touch one fucking hair on her head, I'm coming for you."

Clenching my jaw, I nod, not wanting to have this out with Sawyer right now. Cara is a big girl and can take care of herself. Kind of. Either way, she's not my responsibility. She's a member of The Circle, and it's up to her to learn how to stand on her own two feet. If those other assholes won't give her the respect she feels she needs, then it's her job to demand it and see it through. Holding her hand through all of this isn't doing her any favors, and Sawyer should know that. My only priority is making sure Oakley gets through the next five days.

Unable to help myself, my gaze shifts to Oakley, taking her in on the couch, and a pang of jealousy fires through my veins. I fucking hate that she slept in Dalton's bed last night. She belongs in mine with my arms locked securely around her waist. She always sleeps best in my arms, and without her . . . fuck. I didn't sleep at all. She's ruined me without even knowing, but as soon as the ritual is done, everything can go back to normal.

I hope.

Cara follows me into the elevator, and the second the door closes, the tension thickens between us. I let out a heavy sigh, realizing that she's not going to let this thing between us go, not that there is anything to hold onto. She was a fling, a quick, convenient fuck when I needed to get my dick wet. I should have pulled away the minute I realized she was starting to develop feelings, but it was too easy and she was too willing.

Now I've never regretted anything more. But hell, I was firm with my intentions since the very first time I asked her to fuck, and if she's stupid enough to think it's anything more than what it was, that's on her.

The elevator zooms down to the basement parking, and I stride toward my SUV, Cara scurrying to keep up. "Where are we even going?" she rushes out, hurrying around the opposite side of my SUV.

"I told you," I tell her, trying to resist rolling my eyes. "It's a formality. The Circle members are required to ensure the sacred tomb is prepared and ready for the ritual. It needs to be cleansed with holy water sourced from the Vatican and then blessed with the blood of our people. You'll be required to participate in the ritualistic chants and speak a solemn vow."

"What?" she breathes, gripping the center console and gaping at me as I hit the gas and fly out of the parking garage. "I don't know any of The Circle's chants or vows."

I shake my head and let out a heavy sigh. "Then I suggest you figure it out fucking fast," I tell her. "I shouldn't have to be explaining this shit to you. If you want to survive in this world, then stop giving the other members of The Circle reason to doubt you. Fuck, Cara. Sawyer has known this shit since he was a kid. He used to spend hours reciting the chants and vows."

"Yeah, well, forgive me, asshole. I'm not Sawyer, and my father didn't spend the last twenty-three years preparing me for this shit. He was more interested in making sure I had a good childhood."

"Your father failed you," I tell her, not bothering to sugarcoat it.

"Stop trying to defend his actions. Sure, he might have made sure that you had a great life, and that's more than any of us can say about our fathers, but the bottom line is that he knew the likelihood of you being initiated into The Circle, and he didn't do a damn thing to prepare you. He let you down."

"No, Zade. You did."

I scoff and glance at her. "What the fuck is that supposed to mean?"

"You're the one who put me here, not him. I was happy living in ignorance. Every single member of Empire believed that Sawyer was the rightful heir to my father's legacy. Hell, even Sawyer and I both believed it, but you had to go and make things right. You could have initiated Sawyer into The Circle and no one would have even questioned it. You could have let the secret die with my father."

"But it wouldn't have," I spit through a clenched jaw, not appreciating being questioned. "Apart from the fact that I refuse to start my reign by lying to my people, your father wasn't the only one in on the secret. Your mother knew. She was a liability, and for me to go ahead and initiate Sawyer instead of you, I would have had no choice but to deal with that liability. Is that what you would have preferred? Go ahead and tell me now that I didn't do the right thing, that I, as your leader, didn't make the right decision."

Cara mutters something under her breath before focusing her stare out the window, putting an end to the conversation. She thankfully stays quiet the rest of the drive, not uttering a single word until after I've pulled over on the side of the road, my SUV hidden within the shadows of the nearby woods.

"Where the hell are we?" she says, her gaze quickly scanning the thick brush ahead of us. "I thought we were going to the sacred tomb."

"We are," I say, indicating deeper into the darkness. "It's through there."

"But . . . no. That doesn't make sense. We can't be here already. The meeting doesn't start 'til midnight," she says, glancing down at the clock on my dash. "It's only a little after eight. I figured we'd be driving for hours."

I shake my head, not bothering with a proper response as I get out of the SUV and take a step toward the thick bushes.

Realizing I'm more than prepared to leave her stranded here, Cara scurries after me, hurrying out of my SUV and slamming the door behind her. Rolling my eyes as I listen to her feet rustling through the fallen leaves, I lift my hand over my shoulder and lock the car.

"Wait up," Cara hisses behind me, quickly catching up and invading my personal space as though I could offer her any kind of safety in these woods. "I just . . . can you just lose the chip on your shoulder for one minute and explain what the fuck is going on here? I get it, alright. I'm not good enough to stand as one of The Circle members, but you're not doing either of us any favors by keeping me in the dark. Give me a chance to learn."

I really fucking hate it when other people are right.

Letting out a heavy breath, I lead her through the woods, along the well-memorized path, and out toward the sacred tomb. "You and I both have a lot of enemies, many who are working directly with members of The Circle. They want you dead, Cara. They refuse to accept you as part of The Circle. And me? Well, that's self-explanatory, but tonight's meeting isn't exactly one of Empire's best-kept secrets. If anyone was looking to take either of us out, these woods would be the perfect place and time to do it."

"The fuck?" she gasps, her eyes widening as she scans the darkness, inching even closer. "Why the hell did you bring me out here if there could be people waiting to kill me?"

"Because it's your duty. Whether they're holding a gun to your head or not, you have an obligation to Empire to see this through, and you vowed to do just that during your initiation."

"FUCK."

"Quit panicking," I mutter. "That's exactly why we're here so early. If an assassin was waiting in these woods, he would arrive an hour or two before we were expected to arrive. This way, we beat them to the punch. No one is taking you out tonight, at least not on my watch."

"Thank you," she says, reaching out to me.

I scoff, flinching away from her touch. "Don't thank me," I tell her. "Do not fool my intentions for loyalty or because I care for you in any kind of way. I don't. I'm not doing this for you. If you weren't Sawyer's twin sister, if you were just another member of The Circle, you'd be left out here alone to navigate this shit by yourself, and I can guarantee that you would already be dead and buried in a shallow grave by now."

Cara's gaze falls away, and we walk the rest of the way to the tomb in peace, though I can practically hear her thoughts screaming at the back of my head. Stepping up to the opening of the old tomb, I slip my key into the old lock, having to wiggle it to get it in.

The lock opens, and I step right up to the heavy stone entrance and push it back, sucking in a breath as the lingering smell of my father's charred flesh hits us both in the face. His ashes have been locked down here for almost two months, but time has done nothing to erase the impact of the depraved ritual that took place here.

"Ugghhh," Cara groans, holding her nose. "What the hell is that smell?"

"Trust me," I mutter, stepping through the entrance and lighting one of the old oil lanterns sitting on a nearby table. "You don't want to know."

Cara moves into the tomb, and I close the door behind her before locking it, not wanting to allow access to any uninvited guests. She takes an oil lantern of her own before snatching the lighter out of my hand and lighting it.

With just enough lighting, we start our trek down into the below tomb, following the old stone steps right down into the clearing below. "Shit," Cara says as we reach the bottom, holding her lantern out to take it in properly. "So this is where you're going to perform the ritual?"

"Uh-huh," I say, making my way around the sacred space and lighting all of the oil lanterns that hang off each of the thirteen pillars. Once the open chamber floods with light, all the intricate details of the great tomb are finally visible.

"This is fucked up. You know that, right?" Cara says, taking it all in and scanning over the sacred gravesites of those who have ruled before me.

"What? You think I enjoy this?"

"Hard to tell," she throws back at me.

Cara finally falls silent as my gaze locks onto the pillar in the center of the tomb, the place where Oakley's heart will rest for the entirety of my rule, and fuck, seeing it like this, being up close and personal is really fucking with me. I've always known that's what was going to happen, and I've been okay with that, but now that I know Oakley, know what makes her tick, know what puts the most brilliant smile across her face, the idea of plunging my hand inside of her chest and slaughtering her like an animal is killing me.

Completing this ritual was never supposed to be easy. It was designed specifically to test the loyalty of Empire's future ruler, to challenge him and push him to his limits, because any man who fails in this challenge is not worthy of ruling over Empire. And fuck, I've worked too hard for this.

Cara moves in beside me, staring up at the pillar that will hold Oakley's perfectly preserved heart. "That's where—"

"Yeah," I say, cutting her off, not wanting to hear the end of her question.

"Shit," she mutters. "This all just became a little too real."

Damn straight it did.

Hours pass, and when I hear the familiar sound of the tomb entrance opening, Cara jumps and shrinks back into the shadows, not even a little prepared for what's going to happen here tonight. "Take a cloak and stand in front of your pillar," I tell her, indicating across the room. "There's to be silence in this tomb, not a word until you are expected to recite the chants."

Cara swallows hard, and I watch as she hastily crosses the tomb before placing herself in front of her pillar, the very one her father once stood so proudly in front of.

The old stone entrance closes, and we listen as the newcomer makes his way down the stairs. As he reaches the bottom, I narrow my gaze, not surprised to find that Hartley Scott is the first to arrive, and well over an hour early. Hell, I wouldn't be surprised if he were responsible for leading assassins right to the tomb entrance.

There's no masking the shock on his face, realizing he is far from the first to arrive. Unease flashes in his eyes, and then without a word, he collects his cloak and silently makes his way to his pillar, making for a very uncomfortable hour.

One by one, the other members of The Circle appear at the bottom of the steps, and just like Hartley, they respect our traditions and collect their cloaks before taking their place in front of their pillar until all thirteen spaces have been filled.

The faces of the men around me are all concealed, their long cloaks brushing against the old stone floor, only Cara's is practically draped across it. She's not nearly tall enough to fit the traditional cloak, and it looks like a bad scene out of Harry Potter in here, all we need are wands and we'll be set.

Nikolai Thorne would have been the one to step forward and get this meeting underway, and seeing as though Cara has no idea what the fuck she's doing, I bear the burden and raise my head, spreading my hands out beside me in welcome. "My brothers," I say, my gaze shifting around the hostile room just as the clock ticks past midnight. "Welcome to the sacred tomb of our people, the final resting place of our past and present leaders."

I pause, letting the heaviness sink in. "Tonight, as the sun sets on another day, we take one step further to the birth of our new future. There are four days and four nights until we will gather here again and sacrifice the heart of an innocent, Miss Oakley Quinn."

My gaze shifts to Cara, and I watch as she looks away, bowing her head, unable to meet my stare. "Tonight as we stand as one, we must cleanse our sacred tomb with the blood of our people, wash away the sins of those past, and prepare for a new ruler, a new age, a new legacy."

I let my words fall away as my gaze shifts around the tomb, meeting the eye of every man in the room. "Brothers," I say, drawing the same dagger I used on my palm as I stood over the flames of my father's remains. "Let's get started."

With that, I step forward and hold my palm out flat before digging the dagger deep into my skin and carving the perfect arc. Blood pools in my palm, and I close my fist before turning my hand and allowing my blood to spill on the floor of the sacred tomb.

Next, Ira Abrahms steps forward, and I pass him the dagger before watching him repeat the process. One by one, we make our way around the room, the dagger passing from brother to brother, until it's put into Cara's delicate hand. Her gaze flickers to mine, and I discreetly nod, telling her to get on with it, and as she stares down at the dagger, the faintest "Gross" is heard through the tomb.

She scrunches her face in disgust, then taking a breath, she presses the ancient blade to her palm. She cuts deep, probably a little too deep, and it's clear she's trying to prove some kind of point, but nonetheless, her blood pools in the palm of her hand, and just like I did, she balls her hand into a tight fist before rotating it and allowing it to fall to the ground.

Once the circle is complete and the blood of all twelve members has spilled, I look down at the ground, watching as it trails into the crevices and runs toward the center of the room. It's a slow process, and as we wait, the twelve Circle members begin their chants, proudly speaking the words of those who have stood here before them. Cara just moves her mouth, doing what she can to blend in.

When the last drop of blood has pooled in the center of the tomb, the chanting stops, completing the first step of tonight's ritual.

Breaking formation, Hartley Scott steps away to retrieve the cup of Empire; a large brass, double-handled, diamond-encrusted pot that looks like some kind of Formula 1 trophy. It's filled to the brim with what's supposed to be holy water sourced directly from the Vatican, but honestly, I wouldn't be surprised if it's just dirty creek water from outside the tomb.

Hartley makes his way around the room, starting with me, and without hesitation, I drop my bloody fist into the water, letting it cleanse my hand. I've never really understood this part of the ritual, but I suppose it meant something to the old bastards who created it.

One by one, Hartley makes his way around the circle, allowing everyone to take their turn before handing the cup of Empire to me so that he may take his turn.

The moment he is done, Hartley steps back into formation, and more than ready to get this shit over and done with, I pour the spoiled holy water onto the ground, washing away the pooled blood and cleansing the heart of Empire in preparation for our new beginning, completing tonight's bullshit.

As if on cue, The Circle members begin to flee, knowing these woods are not safe for any of us, not now that we're only days away from completing the transition into new leadership. They're growing desperate, running out of time, but they can't touch me. I'm too strong.

Not wanting to hang out to see what monsters will emerge from the darkness, I nod toward Cara. "Let's go," I say, already one of the last remaining in the bottom of the tomb.

She doesn't hesitate, slipping out of the old cloak and hurrying to my side before pushing in front of me to walk up the stairs first, not wanting to be left with Hartley at her back. But fuck, I'm not particularly fond of having him at mine. But he'd be a fool to try anything on me now, especially in here. He knows what my training was like, and he sure as fuck knows he doesn't stand a chance.

After making our way up the old stone stairs, I pull the heavy door open and step out into the cool night. Cara follows, looking disorientated, and I press my hand to her lower back, leading her through the darkness and back toward my car.

Cara glances down at the deep cut on her hand, sucking in a breath as if only now allowing herself to feel the pain. "That was some real bullshit in there," she tells me. "What the fuck was that anyway? Who the hell goes around sharing the same blade? I'm going to need a visit to the fucking clinic. What if one of those assholes is HIV positive or has hepatitis or malaria or some shit like that? You could have warned me what I was walking into."

"Would knowing have made it any easier?"

"Yes," she spits before reconsidering. "No. Maybe. Fuck, I don't know."

"Just be happy it's over."

"For now," she scoffs. "I'm still going to have to go back in four days and watch a fucking human sacrifice. Not exactly something that was on my bucket list."

Growing frustrated, I don't respond as we continue walking, trying to calm myself, when a noise in the distance has my back stiffening.

Scanning the thick trees, I search the shadows before finally finding what I'm looking for. Damien Santos—A.K.A., The Ghost—Empire's second-best assassin, coming right after me. The fucker has a real gift for disappearing right when shit gets real. Some think he's a legend, but not me. I think he's a fucking coward, terrified of facing the consequences of his own actions. If you're going to do a job like this, you can't be scared to die. And Santos? I don't think I've ever met such a pussy in my life.

I clench my jaw, wanting nothing more than to put this bastard down, especially after the stray bullet he put through Oakley's arm in the warehouse, but my time will come, I'm sure of it. And if it happens to come over the next four days, I might even be nice enough to allow

Oakley to be the one to pull the trigger.

Santos stares heavily, but not in the way he'd stalk his mark, and I realize that he's come to deliver a message. He's too good to be caught out, even by me. He's not here for an attack. This is a warning that he's coming for me.

This is all a fucking game to him, and he thinks he has me right where he wants me. He's trying to gloat, but in my opinion, he's got nothing to gloat about. He could have taken me out the second I stepped out of the tomb, but that would have been too easy. He's looking for the challenge.

Taking me out is going to be his biggest accomplishment, a career move that others could only dream of being skilled enough to make, but I'll never let it happen, not now that I've almost got everything I've ever wanted. He'll never get close enough.

Sensing my unease, Cara looks up at me with wide eyes. "What's wrong?" she demands, her gaze flicking to the shadows. "Is someone out there?"

"No," I tell her, giving her a shove to keep her moving before dropping my gaze away from Santos, knowing he's not something I need to worry about tonight. "Keep walking. We're fine."

Cara nods, and with that, we break out of the woods and back to the side of the road, finding my SUV right where I left it. She scurries to the passenger door, grabs the handle, and impatiently waits for me to unlock it. The second I do, she climbs in and slams the door behind her with fear in her eyes, proving once and for all that she doesn't have what it takes to withstand the ugliness of The Circle.

And without a doubt in my mind, I know this world is going to claim her. It might not be today or tomorrow, maybe not even next week or next year, but at some point, if Empire doesn't beat her to it, she will succumb to the fear and take her own life. I just hope Sawyer is prepared because when she does, it's going to kill him too.

CHAPTER 15

Oakley

The sun rises over the city in shades of pink and gold, promising a beautiful day that I'm finding it hard to take joy in. I lean back and dangle my legs over the side of the DeVil Hotel, taking in the same sky I've spent twenty-one years living under, yet knowing how many sunrises I have left in this world makes this one mean so much more.

Taking a deep breath, I close my eyes and listen to the busy morning below. The breeze breaking through the high-rise buildings, the cars on the road, the dogs bouncing and barking on the end of their leashes, and their owners going about their day without a care in the world. They'll lock their dogs in their fancy apartments and head to their office jobs like every other morning. Maybe they'll stop for coffee or meet a friend for breakfast first, but all of them are blissfully unaware that someone's world is ending.

God, I'd give everything I had to be able to feel that way. To forget about the fresh hell knocking on my door. This morning, I woke in Sawyer's arms to realize there were only four days left. I shouldn't be counting down like this, shouldn't be giving myself a constant reminder, but I can't help it.

Four days.

Ninety hours.

Five thousand, four hundred minutes.

Three hundred and twenty-four thousand seconds.

This is what my life has been reduced to.

Knowing the boys are bound to come looking for me soon, I get up, and as I stand on the very edge of the rooftop, staring out at the world below, the thought enters my mind—I could just throw myself over and put an end to it now. I could finish this on my own terms, have a mostly peaceful death. I won't need to scream in agony. I won't need to feel the torture of Zade's hand plunging inside my chest.

One quick drop to the ground below and it'll all be over.

Fuck.

Tears fill my eyes, and I quickly blink them away before turning on my heel and stalking back toward the private elevator. It's not going to end like this. The boys asked me to have faith in them, to trust that they will find a way to save me, and while that trust is quickly fading, I'm not ready to give up yet, and at the very least, I'm going to enjoy these next few days.

Pressing the call button for the elevator, I lean against the wall and wait the few seconds it takes to come up from Zade's apartment. The door opens, and as I go to step in, I run straight into Easton. He catches me before I break my nose against his wide chest, grinning down at me. "There you are," he murmurs. "I was just coming to look for you."

"I figured as much," I tell him, pressing the button to go back down. "I thought I could beat you to it and get back to Zade's apartment before anyone started to worry."

"Don't stress," he says with a soft chuckle. "It's just me and Sawyer. Zade and Dalton are still asleep, and I figured we'd at least check for you before sounding the alarm. Fuck knows Zade couldn't handle it if you went missing again."

I laugh, able to picture it so perfectly. "Good plan," I tell him as he steps in behind me, his arms circling my waist. Easton drops his lips to the base of my throat, gently kissing me, and I tilt my head, allowing him more space when the door opens to Zade's apartment and we find Sawyer madly rushing around.

Stepping out of the elevator, Sawyer's eyes come to mine and he stops before bracing his hands against the kitchen counter and dropping his head. "Thank fuck," he breathes, letting out a relieved sigh. "I thought something happened to you."

"I'm sorry," I tell him, walking right into his arms before pushing up onto my tippy toes and pressing a kiss to his lips. "I didn't mean to scare you. I just wanted to watch the sunrise from the roof."

"Why didn't you tell me?" Sawyer questions, reaching up and

brushing my hair off my face, looking me deep in the eyes. "I would have come with you."

"You were sleeping so peacefully," I murmur, my hand pressing against his chest. "I didn't want to disturb you. And besides, it was kinda nice just having a moment of peace to myself."

Sawyer rolls his eyes, clearly not satisfied with my answer, but all I can offer him is a wide smile as I step back out of his space and head into the kitchen to make my second coffee of the morning. "I don't buy it," Easton says, crossing the room and heading for Venom's enclosure. "You're not a get-up-early-to-watch-the-sunrise kind of girl. You're a sleep-till-after-lunch girl. You couldn't sleep."

Damn it. That's the one thing I hate about allowing myself to get so close to these guys—they see right through me. "Okay, you got me," I mutter, reaching up for a mug and shoving it under the little spout of the coffee machine. "I heard Cara and Zade get in after The Circle meeting last night, and I couldn't sleep after that."

"Why not?" Sawyer asks, striding across to the kitchen and dropping down on one of the stools behind the island.

"I don't know to be honest," I say, my gaze focused heavily on the coffee machine. "I think I was just allowing everything to get to me. And I mean, we're four days out from the ritual. What else could their meeting have been about? They were probably discussing how best to tear my heart out of my body and figuring out what happens after that."

"They weren't," Sawyer says, pressing his lips into a hard line and looking away, reminding me just how much he knows about the inner workings of The Circle, their practices, beliefs, and traditions. Hell, he was supposed to be one of them until Zade came in and ruined it. "A few days out from completing the leadership ritual, they must convene in the sacred tomb and prepare it. They do some fucked-up blood chants and then cleanse the tomb. It's like a way to farewell the past and prepare for a new rule."

"Oh," I say, feeling a little better about the situation, though it's not like it changes anything. I'm still going to become Empire fodder. "You realize this society you all so shamelessly give your loyalty to is the most fucked-up thing . . . like, ever?"

"Believe me," Easton mutters as Venom circles around his knuckles. "We know."

Taking my mug, I sip my coffee, feeling their heavy stares on my face. They're waiting for me to break, so I make my way around the kitchen island and head down to Zade's room, determined not to waste another day.

Slamming my way through the door, I find Zade fast asleep in his bed, and a smile pulls at my lips. "Rise and shine, asshole," I announce, watching as his eyes spring open, not caring that he only got a few hours of sleep.

Striding through his room, I stop by the tally on his wall and grab the Sharpie before uncapping it with my teeth to avoid having to put my coffee down. Then with a heavy heart, I add another stroke before taking myself into the closet and finding something comfortable to wear.

Emerging from his room, dressed and ready for anything, I stand out in the impressive penthouse, trying to figure out what the hell I can do to fill my day. Usually by now, Zade has come out and barked orders at us all and told us exactly what terrifying task we'll be completing to satisfy his sick and twisted desires, yet I stand here with nothing but time on my hands.

My gaze shifts out the big floor-to-ceiling window, and I sigh heavily. I should be trying to figure out how to make the most of my day, or I could be flipping through the pages of the bylaws in Zade's home office to be sure I haven't missed anything. Instead, all I want to do is spend hours on end immersed in my drawing.

I've always been a whore for charcoal. It's what I used to do to keep my mind off the world, only since Empire decided to invade my life, I've only allowed myself to dabble a handful of times. One of those drawings is now tattooed across Easton's back. I'm not going to lie, every time he tears his shirt over his head and I see my artwork inked on his skin, it's one of the greatest feelings in the world. It gets me so worked up.

My fingers itch to create, and with nothing else planned for the day, I take myself off to Zade's office and search for my charcoal, which is much easier said than done. Zade has an overwhelming need to keep his home tidy. Everything must have a place, and that includes my charcoal. The only problem is, he tends to forget to tell people where those places are.

Finding them in a drawer on his oversized bookshelf, I grin to myself before finding a canvas and taking it out into the living room. In the early hours of the morning, the sun shines right through the living room and the thought of soaking up the warmth is too good to pass up.

Knowing just how messy this can get, I find a bed sheet and lay it across the floor, hoping it isn't some fancy Egyptian cotton worth more than I could make in a lifetime. I place my canvas on top and step back, wondering what the hell I'm going to draw, but I can't help but feel underwhelmed.

The canvas is so small. I'm not in the mood for small.

Since coming to Faders Bay and having my life turned upside down, everything I seem to encounter has been larger than life, big on unbelievable scales. Dalton is a prime example of that. The size of the monster hanging between his legs is simply outstanding. I need to enter him in the annual cock awards, if that even exists, and if it doesn't, it should.

Trying to figure out what I'm going to do, my gaze lifts to the drywall, and my brow arches, a wide grin spreading across my face. Now that's a canvas I can get down with. But then, I've destroyed Zade's walls before, and he definitely didn't appreciate it. Though to be fair, I was marking his walls with insults, but this will be art. Hell, he might even like it enough to keep it here. It's not like I'm a shitty artist. I'm usually quite fond of the pieces I make, and if Zade has even a little bit of taste, he will be too.

Satisfied with my justification, I scootch the old bedsheet across the room to sit perfectly at the foot of the drywall, and without hesitation, I blast my favorite playlist, pick up a piece of charcoal, and get straight to work.

I have no idea what I plan to create, but as the charcoal moves across the drywall, the lines of four ruggedly handsome men begin coming together, and the longer I work on it, the more excited I become. I've never loved a piece so much.

Hours begin to pass, and it's not until my stomach starts to grumble that I take a step back from the wall. It's well into the afternoon, and I haven't eaten since dinner last night. Hell, Zade hasn't even come to scream at me about destroying his home. In fact, I haven't heard a peep out of any of the guys.

Glancing down my body, I find I'm covered almost head to toe in charcoal, and I scrunch up my face before tiptoeing across the penthouse and to the kitchen sink. I slather soap across my hands and arms before scrubbing myself silly, making sure to get all the charcoal out from under my nails. Then for good measure, I dip my head down toward the sink and wash my face too. I can't remember a single time where I haven't accidentally ended up with charcoal smudged all over my face, but that's just one of the many downfalls of creating art. No one ever said it was supposed to be tidy.

Finishing up, I go to pull my destroyed shirt over my head when I glance across the kitchen and find the boys' dirty dishes from lunch and my jaw drops open. What gives? Those big bastards ate without me.

A strange ache settles into my chest, and my bottom lip pouts out, but it's nothing compared to the need to go bust their balls wide open.

Marching through the penthouse, I start searching for the big assholes, and I don't get far before finding Sawyer, Easton, and Dalton chilling out on the massive balcony, probably talking about how hard they're going to take me tonight because, let's face it, what could possibly be more important than that?

My growling stomach all but propels me out the door, and I watch as each of their heads snaps up and those intense gorgeous eyes that I love so much flash right to mine. "What the hell?" I demand. "You assholes ordered lunch and ate without me?"

Sawyer grins, laughter flashing in his eyes. "You're fucking kidding me, right?" he questions. "We asked you if you wanted to eat and got no response, then we ordered for you anyway, and when it arrived, I practically hung it in front of your face and you still didn't notice. You were so caught up in your art, the world could have imploded and you still wouldn't have noticed."

"I, umm . . . Oh. My bad," I mutter, my cheeks flushing. I mean, it wouldn't be the first time I've ignored the whole world while I was busy with a piece of charcoal. "Did you keep it for me? I'm starving."

Dalton cringes and steps toward me. "We tried," he says, guilt flashing in his eyes. "But then Zade—"

"YOU LET THAT ASSHOLE EAT MY LUNCH?"

"Technically," Easton says, lifting his defined arm and locking his hand around the back of his neck. "He's still eating it."

My eyes bug out of my head. "What? No. That's not okay," I huff. "What was it?"

"Your favorite," Sawyer says. "A big, juicy burger with fries."

"And ketchup?"

"Uh-huh."

My heart shatters into a million pieces. "Noooooooo," I cry, before narrowing my gaze on the boys, an idea forming in the darkest pits of my mind. "When you say he's probably still eating it, what do you mean? Like, it's probably almost gone, or he might have only gotten through a few fries so far?"

"No," Easton says, shaking his head. "I know what you're thinking, and it's a bad idea. Zade is protective over his food. He doesn't share."

"Well, lucky for me, I'm not planning on sharing. I'm taking back what's mine, and you're either with me or not. What's it going to be?"

"You're gonna get yourself killed," Dalton warns.

I laugh, a smug grin stretching across my lips. "It's not like he can kill me twice, right?"

Easton blows his cheeks out, still shaking his head when he presses his lips into a tight line, indecision flashing in his stormy eyes. "Fuck," he grunts, striding past me and back to the door. "The shit I do for you, Pretty."

Excitement booms through my chest as I spin on my heels and follow Easton back inside, only to find Sawyer and Dalton coming along for the ride.

"You gotta play this smart," Dalton says as we stand around the dining table as though this is one of the most important meetings we'll ever have. "You can't just walk up to him and take it. He'll see it coming a million miles away. You've gotta be a ghost. In and out without him even noticing."

"How the fuck is he not going to notice her taking the plate right out of his fucking hands?" Sawyer questions.

"Hmmm," Easton says, leaning back as he rubs his hand down his face. "I think I've got it."

My brow arches as all eyes turn to Easton, and we listen as he quickly relays his plan, which is exactly how I end up lying across a skateboard with a rope attached to my ankle.

The smell of my burger assaults my senses, and I will my stomach not to grumble, but damn it's hard, especially as I peek through the opening of the den and watch the way Zade grabs my burger with those big, skilled hands and lifts it to his mouth.

Goddamn. Who does he think he is eating my burger?

Glancing back, I meet the boys' stares. "It's now or never," I tell them. "Let's do this."

Easton nods, and with that, he strides into the den, proving once and for all what a strong man he really is, risking his life for my burger when we could have easily just ordered a new one, but that's beside the point. This is based on principle. That's *my* burger, and if anyone is going to sink their face into it and lick the delicious juices off their fingers, it's gonna be me.

"Yo, you got a second?" Easton says, keeping Zade distracted as I start to roll out into the den, my heart thundering a million miles per hour. "I need to run something by you."

"Yeah, what's up?" Zade responds, still holding onto the burger.

Damn, that was supposed to be Zade's cue to put the burger down. Easton's going to have to try harder than that.

I keep inching closer to the couch, my gaze locked heavily on the plate resting on the cushion beside him. This isn't going to be easy, and so far, it's not going exactly to plan, but I have to have faith that we can pull this off.

Easton walks across the front of the couch and drops down on the opposite side, keeping Zade's attention on him. "It's about Oakley," he says, a strange tone in his voice. "I wanna take her out tonight."

"Ahh, fuck, Cross. Why do you have to go and make shit complicated? You know that's out of the question," Zade mutters with a heavy sigh before putting the burger back down on the plate to give Easton his full attention, completely oblivious to the elation pounding through my veins.

"Come on, man. It's one night," Easton continues as I hold my breath, slowly creeping closer, hoping like fuck he can't hear the subtle sound of the skateboard wheels moving along the tiles. "I was just gonna take her back to my place, maybe cook her dinner or some shit like that."

"I don't know," Zade says as I move in right behind him, my hands shaking. "It's too risky. You know that. Why can't you just cook her dinner here? Why do you need to take her out? It's not like she's the type of girl who needs a man to treat her like a fucking princess to get on her knees. You know she'll still fuck you at the end of the night. Fancy dinner or not."

Ouch. Asshole.

Resisting the urge to smack him up the back of his head, I slowly begin to creep my hand up the couch, mere inches away from my lunch.

"It's not like I'm planning on showing her off in the middle of the city or waving her around like a fucking target. It's dinner in the confines of my home," Easton says. "She's got four nights left. Don't you think she deserves to enjoy them? And besides, my place is like a fucking fortress. It's probably got more security measures than this fucking penthouse."

"Doubt it," Zade mutters just as my fingers find the edge of the plate.

My eyes widen, and I grip it tighter, trying to figure out the best course of action. Do I take my time, slowly pulling the plate to the edge or do I make this fast, steal the plate, and run for my fucking life?

"So what's it gonna be?" Easton questions as I slowly begin dragging the plate toward me.

There's a strange silence and I pause, my heart beating right out of my chest. "Why the fuck are you pushing this so hard?" Zade asks, suspicion thick in his tone. "You know the risks of taking her outside this apartment, and you know how I fucking feel about it."

Fuck. He's onto us.

"I, uhhh . . . FUCK. GO OAKLEY. NOW!"

Shit!

My hand snatches back, spilling fries all over the tiles and barely securing the burger when Sawyer yanks back on the rope attached to my ankle. A terror-filled scream tears from the back of my throat and my eyes widen, watching just how quickly Zade moves, fury in his eyes, realizing he's just been played.

He lunges for me as Easton flies toward him, locking his arms around Zade's body, holding him down. "GO. GO. GO," Easton roars, as the skateboard flies back across the den at a million miles an hour.

I come in like a fucking freight train, clutching the plate and holding it to my chest, terrified my burger is about to be spread from one end of the den to the other. The second the skateboard flies back out through the entrance of the den, Dalton is there, catching me as a howling laugh rips through me.

"Holy fuck," I pant, staring up at the guys before peeking into the den to see Zade and Easton battling it out, Zade's ferocious glare trained on me, and yet all I can do is hold up the plate and grin back at him. "And that, gentlemen, is how you put a bitch in his place."

And with that, I pick up my burger and take a hefty bite, knowing without a doubt that I will pay for that later.

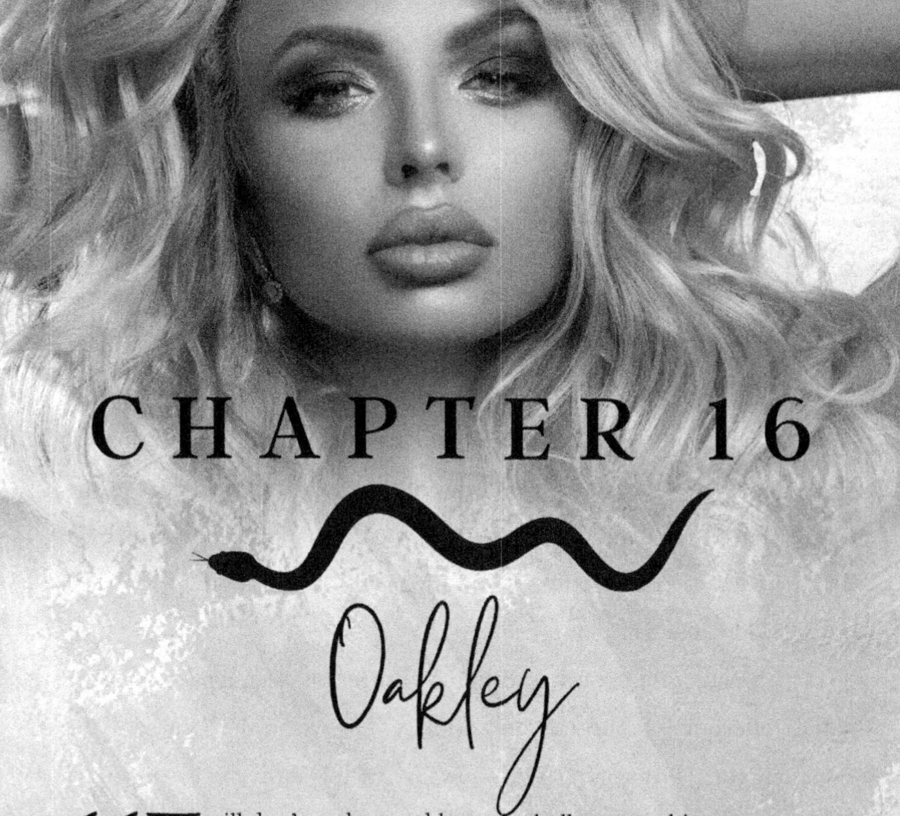

CHAPTER 16

Oakley

"I still don't understand how the hell you got him to agree to this," I laugh as Easton presses his hand to my lower back and leads me into Zade's private elevator with Venom curled around his knuckles. "He seemed pretty adamant that this wasn't going to happen."

"Trust me, when you spend as much time watching people as I do, you figure out exactly how to play them," Easton says as the elevator door closes behind us. "And despite what Zade might think, he can be played just as easily as anyone else."

Easton reaches around me and presses the button for the underground parking garage, and the second the elevator starts its descent, he closes the gap between us, his hands resting at my waist as his lips drop to the base of my neck. I groan and tilt my head to the side, opening up for more. "You wouldn't dare play me like that, would you now, Mr. Easton Cross?"

I feel his grin against my throat, and as his fingers move over my body, I can't help but watch our reflection in the back of the elevator door. "You're here with me instead of spending the night with Dalton and Sawyer buried in that sweet cunt, aren't you? All I had to do was promise you a small window into my life and I all but have you on your knees, mine for the fucking taking. Pretty, I would play you any day of the week if it meant getting to put my hands on your body."

Goddamn. This man.

I groan, leaning back into him as I meet his heated gaze through the reflection of the elevator door. "Then what the hell are you waiting for?" I murmur. "You know, just with Dalton and Sawyer, that everything I am is yours. You don't need to play me, Easton. All you have to do is ask and I will give you anything you want."

His eyes flame like molten lava as his hand sails up my body and clutches the base of my throat. Easton's fingers dig in, clearly disturbing Venom as she unwinds herself from his hand and slithers across the front of my throat, sending a wave of shivers across my skin.

Easton reaches out with his other hand, slamming his palm over the emergency stop button, bringing the elevator to a screeching halt. The momentum of the stop almost knocks me right off my feet, but Easton is right there, his strong arm locked across my front and holding me in place. "Be careful what you wish for, Pretty," he murmurs in my ear. "You don't know what you're asking for."

Grinding my ass back against him, I let him see the hunger in my eyes, knowing how he can't possibly resist. "Then show me, Easton. Show me what it means to be yours because I'm already falling in love with you, and if I only have four days to live, then I want to live them having all of you."

He growls against my skin, the deep sound filled with desperation and leaving me hungry for his touch. My pussy throbs, clenching as I watch his hand release my throat and grip the front of my cropped tank before tearing it clean off my body.

I gasp, never having experienced Easton quite so rough before, but I like it. Hell, I need it. His arm curls around my body, and I watch the way he watches me through our reflection, his heavy stare fixated on my tits as he grabs hold of one, squeezing just hard enough to cause a hint of pain. Then just as Venom curls herself around the base of my throat, Easton's hand plunges down into the waistband of my sweatpants, firmly cupping my pussy.

I groan as he grinds the palm of his hand against my clit, already on the edge "You want to be mine, baby? You want to be my little whore, fucking my friends during the day and hanging off my cock at night?"

Swallowing hard, I nod as my cheeks become flushed, so fucking desperate to feel him inside of me. Reaching up, I twine my hand behind his neck before knotting my fingers into his hair and holding on for dear life.

"Let's be clear, Oakley," he rumbles, slowly grinding his palm over my clit. "You don't want me loving you. I'll give you what you fucking need, but you don't want my heart. It's tainted, not pure enough for you."

Gripping his hair tighter, I demand his attention. "Maybe you haven't been paying attention," I hiss. "If you think for one fucking second that I need pure, then you don't know me at all. I'm not after some nice guy who's going to treat me well and rush in to be my fucking hero. I want a man who's going to slay my fucking enemies and then fuck me in their blood."

Easton growls, and before I know it, my sweatpants are across the elevator and my back is slammed up against the wall, his heavy body keeping me pinned. He leans into me, his head dipped to the curve of my neck as he takes my knee and pulls it up high, spreading me open. "Don't fucking sugarcoat it, Pretty. If you have something to say, then say it."

With my fingers still knotted in the back of his hair, I pull hard, forcing his stare back to mine. "We're not fooling anybody," I tell him. "You say that I can't have your heart, but you and I both know it already belongs to me. You love me, Easton. You have since the second you branded me with your mark. The question is, how much are you willing to sacrifice for me?"

He clenches his jaw, and I see the very second he figures out where this is going. "Don't," he warns.

"Save me, Easton. Be the fucking man I need you to be and save me. Betray your loyalty to Zade and give me a real fucking chance to be yours. You, me, Sawyer, and Dalton. We can start fresh somewhere else, away from all of—"

"ARGHHH," he roars, rearing back and slamming his hands down on the cool metal on either side of my head. "STOP. I will not betray my brotherhood."

Clenching my jaw, I bring my hands up and shove him hard in the chest, putting space between us. "Then you and I are done," I tell him, stepping around him and heading for the emergency stop button to get me the hell out of here. "I'm not going to be your little toy if you can't give me anything in return."

I go to reach for the stop button when Easton's strong arm locks around my waist, hauling me back so hard that my feet are lifted off the ground. My back slams up against the wall, right where I was only a second ago, only this time, my legs are wrapped securely around his waist. "We're done when I say we're done," he spits. "Don't test my fucking loyalty."

"Then give me what I need."

"You don't know what you fucking need," he throws back at me.

"And you do?" I challenge.

Easton growls, and in the very next second he reaches down between us and frees his straining cock from his pants, and just as I feel him at my entrance, he meets my heavy stare, both our chests heaving for oxygen. "I've always known exactly what you need," he tells me before slamming that thick, glorious cock deep inside of me.

I cry out, my head tipping back against the elevator wall as he rams up into me, taking me deep and stretching me wide. "Oh fuck," I groan, clutching his shoulder as my nails bite into his skin.

"You said you were falling in love with me, Pretty," he grunts, thrusting into me as though he'll never get to touch me again. "You can't take that back. Now those words have crossed your lips, you're mine." He pulls back, thrusting again, making my eyes roll to the back of my head. "Say it," he demands. "Tell me this sweet cunt is all mine."

My fingers dig deeper until I'm sure I've drawn blood, and I shake my head, feeling Venom tighten around my throat. "How can I say I'm truly yours when Zade is the one who really owns my heart?" I challenge him, panting with every thrust. "You can take my body any way you want it. Fuck me into submission as much as you need, but no matter what you do, as long as he owns your loyalty, Zade is the only one who has any claim over my heart. Save me, Easton. Save me and it's all yours."

"FUCK," he roars, indecision flashing in his eyes. He doesn't say another word as he fucks me harder, taking me deeper and pressing me against the wall. He takes my thigh and holds it up, giving him more space to move, and as I feel that familiar tightening deep in my core, my eyes start to flutter.

"Oh fuck, Easton," I pant, gripping onto him. "I'm gonna come."

"No the fuck you're not," he demands. "You'll wait."

Oh, God.

Easton is relentless, pushing me right to the edge and holding me there, pressing his thumb to my clit and applying just the right amount of pressure as Venom starts working her way down my body, curling around the outside of my breast.

I throw my head back, the undeniable pleasure too much to bear. "I can't wait," I cry out, feeling my orgasm right there and knowing my body physically can't hold back a second longer.

A deep growl rumbles through Easton's chest, his fingers digging into my waist. "You will."

Shit.

He slowly pulls back, nearly coming all the way out of me until I just feel his tip there at my entrance, and as his thumb applies just a little more pressure to my clit before rolling over it, I all but lose my fucking mind. "FUCK, EASTON!"

He hisses, looking as though dragging this out is almost painful for him, and as he slowly pushes back inside me, I clench down around that glorious cock and watch the way his body reacts. He might think he's in control here, but he should know better by now. Just because I allow him to toss me around and fuck me like some kind of wild animal does not mean for one fucking second that he possesses the control.

"Shit," he pants, his fingers sure to leave bruises.

"I'm gonna come whether you want me to or not," I warn him. "Make up your mind, Easton. You're either along for the ride or you're not. Which is it?"

His cock flinches inside of me and my whole body jolts with undeniable pleasure, then just to prove some kind of point, I clench down around him again, my eyes rolling in the back of my head. "Oh fuck," Easton grunts, his knees all but buckling beneath him. "Come for me, Pretty. Let me feel the way you squeeze my cock."

Thank fuck.

He slams into me one more time and as his thumb works its magic,

I finally let go, my orgasm exploding within me, booming through my body and taking me to new heights. I throw my head back as my toes curl, gasping with the intensity.

Easton roars, shooting his hot cum deep inside my pussy, but all that matters is the way I come undone, the way my walls shatter around him, manically convulsing as my orgasm tears through my body.

"Holy shit," I pant, struggling to keep myself upright as I grip his strong shoulders.

"That's right, Pretty," he murmurs as his thumb continues rolling over my clit, the anger still flashing in his eyes, but damn, it makes this so much better. "Be a good girl and ride out that high."

Fucking hell. I'll be this man's good girl any day of the week, any hour, any minute.

As I come down from my high, Easton inches back, allowing me space to lower my feet to the ground as he folds that big cock back inside his pants. "Let's get one thing straight," he says, not moving any farther away and keeping me crowded in the corner of the elevator. "You and me, we're a done deal. Threaten me all you want, try and walk away, but I won't allow it. I get that you're with Dalton and Sawyer too, and you probably feel exactly the same for them, but that doesn't change a goddamn thing. You're mine, Oakley. You and I have both known it from the beginning, but just because you own everything that I am doesn't mean that I am going to change my values for you. Those I care about are the most important people in my life, and I will not betray a single one of them, even if I don't believe they're doing what's right. Without honor, I have nothing, so hear me when I say that I will stand by Zade's side, supporting him right until the end, but know that I will do the same for you, Pretty. If I can save you, I will, but I will not do it by betraying my brotherhood."

I swallow hard, his dark, intense gaze focuses so heavily on mine that I can't even try to look away, but I wouldn't dare, not when he's opening up like this. Easton Cross is a man of few words, so when he speaks, bitch, you better listen.

Stepping back into him, I lift my hand to his cheek, my thumb brushing across his face. "It's okay," I whisper as Venom slithers up my outstretched arm and down around the back of Easton's neck. "I was out of line. I shouldn't have pushed like that, but you're right. You and I, this means something and I couldn't walk away even if I tried. I want to see this through."

Easton lets out a heavy breath before crowding me back into the corner of the elevator and dropping his lips to mine. He kisses me deeply, every second of it filled with intense passion, only stopping when his phone cuts through the silence.

"Fucking hell," he mutters, pulling back from me and slipping his hand into his pocket. He pulls out his phone and rolls his eyes before showing me the screen with Zade's name in bold letters. "Get dressed," he tells me before finally accepting the call.

"What's up?" he says into the phone as I move around him, finding my sweatpants across the opposite side of the elevator.

I barely get a step before I hear Zade's tone as clear as day through Easton's phone, despite the call not being on speakerphone. "Why the fuck do I have my security on the other line telling me they're watching some little whore getting railed in my private elevator?"

Easton laughs as my eyes widen in horror, not realizing this elevator had a camera let alone a whole security team on the other side watching every fucking second, but why should I be surprised? Easton loves watching, so why wouldn't he invite others to do the same?

"Because some little whore did just get railed in your private elevator," Easton says, grinning as he watches me fix my sweatpants into place before trying to figure out what to do about my torn tank that's been ripped right down the middle.

He goes to offer me his shirt but I wave him off before pulling the torn tank back on and tying the two sides in a knot at the front and deciding it's cute as fuck.

"So, I suppose now that you've gotten your dick wet, you can bring her back up," Zade says. "There's no need to take her out to your place now."

"Fuck that," I say, knowing damn well that big bastard can hear me. "Easton promised me an outing and that's exactly what I'm going to get." With that, I move across the elevator and release the emergency stop before feeling my stomach sink right into my ass as the heavy weight of the elevator begins to drop down to the underground parking garage.

Easton laughs. "You heard her, man," he says, glancing down and checking on Venom around his neck. "I'll have her home in a few hours."

The elevator chimes its arrival at the parking garage, and I smile up at Easton as he presses his hand to my lower back to lead me out, still listening to whatever bullshit Zade is spitting at him. Only as I take a step out of the elevator, Easton pauses, his strong hand curling around my upper arm as his skilled gaze quickly scans Zade's private parking area.

"We're not alone," he rushes out before shoving me back into the corner of the elevator and slamming his hand over the button, trying to close the doors. My heart lurches right out of my chest, panic gripping me, but I don't see a damn thing outside the doors.

I hear Zade yelling through the phone but can't make out a single word he's saying, and just as the doors start to close, I see him—the man from the warehouse, the asshole responsible for the ugly red scar across the top of my arm. I can't remember his name, but I know the boys said something about him being a ghost. He's lethal and terrifying, and fuck, I'm sure just like everyone else, he probably wants me dead.

The seconds start to feel like hours, waiting for the doors to finally close, but he's too far away, he'll never get here in time, but I don't miss the way Easton drops his phone into the pocket of my sweatpants, the call still in progress as he frees up his hands, pulling a gun from who the fuck knows where.

"Fuck, fuck, fuck, fuck," I chant, unable to take my eyes off the asshole across the parking garage, standing motionless, simply staring as though he's waiting for something.

"It's gonna be okay," Easton promises me, just as a hand slams into the closing doors, and like some kind of horror film, an army of men dressed in black tactical outfits swarm the elevator.

"FUCK," Easton grunts, shoving me behind him as he instantly jumps into action, effortlessly taking out men left and right, but there are too many of them. He can't slaughter every single one of them no matter how good he is.

The panic gets to me, and realizing just how much danger Easton is in, I drop to the ground, scrambling toward one of the fallen soldiers, hoping like fuck Zade and the boys get here fast. Snatching a knife off the guy's uniform and prying the gun out of his dead hands, I get to work, hoping I'm doing more good than harm.

With the bodies piling up in the elevator, the doors are unable to close, and we have no choice but to climb over them and run to freedom. The second I step out of the elevator, hands grab me from behind, dragging me back as I let out an ear-shattering scream.

"OAKLEY," Easton roars, struggling to get through the mass of men bearing down on him, all while the asshole across the garage just watches with a smug-as-fuck grin across his stupid face.

"Give up now, girl," someone says in my ear. "It's over for you."

And with that, a black bag covers my head before a fist slams into the back of my ribs. I scream out and crumble to the ground, my knees buckling as the pain tears through me. My hands are bound behind my back with what could only be a thick rope, and not a second later, I'm shoved into the back of a car, the engine already running.

The tires screech through the parking garage, and the momentum of the car has me slamming into the back as I struggle against the ropes. I scream out, terrified by what's to come and what happened to Easton. Is he alive? Did they get me and run or stay to finish him off?

Fuck.

I've already spent days thinking he was dead and it was horrendous. I can't do it again.

A laugh rumbles through the car, a voice I don't recognize, before the familiar sound of an outgoing call connects through the car's Bluetooth system. The call is answered barely a second later, but it's received with nothing but silence. "We got her, boss," someone says from within the car.

"Good. Now bring the bitch to me."

Fuck. I know that voice like the back of my hand.

Aunt Liv . . .

Zade's mom.

CHAPTER 17

Cross

Oakley hangs from chains in front of me, her head lolling to the side, barely kept upright by her arm. They shot her up with something the second we arrived in this shitty underground bunker, and thankfully she's been out cold since, unable to bear witness to the vile torture Santos has been putting me through.

There's not exactly a clock down here in this cold, damp dungeon, but from what I can tell, we've been at this for at least two hours, and so far, I can't figure out what the fuck they want with me. Their end goal is Oakley. If Santos is working for Priscilla DeVil and Matthias Quinn, then why bring me along? I act as Oakley's protection and it goes directly against their game plan in keeping me alive. So why the fuck am I not lying dead in the bottom of Zade's parking garage?

My only guess—Santos has a bone to pick with me, some kind of personal agenda, which makes him nothing but a fool.

The subtle sound of my blood dripping to the floor fills the small dungeon-like prison as I hang from the chains bolted to the ceiling, my only lifeline being the phone I stashed in Oakley's pocket. I can only hope it didn't fall out or that it wasn't found and destroyed before we got here.

Sawyer would have been tracking it before we even left the hotel. They'll find us. Without a doubt. I just hope they do before Santos decides to put a bullet through my brain. Though, it's not like this is the first time I've been caught in this particular predicament, but it's definitely a first being in an underground bunker system. And I sure as fuck have never been chained up with the girl I love, beaten and bruised before me.

Like I said, I'm fucking thankful that she's out cold and not having to bear witness to any of this because it also means she can't feel the pain her body is currently suffering through. But fuck, after asking me to betray Zade, maybe she could use a little pain, but I think I drove that point home and she'll know better than to ever ask that of me again. I get where she's coming from though. Why would she want to be with me when I can't give her what she needs? She doesn't see it though, even with Zade going forward with the ritual, I'd still give everything I am to save her. There has to be a way I can honor my loyalty to Zade and still get the girl.

Fuck. This isn't going to be easy, but I have to try.

The sooner she comes to, the sooner Zade's mom is bound to get the show on the road, and I'm dreading every fucking second of it. But for now, I'm content with Santos using me for target practice because each hit that I take is one less that she won't have to.

Closing my eyes, I let my body go limp as I hang from the chains, needing this time to regroup and conserve what little energy I have left. I have no doubt these assholes are going to try and take out Oakley and when they do, I'll be ready.

Bringing me here with them was the biggest mistake they ever made. More so, putting us in the same fucking dungeon.

My gaze shifts to Venom in the corner of the room, itching for her to come back to me, but she's safer where she is, out of sight, out of mind. She fell out of my clothes when my shirt was ripped off my body. Apparently Santos likes to see the scars he's left on someone. Sick bastard.

With Venom doing alright where she is, I close my eyes again, taking slow, deep breaths until I hear the sound of the heavy metal lock on the door sliding out of place. My eyes snap open, my gaze shifting to Oakley's face, hoping like fuck she's still out.

Finding Oakley still unconscious, I let out a heavy breath before focusing my stare on the door as Santos strides in, a smug-as-fuck grin on his face and a baseball bat firmly in his hand.

Fuck. Where the hell is Dalton when you need him? That fucker would happily stand here and take Santos' abuse. Hell, he'd even like it and ask for more. His father messed him up good. The violence is like a drug to him, but for some reason, since Oakley came running head-first into our lives, he hasn't actively been seeking that thrill. I think she's healing him in some way, something we've all been trying to do for years.

I brace myself for whatever's about to come, a little disappointed that he couldn't find it within himself to even give me twenty minutes reprieve before coming back for more. He must be thirsty for it. Sick fucks like Santos always are. They don't kill out of necessity, they kill for sport. Though I have to admit, the power that fills my veins as I watch someone's life drain from their eyes is the best high I've ever felt. Up until meeting Oakley, I would spend my days craving that rush, but not anymore. Now, all I crave is sinking into her sweet cunt, pushing her to her limits, and watching her beautiful face as she comes on my cock. Hell, my cock, fingers, or tongue. I'll take them all.

To lose that . . . fuck. I'd be a broken man.

Santos looks over Oakley, and judging by the scowl on his face, he's not impressed to find her still out cold, and I'm sure if he had a bucket of ice water, she'd be drenched in it by now. He lifts the baseball bat and rams the end of it into her ribs, rocking her on the chains, but she doesn't budge, doesn't make a single sound as I grit my teeth, knowing exactly what would happen to her if I were to speak out.

He drops the tip of the bat back to the ground before begrudgingly turning his stare on me. He looks at me like a piece of shit he just stood in and can't seem to shake off the bottom of his boot.

Santos takes one step after another, dragging the metal bat that I have no doubt is about to break a rib or two. "Easton Cross," he spits, looking me up and down. "You should have done yourself a favor and let one of my men take you out in the parking garage, but just like your father, you don't know when to fucking quit."

My father? Great. This asshole thinks punishing me is somehow going to even whatever bullshit score he needs to settle with my father. If only he knew that my father doesn't give a single fuck about me. This isn't settling any score, this is only bringing him another problem, one I fully intend to make right.

Santos rears back with the bat and I brace, taking the hit right across my ribs, but I don't give him the satisfaction of screaming out in pain, not even a single grunt. "I worked with your old man three years ago," he tells me as though I actually give a shit. "He was my best fucking client. Sick bastard he is."

"My father is a piece of shit," I murmur, keeping my stare trained on him, all too aware of the work Santos used to do for him, and honestly, it was sloppy at best. "Makes sense that he'd align himself with scum like you. Perfect match. Tell me, did it get you off sucking his dick every night?"

Anger flares in his eyes, and he rears back with the bat again, making it all too clear that this is personal to him. Had this been strictly business, he wouldn't dare allow my taunts to affect him. He'd keep his cool and figure out a way to get in my head. After all, he's supposed to be considered one of the best in the industry, but so far, I'm not seeing anything that gets me hard.

The bat swings right at my ribs again, hitting me in the exact same spot, only this time, I hear the distinct sound of my rib breaking. I close my eyes, the pain making my head spin, but on the outside, I keep neutral, not letting him know just how fucking bad that hurt. And fuck,

I've been in his position before, and there's nothing more frustrating than a man who won't crumble into a million pieces and give me the satisfaction I'm looking for.

Sweat beads on his forehead, and he stumbles back a step, moving closer to Oakley. I watch him closely, not liking the look in his eyes. "She's awfully pretty," he says, lifting the bat to her bare waist and pressing the tip of it to the waistband of her sweats before working them down an inch. "I bet she fucks like an animal."

"Get away from her," I spit.

His eyes shimmer as if only now just realizing that the way to me is through her, and with that, he moves even closer, slowly walking around her until he's at her back. His hands fall to her waist as he steps right into her, grinding himself against her ass. "Mmmm, I could take her right here. Fuck her like the little whore that she is, and once I'm done with her, I'll hand her around to my men."

Oakley's eyes spring open, meeting mine across the darkened dungeon, and it takes barely a second for her to register what the fuck is going down, and without skipping a beat, she uses what little momentum she can get from the chains and slams her ass back into him.

Santos doubles over, groaning in pain. "Ahh, fuck. You little slut," he spits, but all I can do is look at my girl, so fucking proud of her, but at the same time, I wish she'd just kept still. He would have left eventually and then we could have figured out some way out of here, but now that he knows she's regained consciousness, this shitshow is bound to get underway.

"Gross," Oakley murmurs in disgust. "In what fucking world would any woman want your wrinkly old man balls anywhere near them, you sick pervert? Fuck. Can you even get it up without a hit of Viagra?"

Santos quickly recovers and focuses his rage on Oakley, rearing back with the bat and swinging it right across her hip. She screams in agony and the sound tears me to shreds. "I said leave her the fuck alone," I roar, more than prepared to have my ass beat, but unable to bear the thought of her being touched.

Santos looks back at me and laughs, his eyes lighting like fireworks, making it damn clear I just gave him the rush he's been searching for. He moves back toward me, dragging that fucking bat along the cold ground, and as he settles himself in front of me, fixing his grip around the neck of the bat, I focus my stare on Oakley.

She watches me through a pained gaze, her eyes so full of rage and fear, but she's strong. Holding her stare, I watch as she takes a slow, calming breath before finally nodding, letting me know that she's okay.

"You're a fucking joke, Easton," Santos says, ramming the head of the bat into my stomach and winding me. "Pathetic. A child. And you think you have what it takes to stand at the right-hand side of leadership, being Zade's loyal second." He pauses, grunting as he swings the bat at my broken rib. "You're a fraud, all of you. Zade should never have been offered the crown, and now Matthias Quinn will rise in his place, and I will be the one standing at his side."

Oakley scoffs, and I want to strangle her for drawing attention to herself. "Is that what he promised you?" she questions, amusement in her tone. "You do his dirty work while he pretends to be locked up and in return for being a loyal servant, you'll reap the rewards? What a joke. You're more foolish than I thought."

Fuck.

Santos turns on her, his hand whipping out and slapping across her fragile cheek, the sharp sound echoing through the small dungeon. "Do not speak ill of your father, girl."

Oakley spits a mouthful of blood onto the ground before scowling at Santos, not daring to back down. I will her to meet my eye, to stop before he ends her life, but she refuses to look at me, knowing damn well what I would say about this. "I may have been away from my father for a long time, but I know him better than you ever could. He is a manipulative bastard. Anyone who works for him now will be slain the second he steps into power. They know his secrets, know the vile things he's ordered people to do in his name. You're a loose end to be dealt with—not a trophy."

He slaps her again before getting right in her face. "You don't know what you're talking about, but what does it matter? You won't be around long enough to see."

Oakley laughs. "Because you're gonna kill me, right? Don't you get it? My father might want me dead for his own personal gain, but I'm still his little girl, still the baby he raised on his own. You kill me, and he will always see you as the man who took his baby girl's life. You will never stand at his side. You've backed yourself into a corner, and he will never have respect for you."

Santos clenches his jaw before backing up, putting space between them. "If only you knew what fun we have in store for you," he rumbles, the chilling sound almost enough to send shivers down my spine. "Maybe then you'd be smart enough to watch your mouth."

With that, he starts making his way out of the room before stopping, something catching his eye. His stare snaps down to the ground, his gaze narrowed as he finds Venom moving across the dungeon. "Well, well," he says, bending low and scooping her into his hands as my heart lurches in my chest, undeniable fear blasting through my body. "What on earth are you doing here?"

Venom circles his hand as Santos looks back and meets my eye, knowing damn well what she means to me. Every last member of Empire knows about my fucking snakes, but Venom . . . fuck.

I pull against my chains, knowing damn well what he intends to do with her, watching the sick smirk that spreads across his face, the vile, wicked thoughts circling his head. "I swear to God, Santos. You fucking hurt her and I'll end you."

But all he does is smile, knowing he's got me right where he wants me. And with Venom wrapped around his hand, he steps out of the underground dungeon, his voice booming down the hallway beyond. "The bitch is conscious," he yells as my body starts to shake. "Let's get this fucking show on the road."

CHAPTER 18

Oakley

"It's going to be okay," I tell Easton, watching the fire blasting through his dark eyes, terrified of what that sick bastard could be doing to Venom. "If anything, they'll use her against you for leverage."

"For what? They don't need me for anything. There's no value in keeping me or Venom alive," he grunts, thrashing against the chains, desperate to get free, which only sends him into waves of agony from his broken ribs.

"They could use her to get you to lure Zade to them. There's a million things they could use her for, and if anything, Santos is just going to use her to bait you, but it doesn't matter," I tell him, trying to keep him calm, "because you're going to get her back, and when you do, you will slit his throat and take every last ounce of power he thinks he possesses and finally put this shit to rest. You hear me, Easton? We can do this. We just need to get out of these fucking chains."

Easton blows his cheeks out and nods before hanging his head, needing a moment to remember who the fuck he is.

"You need to have faith," I whisper into the darkened room, my arms and shoulders aching from being suspended from these chains. "If something happened to her, you would feel it. You'd know, and besides, you and I both know the boys are coming for us. Zade isn't going to let me slip through his fingers this close to the finish line, but you can be sure he'll never let you try to take me back to your place again."

"Really?" Easton grunts. "You've got jokes right now?"

"Either you laugh at my stupid jokes or I'm going to start crying, and I promise you, it's not the cute damsel in distress cry, this is going to be the ugly, snotty cry that'll have you rethinking every decision you've ever made."

"Okay," he says, hopefully realizing just how on edge I really am. "Your jokes are hilarious, and as always, your timing is impeccable."

"I know," I whisper, taking slow, deep breaths as my gaze lowers down his strong body, hating the cuts and bruises that mar his perfect skin. "How are you feeling?"

"Nothing I haven't handled before."

A small smile pulls at the corner of my lips, knowing damn well he's avoiding answering the question properly. "That's a shitty response and you know it."

"Pretty," he murmurs, his gaze softening. "You look at me like I'm your fucking hero. I'm not about to admit that I'm in so much pain I feel like screaming like a little bitch. I need you to have faith in me, Oakley. I need you to believe that I can pull off the impossible and get us out of here, and if you're too busy worrying about my injuries and how they're going to hold me back, then you're going to doubt me, and that's going to kill me quicker than any of these bastards could."

I nod, understanding exactly where he's coming from. "I get it," I tell him, hating that we're in this predicament at all. "But for what it's worth, I do see you as one of my heroes. You and the boys, you're all bigger than life, and I've been so lucky to be the one you've all allowed to get close."

"No, Pretty. We're the ones who have been lucky. You came crashing into our lives right when we all needed you most. You've saved us each in our own way. I don't know where Dalton would be. He was heading down a bad path, seeking out fights like some kind of violence junkie. He'd be dead by now, and Sawyer? Fuck, after everything that went down with his father and then Cara, he would have crumbled and turned to alcohol. His temper would have been his downfall, but you were there to bring him back."

Warmth spreads through my chest as I worry my bottom lip, hating that I can still taste the blood in my mouth from being slapped. "And you and Zade?" I prompt, his words soothing something within me.

"He'll deny it, but you're forcing Zade to remember that he's still human. You're challenging his every belief and forcing your way into his heart. You're making him feel, and honestly, I think it's terrifying him. As for me, I was hollow before I met you. I had the boys and Venom, and the darkness of my life was consuming me. I didn't care if I lived or died, but you . . . you're giving me something to live for, and I can't bear the thought of never having that."

A tear rolls down my cheek as I hold his stare, a lump forming in my chest. "Is it wrong of me to be so madly in love with you all?"

"No, Pretty. There could never be anything wrong with that."

I pause a moment before meeting his stormy gaze. "I'm not ready to die, Easton," I tell him. "I still have so much I want to do, and with you guys . . . this can't be the end for us."

"I know," he tells me. "We'll find a way."

"Assuming we're getting out of here, of course."

"We are," he throws back at me. "This isn't the first dungeon I've been chained up in, and it sure as fuck won't be the last. The boys are coming for us, so you need to switch over to survival mode because the second they get here, you need to be ready to fight. You're going to have to put all your morals aside and do whatever it takes to survive. You hear me?"

I nod, swallowing over the lump in my throat. "I hear you," I tell him, as a loud clanging comes from outside our fucked-up little dungeon. My eyes widen, fear blasting through my chest as I hold his stare, knowing that whatever is about to happen could be the end for me.

"They're coming," Easton says, his voice calm and prepared. "Don't be scared, baby. Keep your eyes open, count the people in the room, take note of who has easily accessible weapons, and always search for the closest exit in every room. If they separate us, all I need you to do is stay alive. I will find you. I promise you, Pretty. I'm not going to let you die here."

I nod just as the door pulls open and the room fills with men in tactical uniforms, their faces covered. They swarm me, reaching for my binds and unchaining me before letting my body fall heavily to the ground, scratching up my knees and palms.

They're relentless, grabbing at me and starting to drag me toward the door. "EASTON?" I scream, hearing him thrashing against his binds.

"You're okay, Pretty," he says, his voice so clear over the rapid beat of my heart in my ears. "Just remember what I said."

Fuck. Fuck. Fuck.

"What do we do with this one?" I hear one of the uniformed men ask as my body is dragged across the uneven, hard ground, tearing up my skin in the process.

I try to fight them off and free my arms, but there are too many of them, and all I'm doing is wasting what little energy I have. I need to be smart with this, need to conserve what energy I can and use it when it matters most.

I hear Santos through the chaos. "Bring him too," he says, a smug tone in his voice. "He can watch."

Shit.

I'm dragged out of the room before I can see if Easton is actually freed, but I hear the sound of a scuffle and know, despite the pain he's going through, he's doing his part in evening the playing field. I just hope it doesn't cost him his life.

He promised that we will make it through this alive, and I believe him. The question is *how* alive are we going to be?

Someone grabs my arm and yanks me to my feet, my shoulder screaming in protest, and before I can even figure out where I am, I'm pushed hard down a dark hallway. It's cold and reminds me of Empire's prison system, only worse. Much worse.

Heavy chanting comes from the other end of the hallway, and I try to slow my pace, fearing what's coming as I look back over my shoulder, desperately needing to see Easton, but I'm shoved ahead.

One foot forced in front of the other like a fucking death march. My gaze sweeps from left to right, trying to remember the things Easton told me to do, trying to figure out how the hell to survive this.

The chanting gets louder, and my head starts to spin as fear cripples me, creating thick lumps in my throat and making it almost impossible to breathe. My stomach twists and turns, threatening to throw up whatever could be left inside of it.

What am I about to walk in to see? Will my father be there, waiting to slaughter me? Will I be brutally humiliated, raped and played with? Will I be begging for death or will I somehow walk away from all of this unscathed?

The words Santos said back in the dungeon cell have stuck with me—*If only you knew what fun we have in store for you, maybe then you'd be smart enough to watch your mouth.*

Whatever I'm about to step into isn't going to be pretty. It's going to test me, and I hope like hell that I'm strong enough to withstand this torment.

We reach the narrow doorway, the chanting so loud that the walls of the underground torture cell seem to vibrate with their excitement. I'm shoved through the entrance, the grip on my arm falling away as I come to a stumbling standstill, and all eyes are on me. Just as Easton instructed, my gaze snaps around the room, taking a quick assessment.

There's one door. One way in and one way out, and right now, it's surrounded by the enemy. There are men from left to right, filling the outside of the room, and I quickly realize these men in tactical uniforms must be my father's loyal followers.

There must be at least fifty of them, each one watching me a little too closely as they stand around the outside of the room, creating a circle with one lone chair situated right in the center. I can only assume that's for me, but like hell I'll volunteer myself to sit in it.

Santos strides into the room, and the chanting begins to fade, but judging by the way some of them continue, it's clear he doesn't have everyone's respect. My heart races as Santos walks right up to me and grips my arm, his fingers biting into my flesh. He yanks me forward, forcing me toward the chair before easily overpowering me and shoving me into it.

My ass hits the hardwood, and he yanks my arms behind me before binding them together with rope. I quickly scan the room, trying to remember Easton's other instructions. Exits. Weapons. Fight.

Santos has a gun on his hip, but with my hands tied, getting it almost seems impossible, and what would I do with it then? Take a few shots, maybe take out a few of the assholes in the room before running out of bullets then being put right back here? No. That plan isn't even close to acceptable. I'm too outnumbered. There's no hope for me now.

A noise erupts at my back, and I whip around, my eyes wide as I find Easton being shoved into the room. His gaze comes to mine first, his jaw clenched so tight he's probably breaking his teeth under the pressure.

Relief flickers in his eyes, finding me still breathing, and with that, he starts his assessment of the room, probably a shitload better than mine. Before his gaze has even finished working its way around the room, one of the assholes in black tactical clothing rams his fist right into Easton's stomach, dropping him to the ground.

Laughter erupts throughout the room, but Easton keeps his gaze locked on mine the whole time, not letting the bullshit affect him. He's in the zone, ready to strike the second he can.

A million messages pass between us, and with every second I'm left sitting here in the center of the room, the tension grows, knowing that the reason I'm here is about to come to light.

Silence fills the room, and I swivel to follow their line of sight. At the only exit, I find Aunt Liv looming in the doorway, and I suck in a breath, her betrayal sending another painful pang through my heart. She strides toward me, dragging a hardback chair in one hand and a revolver in the other. The woman I learned to love like a mother has her cold gaze glued to me with disgust and amusement.

Fear erupts through my body, and the weight of her betrayal brings tears to my eyes. I try to blink them away, not wanting her to see me cry. She's already proved back in Missouri that she doesn't care if I live or die. She tried to use our relationship against me, and unfortunately for her, that backfired, but I'm not about to let her try it again.

This is not the Aunt Liv I once knew. This is Zade's mother—a vile, twisted leech who needs to be put down.

She wears a fancy pantsuit and high heels, looking like the CEO about to dominate a boardroom, and I watch her closely, taking note of every step, the same way Easton does. Only instead of betrayal flashing in his eyes, there's nothing but pure disdain, probably remembering the little boy he once knew suffering through the loss of his mother.

She makes her way across the room until she's standing right in front of me, and even though she settles her chair facing mine, she remains standing, looking down on me as every eye in the room focuses heavily on us.

"I'm glad you could join us, Oakley," she purrs, her voice cold and calculating, so different from the one I once knew and loved. "You've certainly put up a good fight over these past few months, but now your time has come to say goodbye."

"Quit the fucking act. I know you're not my aunt, and I know you don't give a shit if I live or die, so why even bother pretending?"

"You're right," she says, allowing the coldness in her eyes to shift into something even more chilling. She takes a seat, fiddling with the revolver in her hand and emptying six bullets into her palm. "I suppose old habits die hard. I'm so used to having to cater to you and your insignificant problems."

"Why bother? You should have just left me. I didn't ask for your help."

"Tsk tsk. This is my show, and I'll be the one controlling the narrative," she says, lifting her finger and waving at me in the universal sign for shut the fuck up. "Now, this is how this is going to go. You're going to die, Oakley. Right here and now. There's no escaping this. Your death has been on the cards since the day your father was locked up and realized his potential to take leadership. It's written in the stars. There are no hard feelings, my darling. This is purely business."

I shake my head. "You're insane if you think *I'm* the one dying today."

"What did I say?" she demands. "This is my show. You will have your chance to ask questions. As for now, you will shut up and listen."

I swallow hard and do as she asks, more than aware that she's the one with the upper hand here. "You and I are going to play a little game," she continues. "For old time's sake. I know how you like to play, but I've always played by your rules. Tonight, Oakley, you will play by mine. Understand me, if you behave, we can do this humanely, but mess with me, and this little game might be over a lot sooner than either of us could have anticipated."

I watch as she inserts one bullet into the revolver and then spins the chamber, then in a flash of lightning, she raises her arm, aims right between my eyes and pulls the trigger.

CLICK!

I scream, my whole body jolting with fear as Easton roars in fear. He fights off his captor and gets to his feet, racing toward Zade's mom, but Santos steps in with a taser and brings my hero to his knees.

He convulses on the ground beside me, and I cry out, desperately trying to reach for him, only with my wrists bound at my back, neither of us are going anywhere. "I'm okay," I tell him, the clicking sound of the empty shot something that will forever haunt me. "I'm okay."

Santos releases him from the electrical current, and Easton lets out a heavy breath on the ground beside me. I meet his eye for just a moment before the guys in black tactical uniforms drag him back to the edge of the room.

"Oh God, that was a rush!" she says, demanding my attention, and as I turn back to her, I find her inserting a second bullet. "I'm sure you must have some questions for me," she states as though we were casually sitting around the dining table with a pizza on a Saturday evening.

"No shit."

"Tsk tsk," she says. "Watch your language. I understand our predicament perfectly well, but that does not mean that I did not raise you to be a lady."

"A lady? You raised me to be an easy target."

She shrugs her shoulders, spinning the chamber again. "Possibly."

I swallow hard before glancing back and checking on Easton, wondering how long I can drag this out. "I don't even know who you are," I say, my chest heaving. "I mean, I know you're Zade's mom, and I know you abandoned him when he needed you most, but I don't even know your real name."

She lifts her chin, so different from the carefree aunt I grew up with. "My name is Priscilla DeVil, the wife of our late leader, Lawson

Michael DeVil the Third."

"You're working with my father."

Her gaze narrows and she spins the revolver again before pointing and shooting. My eyes widen with fear as my whole body jolts again.

CLICK!

My heart races, and I start to shake, but Priscilla just watches me, unfazed. "How did you come to that conclusion?"

"You left a photo of the two of you together in your home out in the country," I explain. "We put the pieces together, but it leaves me with more questions than I started with."

"Like what?"

"In the photo," I say. "It's obvious you're in love with him, and I guess that leaves me wondering just how long that's been going on. I mean, I never knew who my mother was—"

CLICK!

She shoots again, and the eager spectators laugh as a terror-filled scream tears through my chest. "No," she says, rolling the other four bullets around her palm. "I know where you are going with this, and absolutely not. I am not your mother. I birthed one monster in order to complete my duty to my husband by offering him an heir, and I certainly had no plans to birth another. I was never meant to be someone's mother. Zade was a lost cause since the day he was born, and he's clearly just as foolish as his father thinking he can take the crown of an organization that was never his to take. The second my husband got his talons into that child, he meant nothing to me. He was useless. Besides, I always knew I was destined for greater things, and now here I am."

Her words sting, but I don't question it as I watch her insert a third bullet into the chamber. I've been lucky, but there's only so much luck one girl can have before it runs out.

"You've come far," she starts telling me. "And despite what you think, I do regret that I must end your life now, but what your father needs is much bigger than you or me, and unfortunately, the only way for him to take that step is to remove you from the equation. You understand me, don't you? He's going to go on to do great things with me at his side, just as it always should have been. My late husband, he didn't deserve the love I gave him. He was an unworthy fraud. But the blood of Empire pulses through your father's veins, and I will do everything in my power to ensure that he takes the crown."

"You're insane."

CLICK!

Fuck.

I catch my breath, swallowing hard.

"I warned you what would happen if you didn't behave," she says.

"I know, I know," I say, trying to breathe through the fear. "I'm sorry. I'll behave. But I just . . . there's something that I don't understand."

"What's that?"

"The ritual where Zade's father was to sacrifice you. It doesn't make sense. I've been trying to wrap my head around how you could have survived it, but it's not possible. There are no loopholes in the bylaws, and Nikolai Thorne said that he watched you die, but he couldn't have, not when you're . . ." I nod toward her, not needing to finish my sentence.

A smug grin stretches across her face, and I watch as she stands. "Trust that old bastard to take The Circle's darkest secrets to the grave," she says, clearly not knowing the *old bastard* as well as she thought, considering that he couldn't seem to keep *any* secrets before his execution, going as far as to put a target on his own daughter's back.

Priscilla begins unbuttoning her suit jacket, and I watch her with curiosity as she allows it to hang open, then curling her fingers around the remaining bullets in her palm, she starts working the buttons of her silk blouse. "I did die that day," she says, her tone gravelly and filled with disdain.

My brows furrow, confused until she opens her blouse across her chest, showing off a sickening scar that runs right through the center of her chest, a scar I've never seen in my life. "I was forced to the dirty floor of that tomb, my arms and legs bound like an animal as my husband took a hunting knife and tore through the center of my chest. I paid the ultimate price for his chance at leadership, and for what? For a fraudulent leader? He broke me, and I will never forget the agony of that night."

I shake my head, unable to take my eyes off the angry scar, not able to comprehend how I missed that all of these years. I never saw it when we went to the beach, and she would even wear a bikini. I never saw it when she would dress up in plunging outfits, or the handful of times I accidentally walked in on her in the bathroom. Was it always there and I just didn't notice, or was she going out of her way to keep it hidden? "I don't . . . I don't understand. How are you still alive?"

"Because my husband was not the man he portrayed himself to be. He was weak, and when it came down to shoving his hand inside my chest and taking my beating heart into his hand, he couldn't do it. He couldn't rise to the test. He failed, and instead of stripping his title, The Circle buried his indiscretion and allowed him to rise in power in order to avoid a rising war."

"How do you mean?"

Priscilla steps back, adjusting the buttons of her silk blouse and fixing her suit jacket back into place before adding the fifth bullet to the chamber. "Because at the time, there was no knowledge of another heir. My son was too young and inexperienced to take the crown. He was barely eight and would never have made it through the ritual, let alone holding the weight of Empire on his shoulders. If Lawson did not rise in power, we would have been left with the very same predicament we have today. Only unknown to the members of Empire, we do have an heir waiting in the shadows, waiting for my son to fail. And he will."

I shake my head. "He won't," I tell her, lifting my chin. "If you think something like this is going to keep him from taking Empire as his own, you don't know him well enough."

"Tell me, sweet cheeks. How is he going to rise in power when the heart of the innocent he needs to sacrifice is already dead and buried?"

"He'll find a way," I tell her, more adamant than ever. "History has a habit of repeating itself. If Lawson can walk out of that tomb without completing the ritual and still rise in power due to The Circle's fear of war, then Zade can too. Nothing has changed. There is still a war brewing, and if Zade doesn't rise in power in the next few days, then Empire will all but burn itself to the ground."

"Your faith in my son is severely misplaced," she says, making a show of spinning the chamber again. "He will fail. I promise you that. The Circle will not make the same mistakes they once did, and now that news of Zade's lineage is starting to spread, he's got nothing. With or without you, he will still fail."

Priscilla gives me one last haunting smile, and I know this is it. My time is up.

She strides toward me, tilting her head to the side and looking like some kind of messed-up psychopath. "It's been a pleasure, Oakley," she says, lifting the gun right to my temple. "We had a few good years together, but it's time for a new adventure. You and your father were both destined for bigger things, and unfortunately for you, only one of you is ever going to achieve it."

BANG!

CHAPTER 19

Zade

My knife slices across the guard's throat, and I watch as he crumbles to the ground at my feet, blood spurting across the entrance of the underground bunker. Usually, I'd stand here a minute and really take in the artistic splatter against the wall, but not tonight.

It's already taken us too long to get here.

"Come on," Sawyer says, pushing past me and stepping over the fallen body, eager to get inside and find her, but fuck, I don't know what we're about to find. It's been nearly three hours since they were taken from my parking garage, and for a while, we were able to track them from Cross' cell, but after twenty minutes, that signal went dead, which could only mean they'd either found the phone and destroyed it, or they'd gone deep underground.

In my professional opinion, if I needed somewhere to hide an army, I'd go underground too. Though, who knows just how many followers Matthias Quinn actually has now. Because Cross sure as fuck left a good chunk of them bleeding out in my parking garage.

I don't blame him though. At first, I was furious that he even considered taking her away from the safety of my penthouse, away from the safety of my protection, but he couldn't have seen that coming, and at that magnitude too. What it really comes down to is that Cross came to me first. He asked for approval to take her to his home, and I willingly accepted. Well, kind of. It was more of a begrudging acceptance. Either way, Oakley was down in that parking garage on my say-so, and I can only hope that Cross has been able to do his part and keep her alive.

I know I need her for the ritual, and I'll try and convince myself and the boys that's the only reason why I need her unharmed, but fuck. She's breaking me down. These past few nights not having her in my bed, tucked in my arms has fucking eaten at me. But who the fuck am I to tell the boys to give her up when I'm about to take her from them for good? They deserve what little time they can have with her, even if it means giving her up for the night. I fucking hate it though.

In a perfect world, I would have claimed Oakley Quinn as my own the first fucking second I laid my eyes on her. I've been doing everything in my power to keep her at arm's length, to keep myself from wanting her the way I do, but with only a handful of nights left before the ritual, I'm starting to realize exactly what I'll be missing.

Fuck. I've got to get my head in the game.

Following Sawyer through the entrance with Dalton at my back, we make our way into the underground compound. The cheap lighting fades in and out the further we get, and there's a muffled chanting coming from deeper in the compound.

We follow the sound, silently taking out Matthias's army one by one, picking off the stragglers caught in the long, damp corridors. We make our way down, like a fucking maze leading us into the darkest pits of hell, but the further we get, the louder the chanting becomes.

It reaches an all-time high before suddenly falling silent, and we pause, both Sawyer and Dalton glancing at me. "Whatever they were preparing for," I mutter, my stomach twisting in knots, "it's showtime."

Dalton grunts, his face scrunching with horror. "Fuck."

We forge ahead, my feet pounding against the ground. I glance left and right, peering into each of the rooms we pass, taking out as many of these assholes as possible, but one room has me pulling up short.

Peering in, I find a small room that looks as though it's been carved right out of rock. There are thick hooks embedded in the rock above with two of them sporting thick chains, and fresh blood drenches the ground below.

"This has got to be where they were keeping them," Sawyer says, his face turning white at the sight of their blood, and not because he's squeamish. I know exactly where his mind has taken him, probably the same place that mine and Dalton's have, but we can't think about that. I have to believe that the blood is Cross', not that I'd ever want harm to come to him, but because if it did, I know he'd be able to handle it.

That kind of blood loss for someone as small as Oakley . . . well fuck, it could mean we are too late.

A blood-curdling scream tears through the underground compound and my head whips around, the piercing sound one I've heard a million times before.

Oakley.

Without a word, we all take off at a sprint, racing down the long corridor as fear blasts through my veins. I can't lose her like this. This isn't how it is supposed to go. We still have two days, two short days before I have to let her go, and I promised that I would protect her. I can't let her down again. And what's more, I can't let her go while she still hates me like this. The idea of her leaving this world without knowing how fucking much I need her kills me. She needs to know that despite everything, she owns me.

Fuck, she owns every single piece of me.

Men linger at a door toward the end of the corridor, booming laughter coming from within, and judging by the way they move around each other, trying to peer over one another's shoulders, I can only assume that the room inside is packed with men, each of them desperate to see the show inside.

There's so much noise coming from within the room that the men at the door don't even hear us coming, and before they've even looked back, I'm on one of them, my knife delicately slicing across the front of his throat as Dalton effortlessly snaps the neck of the guy to my right.

We shove the bodies aside, quickly picking off these assholes one by one when a familiar voice cuts through the room. "It's been a pleasure, Oakley."

Fuck. My mother.

I should have prepared for this. Should have known she was behind this.

Peering through the gaps in the bodies before me, I try to get a glimpse of what the fuck is going down when terror fills every inch of my veins, almost bringing me to my knees.

Oakley sits in the center of the room with my mother holding a revolver to her temple, and the determination in her eyes tells me this is no bluff. My grip tightens on the knife in my palm, quickly surveying the rest of the room and finding Cross on his knees, blood covering his body and a darkening bruise to his ribs, clearly broken.

He thrashes wildly with Santos at his side, a smug grin across his face as he uses a military-grade taser against him. "NOOOO," Cross roars, everything happening in slow motion.

I break through the crowd, Dalton and Sawyer desperately slaughtering the men around us as my mother continues her ridiculous speech. "We had a few good years together, but it's time for a new adventure," she says, just as Cross breaks through the agony, reaching up and gripping the hilt of a knife in one of his captors' tactical belts before spinning on Santos and moving like lightning. His hand strikes out in a perfect arc, whipping toward Santos with incredible speed, the blade slicing straight through Santos's wrist, his whole fucking hand dropping to the ground while still clutching onto the taser.

Santos roars in agony and then without skipping a beat, Cross is on his feet, racing toward Oakley as I rear back with my blade. My heart pounds erratically in my chest as fear like I've never known holds me captive.

"You and your father, you were both destined for bigger things," my mother continues, unaware of Cross barreling toward them, roaring in agony with every step he takes, "and unfortunately for you, only one of you is ever going to achieve it."

The blade leaves my fingers, soaring through the room and just as she pulls the trigger, Cross slams into Oakley, his big arms wrapping around her as his momentum sends them hurtling to the ground, the wooden chair splintering beneath the weight.

BANG!

Oakley's scream tears through the room just as the blade of my knife sinks deeply into my mother's chest. She stumbles back and drops the revolver as her wide stare snaps up in horror, meeting mine across the room. She knows damn well that this is it for her.

As if not being able to comprehend what the fuck just happened, her gaze drops to the hilt sticking out of her chest, betrayal flashing in her eyes, and in a flash of fury, her head snaps back up, a battle cry tearing from the back of her throat. "KILL THEM ALL!"

A war erupts, the room so fucking crowded that only a handful of people can get to us at a time, but it's nothing my boys can't handle. Our reputation precedes us, and I'm not surprised to find many of these assholes fleeing in fear, knowing the likelihood of any of them making it out of this alive.

Cross scrambles to his feet, keeping Oakley at his back, but in the center of the room, she's still not protected. We forge ahead, working our way through the thick crowd of murderous rage until we're surrounding her, protecting her at all angles.

"You good?" Dalton calls over the noise as Oakley tries to get to her feet, gunshots sounding every few seconds through the room.

"I . . . I don't know," she says as she struggles, her wrists still bound behind her back as her hand clutches onto a piece of splintered wood, a makeshift dagger ready to be used at her disposal like the fucking warrior she is. Then needing to give her every chance to save herself, I whip around, step inside our circle, and grab the knife at Sawyer's back before slicing it straight through the rope and freeing her hands.

Her gaze briefly meets mine before going wide and searching over Cross' shoulder. "Your mom," she rushes out. "She's getting away."

Oh, fuck no. Not today.

Glancing across the room, I find my mother shoving her way through the crowded bodies, trying to scramble over the fallen ones while looking around frantically, clearly out of her depth when the control isn't in her hands. She's a fucking leech clinging to power, but in reality, she's got nothing.

Shoving people out of my way, I go for her, catching up to her with ease before gripping her hair and yanking her back, dragging her over the fallen bodies, and shoving her to her knees. "Zade," she cries, holding her hands together and pleading for her life. "Zade, my precious son. Please. I was only doing what I had to do. Spare me."

Oakley appears at my side, her hand clutching my arm as if trying to save me from something I might regret, but her foot connects with the dropped revolver, she scrambles to pick it up, needing every advantage she can get in this room.

"Zade," she breathes. "You can't."

"Zade, listen to her," my mother says, short of breath, the blade in her chest surely having nicked a lung. "I know you may hate me, and you may never forgive me for the years I abandoned you, but I was only trying to do what was right for you. I know you, son, better than anybody. If you kill me, you'll never be able to look yourself in the mirror again. Please, my precious boy, spare me. I know I can make this right."

I laugh and look down at her with pity. What a foolish woman to think her life would mean anything to me. "My mother died when I was eight years old. I grieved her years ago, and you . . . you are not that woman, but you are right. I won't kill you, not because I can't, but because I'm not the one who deserves to."

Her brows furrow and I glance down at Oakley. "Take your shot, Lamb," I tell her. "And make it count. She's survived worse odds."

Oakley looks up at me, clearly in pain before glancing back at the woman who raised her since she was a child. "Are you sure?" she whispers, her voice somehow traveling through the room. "You won't hold it against me?"

"No, Lamb. Now take your shot."

And with that, Oakley focuses on the woman before her, the stranger who wears my mother's face, and raises the gun directly between her eyes. "Rot in hell, Aunt Liv," she says, giving her a sad smile before the sweetest sound fills the underground compound.

BANG!

The bullet penetrates straight through my mother's skull, and the second her lifeless body falls limp to the dirty ground, relief settles through my chest, and for the first time since discovering she was alive, it's a little easier to breathe.

Priscilla DeVil should have stayed dead. Aligning herself with my enemy was the biggest mistake she ever made.

Turning back, I find the boys have nearly cleared out the room, bodies lying from one end to the other, and I grab Oakley's arm, pulling her back toward the boys, only she stops, grunting in pain. I look back at her, my brows furrowed as my gaze sails over her body.

"Get her out of here," Cross calls over the chaos. "She's injured. Santos swung at her with a baseball bat. We can handle this."

Looking around, I see that Cross is right. Most of Matthias's army has been dealt with, while the rest of them have fled with their tails between their legs, knowing damn well what standing against any of us would result in.

Trusting the boys to have each others' backs, I clutch Oakley's arm tighter and pull her closer into my side before meeting the boys' stares. "If anything goes down, get your asses out of here. Understood?"

Cross scoffs. "I ain't leaving until I've found Venom."

"Shit," Sawyer sighs, adding a little extra punch into his kill and clearly realizing that tonight is about to be longer than any of us anticipated.

Glancing down at Oakley, I pull on her arm. "Come on," I say, when she hesitates, glancing back at the guys, not wanting to leave them here. "They can handle themselves, Lamb. They were trained for this," I remind her. "You're not. Now walk before I'm left with no choice but to carry you out of here."

She lets out a resigned sigh before finally agreeing and hurrying along beside me, trying not to let on just how much pain she's in. We pass a few of her father's followers, and I'm relieved when they simply allow us to pass without causing any issues, and before I know it, we're breaking out into the fresh air of the night.

With the threat now behind us, I slow our pace and Oakley lets out a pained groan. "Fuck," she grunts, doubling over and bracing her hands against her knees. "I just need a second."

"We don't have a second," I tell her, stepping back into her and scooping her into my arms, pulling her tight against my chest. "We're easy targets standing out here, and I didn't go through all of that just to clip a bullet in the back of my head on the way out."

She rolls her eyes and settles against me as I get us out of here, slipping into the darkness and concealing us as best as possible on our way back to my SUV. "I just want this shit to be over," she tells me. "I'm sick of running and constantly fearing for my life."

"Trust me, I'm fucking sick of it too."

The rest of the walk back to my SUV is silent, and as we finally reach it, I open the back and sit her in the trunk before stepping into her and looking over her injuries. My fingers skim across her ribs, taking in the heavy bruising before trailing down to her hip.

Oakley hisses in pain, trying to hold in her groans of protest as she clutches my arm, her nails digging into my flesh. "You'll be alright," I tell her, glancing up and meeting her big blue eyes. "Nothing's broken, just bruised."

"You sure?" she asks as my hand falls to her thigh. "It feels like I've been hit by a train."

"Positive," I say, refusing to step out of her space.

Oakley presses her lips into a hard line, looking deep in thought as if trying to convince herself not to say whatever's on her mind. "Thanks for coming for us," she finally says, dropping her head and glancing up at me through those thick lashes. "I mean, I know you were coming either way, but there were a few moments where I thought you weren't going to make it in time, and I just . . . having that gun against my head like that . . . I don't think I've ever been that close to death before."

"Trust me," I say with a scoff, my lips twisting with amusement. "When you come at me with that bullshit attitude of yours, you've been a shitload closer to death than you could have ever known. Especially when we first met."

Oakley smiles, her eyes sparkling with silent laughter. "You mean that night in your shitty fake apartment when I found the calling card and all of my details in your bedside table?"

"Damn straight," I tell her, my hand tightening on her thigh and pulling her closer to me. "That mouth of yours has always been my biggest enemy. I didn't know if I wanted to wire it shut or fuck it."

"When in doubt," she says, "always fuck it."

I laugh as she falls silent, a seriousness coming over her as she places her hand on my chest and looks up at me again, her gaze filled with the deepest fear I've ever seen. "Zade," she murmurs, her hand visibly shaking against my chest. "I've been trying so hard to hate you. Every time you open your mouth, you infuriate me, and I use that as fuel to keep hating on you, but then you go and do this. You hold me in your arms at night and touch me without even realizing it and . . . I'm falling in love with you, Zade."

Horror grips my heart in a chokehold, squeezing tighter until I can't breathe. "No," I whisper, shaking my head as I lean into her, my hand cupping the side of her face. "You can't."

Oakley lifts her chin, closing the gap between us and catching her lips in mine, kissing me gently. I know I should pull away, but goddamn it, I can't. She's too perfect. The forbidden fruit I've tried to avoid, but she's breaking down my walls and forcing herself in, and now those words . . . *I'm falling in love with you.*

Fuck. They tear at my soul knowing what I have to do to her in the next three nights.

I kiss her tenderly, and with every passing second, the passion amplifies between us, the connection that's been dormant for the last two months striking up and burning brighter than it ever has before.

Knowing this can't happen, I pull back and shake my head, the taste of her lips on mine like the sweetest drug. "You shouldn't love me," I warn her. "I don't deserve it."

She considers me a moment, her hand falling on top of mine on her thigh, clutching onto it as though it were her only lifeline. "I wish you could see yourself the way that I do," she tells me, her heart breaking right in front of me. "You're so much more than the asshole you portray yourself to be."

Meeting her eyes, I go to correct her when I hear someone approaching in the distance. I whip around, blocking her body with mine, when I realize it's just Cross and Dalton. Peering further into the darkness, I see Sawyer coming from the opposite side of the property. Then as one, both Cross and Sawyer hold up their hands. "Got her," they say in unison, both of them holding a black snake in their hands.

"Uuhhhh, what?" Oakley grunts, leaning around me and looking back at the guys. "Did they both just say they had Venom?"

"Uh-huh."

"They both can't have her," she murmurs as if thinking out loud. "That could only mean that one of them has some random snake they found."

"Yep. My money's on Sawyer," I tell her. "Cross could identify Venom in a sea of a million black snakes. He'd still find the right one."

Cross's brows furrow, probably assuming he heard Sawyer wrong, and he quickly catches up to us with Dalton at his side, both of them looking like they've been through hell and back to get that snake. Venom curls securely around Cross' hand as I step out of the way, allowing the boys space to check on Oakley as we wait for Sawyer to catch up.

It only takes another minute before he's standing at the back of my SUV with us, and just as he goes to hold his hand out to Cross, the snake strikes, plunging its fangs right into Sawyer's palm. "Ahh fuck," he grunts. "This little bitch. I swear, she's never liked me."

Cross smirks at Sawyer. "Yeah. No shit. That's because that's not Venom," he says, holding his hand up to show Venom curled between his fingers. "I think that's a baby black king snake, which isn't venomous, but it's dark, man. I don't wanna risk that I'm wrong."

"Fuck," Sawyer panics as Oakley gasps in horror.

Fucking perfect.

Sawyer goes to shake the snake off him when Cross hurries in. "Hey, don't hurt her," he says, unwinding her body from Sawyer's wrist, though I can't help but notice just how fast he moves, telling me this might be a little more serious than any of us anticipated. "She's still precious even if she has bad taste in men."

Cross chuckles to himself as he skillfully releases the snake's fangs from Sawyer's wrist and then studies her like a kid in a candy store. There's only ever been a few times where I've seen Cross lose the chip on his shoulder, and that's either when he's with Oakley or he's adding another snake to his collection, and I don't doubt for one second that this little bastard is coming home with us.

Sawyer ties a tourniquet around his forearm and grabs a compression bandage from the first aid kit in the trunk of the SUV and gets in the backseat with Dalton, taking all measures to keep the blood circulation from spreading from his hand and through the rest of his body.

Cross gets in the front passenger seat with his new pet, and with not much more space, Oakley comes with me, climbing right into my lap and clinging onto me like a baby koala as I drive our asses toward the ER, her head resting against my chest as she watches the world pass us by.

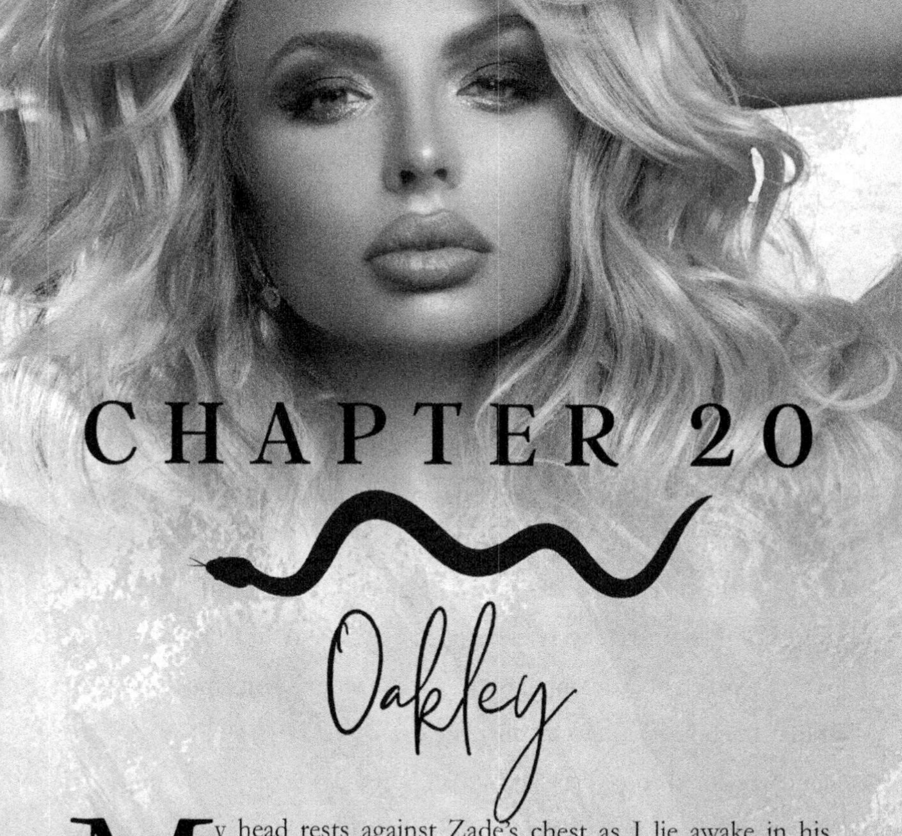

CHAPTER 20

Oakley

My head rests against Zade's chest as I lie awake in his arms. It's three in the morning and technically only two days before my brutal execution, and with every passing second, the heaviness continues to weigh me down.

"Go to sleep, Lamb," Zade murmurs, making me jump. We've been lying here in silence for hours, and all this time I thought he was asleep.

"Can't," I mutter into the night, so many things rushing through my mind, like what the fuck I was thinking telling Zade that I was falling in love with him. What the hell is wrong with me? Though, it's not like he entirely freaked out. But he was right about one thing, he doesn't deserve it . . . kind of. Two months ago, I would have agreed wholeheartedly, but now that I've gotten to know the man hidden inside, the one screaming for help, I see him in a different light. He's fearlessly loyal and will do anything to protect those he loves, even if it means putting his own life on the line.

The boys have told me they think he loves me, and up until tonight, I wasn't so sure, but sitting in the back of his SUV, I saw it in his eyes. Despite doing everything in his power to try and ignore it, it's still there, like an invisible string tethered between us, growing stronger every day.

For the first time, I feel myself feeling for him, for this fucked-up situation he's in. If I were a stranger, some random woman plucked off the street, he wouldn't have had an issue sacrificing me during the ritual, but now he has to sacrifice the woman he loves, and I'm not sure any man could come back from that.

Zade's hand moves across my back, gently roaming over the new bruises that I've added to my collection. "What's on your mind?" he questions in a deep, rumbling tone.

"Sawyer," I admit, my fingers tracing small circles across his chest, not ready to admit what else had been on my mind. "Do you think he's going to be okay? I don't really know anything about snakes, but aren't they lethal?"

"Not all of them," he tells me, a strange tone in his voice as if trying to sugarcoat the seriousness of the situation, "but I'm sure Sawyer is fine. Cross is rarely wrong about a snake breed, they're just in the hospital as a precaution until they can identify the snake's breed. If anything, Sawyer's probably passed out in his hospital bed. He'll probably be home by morning."

I nod, his words putting me at ease. So at ease that it gives me the courage to lift my head and meet his eyes. "Zade?" I question, a strange reluctance in my tone.

"What's up?"

"You know what I told you outside my father's base?"

He nods, understanding in his dark eyes. "You didn't mean it."

"What?" I mutter, my brows furrowed as I lift my head off his chest a little higher, only that doesn't seem like enough. I need to face him properly, need to really say what I know to be true, and with that, I pull myself up and scramble onto him, my knees on either side of his hips as his fingers brush my thighs. "I meant every word," I tell him, making sure he truly hears me. "I think I've known it for a while, but I didn't want to believe it. You're the man who's going to end my life, and I've convinced myself that it's wrong of me to feel this way. I should be trying to run from you and plot your untimely demise instead of thinking about how good it feels to be in your arms. I'm in love with you, Zade, and I know I shouldn't be, but that's not what this is about."

He watches me, his brows furrowed as he takes in my words. "Then what is it?" he questions, his eyes filled with wariness as if knowing exactly what's about to come out of my mouth.

"I think you love me too."

Pain flashes in that dark, bottomless gaze, and his stare turns hard, preparing to push me away, to tell me I'm wrong, but I won't accept it. "Don't make this harder than it needs to be, Lamb," he murmurs through the night, his hand lifting from my thigh and softly caressing my face. "Isn't it enough that you have Dalton, Cross, and Sawyer falling for you?"

"Maybe," I tell him honestly. "I'm content with loving them. They're the most incredible men I've ever met, and you're so lucky that you get to spend the rest of your life being able to call them your brothers. But there's this hollow part inside my chest that is holding out for you, needing you to make it feel whole, and while I know I will be content if this never goes anywhere, I can't help but need to know how it feels to love you."

"Lamb—"

"Don't," I cut him off, seeing the refusal in his eyes. "You and I have come so far just to get to this point. You've done unspeakable things. You've lied, you've manipulated me, you've lost my trust over and over again, and I'm still here willing to give myself to you. So please, just this once, be honest with me. If I'm making this all up in my head then tell me now. Tell me that you're not in love with me too."

Zade sits up in bed, curling his arm around my waist and pulling me in closer, his eyes lingering heavily on mine. "I can't do that," he tells me, confirming what I already know to be true, only he's not there yet, not ready to say the words out loud.

Warmth spreads through my chest, and I dip my head forward, my forehead resting against his as I breathe him in. His arms are so tight around me, squishing against my bruises, but I don't dare say a word. I need to feel him like this.

The conflict within him flashes behind his eyes as he struggles against what he needs and what he believes to be right, but I know he feels this too. How could he possibly deny it now?

"Is it wrong for me to feel this way?" I murmur, my voice barely audible through the darkness.

"Yes," he tells me, not bothering to sugarcoat it. "But there's not been a damn thing right about any of this."

I swallow over the lump in my throat, nervousness building within me, unsure how this is going to go. "I'm dying in two days, Zade," I remind him, in case that message didn't quite get across. "And I know that you know how desperately I want you to save me, and I know that you've looked through every bylaw Empire has trying to do that, so I don't want you to think that I'm asking this of you as some kind of way to manipulate you. That's the last thing I want, but I don't want to die without knowing how it feels to be with you."

He pulls back slightly, his heavy gaze resting on mine. "You want me to fuck you?" he questions, pushing my hair back to see my eyes.

"No," I tell him, my stomach twisting in knots. "I want you to give me all of you. I don't just want you to make me come, I want to *feel* you. I need that connection with you. I want to be your whole world."

His stare lingers on mine, a rich need and craving flashing in his eyes as his hands fall to my waist, his fingers tightening as if trying to resist, but that simply won't do. I need this too much. I thought I was fine resisting him, thought I was fine living in denial, but now that those words have slipped out of my mouth, I want to go the distance. I want to be his whole fucking world.

Leaning in, I close the distance and press my lips to his, the same way he kissed me in the trunk of his SUV, and the second his warm lips move against mine, the fireworks explode between us. His grip tightens on my body, pulling me in even closer, and goddamn, it feels just as good as I knew it would.

He's kissed me before, but those times were out of pure desperation when the overwhelming desire became too much to control. This is different. Just like in the back of the SUV. This is controlled and thought through. Intentional. And damn, I could really get used to it. Don't get me wrong, I love the spontaneity of the other kisses, the fierce desperation and hunger when he slammed me up against the wall of the tunnels in Empire's underground cells. Nothing can compare to that kind of need, but there's something different about this, something so cautious like we're finally allowing ourselves to truly push the limits of our relationship and finally take this somewhere neither of us ever thought possible.

"We shouldn't," he warns me, pulling back just an inch as I catch my breath. "If I allow myself to really touch you, to taste you, there's no going back for me."

"What does it matter at this point?" I whisper, pressing my chest firmer against his. "Spend the next two days buried in me if you have to."

"Fuck."

His arm tightens right around my waist before lifting me just enough to roll us on his bed, his lips right back on mine as he hovers over me, his straining cock grinding against my core as my arms lock around his neck, holding him to me.

His tongue sweeps into my mouth like the most exotic intrusion, and I welcome it eagerly as my thigh hooks over his hip, needing to feel so much more of him.

Zade DeVil doesn't strike me as the kind of man to willingly give himself over in the way I've asked. He's definitely a hard, fast, and wild kind of fuck. I imagine him as the type who enjoys making a woman scream, seeing just how far he can push her as his fingers tighten around her throat, and I'm not opposed to it. Hell, I need it more than I need my next breath, but that isn't what this is about.

Tonight, I just need him, the real Zade DeVil. Not the future leader of Empire, not my executioner, or the man who bears the weight of the world on his shoulders.

His rough, calloused hands slip up inside my tank, skimming over my skin and leaving a trail of goosebumps in their wake. Then needing more, Zade breaks our kiss and takes the fabric of my tank before pulling it over my head and leaving me exposed. His lips drop back down, detouring to the base of my throat and working their way up to the sensitive skin just below my ear. I can't help but turn my head, allowing him more access as my hands roam over his strong, defined back, my nails digging in and claiming every inch of him.

He's barely started, barely even touched me, and it's already too much, too good. How the hell have I been living without this these past few months?

My eyes flutter, and I close them before tipping my head back and arching up into him, needing his touch to claim every inch of my body. My hand trails down his back and pushes into the waistband of his sweatpants before grazing over his defined ass, so fucking perfect. I don't know what it is about a man's ass, but when it's sculpted to perfection like this, I'm a fucking goner. I could just bite it.

Zade starts working his lips down my body, and I groan as his palm curves around the side of my breast just moments before his warm lips close over my nipple. He sucks hard before flicking his tongue over the pebbled peak, and a thrill shoots through me, sending shockwaves pulsing through my body and right down to my core.

God, I need him to touch me.

"Zade," I pant.

"I've got you, Lamb."

He makes his way further down my body, touching and tasting every inch of my skin before hooking his thumbs into the waistband of my sweatpants. He slowly drags them down my thighs, the anticipation killing me as my pussy craves his touch.

My pants hit the ground and then he's right there, his soft breath brushing against my core. His gaze sails up and down my body, really taking me in, and while I know he's seen every inch of my body as I've taken his friends, this is different. Now it's his hands on my body, his breath against my skin.

His fingers brush over my hip, taking his damn time before finally dipping between my legs and making my body jolt as they skim over my clit. He does it again, and I suck in a breath as a soft groan tears from deep within my chest. "Be a good girl and open wide, Lamb," he rumbles. "Let me see that pretty cunt."

Butterflies explode deep in my stomach as I spread my legs further apart, exposing every inch of my body to him. Zade's eyes flash with a deep hunger, and when he settles himself between my thighs, taking one and hooking it over his shoulder, I know this is going to be some kind of magical tongue work that only women personally blessed by the gods could ever be so lucky to experience.

Zade growls deep in his chest before his fingers trail down to my entrance and slowly push inside. My eyes roll in the back of my head, and I arch up off the bed, my hands skimming over my waist before firmly gripping my breasts. "Oh, God. Yes," I breathe.

He's barely pushed all the way inside of me when his warm lips come down on my body, closing over my clit and gently flicking with his tongue, sending a wave of electricity pulsing through me and bringing me to life.

My fingers knot into his hair, holding on for the ride, and reading my response to his touch, he gets to work. His tongue is skilled, just as I knew it would be, and I'm quickly sent into a world of bliss, even more so when his fingers part inside of me, massaging my walls while moving in and out, so fucking sensual and erotic.

God, I always knew he'd eat pussy like a pro, but I never could have imagined it'd be like this.

Zade sets my body on fire, taking me to new heights as his tongue works over my clit. I can't keep still, my body flinching and jolting with every swipe of his tongue, every firm suck and thrust. My eyes roll in my head, and as I groan his name, my fingers tightening in his hair, I feel that insatiable burn building within me, threatening to destroy me in the best possible way.

"Zade," I pant, my back arching as I squeeze my breast, my thumb stroking over my pebbled nipple. "I'm gonna come."

He groans, peering up at me with that devilish stare, and it's all I can do not to fall to pieces. His stare has such an effect on me, and as that skilled tongue flicks over my sensitive clit one last time, I'm thrown right over the edge, my orgasm exploding through my body and sending the most satisfying electric currents pulsing through to my core.

I cry out, throwing my head back as I come on his fingers, my walls convulsing around him, but he doesn't dare stop. He keeps working me, keeps pushing me past my limits until I crumble. Fire pulses through my body, spreading right through my fingers as I clutch his hair and down to my toes, making them curl, but all I can concentrate on is the way his lips move over my clit, branding me with his touch.

He gives me his all until I finally come down, gasping for sweet oxygen, and when he slowly removes his fingers from inside me, I could cry. But then he's right there, climbing back up my body until his lips are barely a breath away from mine and his fingers are pushing inside my mouth. "See how sweet you taste," he murmurs, his eyes hooded with a deep seduction.

I roll my tongue over his fingers, and as he pulls them free, he quickly replaces them with his kiss, his tongue delving into my mouth and fighting for dominance.

I feel his cock grinding against me, and despite the earth-shattering orgasm he just gave me, I've never been so ready for more. I need to feel him inside of me, need to feel the way my walls stretch around him.

Not being the type to hesitate with what I want, I reach down between us, slipping my hand inside his sweatpants, more than ready to repay the favor and make him feel just as good. I'd give anything to taste him, to feel the way he fills my mouth, taste him as his warm cum trails down my throat, but something tells me we're not going to make it there tonight.

My fingers curl around the base of his thick cock, and I can already feel the angry veins that trail up to his tip. He's big. Hell, I already knew he was. I wake up nearly every morning with his cock pressed firmly against my ass, but actually feeling him in the palm of my hand I can see just how big he really is.

He's thick and long; the kind of cock that women can only dream about. Hell, the kind of cock that women have in their bedside drawers, hidden from their partners because they know they'll never be lucky enough to find it in person. Yet here I am, ready to take everything he's got.

"Zade," I breathe between kisses. "I need to feel how you stretch me."

He groans against my neck, the anticipation killing us both, and with my other hand, I shove his sweatpants down as far as my arms will reach before he takes over and kicks them off the end of the bed. My hand continues pumping up and down his breathtaking cock as he grabs my thigh and pulls it up high, hooking it over his hip and spreading me wide.

His hand closes around mine over his cock and he guides his tip to my entrance, teasing me with what's to come before slowly pushing inside. I suck in a breath, my head tipping back, each inch he takes me getting even better.

Zade's lips come down on mine, swallowing my shallow gasps as he groans into my mouth. His hand finds my hip, and he holds me still, taking me so damn slow as my body adjusts to his size, truly needing to stretch to accommodate his length.

"Fuck, Lamb," he mutters, putting just a breath between us as he drops his forehead to mine, wanting to take his time and truly savor the feeling of my walls so tight around him, something we've both been so desperately craving since the moment we met.

My arm hooks around his neck, holding him close, and as I clench my walls around him, his gaze snaps to mine, fire burning within his intense stare. His lips begin to pull into a wicked grin, and with that, he kisses me with everything he's got and finally starts to move.

He's dominant and intense, each thrust delivered with both a fierce determination and the sweetest tenderness. His hand grips my ass as we quickly grow sweaty, his lips not once stopping against mine.

Zade takes me deep, working me just right as he rolls his hips, his hands forever roaming over my body and setting me alight. The intensity burns between us, gasping for air as my pussy shatters around him, taking everything he's got to offer.

Then just when I thought it couldn't possibly get any better, he reaches down between us, his fingers gently pinching my clit and sending hot bursts of electricity pulsing through me. "Oh God," I cry out as he takes the opportunity to drop his lips to the base of my throat, making my eyes roll in my head. "ZADE!"

"Fuck, Lamb. That's right," he praises. "Take it all."

God. I'd take it all and more if I could.

That familiar build returns and before I even get the chance to warn him, I come hard, an intense, crippling orgasm. It rocks through my body, and I cry out his name again, my walls convulsing around him, squeezing him tight as my eyes roll in the back of my head.

"Oh God," I pant, feeling the high continue to wreck me, making me jolt and spasm beneath him. Then with a delicious groan that will forever change me, Zade comes right along with me, emptying himself into me as he slowly rocks back and forth, allowing me to ride out the high as I hold onto him.

He drops his forehead back to mine, both of us panting as we try to catch our breath, and I realize just how right I was—I am unequivocally in love with Zade DeVil, and despite his reluctance to say the words out loud, he's in love with me too.

Keeping his weight on me, he comes down, our legs tangled as one as his fingers brush my hair off my face, both of us covered in a light sweat. "I didn't know it could be that good," he murmurs in my ear, his lips brushing across my lobe.

My arms tighten around him, and I hold on with everything I've got, terrified of the moment he inevitably pulls away and tells me how we shouldn't have done that. "That's how it's *supposed* to feel," I tell him, not needing to clarify my meaning—that this is how it's supposed to feel when you're with someone who matters, not just some woman you met on the street, or your friend's twin sister who you see as nothing more than a convenient screw.

Zade nods, and I feel the exact moment he starts getting lost in his head. "Come on," I tell him, reluctantly shoving him off and rolling him onto his back before curling into his side and hooking my thigh up over his hip. My fingers trail over his chest, desperately trying to keep him from sinking back into the darkness that lives inside his mind. "It's been a long night. Go to sleep and then you can give me whatever lecture you're coming up with in the morning."

"There's no lecture, Lamb," he says, his hand settling on my thigh.

"I'll believe that when I see it," I say, a fond smile stretching across my face, unsure if we've just crossed a line we can't come back from. After all, Zade set the boundary for a reason.

His thumb roams back and forth over my thigh, and within seconds, the exhaustion of the day catches up with me, and as I listen to the steady rhythm of Zade's heart, I drift off into unconsciousness, terrified of what the upcoming days could bring.

CHAPTER 21

Oakley

A heavy arm drops over my bruised ribs, and my eyes snap open as pain rocks through my body. "Ahh, fuck," I mutter, scrunching my face and trying to breathe through the pain, realizing Zade rolled over in his sleep, and in his attempt to hold me, he nailed me right where it hurts.

The big bastard.

Though what does it say about me if I can't handle an accidental rib touch? Zade's going to tear my chest open in less than forty-eight hours, and I can only hope that I pass out from the pain and die before having to suffer through too much agony. Hell, I doubt the bylaws say anything about me not taking a few sedatives beforehand. I mean, just what kind of state of aliveness do I need to be in for this?

Ugh. I don't want to think about the pain. Today is a new day, and despite my impending doom, I want it to be as normal as possible. I want to spend every second with the four loves of my life. I want them to screw my brains out and make me feel more alive than ever, maybe splurge on something delicious, and at the end of the night, fall asleep in all of their arms because it will be the last chance I get.

Fuck. Okay, cue the waterworks.

Today was supposed to be a good day. Don't tell me I'm getting all sentimental now. I've come this far. I just need to hold it together for two more days.

Knowing there's no hope of getting back to sleep, I glance at Zade's alarm clock, and while it's still early by my standards, it's mostly acceptable to get up for the day. I sneak out from under Zade's arm and dash into the bathroom for a quick shower and to get ready for the day. Every passing second my brain replays my night with Zade, remembering the way he touched me and how he felt pushing inside of me. I asked him not to just fuck me, but to give me more, and he delivered in a big way. It was perfect, everything I needed from him and more.

Finding one of Zade's shirts, I pull it over my head before trudging out of the bedroom and leaving him in peace to sleep. He's a light sleeper, so I don't think it will be long before he realizes I'm not there and comes searching for me, but until that happens, I'll be spending my morning with my head buried in the bylaws in a last-ditch effort to try and save myself.

Striding out into the living room, I see Cara in the kitchen, busily helping herself to the coffee machine. "Want one?" she asks with a yawn, her gaze dropping to Zade's shirt with a hint of jealousy.

"Please," I say before indicating toward the hallway. "I'm just gonna check on Easton and Sawyer first. We had a rough night."

"Yeah, I heard about that," she says. "Are you okay? I can't imagine the shit you went through."

"Honestly," I say with a shrug of my shoulders. "It's just kinda bouncing off me at this stage. I mean, in comparison to what's going to happen at the ritual, a little kidnapping and torture is child's play."

Cara nods, her lips scrunched in concern. "That's umm . . . yeah, that's disturbing," she says. "You need professional help."

"Believe me, I know," I mutter before darting down the hallway toward the boys' bedrooms and bypassing Dalton's knowing he's perfectly fine in there. And honestly, if I walk in there with no pants on, I'm going to end up spread wide across his bed with his face between my legs and his piercing somewhere in my esophagus. While I couldn't think of anything better, if I allow myself to venture through his door, I'll never get a chance to check on Sawyer and Easton. Besides, it's a busy day, and I have a plan to stick to.

Starting with Easton, I quickly turn the handle before peeking inside to find him already sitting up in bed, studiously studying the new snake in his hands. "You better be careful," I tell him. "Keep paying so much attention to that thing and Venom might get jealous."

"Will Venom get jealous, or is it you?"

"Wow, barely even seven in the morning and already bringing out the claws," I say, striding through his room and dropping my ass to the edge of his bed, keeping a healthy distance from the little nope-rope who I'm sure will one day turn into the most terrifying snake I've ever seen. Not that I'll get a chance to witness it.

Easton reaches over and places the snake into a small portable enclosure beside his bed before curling his arm around my waist and dragging me up his bed. "You good, Pretty?" he questions, taking the hem of Zade's shirt and lifting it enough to check my injuries.

I smile at him before dropping my gaze down his bare chest to his broken rib, which he seems to be handling a shitload better than my bruised one. "I came here to do the same thing," I tell him, glancing up to meet his heavy stare. "Yesterday sucked. I hated seeing the way he hurt you. It killed me, but your stupid ass was practically provoking him. Do you have any sense of survival?"

Easton laughs and pulls me in close enough to brush his lips over mine in the sweetest kiss. "If I didn't provoke him, he would have set his attention on you. Besides, he wanted it. Whether I provoked him or not. He was trying to prove some kind of point, otherwise, he would have put a bullet through my head in the parking garage."

"Biggest mistake of his life."

"You can say that again."

"I just . . ." I pause, letting out a heavy sigh as my fingers knot with his. "In the future, when you decide to get kidnapped again—because let's face it, you will—can you do me a favor and just . . . I don't know, not provoke the asshole who holds your fate in the palm of his hand?"

Easton laughs, his lips kicking up into a wicked grin. "Pretty, you know I'd do anything for you, walk through the darkest pits of hell just to see you smile, but not provoke my kidnapper? Nah, babe. What's the point of getting taken if I don't get to enjoy it?"

I gape at him, my jaw dropping wide. "You can't be serious," I grunt. "You actually enjoy that shit?"

"What can I say?" he chuckles, a smirk playing on his inviting lips. "We're all a little fucked up."

"Speak for yourself," I say, leaning in and kissing him again before getting up. "I'm going to spend a few hours digging through the bylaws if you want to help me."

Easton nods. "Sure thing, Pretty," he says. "Give me ten and I'm all yours."

After kissing him again, I stride out of his room before heading over to the next one to find Sawyer still fast asleep, and I go to walk in before thinking better of it. After the snake bite last night, I'm sure he needs the rest.

I go to step back out when his thick tone fills the room. "Where the fuck do you think you're going?" Sawyer murmurs, his eyes still closed. "Get your ass over here."

A soft smile pulls at my lips, and I hurry through his room before scrambling across his bed and pulling the blankets up over me, snuggling into his side, his body so warm around mine. "I was just coming to check to see if that teeny-weeny little nope-rope managed to take out the great Sawyer Thorne."

Sawyer scoffs, amusement in his tone as he pulls me a little closer and presses a warm kiss to my temple, his lips lingering for a moment as my heart flutters in my chest, making me feel like a teenage girl with her very first crush. "I'm fine. Cross was right. It was a baby black king snake. They're not venomous. I'm just pissed it took them so long to decide I was fine and send me home," he explains, making it easier to breathe. "Besides, it'll take more than a little snake to take me out, Doll."

"Really now?" I say. "Why does that sound like a challenge?"

Sawyer laughs and pulls me in closer. "You think you have what it takes to bring me down?" he says. "That's cute."

My tongue rolls over my lips, and with that, I climb over him, letting him see the clear challenge in my eyes. "You don't think I could bring you to your knees?" I question, rocking my hips over his hardening cock and proving just how much power I really have.

Sawyer groans, reaching for my body, but I catch his hand in mine, threading our fingers together as I reach down between us and free his thick cock. My fist pumps up and down, watching the way his head tips back, already a goner.

Rising up on my knees, I guide him to my entrance before slowly lowering myself down over him, both of us gasping as I take him deep, my walls so perfectly fitting around him. Taking our joined hands, I place his on my hip as I clench around him, loving his sharp inhale of breath. Then with that, I reach down between my legs and slowly massage my clit as he watches me, fire burning in his gorgeous green stare.

I start working up and down his cock, my pussy clenching around him as every part of me holds him captive. He flexes his hips, raising them up to take me deeper, and I groan, knowing damn well I'm giving him the best morning ride of his life.

I take my time, not wanting to rush and turn this into something it isn't as I lose myself to the feel of his thick cock inside of me. My pussy clenches and as his fingers tighten on my hip, I know I've got him right where I want him.

We come together, both of us panting. Life simply doesn't get better than this . . . you know, apart from the obvious. Then hearing Easton out in the hallway, I lean down over him and brush my lips over his. "You know, I kinda love you, right?" I say with a smile. "I'm glad the little nope-rope didn't take you out, but next time you want to challenge me, remember just how much power this tight little pussy wields."

"Careful now," Sawyer warns. "Keep talking like that and I'll have no choice but to teach that tight little pussy a lesson."

"I look forward to it," I say, leaning in and kissing him deeply before pulling back and gazing into his bright green eyes. "Did you want to go back to sleep?"

"Nah, it's okay," he says, sitting up. "I don't want to waste any of this time with you."

"Okay," I say with a smile. "If I don't get coffee in my system soon, I think I might explode."

Sawyer laughs and allows me to pull him out of bed, and I wait a moment for him to find a pair of sweatpants before taking his hand and striding out into the hall. Only I get three steps before doubling back to his room and racing into the bathroom when his cum starts spreading between my thighs.

Coming back out into the hallway, I find Sawyer waiting for me, a smug grin across his face as he loops his heavy arm over my shoulder. He makes it a point to slam his fist against Dalton's door on the way past. "Get up, Eros," he calls. "It's a new fucking day with our girl."

Warmth spreads through my chest at how accepting the guys have been of the strange little arrangement we have here. They don't get jealous, don't care when I spend the night with one instead of another. It's as if they just know what I need when I need it and ensure the right man is there for the job.

Making our way out to the kitchen, I find my coffee already on the counter waiting for me, and I all but run toward it, desperate to get the yummy goodness into my system. Cara is already hovering over her paperwork that's spread across the dining table, still busily organizing the mass funeral following the explosion. It's planned for a few days after the ritual. The boys all agreed it was best to give Zade a few days to come to terms with his grief after taking my life before forcing him in front of a crowd of people and expecting him to seem somewhat sane.

Not wanting to waste time, I make my way into Zade's office and find the bylaws. Then with a stack of heavy books in my arms, I venture back out to the dining room and dump them at the opposite end of the table from where Cara is working, not wanting to bother her.

Sawyer sits across from me, my feet in his lap as Easton grabs one of the books and starts flicking through the pages, then just when everyone falls silent, Dalton strides out from the hallway, his sweatpants riding dangerously low on his hips and making my mouth water. But more than that, I can see the perfect outline of his cock and piercing through his pants.

He yawns as he makes his way toward the kitchen. "Why the fuck are we up already?" he mutters. "I barely got a wink of sleep after spending all night jerking off to the sound of Zade eating out my girl."

My cheeks flush bright red as all eyes in the room turn to me, all except Cara, who focuses a little too closely on the work in front of her. "No shit," Sawyer says. "Finally sealed the deal with him, huh? Not gonna lie, Doll. I know you could convince any man to want you, but I really thought Zade was a lost cause."

I shrug my shoulders. Last night feels too private to share with everyone. "He's not a lost cause," I say, defending the man who's going to kill me. "He was just doing what he could to make this easier for everyone, and having boundaries between us was working for a while, but now . . . I don't see the point in resisting when I'll be dead in two days. He makes me feel something, and I would have hated getting to the end and not really understanding what that was, and now . . . I know, and it's not something I'm willing to let go of."

"What's that supposed to mean?" Dalton asks from the kitchen, another yawn tearing through him.

"It means," Cara states in a flat tone, "that she's finally figured out that she's in love with Zade."

I press my lips into a hard line, not seeing the point in trying to deny her. She's right, not that it's any of her business, but considering my relationship with the rest of the guys, I think it's only fair for them to know where I stand with each of them.

My gaze flicks up between Sawyer and Easton, knowing damn well that Dalton won't mind. "Is that going to be an issue for either of you?"

Easton shakes his head. "Pretty, I don't care who you're fucking or who you're in love with as long as it makes you feel like you have everything you could have ever wanted. All I want to know is if it's going to change anything. How far does his change of heart stretch?"

"Not as far as you're hoping," I tell him. "He's still planning on going through with the ritual, but now it means it's just going to be that much harder for him to see it through. He's going to need you guys even more afterward. I know he's strong, probably the strongest man I know, but doing this . . . it's going to kill him."

"It's not going to get that far," Sawyer promises, his hand falling to my foot and giving a firm squeeze. "We still have two days to figure something out, and I'm not giving up until it's already too late."

"Thanks," I say, giving him a warm smile before turning my attention back to the bylaws, not wanting to tell him how much his faith in his ability to find a solution kills me, because let's be honest, if we haven't found anything yet, then it's never going to happen.

I start flicking through the pages and quickly get lost in the ancient text, trying to learn the old phrases and chants. I get stuck on the page that details the ritual. It's not exactly one of the bylaws, but more of a guideline of how the ritual will be performed, and it sends chills down my spine.

I find myself looking over it for at least an hour, taking in every little part, learning the chants and meanings behind each step of the ritual when Zade emerges from his room, looking as though he's slept better than he has in weeks.

His gaze immediately lifts to mine, looking over me in his big shirt, a million messages passing between us. He doesn't say a word, but it's clear what's on his mind. Though I can't tell if he's thinking about doing it again or ready to explode with regret. He's always been impossible to read.

He makes his way into the kitchen, and my gaze drops back to the ancient text, unable to get past it. I scan over it again and again when I finally figure it out. "Hey, I think I've found something," I say, a little unsure. "Maybe a loophole. I'm not sure."

All heads snap toward me as Zade stops motionless in the kitchen, not a single sound, not even a breath to be heard. "What is it?" Zade rushes out, his eyes slightly widening as he snaps back into it, striding toward me and walking around the table until he's hovering over my shoulder, staring at the pages he's probably studied a million times before.

"I . . . I don't think it's moral," I warn him as the guys seem to hang off my words.

"These people want me to carve your still-beating heart right out of your fucking chest and you want to worry about what's moral?"

"Right," I say, shaking off the thought and going for it, pointing out the section of the ritual I'm referring to. "This here says the ritual will commence at exactly midnight on the night of the sixtieth moon where The Circle will bear witness. All twelve members must be present to perform their part of the ritual, but . . . hypothetically .

. . what happens if just one of those Circle members just happened to fall and accidentally slit their throat? They obviously wouldn't be there for the ritual, and it won't be able to commence. I wouldn't be sacrificed."

"Correct, you wouldn't be sacrificed," Zade says with a heavy sigh, disappointment heavy in his tone. "But it also means that I can't complete the ritual, despite being there and present. I'd forfeit my claim and everything that I've worked toward, which isn't an option for me. And more so, it means your father will gain control of Empire."

My shoulders slump, not having considered that. "I'm sorry," I whisper. "I didn't mean to give you false hope. I just thought I was onto something."

"You were," Zade says, his hand falling to my shoulder and giving it a tight squeeze. "Trust me, you have no idea how many times I've considered that very thing just to save you, but in reality, if you somehow survive the sixtieth moon, you're still not home safe. Your father will continue to hunt you. We can't be wasting time searching for a temporary fix. We need something permanent. Something that ensures we each get what we need."

"I—" I cut myself off, my brows furrowed as I twist to glance up at Zade. "How sure are you that if you fail the ritual, you won't take the leadership?"

"Positive," he says as Easton glances at me, probably remembering the same conversation I had with Priscilla DeVil while she played the most fucked-up version of Russian roulette I'd ever seen.

"Are you sure?" I push, twisting in my seat to face him better.

"Last night in that underground compound, before you guys came in, I was asking your mom about your father's ritual because I've never been able to work out how she survived, and it turns out, your father failed. He didn't use some decoy, he sacrificed your mother. She showed me her scar. He tore open her chest, but when it came time to take her heart out, he couldn't do it. He failed, and without a suitable replacement and the fear of a brewing war, they turned a blind eye. The Circle still allowed your father to rise in power. Who's to say they won't do the same for you?"

Zade drags his hand down his face. "I don't know," he says. "But I don't want to risk it all on a possibility. When my father rose, it was a different time. His only heir was a child. If he didn't take leadership, Empire would have crumbled. But now, if I don't rise, there's someone waiting in the wings, ready to fill my shoes. Not to mention, there's you as well, a real blood heir. There's plenty of other options The Circle could take, and I'm not willing to risk it all on the idea that they might just let it pass."

"Shit," I mutter, feeling hopeless as I brace my elbows against the table before dropping my face into my hands. "It's useless. I'm not finding anything."

"We're going to figure it out," Dalton says, dropping down in the space beside me, bringing me another coffee as tears fill my eyes. He takes the old book from in front of me and slides it in front of him, picking up where I left off. "I'll go over this one," he tells me, giving me a warm smile that brings back just a little bit of that hope. "Go take a break, look up some monster porn or something that'll get that tight little cunt of yours all worked up, then come back and we'll do this together."

Letting out a heavy sigh, I have to strain to fight the smile that threatens to spread across my face, and I get up, fixing Dalton with a heavy stare. "That's not fair," I tell him. "You're not supposed to make me smile while I'm trying to fall apart."

"My bad," he says with a stupid smirk. "Next time, I'll be sure to make matters worse. Until then, I may or may not know someone who has a small business making monster-shaped mega dildos. So, if you need a link, all you gotta do is ask."

I scoff, rolling my eyes as I make my way into the kitchen and open the fridge. Pausing, I glance back at Dalton, seeing his expectant gaze still lingering on mine. "You dirty little whore. You want that link, don't you?"

Fuck.

My cheeks flame, and I shrug my shoulders. No point in denying it now.

"Damn straight I do," I tell him. "And they better have overnight shipping because I'm gonna need to try that."

"Fuck yeah," Dalton says. "Why not buy the whole collection? But babe, you better be ready because if we're doing this, then I'm using every last one of them on you, and you better fucking love it."

"You've got yourself a deal," I tell him, a smug grin stretching across my face, amusement thick in my tone. "But fair warning, whatever you get to use on me, I get to use on you."

Dalton laughs, but it quickly fades away as his face drops, realizing exactly what I mean, but before he can say a damn word, I scurry out of the room with a skip in my step, more than ready to explore the ins and outs of monster dildos.

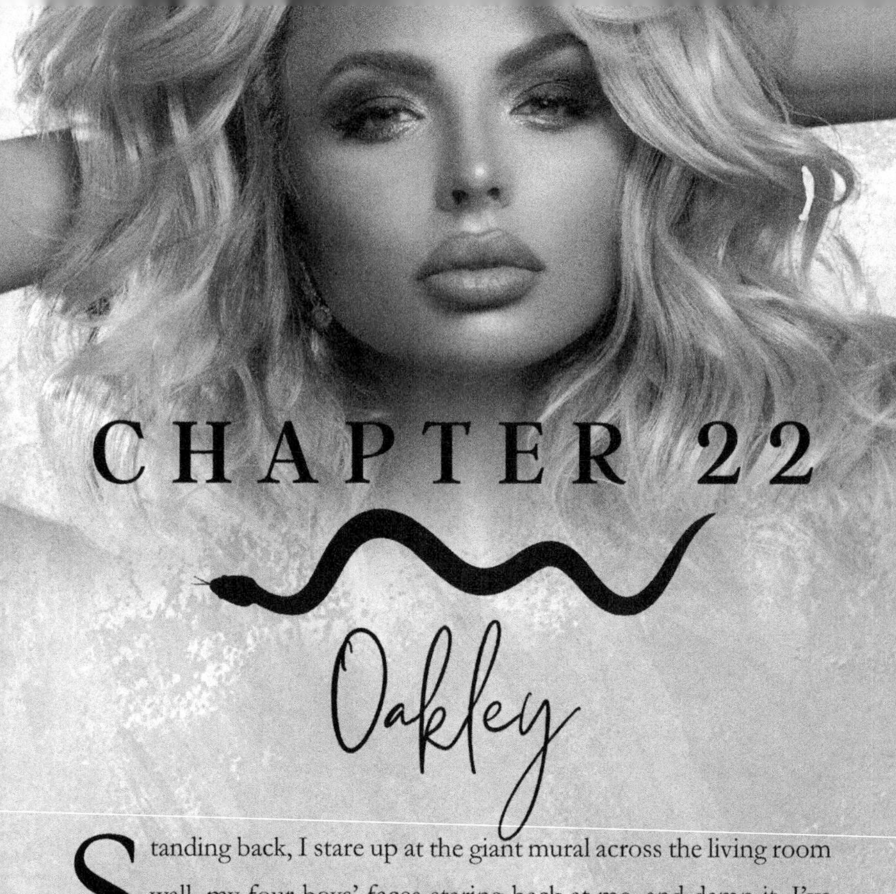

CHAPTER 22

Oakley

Standing back, I stare up at the giant mural across the living room wall, my four boys' faces staring back at me, and damn it, I've never been so proud. "You finished?" Dalton asks, stepping in behind me, his hands falling to my waist as I feel his wide chest pressing against my back.

"I think so," I murmur, taking it all in as he drops his lips to my neck. I lean back into him, my heart fluttering with undeniable joy at simply being in his warm arms. "Promise me you won't let him paint over it," I whisper, not needing to clarify who he is.

"He wouldn't dare," Dalton tells me before turning me in his arms. His bright blue gaze comes straight to mine before an amused grin stretches across his delicious, full lips. "You're a mess," he laughs, reaching up and trying to rub charcoal from my cheek before cringing. "Oh fuck. I just made it worse."

A devilish grin settles across my lips as I feign a gasp. "You didn't," I demand.

He shrugs his shoulders, not sorry in the least. "My bad," he grins, that wicked grin making everything clench with hunger. "But you know I love it when you get dirty."

"Really, now?" I question, my eyes sparkling with mischief as I snap my hands against his face and drag my fingers down his cheeks, the lingering charcoal rubbing off on his beautifully tanned skin. "It looks like I'm not the only one who likes getting dirty."

Dalton grins, shaking his head as he grabs my ass and hoists me up into his arms before turning on his heel and striding through the penthouse. He takes me down to his room and through to his private bathroom, stepping right into the shower, clothes and all.

The water streams down over us as he presses my back against the cool tiles, working tirelessly to get my wet tank up and over my head as I laugh, clinging onto him as though I'll never let him go.

The rest of our clothes come off, and just when I think the need for him is going to kill me, he pushes up inside of me, both of us gasping for air as I stretch around him. "Fuck, Firefly," he hisses, really starting to move as I feel his piercing working its magic inside of me.

He fucks me with urgency, both of us desperate to feel that release, and as he pushes me right to the edge, my world explodes around him. Dalton comes with me, shooting hot spurts of cum deep inside my cunt as my walls convulse uncontrollably around him.

Then only after I'm completely satisfied and have had more than my fill of him does he set me back on my feet and wash the charcoal from my body. He's thorough, making sure to soap up every inch of skin until I simply can't take it any longer and jump him again.

Twenty minutes later, I stand in front of Dalton's bathroom mirror, my gaze sailing over the scars and bruises covering my body. I've had more injuries over the past two months than I've had my entire life. My body is covered from head to toe, a map of the hell I've suffered through since meeting the boys, but nothing will be worse than the damage Zade will inflict on my body.

Dalton stands behind me, watching as I survey myself, a frown settled on his lips. I twist, taking in the more recent bruising on the back of my ribs and hip, courtesy of Santos. I've suffered through cuts, scrapes, explosions, and a bullet wound, and yet none of them seem to have bothered me in the way this fresh bruising does.

"You good?" Dalton asks, his thumb gently brushing over the dark purple and blue hues across my skin.

"Yeah. These ones are just really tender," I tell him. "I don't know if it's the positioning or maybe it's just really deeply bruised, but these new ones really suck."

"Maybe you need to put some ice on them," he suggests, his concerned gaze dropping back to my ribs. "There's still a lot of swelling, and the bruises are only going to get worse over the next few days."

"Damn. I need some kind of magical cream that I could apply to make them simply disappear," I tell him, reaching for his discarded shirt and pulling it over my head, the fabric hiding the cringe of pain on my face as I lift my arms up high.

"I mean, it's not a magical cream that will make them disappear, but I've got the next best thing at my place. You won't even know the bruises are there."

"Sounds good, but the last outing I went on ended with me hanging from chains in an underground compound," I remind him. "And despite my abilities to charm Zade into agreeing to things he knows better about, I doubt he's going to sign off on this little adventure."

"I thought that might be the case," he says, leaning forward and pressing a kiss to my cheek. "I'll head home and grab it, and if you're lucky, I might even grab the joint I've got hidden in my bedside drawer."

I gape at him through the bathroom mirror, my hand resting against my heart. "My, oh my, Dalton Eros, you spoil me."

He rolls his eyes and laughs before striding out of his bathroom and to his closet, finding something to wear before pinching the keys to his beloved Harley, Candice, off his bedside table. "I'll be back in twenty," he tells me, walking to his door and glancing back at me, his face scrunched with indecision. "If Zade or the boys ask for me, just tell them I'm shooting hoops. I can't imagine this is going to go down well."

I make a show of zipping my lips and locking it before tossing away the key and watching that fine ass walk away. Following him out, Dalton makes his way down to the elevator as I stop by the kitchen, more than ready to start thinking about dinner.

I hear the elevator chime its arrival and glance over just in time to see Dalton step in and press the button for the parking garage, he turns to face me and sends me a devastating wink just as the doors close him in.

Butterflies swarm through the pit of my stomach, and I hate how obvious I am, but there's no denying just how crazy I am for Dalton Eros. He's everything a girl could want. He's so chill and delicious, down for whatever, and will also go to the ends of the earth just to see me smile.

The ritual is going to tear him to pieces, but given time, he'll start to heal. Then one day, maybe he'll make another girl as happy as he makes me.

A pang of jealousy bursts through my chest as I help myself to Sawyer's snacks in the fridge. I'm busily scarfing them down when movement out on the balcony catches my eye, and I find Zade standing alone, staring out over the busy city.

I want to go to him, only I hesitate, not really sure where we stand after last night. He doesn't exactly strike me as the type to get on his knees and confess his undying love, but I know it's on his mind. It has to be, right?

My hands shake. I felt so brave last night, but I had the adrenaline of being kidnapped and rescued pulsing through my veins. Plus, under the cover of darkness, I could keep myself concealed. He wouldn't have been able to read me the way he can in broad daylight.

Not willing to just forget it ever happened, I let out a shaky breath before making my way out to the balcony and closing the door behind me, offering us a little privacy. I silently stand next to him, not quite touching, but closer than I would usually, and as I go to glance up and meet his eyes, the loud roar of a Harley Davidson rumbles through the streets below.

My gaze drops, cringing as I watch Dalton flying through the streets. "Where the fuck is he going?" Zade questions, shaking his head.

"Who? Dalton?" I question, avoiding his heavy stare. "Oh, that wasn't him. You must be confused. Dalton was heading up to the roof to shoot hoops. He's definitely not heading home to find the joint hidden in his bedside drawer."

"The fuck?" Zade mutters.

"He's a big boy," I remind Zade. "He can handle himself. Besides, it's not as though he took me along with him. I'm still right here where you can see me. Though props to you for not keeping me chained up. We've come so far."

"You're infuriating, Oakley."

A stupid smile stretches across my face as I turn my gaze back to the busy city, taking it all in as the sun slowly begins its descent. I inch in closer to Zade, needing to feel that closeness from him while not knowing what the hell to say. I need to know where we stand, if last night was just a one-off, or if this thing between us is as real as it is with the others, but he's not exactly the easiest man to talk to. Our track record hasn't been great.

I worry my bottom lip, trying to convince myself that I'm content with just being near him when he lets out a heavy sigh and reaches for me, pulling me in front of him as his hands fall to the balcony on either side of me, keeping me caged.

"I don't know how to do this, Lamb," he tells me. "I don't know how to be with you while knowing that I have to be the one responsible for tearing your heart out of your fucking chest."

"Then don't," I say, spinning in his arms and meeting his dark stare. "Let's take off. You, me, and the boys. We can get out of here, put Empire behind us and start fresh in a new place, not having to worry that someone is trying to end my life every second of the day. We could have a real future together."

Zade pushes back from me, his hands fisting in his hair. "FUCK."

He starts pacing, moving up and down the balcony before his intense stare comes back to mine. "This was supposed to be easy, Oakley. I was supposed to watch over you for two months, keep you at a distance and then sacrifice you. This . . . you and me . . . this was never part of the plan. Before I met you, I could see it all so clearly. The leadership was right there in my grasp, and now I'm barely holding on to it. You're fucking everything up. You're making me question everything I've worked for."

I shake my head, stepping toward him, willing my eyes not to fill with tears. "Falling in love is never supposed to be easy," I tell him, reaching out to take his hand, only he pulls it away. "It's supposed to challenge us, force us to find a compromise. Love isn't selfish, Zade. It's raw and honest. It's about giving your heart in the purest way and hoping that person doesn't destroy it."

I step into him again, this time forcing him to stop and accept me as I press my hand to his chest, feeling the rapid beat of his heart beneath my palm. Looking up, I let him see the sincerity in my eyes, the raw truth. "I am literally giving you my heart, Zade, and I'm begging you not to break it."

He holds my stare, his chest heaving with heavy breaths, and as I look into his eyes, I see the real Zade DeVil, the little boy screaming for someone to save him, and it breaks me. "It's okay to be scared," I whisper. "To question everything you've always believed. That's how we grow as people, how we learn and change."

Helplessness enters his gaze, quickly consuming him as he steps even closer, his hands gripping my forearms as his forehead drops to mine.

"Just know," I tell him. "No matter what you decide to do, whether you end my life in two days or we find ourselves running from this place, that you'll do it with me by your side. You obviously know what outcome I'm hoping for, but if you have to go through with it, if you decide that you can't turn your back on everything you've been working toward, I'm not going to hold it against you. I'm going to be proud of you, and I'm going to look down on you, knowing that you'll be the greatest leader Empire ever had."

"You won't hold it against me?" he murmurs, the words seeming to break him.

I shrug my shoulders, a sad smile pulling at the corners of my lips. "I mean, I might hold a little bit of a grudge for a while, and I'll definitely be haunting your ass every chance I get, but deep down, I'll know why you had to do it, and I'll have no choice but to be okay with it."

Zade shakes his head, looking at me in wonder. "The idea of ever hurting you . . ." he says, his sentence trailing off as though not able to find the words that could possibly describe the turmoil this has been putting him through. "Don't you understand that you're my weakness?"

Pushing up onto my tippy toes, I press my lips to his as I curl my arms around his neck. "I don't want you agonizing over this," I tell him, my lips moving over his. "We have two nights together. Let's make them count."

Zade deepens our kiss as he walks us back to the balcony until I feel the early evening breeze on my skin. His hands roam down my body until they're slipping under the fabric of Dalton's shirt, and as his warm hand brushes along my skin, the butterflies begin to flutter deep in my stomach.

My fingers knot into the back of his hair, holding on tight as I desperately wish for some way to ease the demons that torment his mind, but I suppose all I can really do is be here for him.

As his tongue sweeps into my mouth and his hands tighten on my waist, I hear the familiar roaring sound of Dalton's Harley flying through the city. I try to tune it out and focus all of my attention on Zade and it's just about to work when a loud screeching tears through the night, quickly followed by a sickening crash.

My eyes widen, fear blasting through my chest as I whip around, clutching the balcony and glancing down at the street just in time to watch as Dalton is flung across the street, his Harley knocked on its side and skidding across the road after being T-boned at the intersection.

"DALTON," I scream, watching with wide eyes, sick to my fucking stomach and hoping that he's alright.

I spin on my heels, ready to get down there, when Zade catches my elbow, yanking me back. "Wait," he says, his gaze flicking up and down the street, so calculating and suspicious. Then as if on cue, gunshots sound in the street below, and Dalton springs to his feet, clutching his shoulder.

"My father," I breathe, watching as a black Escalade pulls up and the bastard steps out, striding toward Dalton with purpose.

"The fuck is going on?" Easton roars, barging through the door and all but hanging over the balcony to see the fresh hell below, Sawyer quickly following on his heels.

I shake my head, the horror too great to form words as bullets continue whizzing toward Dalton, the other people in the street screaming and running in fear.

Dalton hides behind a postbox, but it doesn't offer him much safety, and I watch in horror as he grips his shoulder and violently slams back against it, realizing too late that he's putting it back in place. "Why aren't we doing anything?" I demand. "We have to help him."

"It's a trap," Sawyer says, taking in the scene below. "There's nothing we can do, and by the time we get down there, he'll already be gone."

"What? What do you mean *gone?*" I rush out, struggling against Zade's hold.

Then like lightning, Dalton whips out from behind the postbox with a gun in his hand, his arm already outstretched as he aims at my father's chest, but as if expecting Dalton's very move, my father is there, his fingers already pressing on the trigger.

The loud gunshot echoes through the street, and I scream as Dalton goes down, terror pounding through my veins. "NO," I wail, my knees buckling under me, and all I can do is watch as my father strides up to him, not knowing if Dalton is alive or dead.

He grabs Dalton's heavy body and hauls him over his shoulder before striding back to his Escalade and ceremoniously dumping him in the trunk. Then just like that, my father walks back to the driver's door, and just before sliding in and hightailing it out of here, he looks up to the sky, his familiar gaze locking right on mine.

A smirk plays on his lips as he salutes me, and with that, he finally gets in his Escalade and races away, and all I can do is stare at him, his taillights quickly disappearing into the busy city below.

"FUCK," Easton roars, quickly pacing the balcony as my head spins, and Zade finally releases his death grip on my elbow.

"We have to do something," I demand, unable to wrap my head around why the fuck we aren't making a move.

"I told you," Zade snaps, frustration thick in his tone. "It's a fucking trap. He took Dalton to lure you out. We have to play this smart. We can't just go racing in and hope like fuck we make it out alive."

"The hell we can't," I say, shoving his chest. "This is Dalton we're talking about. He'd do it for you."

"Trust me, that isn't fucking lost on me," Zade says, turning back to face the street and gripping the railing, his knuckles turning white, clearly deep in thought and trying to think this through rationally, something I'm clearly not capable of right now.

A moment passes before Zade turns back and looks over both Sawyer and Easton, his face scrunching, not liking whatever he's about to say. He focuses on Easton, his gaze quickly flashing down to his broken rib. "You stay here with Oakley," he orders before glancing at Sawyer. "You good to go?"

Sawyer nods as I shake my head, not down with this plan at all. "You want to split up?" I question, horrified by the very thought as I gape at Zade. "Haven't you learned that bad shit happens when we're not all together? Besides, I know my father. He's a manipulative bastard. I know going after Dalton is a trap, but my father has been ten steps ahead of us this whole time. We're too close to the finish line and he knows you're not about to put me at risk now. He'll anticipate that you'll leave me behind, and when you do, it's the perfect time to strike."

"FUCK," Zade grunts, knowing I'm right.

Sawyer lets out a heavy breath. "She's right, man. You're damned if you do and damned if you don't."

I nod, holding Zade's stare, my heart pounding faster than ever before. "What's it going to be?"

Zade glances at Easton, his jaw clenched, clearly not liking this plan, but what other choice do we have? We've already proved time and time again that we're better working as a team. If Zade and Sawyer left me here, they wouldn't be focused, they'd be wondering if I was right, if they'd just let me walk straight into another one of my father's traps. "How's your rib holding up? Are you good for this?"

"I'm fucking ready," Easton declares, fire burning in his eyes.

And with that, Zade nods, grabbing my arm once again before racing back inside, more determined than ever to prove to Matthias Quinn that we can't be fucked with.

CHAPTER 23

Dalton

Wow. The fucker isn't even trying to hide the fact that this is a trap.

I hang in the same underground compound that Cross and Oakley were held captive in barely twenty-four hours ago, in the same fucking room, held up by the same fucking chains. Unimaginative if you ask me.

The only problem is that Zade is backed into a corner. He's not about to turn his back on me and allow Matthias to slaughter me. He's coming, and logic would have him leaving Oakley back at the penthouse with Cross. The only problem there is that it leaves them vulnerable.

Zade has no choice but to bring Oakley here with him, and when he does, they'll be ambushed. Matthias Quinn is a cunt like that. At least, I can assume he is judging by the bullshit salute he sent Oakley out on the street.

I could hear her tormented scream all the way up on Zade's balcony, and I fucking hate that she had to witness that, but hell, what's a simple gunshot wound after a nice evening ride? It's nothing I haven't had to suffer through before, and I'm sure as fuck it'll happen a million times more, assuming Zade gets here before these bastards decide to take me out. Though I know he will, risks and all. That's just who Zade is.

Not gonna lie, I'm more pissed about my fucking bike. Candice was one of my prized possessions, simply stunning with sleek curves, and the way she rumbled when I rode her . . . fuck. She was perfect, and now she's nothing but a twisted heap of metal destined for the junkyard. I'll have to figure out which one of these bastards was responsible for sending her to an early grave, and when I do, I'll be sure to return the favor.

Taking slow, deep breaths, I do what I can to preserve my energy. I've only been here fifteen minutes at most, but it's more than enough to know my shoulder doesn't fucking enjoy hanging from these chains like this, but if I have to endure it a little while longer, I will. The gunshot wound, on the other hand, that's a fucking bitch. I can't lie, that bastard stung, and the fact that it's still embedded in my chest isn't exactly something I'm particularly fond of. But like I said, it's not the first, and it sure as fuck won't be the last. I'm just glad it hasn't seemed to puncture anything important, and with the bullet still lodged in there, it's acting as a plug, keeping the blood loss to a minimum.

Hearing the heavy clanging of the door, a twisted grin tears across my face, more than ready to get this show on the road, the adrenaline already pumping wildly through my veins. The door opens, and I'm pleased to find the one and only Matthias Quinn before me, and I have to be honest, I had him pegged as the kind of guy to send someone to do his dirty work. I'm impressed.

I guess it's finally time to see just what this asshole is made of.

"Ahh, Mr. Quinn," I say, welcoming him into my humble abode. "What an honor to see you again. Did I mention how well you're looking for a dead man?"

He doesn't waste any time, stepping right into me and slamming his fist right into my gut, winding me.

"Woah, Mr. Quinn," I laugh, the adrenaline now soaring, sending a fiery thrill straight through me. "I thought you'd at least buy me dinner before taking me to bed. You naughty boy, you."

He steps back, confusion flashing in his eyes, but hell, how was he supposed to know that a good beating is one of my favorite kinks? He's about to though, he's about to know me real well.

"I don't know what you're so happy about," he says. "You'll be dying here tonight."

"Oh yes, I'm sure I will," I agree in a condescending tone. "Go big or go home, right? Though, if that cheap shot to the gut is all you've got, give me the heads up so I can add a few grunts and groans into the mix to make you feel like the big man on campus. After all, I'm sure Oakley will be here sooner or later, and you're going to want to impress your little girl with your skills, right?"

Anger flares through his eyes, and I hate how much those eyes look like Oakley's, and without warning, he nails me again, only this time he clocks me across the jaw before sending one to my ribs, really getting me hard. "Don't you speak her fucking name," Matthias growls.

"FUCK YEAH," I boom, ignoring his jab about Oakley. If anyone shouldn't be speaking her name, it's this motherfucker right here. "That one was good, but you're gonna have to try harder than that. My father was giving me better beatings at nine years old. Oh, have you got any brass knuckles? Now that'll really get me going."

"The fuck is wrong with you?" Matthias spits, looking me up and down. "Is this the kind of filth my daughter's been spending her final days with?"

"Damn straight," I tell him, about ready to start begging him for more. "That girl of yours . . . fuck. She's a little firecracker. You should have seen the way she took my cock this morning, up against the shower wall. She's such a good little girl, and so damn pretty when she's down on her knees."

His fist flies right at my face, splitting my brow and probably fracturing my eye socket too, but goddamn, it feels good. He hits me again and again until I'm in a daze, the endorphins working their magic.

Matthias stumbles back, out of breath and quickly realizing he's not getting what he needs out of me, but honestly, I don't know what the fuck that is. I'm here solely as a tool to lure Zade and Oakley out of the penthouse, so I really don't know what he gets out of this apart from a cheap workout.

"Oh, you're done so soon?" I question, letting out a heavy sigh.

"I could go another round, but do you have someone else? Santos perhaps? All those years in lock-up have you lacking. Don't get me wrong, you throw a good punch, but you could definitely use a little training just to sharpen up a little."

"You have no fucking clue what's good for you," he tells me, shaking out his fists, his knuckles covered in my blood. "Do you ever shut up?"

"Shut up?" I gasp. "Why the hell would I do that when I'm chilling out with my girl's dad for the first time? I mean, fuck. What better chance to get to know one another? You know, I intend to marry her one day, if she'll have me, of course. I'll have to beat my boys to the punch though, but I think I'm in with a good chance."

"Foolish child," Matthias says, shaking his head. "I commend your positivity, a glass-half-full type of guy, thinking that she will ever live to see another day after I'm through with her. Let me break the news to you now and save you the heartache. My daughter will die tonight."

"Yeah . . . I don't know about that," I tell him, my shoulder silently screaming. "I've gotten to know her quite well over these past two months, and she's really not down with the idea of becoming someone's bitch, but I commend you for trying. You must be a glass-half-full kinda guy too. Seems we have that in common."

"Okay, I've had enough of your bullshit," he says, reaching behind him and drawing his gun. "Any last words?"

"Umm, what about a question?" I ask. "You've got me curious. I think I've pretty much worked you out, but there's just one thing that isn't adding up for me."

"Dare I ask?"

"Well, it's clear that you've been orchestrating all of this for quite some time. You infiltrated The Circle, got members on your side, working from within while you rotted away in that cell. You spent years building an army of loyal followers, people who will have your back when you attempt to rise in power," I say, filling in the pieces as I go. "You've watched Oakley from afar, put people in her life to ensure she was right where you wanted her when the time came to finally take her out because you're threatened by the potential power that pulses through her veins. Terrified that she would have taken your crown the same way Zade took his father's."

"What is your point?" Matthias questions. "I'm growing bored, and in case you have not quite worked it out, I have an army to rebuild and only a few measly days to do so."

"My point is that you have orchestrated every step of this. You've been the mastermind behind it all along, though I'm sure you didn't count on Zade taking out his father quite so soon," I say, knowing damn well that none of us were quite prepared for it, though we knew it was inevitable. "You have a reason for everything you do, every step is so meticulously planned out, and everything has a rhyme or reason, but the one thing I can't quite figure out is, why the explosion at Cara's initiation ball? Why put the people of Empire through such turmoil when you will eventually need to acquire their vote to claim leadership?"

"How did you figure it out?" he questions. "How'd you know I was responsible for the explosion when no one else has even whispered a breath of it?"

"Oakley ran that night," I explain. "I spent hours filtering through city surveillance, trying to figure out where she went, and unfortunately for you, I have all the proof I need to keep you out of leadership."

"What are you talking about?"

"When was the last time you brushed up on the bylaws?" I question. "In the event that Zade forfeits leadership, leaving no known blood heir, candidates may put themselves forward and campaign for votes. Unless you can prove your true lineage, you'll be left to campaign, but I can only wonder how successful your attempts will be once the footage of you setting the bomb which killed countless members of our organization gets into the hands of the voters."

Matthias narrows his gaze at me, fury burning in his stare, but he doesn't respond, doesn't give me what I'm looking for, so I push harder.

"You will be executed on the spot, no private trial, no chance to fight your way out, and then all of this would have been for nothing. You would have destroyed your relationship with your daughter for nothing."

Matthias steps back, returning his gun to the back of his pants, not willing to risk taking me out just yet when there's a possibility I hold the key to his demise. His gaze narrows, and I see him deep in thought, trying to figure out his next move when an alarm sounds through the underground bunker.

A smile pulls at his lips as something flashes in his eyes, and I realize my rescue team has just been discovered. "We'll continue this conversation at a later date," he tells me. "I have a daughter to ambush and kill."

Ahh, fuck. I hope Zade and the boys know what they're doing because if even one hair on her head is hurt tonight, I'm going to be pissed.

Matthias slips out of the room, leaving the door wide open as I dangle in the darkness, quickly growing bored. "Hey," I call out to the men dashing past my dungeon cell.

One of them stops, peering in, his brows furrowed. "Me?"

"Yeah you," I say. "Come here."

He scoffs and goes to hurry away when I call after him again. "Just wanted to let you know that I fucked your wife last week," I say, taking a shot in the dark. "She told me all about you while I bent her over and took her right there on your bed. But fuck, man. She goes wild. I think I'll go back for more."

The man stops and whips back around, his jaw clenched. Clearly I've struck a nerve. After all, the divorce rate in America is nearly fifty percent, with a good chunk of those being due to infidelity. If it didn't work on this asshole, it was bound to on the next.

He takes a swing at me, and I welcome it with open arms . . . figuratively. My arms are well and truly stuck above my head. I'm pleased to find this guy has a decent swing on him, and I let him get a few more hits in before getting the show on the road.

My legs whip up, my knee hooking right around his neck and coming down hard, snapping it in one fell swoop. The guard's body drops heavily to the ground, and I groan, needing to roll him with my feet to get access to the gun at his belt.

Getting him right where I need him, I shimmy the gun out of the holster with my foot before using my other to find purchase on it. I take a breath, and with that, I bring my feet right up until I'm hanging upside down on the chains, like a kid on the playground, my feet and the gun up by my hands.

I grunt and groan, not exactly as flexible as I need to be to do this, but I'm gonna have to give it the good old college try. Straining to reach, I keep pushing myself until I finally feel the cool metal of the gun pressing into my palm.

I clutch onto it before letting my body dangle back down, the guard's body acting as leverage for me to stand on, taking the weight off my shoulder. Then not wanting to waste another second when Oakley is out there somewhere, I raise the gun to the rock ceiling and get to work, shooting out the chains. The sound is deafening in this underground dungeon, but damn, it's effective.

Shooting out the links in the heavy chains, I finally come free from the ceiling, the majority of the chains still bound to my wrists, but until I can find a metal grinder, I'm going to have to get used to them. Hell, I might be able to use them to my advantage.

Balling up the chains in either hand, I break free of the room and race out into the long corridor, following the sound of the alarm, taking me in the opposite direction from where we found Oakley last night. Though after spending nearly an hour searching for Venom down here, I consider myself pretty fucking familiar with the layout.

Considering this is some kind of ambush, I can only assume

they're going to need a large space to pull it off, and I hurry up the long corridor, winding my way back toward the top and out through the back entrance.

This compound is massive, the underground system like a fortress while the above-ground part of it expands for miles. I can only wonder if this property belongs to Empire, forgotten land that only a handful have known about because there's no way Matthias would have had the means, the man power, or the funds to have built all of this himself.

Slipping out through the back, I expect to find Matthias's army with Zade and Oakley in a chokehold, backed into a fucking corner, but instead, I look around in awe, finding Matthias's army huddled in the center of the courtyard, their guns abandoned on the ground.

Each of them kneels with their hands raised in surrender, and I follow their gazes up to the roof of the compound, finding my girl and my brothers running this fucking show. But what makes it even better is the way Zade holds Matthias in front of him, on his knees with a gun pressed firmly at his temple. Though it doesn't go unnoticed how none of those bastards thought to come and help me.

I can't help but laugh, and all eyes turn to me. "Where the hell have you been?" Oakley demands, her gaze raking over me. "We've been waiting forever for your bitch ass to show up."

"Your dad was busy getting me hard," I call back, a wicked grin stretching across my face, knowing only my boys and Oakley would truly understand what I could possibly mean by that, while Matthias's army is probably wondering why the man they've sworn loyalty to is fucking the prisoners.

My sweet little Firefly groans, disgust etched into her face. "I didn't need that visual in my head," she tells me. "Now would you hurry up and get over here so we can get this over and done with?"

"Oh, yeah," I say, hurrying through the courtyard, squeezing my way through the surrendered army. "Coming through," I say, tiptoeing around them and clipping a few with the chains braced around my wrists. "Excuse me. Hey there. Hello. Don't mind me. How ya doing? Oh, nice ring," I say, stopping by a woman and gazing at the massive fucking rock resting on her petite finger. "I'm gonna need that."

"What?" she breathes.

"You heard me."

The woman sighs, and not a moment later, slips the rock off her finger and presses it into the palm of my hand, and with that, I scurry the rest of the way, not wanting to hold this up any longer than necessary. After all, Oakley only has what's left of tonight and tomorrow, and I'm sure she doesn't want to be wasting it here.

Reaching the roof, I step in toward Cross's left side, and I don't miss the way his gaze drops to the bullet wound in my chest that's still steadily bleeding. "You good?" he questions, studiously ignoring the bruises covering my skin, knowing damn well they were provoked.

"Fine," I say. "Let's just get this done."

Turning my attention to Zade, I watch as he looks out at the army before him, committing every last face to memory and making a note of his enemies. "In a little over twenty-four hours, I will ascend Empire's great throne and inherit the crown," he calls over the night. "This is your only warning that those who stand against me, those who betray their leader will be punished to the full extent of our law, and I intend—"

"Fuck. Get down," Cross roars. His booming voice has us all dropping to the ground without question, and as Santos emerges from the crowd, a loud gunshot echoes through the courtyard. My hand whips behind me, the heavy chains slowing my movement, but Zade is already there, firing back, the gun once held at Matthias' temple now aimed at Santos.

Zade lets off two shots, and in his moment of distraction, Matthias throws himself off the roof and lands in a sea of his loyal followers below. They quickly form a cluster around him, protecting him with their lives. Some of them grab their guns while others flee. Not wanting to risk Oakley getting hit by a stray bullet, we take off, darting across the rooftops and keeping to the shadows.

Gunfire follows us, but they're shooting blind, and I can't help but zero in on the sound of Oakley's booming laugh as Sawyer clutches her arm, making sure she doesn't fall behind. "I'm so pissed we didn't get him, but that was fucking awesome," she says.

"You'll get your chance," Cross tells her.

"I had a whole speech planned out and everything."

I can't help but laugh, and as the bullet wound in my chest really starts to bother me, I pull myself together, zipping my lips and not exerting any more energy than necessary. My focus needs to be on getting my ass back to the car.

Reaching the end of the roof, we launch ourselves straight off the edge and fall to the ground as Oakley hesitates, waiting a moment for

Sawyer to stop and hold his arms out to her. She takes a breath, and then remembering who the fuck she is, Oakley takes the plunge and jumps after us, looking like a fucking goddess as she goes.

With one final trek through the thick bushes surrounding the compound, we try to get a move on, but my pace quickly starts to slow as I grow light-headed. Zade hovers closely by my side, ready to push me along if need be. It's agonizing, but I make it all the way to the car, and the second I fall through the back door of Zade's SUV, Oakley takes my hand, and just like that, unconsciousness claims me.

CHAPTER 24

Oakley

A heaviness rests on my heart as I stand out on the roof of the DeVil Hotel, tears welling in my eyes as I watch the sun slowly set and the sixtieth moon rise in the late afternoon sky.

This is it. Tonight is the night. The hour before dawn will end it all.

I've been hollow all day, and the guys have been tiptoeing around me, too scared to say the wrong thing and leave me a wreck, but honestly, they're feeling it too. It's been a heavy day. I've cried, laughed, forced smiles, and then cried some more.

Each of the guys has been just as broken up, not ready for this to be goodbye, but in a little under nine hours, Zade is going to take my hand and lead me into his private elevator, taking me away from them for the final time. He's going to drive me out to Empire's sacred tomb, and just like that, the start of the end will be here.

I spent a good chunk of yesterday memorizing what's going to happen during the ritual, but right now, I can't seem to remember a single thing. All I can think about is how easy it would be to just throw myself off this roof and end it all now, end it before the pain, before the fear and the heart-shattering goodbyes.

How am I supposed to just get in that elevator without them? How am I supposed to walk to my death without Dalton's hand in mine, without Easton's sweet, murmured words or Sawyer's bright green eyes making me feel like the strongest woman in the world? But more so, how am I supposed to meet Zade's eyes as he plunges the dagger into my chest and pries it open?

I've been up here alone for an hour, the boys checking on me every now and then, and in all honesty, the only reason I think Zade has allowed this is because maybe he's hoping I do jump. That I take myself out of the equation and save him from having to do it himself, save him from a lifetime of despair and guilt, knowing exactly what he gave up for the crown.

The tears fall down my face, and as the moon becomes more prominent in the night sky, I find it harder to look at and have to tear my gaze away. I've looked at that same moon a million times before, but tonight, it symbolizes a future I will never have, a life, love, a family of my own. So many things I'll never get to experience, so many things I'll have to go without.

The tears become too much, and I collapse into a ball on the ground, my face buried in my hands. My eyes are puffy and sore, red-rimmed from a day of tears, yet despite all the time I've already spent crying, I just can't stop myself.

Wiping my sore eyes on the back of my sleeve, I try to pull myself together, and realizing it's not going to happen, I clamber to my feet and turn away from the moon, unable to look at it a second longer. Then moving away from the edge of the roof and taking the idea of jumping off the table, I head back to the elevator and make my way down to the boys, needing their undeniable comfort.

I stop by the bathroom and splash cold water over my face, needing another moment to myself before finally finding the courage to face them, but they're not here, at least not where I can see them. The balcony is empty, and only Cara sits in the living room beneath a blanket, her knees pulled up against her chest and her arms wrapped tightly around them. Thoughts of tonight rest heavily on her shoulders too. Hell, if I were in her position, I'd feel sick to my stomach. The things she's going to have to witness tonight will forever change her.

She doesn't look up, her gaze locked out the big window, but I don't really think she's seeing any of it, and not wanting to disturb her and send her into another round of tears, I slip through the kitchen and out the other end before finally hearing the subtle murmurs of a whispered conversation.

Following the sound to the den, I find the guys on the couch, Dalton and Sawyer to the right of the room with Easton and Zade to the left. The second I appear in the doorway, their conversation falls away, and I force a smile to my lips, trying not to let on how fucking terrified I really am.

Judging by the sudden halt in the conversation and the tension in the air, it's clear they were discussing the ritual and don't want to set me off. "It's okay," I tell them, striding into the room and settling on the couch between Dalton and Sawyer, snuggling into Dalton's side and clutching his arm like it's my only lifeline. "I'm a big girl. You don't need to stop talking on account of me."

"Yeah, we do," Easton says, adamant in his tone. "Today is already hard enough. We don't need to be making it any worse for you."

My bottom lip wobbles, feeling myself about to break, but I manage to hold onto control.

"How are you feeling?" Dalton asks, his fingers caressing my cheek as my gaze slowly circles the room, taking in each of the guys, committing their features to memory in case I somehow get to take that with me into the afterlife . . . or whatever comes next.

I shrug my shoulders, not knowing how I feel or even where to begin to describe it. "I feel like this is all some big cosmic joke. It doesn't feel real, but on the other hand, it feels all too real. I don't know what I'm supposed to be thinking or what to even say to each of you. I'm not ready to say goodbye."

"I get it," Dalton murmurs. "But I suppose there's no right or wrong in any of this, just feel whatever feels real to you. Whatever you want. If you need to cry, then do that. If you want to fall to pieces, then that's okay too. We're not going anywhere, Firefly."

I nod against his chest, not sure I'm able to find the words, but as I lift my hand to his heart, feeling the steady rhythm through his shirt, my fingers brush along the bandaging from his bullet wound. Getting him home was interesting. We had to lay down the backseats of Zade's SUV, and Sawyer hoisted Dalton across them as Easton found the first aid kit stashed in the trunk.

I watched in terror from the front as Easton dug the bullet out of him, but the second he said that Dalton was in the clear, it was suddenly so much easier to breathe.

I can't help but catalog all the times the guys have gotten injured under the name of protecting me, and I fucking hate it. No one should have to suffer for me, and while I truly appreciate the many times they've been there to protect me, the fact that they had to in the first place tears me apart. Perhaps my untimely demise has a few benefits after all. The boys will finally rest easy, knowing no one is coming for their throats, and Zade will have all his dreams come true.

Dalton pulls me onto his lap, his hands slipping beneath the fabric of my shirt, roaming up and down my back as I curl into his chest, and without hesitation, Sawyer scooches over on the couch, keeping close enough that he can take my hand, his thumb moving back and forth over my knuckles.

"I'm not ready," I whisper into Dalton's chest, tears brimming in my eyes. "The idea of losing you all . . ."

Zade leans forward, bracing his elbows on his knees and dropping his face into his hands, truly looking tortured by what he has to do tonight. Hell, his whole face is turning white. Then as if on cue, he gets up and strides out of the room, gently squeezing my shoulder as he passes.

"Is he okay?" I ask.

Easton shakes his head and gets up, striding over to us and dropping down on the coffee table just behind me, bracing his elbows on his knees, much like Zade was just a moment ago. "No, Pretty," Easton murmurs, reaching out and wiping the tears off my face. "He's not. He's barely holding on."

"Should I go after him?"

"Nah, just give him some space. He needs to work it out of his system," Sawyer tells me, squeezing my hand.

I nod, sitting up on Dalton's lap, my gaze fixated on his shirt, not able to meet any of their intense stares. "I don't know what to do," I admit. "I feel so . . . empty."

Dalton lifts his hand to my chin, his warm fingers forcing my gaze back to his. "You don't need to do anything, Firefly," he murmurs. "Let us help you feel something."

I nod as Easton gets to his feet behind me, leaning over me as his hand curls around the back of my neck, turning my face to his before pressing his warm lips against mine in the most passionate kiss. I feel Dalton's eyes on us, his hand slowly brushing over my waist from beneath my shirt as Sawyer's hand shifts to my thigh, trailing higher and sending a wave of goosebumps across my skin.

Easton reaches down, thumbing the fabric of my shirt before slowly lifting it over my head, exposing my body inch by inch. He tosses the shirt aside, and as he continues to kiss me, his tongue sweeping into my mouth, Dalton's hand skims across my bare breasts, my nipples pebbling under his soft touch, but nothing is more intense than his heavy stare lingering on my body.

He makes me feel alive. They all do, and I need so much more.

Sawyer's fingers work their way up between my legs, his hand firmly cupping my pussy before he rubs me over my underwear, making me grind down on Dalton's lap. I groan into Easton's mouth as my hands fall against Dalton's chest, fisting his shirt into my fingers and pulling it over his head.

The sweetest bliss begins pulsing through my veins, my eyes rolling in the back of my head, then reading my body and knowing how much more I need, Sawyer fists my lace panties in his hands and tears them clean off my body. I gasp as he presses his fingers to my needy clit, applying just the right amount of pressure before rolling them and making my body jolt.

I moan into Easton's mouth as I reach down before me, freeing Dalton's thick cock from his pants. My hand circles his base, my fingers not quite able to close fully, and I work my fist up and down, watching the way his head tips back on the couch in ecstasy.

Sawyer dips his fingers lower, pushing them inside of me, and I grind down against him, groaning as they roll and massage my walls. As the undeniable pleasure rocks through me, I pull back from Easton's kiss, my eyes rolling in the back of my head. "Oh God, Sawyer," I pant.

"You like that, Doll?" he murmurs, reaching inside his pants and fisting his cock, slowly working up and down as his gaze lingers on me, his thumb rolling over my clit and making me gasp.

My walls clench around Sawyer's fingers as I start to pant, desire blasting through me. "I need more," I tell them, desperate to feel them inside me, making my world explode into a million tiny pieces.

"You ready, Firefly?" Dalton asks.

"Oh yeah," Sawyer murmurs, slowly pulling his fingers from me and licking them clean as his lips pull into a wicked grin. "She's ready."

My cheeks flame as Dalton locks his arm around my waist, turning me around and pulling me until my back is against his chest, my knees wide open. Easton drops down before me, and his hungry gaze locks on my exposed cunt.

A thrill shoots through me as I watch him fist his cock and work it up and down before closing the space between us. His warm mouth closes over my clit, his tongue flicking the tight bud and testing me to no end. He sucks hard and reaches below, pushing two thick fingers inside of me.

"Oh fuck," I groan, leaning right back against Dalton, reaching up and curling my hand behind his neck. I knot my fingers into his hair as he caresses my breasts, gently pinching my nipples and feeling how they pebble beneath his touch.

He grinds his cock against me as Easton spreads my wetness right down to my ass, teasing me there and preparing me for what's to come. A thrill shoots through me, and I've never wanted it more, but before I even get the chance to tell them what I need, Easton's tongue flicks over my clit again and my orgasm blasts through me, shocking my system as my pussy shatters around Easton's fingers.

"Oh God," I groan, gasping and panting as I watch the way he works my clit, pussy, and ass at the same time. Dalton drops his lips to my neck, continuing to torment my nipples with the sweetest caress, and my orgasm intensifies, my eyes fluttering with undeniable pleasure.

"So fucking beautiful when you come," Sawyer murmurs beside me on the couch, slowly working his cock, knowing damn well we're only just getting started. I can't help myself, reaching for him and closing my hand around his thick cock before roaming my thumb over his tip and living for the breathy groan that's forced through his clenched jaw.

I come down from my high, but I'm so desperate for more, so determined to feel the way Dalton fills my ass. And he doesn't let me down, tightening his arm around my waist and lifting me before guiding his tip to my entrance.

Knowing just how much Dalton is going to stretch me, Easton continues working my clit, slowly massaging my inner walls and keeping me relaxed as I prepare to accommodate his delicious size.

Dalton begins lowering me down, and I groan, feeling his tip pushing through my entrance. He takes his time, slowly stretching me as my fingers tighten in his hair. "You can take it, Firefly," Dalton murmurs, his lips moving over my neck as he lowers me right down. He pauses, neither of us moving as he gives me a chance to get used to his intoxicating intrusion, and then finally, I let out a breath, fully relaxing around him.

"Damn right, I can," I say as he flexes his hips, taking me a little deeper and making me gasp.

He slowly lifts me up and down, then needing more space to move, he adjusts us on the couch until he's laying down. Sawyer watches us before moving between my thighs, his heavy cock resting against my hip as he takes my thighs and pushes them back toward me, folding me over like a fucking pretzel.

His tongue rolls over his bottom lip, hunger bursting in his heavy stare. "Are you ready for more, Doll?"

"God, yes," I pant. "Fill my little cunt. Fuck me hard."

Sawyer doesn't hesitate, guiding his tip to my pussy and slowly pushing inside, filling me just the way I need. He takes his time, matching Dalton's rhythm, pushing in just as he pulls back, sending my system into overdrive, the undeniable pleasure like nothing I've ever felt.

Sawyer grunts, the sound sending shivers trailing over my skin, then just when I think it couldn't get any better, he presses his thumb to my clit and starts circling it, forcing a deep, breathy groan to rumble through my chest.

"Oh shit," I pant, Dalton's skilled fingers still teasing my nipples and sending wild bursts of electricity shooting through my veins, heading right down to my core.

"Come on, Pretty," Easton says on his feet beside me, his delicious cock hovering right by my face. "Don't lose control just yet. You've still got work to do."

Damn right, I do.

I eagerly lick my lips as I meet his intense stare. "Then what are you waiting for?" I purr, a silent promise to blow his fucking mind. "Come and take it."

His eyes become hooded, and he squeezes his cock firmly before stepping in even closer. Gathering my hair in one hand, he curls his fist around it, taking full control of my neck, and as his tip hits my lips, I quickly lap up the small bead of moisture, claiming it all.

"Open wide, baby girl," he murmurs, and I do just that, eagerly taking him right to the back of my throat as my tongue gets to work. I grip the base of his cock as Dalton tightens his hold around me, keeping me balanced.

Sawyer rolls his hips, taking me at a new angle that has my eyes rolling in the back of my head. "Oh fuck," I murmur around Easton's thick cock, my pussy clenching, not knowing how much longer I can handle the intensity.

Dalton grunts, right on the edge as we start to grow sweaty, the wild pleasure like nothing I've ever known. I've never been so full or pushed so close to the edge. I don't know if I can take it. Sawyer slams in and out of me, thrusting and rolling as his cock glistens with my arousal. His thumb relentlessly works my clit as Dalton continues to take my ass, picking up his pace as we all grow desperate for a release.

I squeeze Easton's base firmly as I work my fist up and down his length, letting him push past my gag reflex to the back of my throat as his grip tightens in my hair.

It's fucking glorious—like angels singing in the sky, and as I feel that familiar pulse starting to grow deep in my core, I know I only have moments left.

"Mmmm," Sawyer grunts as my pussy tightens around him, glancing at Dalton over my shoulder. "You feel that? She's close."

"Of course she is," Dalton praises, his words pushing me even closer to the edge. So fucking close I could fall at any second, but fuck. I don't plan on just falling off this cliff, I plan on flying.

Easton groans, clenching his jaw as he starts to lose control, and as Sawyer rolls his fingers over my clit while Dalton pinches my nipples just that little bit harder, my orgasm comes shooting through me, reaching new fucking heights.

"FUCK," I cry out, my world exploding as my ass and pussy clench, convulsing around the boys' cocks, and they come right along with me, filling me with hot spurts of delicious cum. Then not willing to miss the party, Easton lets go, and with a loud groan, he spills his load right down my throat.

I eagerly suck him dry, tasting every last drop he has to offer as my walls furiously convulse around Sawyer's cock, feeling as though I'm about to spontaneously combust. He keeps working my clit as he pulls out of me, watching the way his cum leaks from my spasming cunt.

"Fuck that's hot, Doll," he murmurs with a deep growl as my body finally begins to wind down.

Easton pulls free of my mouth, and I hold his stare as his thumb swipes across my bottom lip, his grip loosening in my hair. Dalton eases up on my nipples, cupping my breasts instead, his thumbs gently caressing their full curves.

"Fuck, Firefly," he says as I collapse back against his wide chest, hoping like fuck I'm not hurting him. "That was intense, but goddamn, I wanna do it again, only this time, I want to take that sweet cunt."

I groan, a smile pulling at my lips. "You're more than welcome to go again, but I'm a walking cream pie, so as long as you can all find a way to take me in the shower at the same time, then I'm all yours."

The boys look at each other, wicked grins stretching over their faces, and not a second later, Easton scoops me off Dalton and pulls me into his strong arms, more than ready to see this through right to the end.

CHAPTER 25

Oakley

Cara stands behind me, brushing through my long blonde curls as my gaze flicks toward the clock for the millionth time tonight, my heart so completely broken and devastated.

It's quickly approaching three in the morning, leaving me a little over two hours left on this green earth.

How did this come so fast? I was supposed to have more time to figure this out, more time to live, learn, and be free. God, what I wouldn't give to be able to spend more time getting to know the boys, being able to spend long days and nights between the sheets with them, our bodies moving as one. I would get to know them on a deeper level, learn all about their lives growing up and who they dreamed of becoming. I wanted to spend a lifetime giving them all of my heart and receiving theirs in return. We could have been so happy. I'm sure there would have been a few things we'd have to work out, but we would have worked through it and figured out a way to live in harmony, even with Zade.

Despite having worked through the last knot in my hair at least ten minutes ago, Cara continues to brush through my long golden locks, both of us sitting in silence as I watch our reflections through the floor-to-ceiling window of the dining room, the night sky creating the perfect mirror.

"I know you don't have any reason to trust me," she murmurs, the brush pausing in my hair as she meets my gaze in our reflection. "But you have to know that I never wanted this for you. If there were some way I could change your fate and take back all the hurt I caused you, I would."

"I know," I tell her with a sad smile, trying hard to find the courage to face this straight on and not break. "These past few days have been a straight-up cluster-fuck, and I haven't had a chance to tell you that I forgive you."

Her eyes widen, and she sucks in a small gasp. "You do?"

I nod. "Don't get me wrong, if I had time on my side, I would have drawn it out, made you really sweat it, but I don't want to die tonight and leave things unsaid. Despite what you did and how you hurt me, I can't accept that you would be left with regrets, always wondering how I felt. That's no way to live your life, and I think you need to take me as an example of just how short life can really be. If this world isn't doing it for you, then get out. Turn your back on Empire and find somewhere new. Find a man or four who are going to treat you like their queen and blow your mind every damn night because that's what you deserve."

"I—"

Cara cuts herself off as Zade appears in the reflection behind us, a long white gown resting in his hands. A heaviness rests in his eyes, and as I turn back to face him and really look into his eyes, I see just how broken he really is. "It's time," he says, reluctantly making his way toward me.

He clutches the dress as I get to my feet, my hands shaking. My eyes fill with tears as I take in the white gown and slowly creep toward him, fearing taking this step. He places the gown on the dining table before taking my arms and pulling me into him, his forehead resting against mine.

A moment passes between us, and I simply breathe him in, not ready to say goodbye. I feel myself beginning to break, and without another word, Zade reaches down and grasps the hem of my shirt before dragging it up over my head.

I silently weep as he tosses my shirt aside and takes the dress in his hands, bunching up the fabric and threading it over my head. The beautiful white silk flows down my body, falling into place as the hemline skims the expensive tiles. Zade turns me around, his fingers brushing over my waist before working the small buttons on the back.

When he's done and the dress is firmly secured around me, he simply stands there, his fingers brushing my shoulder before lowering his lips and kissing me gently below my ear. "I'm sorry," he whispers, knowing just how hard this is for me.

I wipe my eyes, my spilled tears already staining the flawless silk gown, and as I turn back to face him, I find Dalton leaning up against the kitchen counter, his hopeless, broken stare lingering on me. The despair in his eyes tears me apart, and I step out of Zade's arms and go to him.

Dalton immediately pulls me into his chest, his strong arms wrapping around me, holding me so tenderly against him, one hand around my waist, the other fisted in my hair as though he'll never let me go.

"I don't know how to say goodbye to you," he tells me, his lips pressing against my forehead as his voice breaks. "You're the love of my life, Firefly, and I've failed you. I've let you down."

I shake my head. "You could have never let me down," I tell him. "These past two months have been some of the hardest times of my life. The things I've had to do and witness in the name of survival have terrified me, but you've been there every step of the way, giving me life and putting a smile on my face despite my darkest days. I love you, Dalton, and if I had the rest of my life ahead of me, I would happily live every single one of those days with you."

Dalton takes my face in his hands, tilting my chin up toward his and kissing me deeply, his lips lingering on mine as the tears roll down my cheeks. Breaking our kiss, he drops his forehead back to mine as he takes my hand in his before sliding a beautiful ring onto my finger.

My eyes widen, taking it in as I gaze at the beautiful diamond ring. "I . . . I don't understand," I tell him, gazing up into those conflicted blue eyes.

"I fucking love you, Oakley, and I know this might not mean anything now, but I need you to know that I see my whole future in your eyes. If I had my way, I would run with you now, take you away from all of this and truly make you mine. I would marry you in a heartbeat, Firefly, and while this ring is nothing but a token, stolen off the finger of another woman, I want you to take it with you."

My brows furrow, and I wipe away my tears as I listen to his words, his heart on his sleeve. "When Zade plunges that knife into your chest and the agony is unbearable, when you're ready to give up and feel yourself slipping away, I want you to hold this ring and remember how much I love you. Remember how much you mean to me and how your smile alone could light the whole freaking world."

My tears come faster, and I bury my face against his chest, my heart shattering into a million pieces. "I'm going to see you again, Firefly. I promise you that," he says. "Whether it be ten years from now or next week. This isn't the end for us. We'll come together in another life, and when we do, we'll finally get the ending we deserve."

I nod against his chest when a hand falls to my lower back, and I look up to find Sawyer at my side and reluctantly step out of Dalton's arms, straight into Sawyer's loving ones. He rests his chin against my head for a moment, the two of us so content in one another's arms. "I've known this was coming since the very beginning, yet no amount of time could have prepared me for how much this hurts," he tells me. "I truly thought that we would have found a way to save you, and I gave you my word. I told you I would save you, and now I have to sit back and watch as Zade takes you away."

My hands slip up the back of his shirt, my palms against his bare skin, not wanting to let go. "It wasn't fair of me to demand that you give me your word to save me," I tell him. "It was an impossible task, and I put the weight of the world on your shoulders when you were already grieving the loss of your father and dealing with Cara's initiation. I never should have done that."

"I'm not going to allow you to apologize for trying everything you could to save yourself," he tells me. "I would have done the same thing. I just hate that I resisted you so much in the beginning. I wasted so much time when I could have been standing at your side, but I hate it even more that we've come this far and I'm only now for the first time telling you how much I love you."

My eyes widen, lifting my gaze to his, hating the devastation in his eyes, but damn, it's so identical to mine. "You do?" I whisper, the tiniest sliver of my shattered heart healing. His words mean so much more than he could ever know.

"I do, and you damn well know it," he tells me, pulling me in even closer. "Losing you is going to fucking destroy me."

Pushing up on my tippy toes, I press my lips to his and kiss him with everything I've got, tasting my tears as they roll down my cheeks. "God, I wish I had the chance to live the rest of my life with you."

"You don't know how fucking badly I wish we could."

"Oakley," Dalton murmurs, drawing my attention. I glance up to meet his shattered stare, and as I do, he nods toward the balcony to where Easton stands out in the night, his hands braced against the railing and his head hung low.

Every last part of me breaks, and I turn back to Sawyer, giving him another soft kiss before stepping out of his arms. He holds onto my hand for as long as he possibly can before I move too far away and our hands fall down to our sides.

Crossing the dining room, I catch my reflection in the floor-to-ceiling windows and stop, taking myself in. I look like a bride in this dress, and it's almost funny. This gown for the ritual is supposed to signify my purity, my innocence, the same way a wedding dress would, and yet the occasions are so vastly different.

I hate it.

There's no doubt that the dress is beautiful, hauntingly beautiful in fact, but what it represents terrifies me. Though I suppose it doesn't matter. In two short hours, I'll be dead and all of this will be nothing but a painful memory to those I'm leaving behind.

Taking a shaky breath, I push through the door and step out into the night, my heart heavy as Easton glances back over his shoulder. His gaze trails over the dress, taking it all in, and for a moment, I'm wondering if he's seeing me as the bride he'll never have.

"How do I look?" I question, the soft night breeze blowing my hair back behind me.

He turns to face me properly, walking right into me and pulling me into his warm arms. "Like a fucking nightmare," he tells me, his fingers lifting my chin and bringing his lips to mine. He kisses me deeply, filled with passion, love, and fire, but there's also an intense sadness that acts as a constant reminder of exactly what I'm losing tonight.

His lips move against mine when a pained sob tears from the back of my throat, cutting our kiss short, and he pulls me hard into him, his bruising hold crushing the breath out of my lungs. The pain tears at me, and before I know it, Easton and I are crumbling to the ground, his face buried in the curve of my neck.

"Don't think about the pain," he tells me, agony thick in his tone. "It'll burn at first, and you'll scream to the point of spitting up blood, but Zade will make it quick. He won't draw this out. Once the adrenaline hits, it will quickly morph into a dull ache, and with any luck, you'll pass out before he cracks your ribs to reach your heart."

"Easton," I whisper, my lips trembling.

"No," he says, cutting me off. "You need to be prepared, Oakley. I know you're fucking terrified. Hell, I'm terrified for you, but I don't want you going in blind. These are your final moments, and I need to know that when your life is slipping away from me, when I lose you, you're going to be brave and prepared. That you'll leave this world with your head held high. Every eye of The Circle is going to be on you, and when they are, I want you to be strong and not allow them to see you fall apart."

I nod, but that's not enough for him, and he takes my face in his hand, staring right into my eyes. "Promise me, Oakley. Promise you won't let them see you fall apart."

"I promise," I tell him. "Even in death, I'm going to stick it to those old bastards."

"That's my girl," he murmurs, brushing his thumbs across my cheeks and wiping away the lingering tears.

Soaking in the warmth of his hold, I meet his haunted stare. "I want you to fall in love, Easton. Sawyer and Dalton, I know they'll be okay. It'll hurt for a while, but eventually they'll be able to move on and find their new version of happiness, but I worry about you. Your heart has always been so closed off, so terrified to let anybody in, and I don't want that for you. I can't stomach the idea of you never finding someone to spend the rest of your life with."

"I did, Pretty," he murmurs, brushing his knuckles down the side of my face. "I found you, and I know we didn't get forever, but we got a little while, and having you for just a little while is better than never having you at all. I'm not about to throw that away to find some other girl. I'll be okay, Oakley. I gave my heart to you, and it will always be yours."

Letting out a breath, I drop my forehead to his and hold onto him a moment longer when Zade steps out into the night, regret shining in his dark eyes. "I'm sorry, Lamb. We need to go."

Undeniable fear blasts through my chest as Easton scoops his arms beneath me and lifts us both to our feet. My whole body shakes, and as the tears stream from my eyes, Zade takes my hand and pulls me into his chest. "I've got you, Oakley," he tells me. "I'm not going to let you go."

I swallow hard and nod, allowing him to lead me back inside.

Easton follows on our heels, and I stand near the dining table, the boys rushing in and holding me one last time, tears welling in their eyes as they try to fight them back. They kiss me, hold me, and whisper goodbye.

One last touch.

One last kiss.

One last whispered admission of love.

Then all too soon, Zade takes my hand again and leads me toward the elevator with Cara heavy on our heels. I glance back, watching as my three heroes stand defeated around the dining table. Easton's head hangs low as he grips the back of the chair, and Sawyer crumbles against the floor-to-ceiling window. Dalton clenches his jaw as he paces, and his hand ferociously sweeps toward a crystal vase as he passes it, sending it soaring across the penthouse with a ragged, pained cry.

Their heartbreak destroys me, and as the elevator chimes its arrival and Zade leads me in, pulling me in tight against his chest, all I can do is weep as I prepare to meet my fate.

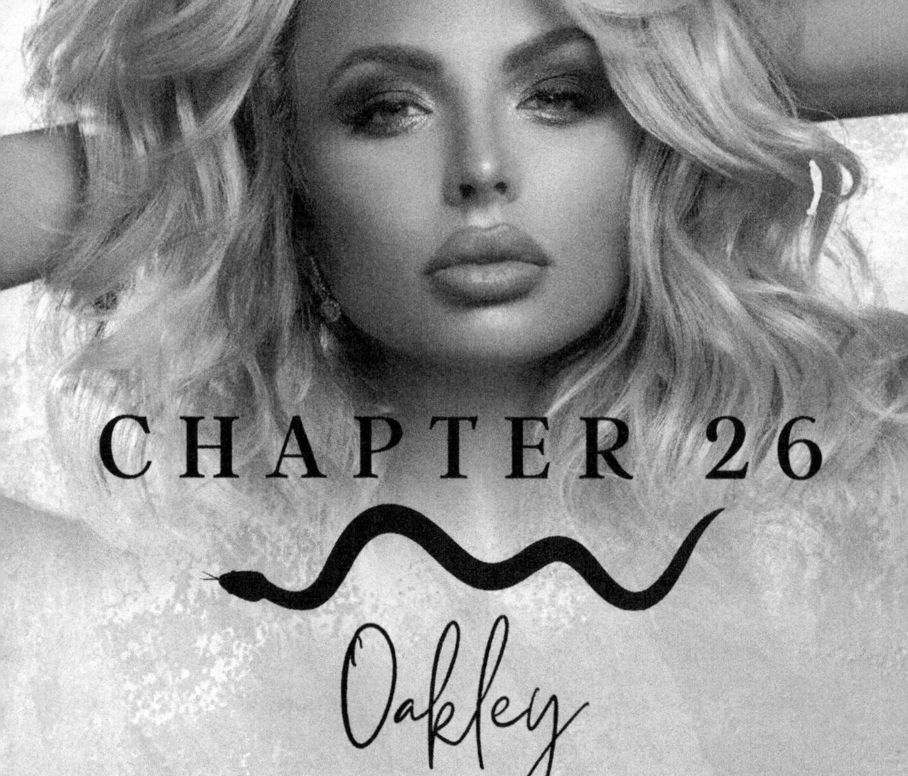

CHAPTER 26

Oakley

The walk through the thick woods to the tomb is terrifying. I hear people in the trees around us, threats at every corner, enemies wanting one last ditch effort to keep Zade from rising in power, to force him to forfeit his claim to the crown. Not that he truly has one.

I wonder what they would think if they knew that when they attack me, they're attacking the true blood heir of the organization they claim to be so loyal to. It's almost ironic . . . downright laughable. To attack a blood heir is a direct betrayal against the blood, punishable to the full extent of Empire's law, punishable by death. I bet if they knew that, knew the lineage and purity of my blood, they wouldn't move to attack me so quickly.

The fallen leaves rustle under my feet as I walk as close to Zade as humanly possible, my heart pounding so loudly in my ears that I can barely hear anything around me. Cara stands on his other side, probably the closest she's been to him in weeks, and I know it's solely out of fear. She's well aware of the enemies in the thick bushes, waiting to strike, but like me, she has no choice but to trust that Zade will protect her. Unfortunately for her, if someone was shooting at us, I know undoubtedly which one of us Zade will throw himself in front of, and I don't say that to be a cold bitch, it's simply fact. Something she must be aware of.

The walk is long and cold, and after such a long day, I'm already exhausted, but as far as last days on earth go, it was a good one. The emotions were overwhelming, and saying goodbye to the boys was the hardest thing I've ever had to do, but on the other hand, they went out of their way to ensure I had a good day, to truly make me feel alive. Hell, even now I can still feel them between my legs, and what better way to go? Not going to lie, my ass could use a cold compress and an ice bath. It was worth it, though.

The idea that my father could be in these woods surrounded by his army eats at me, and when a shiver trails down my spine, Zade glances at me, pulling me in even closer, lending me his warmth. "Are you okay?"

I shake my head. "I can hear them around us," I tell him. "Lying in wait, wanting to take one last shot."

"There's no one out there," he comforts me. "I mean, there is, but they're my people, security put here by me to patrol the area and watch our backs when I can't. I'm not taking any risks, not with you. I anticipated this, Lamb. I've meticulously planned this out. You're the safest person out here in these woods."

"Do you think my father will show up?"

"I have no doubt," he tells me. "But he won't be able to get to you once we're inside the tomb . . ."

"I won't be coming out," I finish for him.

He lets out a heavy breath, the hopelessness growing between us and weighing on my shoulders. "Please forgive me, Lamb," he begs, his tone filled with the greatest agony, absolute disgust for himself flashing in his eyes. "If there were another way, if I could save you—"

"I know," I whisper through the trees.

"No," he says, grabbing my arm and pulling me to a stop, forcing me to meet his haunted stare. "I don't think you do."

As I stare up at him, my baby blues locked onto his dark gaze, I see that terrified little boy inside of him, the one clawing to get out, and it breaks me.

"I scoured the fucking bylaws, spent sleepless nights agonizing over how the fuck I could have saved you, and now we're standing right here, barely a few feet from the tomb, and I can't fucking do it. I can't save you and be the man you need me to be." He closes his eyes, and in a fit of despair, drops to his knees before me, clutching my hands with everything he's got. "Please, baby. Please tell me that you'll forgive me. Know that if I was physically capable of walking away and offering you a life of freedom away from all of this, away from me, I would give it to you in a fucking heartbeat. I don't want to do this to you, but fuck, I have to, Lamb. I have to see this to the end."

My heart races, and I feel myself breaking, seeing the strongest man I know fall to pieces at my feet, but I won't fucking allow it. He's about to be the leader of this fucking organization, one of the most powerful men in the world, and if he's about to make the decision to sacrifice me to get it, then he doesn't get to fall apart. He doesn't get to send me off into an excruciating death after telling me how he doesn't want to do it. If we're doing this, if he's really plunging a knife through my chest and prying it apart with his bare hands, then he's going to do it with pride for the crown that he's so tirelessly worked for.

"Leaders don't kneel to anyone, Zade DeVil," I say, raising my chin. "Get up."

He swallows hard, agony consuming him, and I watch as he clutches my hand and gets to his feet, that lost little boy desperately crying out, needing me to save him, but I can't offer him that, not anymore.

"I know you're hurting," I tell him. "I know this decision has eaten at you since the moment you met me. I get all of that, but I need you to be strong. I need you to hold me together because I do not want to walk into this with fear. I need to know that you'll hold my hand and be there every step of the way, despite the fact that you'll be the one holding the dagger. I need your strength to get through this. Hear me, Zade. You can't fall apart on me, not now."

He holds onto me, clutching my waist, his forehead pressed to mine, breathing heavily as he struggles with his demons, and despite not saying a word, I know the second we step into that tomb, he'll transform into the leader I need him to be. He'll become both my savior and executioner, and as he slaughters me, he'll hold my hand, walking me through every second of it until the life finally fades from my eyes.

"Come on," Cara says, her voice breaking as she moves into us, giving us a gentle nudge. "We need to get out of these woods. We can't have anyone seeing you like this."

Knowing just how right she is, Zade starts walking again, his fingers threaded through mine, holding me close to his body, and before I know it, I'm staring up at Empire's sacred tomb as a chill sweeps through my body.

Zade unlocks the heavy door before sliding it back out of the way, the stone scraping against the ground. Then offering me his hand again, Zade leads me to my death.

The tomb is colder than I expected, and there's a foul, musty smell that lingers in the air. I can only imagine where it's coming from or what I might find down there. Old oil lanterns send waves of light through the big tomb, showing off just how extravagant this place is, but I would expect nothing less of Empire.

We make our way down a set of old stairs, spiraling right down to the bottom as both Zade and Cara hold out their oil lanterns, leading the way. It's eerie down here, each of our footsteps echoing through the tomb, the sound going on for miles.

We're the first to arrive, and that much is clear as we reach the bottom of the stairs. It's pitch black down here, and as I walk out into the main part of the tomb, I sense the ghosts of the innocent lives sacrificed before me.

My whole body shakes, and I watch as Zade makes his way around the tomb, lighting lanterns that hang from pillars, sending dull beams of light through the tomb. There's writing on the walls, names of the men who have stood here before Zade, each of them proudly taking their position at the head of Empire, each of them willingly slaughtering an innocent life in order to gain their power.

Unshed tears linger in my eyes as my gaze settles on a stone block with chains in all four corners, and without a word of confirmation, I know this is where it will happen. My wrists and ankles will be bound to these chains, and it's there that my life will end.

"Hey," Zade says, stepping into me, wrapping his arms around me, and forcing my stare away. "Just be here with me."

I look up into his eyes, needing the world to fade around us like it usually does when he peers into my eyes. Usually, it's as though he can see right through to my soul, but right now, it's impossible. I can't block it out, and all that's left is fear.

"How much longer?" I ask him.

"The Circle members should start arriving soon. They will each take their place, and at exactly the hour before dawn, the ritual will start."

"How long until that?"

"Less than forty minutes."

I whimper, my knees buckling beneath me as I fall into Zade's strong arms. "Shit," I tremble, my forehead falling against his chest as his hands slowly roam up and down my back, trying to keep me calm.

"Remember to bury me somewhere nice. Maybe by the water or in a tulip field. Somewhere the boys can come visit me in private. I don't want some shallow unmarked grave," I say, my tone shaky as the tears really start to fall, a huge lump forming in my throat as the desperation claims me. "And don't let any of those assholes touch me afterward. Just you, okay? Don't leave me here alone. I don't care what the bylaws state. I can't be left here to rot."

"I got you, Lamb," he murmurs, his hand curling around the back of my neck and holding me still. "You're safe with me."

"And cover me up, okay?" I whisper, needing to lower my voice to physically get the words out. "I know the boys are going to want to see me, to say goodbye, but I don't want them seeing me like that . . . without a heart."

"I'll brush your hair," Cara says from her position across the tomb, standing in front of her pillar, a black cloak draped over her shoulders. Tears fall from her eyes as her tone wavers, desperately trying to hold it together. "Before the boys see you, I'll make sure you look breathtaking, and maybe," she pauses, swallowing hard, "maybe Zade could help me put you into a nice dress. Nothing white like this. Something that truly represents who you are."

"Okay," I say shakily. "Yeah, I'd like that."

Cara nods, furiously wiping the tears on her cheeks when we hear the tomb door open, the heavy stone scraping against the ground. "This is it," Zade tells me. "Now they're starting to arrive, I have to bind you to the altar of sacrifice, and once I do, you will not be permitted to speak. I won't leave your side, Lamb, I swear. I'll be right here the whole time."

I swallow hard, and with that, he drops his hand to my lower back and leads me across the tomb before helping me up onto the sacrificial altar. He helps to lay me down, his touch on my body more gentle than he's ever been since coming into my life.

He takes my wrist and pulls it up above my head, gently binding it to the stone before walking around my other side and repeating the process. I don't take my eyes off him, and I know he feels me shaking, the fear truly crippling me. My ankles are bound next, and as I hear someone on the stairs, the eerie echo of footsteps fills the tomb, and my blood runs cold.

Zade strategically positions himself in front of me, keeping as much of my body hidden behind his large frame as possible, knowing damn well that we can't trust a soul within The Circle. He stands with his hands behind his back, his fingers touching my waist, and to anyone walking down those stairs and looking on, they'd never know how he was honoring his promise to stay with me this whole time.

The first Circle member appears at the bottom of the stairs, and he takes a quick look around, his gaze sailing over me with curiosity. Taking a black cloak, he silently moves across the tomb before positioning himself in front of a pillar.

Hartley Scott is the next to appear, and judging by the scowl on his face, it's clear that he had no intention for us to make it this far, and now, there's not a damn thing he can do.

Silent tears stream down my face as every last member makes themselves known, and once the circle is finally complete, they stand in silence, patiently waiting for the precise moment to get the ritual underway.

My silent tears have turned into soft weeping, and my subtle shakes have become full-blown trembles, and if it weren't for Zade's thumb slowly trailing back and forth over my waist, I would have surely died from fear already.

I try to remember Easton's words, try to find the strength he willed me to have, desperately wanting to go out with my head held high, and as Dalton requested, I think of how much he's loved me, of the beautiful diamond ring circling my finger. I think of Sawyer, of the grief he's already suffered through at the hands of this organization, and how I would have done anything to take that away. But mostly, I find myself hoping that I was enough for them.

Movement catches my eye, and my heart stops, watching as Hartley Scott strides into the center of the tomb, an oil lantern in his hand. His head remains bowed, and it's clear that whatever is about to go down here, despite the outcome, each person in the room has a great respect for the process. All but maybe Cara.

Hartley raises his stare to Zade, his gaze briefly flickering to me before finally getting on with it. "It is time," he announces. "Let the ritual begin." And with that, he drops the oil lantern to the ground, and an inferno spits up into the air.

Hartley returns to his position around the circle as the roaring flames quickly spread warmth through the chilling tomb, but it doesn't matter. Zade commands the room, and his authoritative tone demands loyalty.

"We gather here in the sacred tomb of our people, amongst the spirits of our great past leaders," he starts in a booming tone, my stomach turning with unease. "The official reign of my father, Lawson Michael DeVil, has ceased, and I stand before you, the true heir of the founding Circle and proclaim my intention to rise as the leader of our fearless organization and claim what is rightfully mine."

As if on cue, The Circle members begin to chant, and I watch in fear, only just now realizing how fucked up this is going to be. I knew there would be chants and fire and probably a blood oath taken by each of The Circle members to declare their loyalty to their new leader, but reading about it in an old book and actually witnessing it are two very different things.

"The flesh of my flesh will perish in flames, but the blood will forever reign."

The chant is repeated two more times before Zade moves on, that same tone turning my blood cold. "Tonight I stand, offering my soul to my people in the greatest sacrifice. A show of loyalty, a sacred vow in which shall bind me to Empire and my subjects, and with this sacrifice, I will rise as the rightful leader, my power indisputable until the time of my natural death."

As one, The Circle drops to one knee, each of their heads bowed. "Zade Alexander DeVil," they say, Cara's voice coming out as a whimper. "We acknowledge your intentions, and on this night, after sixty suns and sixty moons, in this final hour before dawn, you are welcomed before the spirits of our past leaders to sacrifice the heart of an innocent and swear your unconditional loyalty to your people."

The Circle remain on their knees as Zade raises his chin and walks around the back of the sacrificial altar, exposing me to The Circle, but what does it matter at this point?

Tears stream down my face as Zade's broken stare locks on mine, regret heavy in his eyes. He reaches under the altar, and everything within me shatters as he produces a beautifully crafted dagger, the blade designed with intricate patterns, ones that are so similar to the lines Zade and Easton have tattooed on their bodies.

I hear Cara's whimper across the tomb, but I only have eyes for Zade, my complete, undivided attention locked on him.

This is it. The moment both Zade and I have counted down to, the moment that has haunted us each for such different reasons. As he holds my stare, I see the plea in his eyes, begging me to continue to love him through all of the pain, through the fear and the unknown, and move on into death with courage.

"My sweet Lamb," he murmurs, his voice so low that above the raging flames, only I can hear it. He leans down to me, pressing his lips to mine in the sweetest, lingering kiss. "I love you, Oakley," he confesses, saying those three little words I never thought I would hear and repairing something broken within me. "Every part of me wholeheartedly belongs to you. It has since the moment I met you, and I have feared this moment, feared what would become of me."

He closes his eyes, needing a moment to find his composure before looking back down at me. "I will make it fast," he promises as I feel the tip of the blade so subtly resting against the center of my chest.

I tremble, and with his other hand, he reaches up and grasps mine, threading our fingers and squeezing tight just as he promised he would. I feel the slightest pressure against my chest, the tip of the dagger drawing the smallest bead of blood, and I whimper, my heart racing faster than ever.

Then just as Easton said, I feel the adrenaline start to pour through my veins, and when Zade kisses me one last time, a silent goodbye on his lips, I know my time is up.

He meets my fearful stare and as I gaze into his eyes, I see the exact moment that scared little boy disappears, and I'm met with the ruthless new leader of Empire. The sharp pinch of the dagger lifts off my chest and as Zade's muscles flex, ready to plunge the dagger deep into my chest, I let out a blood-curdling scream.

He moves like lightning, the dagger hurtling toward me, only he flicks his wrist, releasing the hilt and sending the dagger flying across the tomb, the sharp blade sinking deep into Hartley's chest, committing one of the greatest betrayals Empire will ever know.

Cara screams, and as if on cue, the sacred tomb turns into a fucking war zone as Zade officially forfeits his claim to leadership, leaving it wide open to the likes of Matthias Quinn.

Zade presses his hand beside my waist on the altar and launches right over it, taking a protective stance in front of me as the sound of Hartley choking on his own blood fills the tomb, and before he's even fully situated in front of me, The Circle members are already on him, coming at him with the type of skill you only see in movies.

Zade does a good job of putting distance between them and me, and I don't miss the way that Cara drops to her knee and scrambles through the tomb, terrified of being slaughtered right along with

Hartley.

My eyes widen, barely able to comprehend what the hell is happening, watching as Zade snaps the neck of Ira Abrahms, and with a lethal blow, sends his lifeless body spiraling toward the roaring fire.

A hand grips my wrist, and I let out a scream, thrashing against my chains, but when I look up, I find Cara furiously trying to release me. That's when I see them.

Sawyer, Easton, and Dalton storm the tomb, but they don't come from the stairs above. They're racing from one of the dark tunnels that lead deeper underground, but that doesn't make sense. How? Unless they've been here this whole damn time. This was their plan all along.

"Hurry," I panic, these brief moments possibly being the only ones we have to save ourselves because, let's face it, if anyone in this tomb survives, Cara will be executed right along with us.

The boys quickly rush into battle, The Circle members definitely more skilled than the pathetic army my father amassed, but the boys quickly start to gain the upper hand, and The Circle members begin to fall before my very eyes.

Cara finally frees my right wrist, and just as she races for my ankles with trembling hands, Sawyer's booming roar fills the tomb. "CARA. GET DOWN."

She squeals, quickly dropping just as a cloaked member rushes toward her back, the dagger from Hartley's chest now clutched in his palm. He doesn't get another step as Sawyer launches a knife clear across the tomb, the blade sinking straight through his skull, the hilt sticking out between his eyes.

The Circle member drops to the ground behind Cara, and she squeals again, not quite as used to witnessing this level of brutal murder that I'm starting to become accustomed to. "Cara," I call, pulling on my binds, both my ankles still tied down. "You can book a therapy session the second we get home, as for now, help me the fuck out of these chains."

The battle rages on around us as Cara finally scrambles back to her feet and starts working the chains around my ankles, and I reach over to my other wrist, desperately trying to release myself.

When I finally have my wrist free, I sit up to reach my other ankle, but a blazing force slams into my chest and knocks me back to the altar. A burning sensation quickly spreads through me, and my gaze snaps down in terror, seeing a gold, diamond-encrusted dagger protruding from my chest.

"OAKLEY!" Cara screams as the pain becomes dizzying.

The terror in her tone has all the boys glancing my way, but the moment of distraction costs each of them dearly as Dalton takes a knife below his ribs and Sawyer is thrust toward the fire. Easton's pained grunt fills the tomb, but all I can focus on is the warm trail of blood seeping from my chest and pooling beneath me.

Then on instinct, my hand curls around the hilt with a pained cry, and I tear it out, the blade clattering to the ground as I hear Zade's angered roar telling me no.

"HELP HER," Sawyer roars at his sister, but she's already there, scrambling on top of me, straddling my waist as she presses down over the wound. She tries to gain control of the bleeding, but the more she presses down over my chest, the harder it becomes to breathe.

"Oakley," Cara demands as my eyes grow heavy. "Don't you dare go to sleep."

My head lolls to the side, and I gaze at the boys, coming to the realization that this really is it. It wasn't the terrifying slaughter I'd prepared for, but tonight will still mark the end of my life, the end of my story. I'm just grateful I got to see the boys one last time.

Nothing could ever beat that.

Taking out the last remaining Circle members, Dalton comes racing around the sacrificial altar, his skilled fingers working the chains on my ankles in a flash as Sawyer races to my other side, locking his arm around his sister's waist and all but throwing her to the ground in order to scoop me into his strong arms.

"LET'S GO," he says, his booming voice echoing through the old tomb.

Sawyer takes off at a sprint, and as Zade puts the final nail in the coffin, finishing The Circle for good, I peer back over Sawyer's shoulder. The boys hurry behind us, terrified panic in each of their eyes as they sprint toward the old stairs, desperate to get me out of here, and just as Sawyer hits the bottom stair, I see a familiar face hidden in the shadows.

A wicked smile stretches across his face, and as I fade from this world, I know without a doubt that my father, the man who raised me from a newborn into a curious little girl, was the one responsible for ending my life.

Then before Sawyer has even reached the top of the stairs, I fade from existence, my last breath expelled from my lungs as I silently die in his loving arms.

CHAPTER 27

Sawyer

"NO," I roar, my boots slamming against the hard earth and propelling me through the thick woods as my girl lies motionless in my arms.

The boys race around me as Cross practically drags Cara to keep up and fuck, if she weren't my twin sister, if she didn't share my blood, she would have been left behind. We don't have time for stragglers, especially when Oakley is dying in my arms.

I have to get her out of here.

We didn't just slaughter the whole fucking Circle only for Oakley to die on her way out the door. That is not how her story is supposed to end.

Panic tears at my chest, a raw desperation I've never felt before gripping hold of my throat and squeezing it tight, making it impossible to breathe. "Oakley," I grunt, rattling her as I barge through the thick brush, the low-hanging twigs scratching up my face and arms as I sprint past them. "Come on, Doll. You're not fucking dying like this."

"Does she have a pulse?" Zade demands, racing out in front of me as we clear the thickest part of the woods, passing the bodies of Matthias's army left carelessly by Zade's team in the thick shrubbery.

"I don't know," I respond, knowing he hears the raw, unfiltered panic in my tone, letting on just how fucking bad this really is.

We finally break through the woods to Zade's SUV parked up on the curb, and he unlocks it, racing around to open the back door just moments before I go flying through it, laying Oakley down across the back.

Cross scrambles for the first aid kit as Zade hits the gas, the back doors still hanging wide open. Cara squishes in the trunk as Cross and I hover over the backseat, my fingers pressed firmly to Oakley's throat as Dalton hangs over the front passenger seat, his eyes glued to Oakley's face.

Everybody rushes out demands, needing to know if she's alright, and I zone them all out, only able to hear the rapid beat of my heart in my ears. Then finally, I feel it, the light flutter beneath her skin that tells me we still have a fucking chance. "I've got a pulse," I rush out, hearing the collective sound of relieved sighs throughout the SUV, prompting Cross to get stuck straight into first aid. "It's weak, but it's there. She's just out cold."

"Thank fuck," Zade grunts, pushing even harder on the gas, more determined than ever to get her to the ER.

"Look at her chest," Cross says as Cara hangs over the backseat and grabs Oakley's hand, clutching onto it for dear life, tears streaming down her face. "She's trying to breathe, but she can't."

"She's got a collapsed lung," Dalton suggests, tearing off his shirt and holding it against the stab wound at his waist, trying to control the bleeding as his face turns white, but considering he hasn't passed out and managed to make it all the way back to the SUV, I can only assume it's just a flesh wound, same as the burn to my arm.

Cross tears the bloodied silk gown from Oakley's chest, getting a real look at the deep stab wound, and it makes me sick, not because of the blood or the injury itself, but because it's Oakley. I would have endured a million stab wounds if it meant saving her from just this one.

Applying pressure to the stab wound, Cross hovers over her before adjusting himself to straddle her waist, and while he's able to gain control of the bleeding, there's no telling what the fuck is happening inside her body right now.

"Come on, Doll. Open those pretty eyes," I murmur through the car. "You're not ready to give up yet."

The drive to the emergency room seems far too long, and I will Zade to go faster, but he's pushing his SUV to the kind of limit that would have any lesser driver already dead in a shallow grave.

"She's gonna need surgery," Cross says, "and after taking out the whole fucking Circle, we don't have that kind of time on our hands. Maybe an hour, two at max before word starts to spread and it turns into a fucking manhunt."

"We'll figure it out," Zade says. "We'll lock down the whole fucking hospital if we must, but whatever happens, she does not leave our sight, understood? If Empire comes for us, then we deal with it, pick them off one by one until it calls for something more. Until then, we focus on Oakley getting better. We're on the run now, our faces will be plastered all over the fucking country, and she needs to be in a place where she can run right along with us because now that Matthias has a legitimate chance at claiming leadership, he won't stop until she's dead, even if it takes years."

"Agreed," Dalton says just as Oakley's eyes start to flutter.

I suck in a gasp, all eyes falling to Oakley and watching as she finally comes to, fierce relief pounding through my veins. "Oh thank fuck," I breathe, my hand slipping into hers and giving a gentle squeeze, letting her know I'm right here and that she doesn't need to be afraid.

Her gaze lingers on my face, a dreamy smile pulling at the corner of her lips. "This must be heaven," she croaks, the words struggling to come out with her lack of oxygen. My brows furrow, her comment odd before quickly realizing that she thinks she's dead.

"Yeah, Doll," I tell her, preferring her to believe that she's got us all in heaven over the reality of the fact that her injuries are near fatal. "Everything's alright now. The worst is over, and now you're free. You're going to be just fine."

She smiles up at me, her eyelids growing heavy just as Zade pulls up in the ambulance bay and shoves his door open wide, frantically calling out to anyone who'll listen. "I NEED HELP OUT HERE."

CHAPTER 28

Oakley

The rhythmic beat of my heart rate monitor fills the room, and I try to open my eyes as a dull ache pulses in my chest. My throat hurts, and I feel groggy, but I try to push past it as I peer into the room, finding the faces of my four boys, terror etched into each of their haunted stares.

I want to put them out of their misery, to throw myself from the bed and race into their arms, telling them that I'm alright, but I can't. All that matters is that rhythmic beat, that repetitive subtle *beep* telling me that for now, my heart is still where it belongs.

I'm alive against all odds. I've defied fate and live to see another day. I get to love again, hold the boys' faces in my hands and kiss them until the end of time with their warm arms wrapped around me.

Since the day I moved back to Faders Bay, there's been a countdown on my life. I was never supposed to have luck on my side, yet in that tomb, Zade made the split-second decision to throw away everything he's worked for. He chose me, he chose our love, and he gave us the future we were always supposed to have. But what exactly is he risking in order to give me that? What exactly has he sacrificed?

My head pounds, and as I open my eyes enough to truly take in the room, I find Easton sitting directly at the end of my hospital bed, his head in his hands as Zade paces the door, his gaze constantly flicking out the window and down the busy hospital corridor as if waiting for some kind of attack.

Sawyer is to my right, his elbows braced on his knees, fidgeting with his fingers as his gaze remains fixed on the end of my hospital bed. He looks stressed. Hell, they all do, apart from Dalton, who's directly to my left, his hand clutching mine, two of his fingers stretched out to my wrist, and while most people wouldn't think anything of it, I know he's really tracking my pulse, not willing to trust the heart rate monitor beeping through the room.

My eyes flutter, slipping in and out of consciousness, but I push through it as the desire to put the boys at ease thrums through me. My memories may be hazy, but I recall the way they erupted from the shadows. It was as if they'd been there the whole time.

They knew to be there.

They knew Zade was planning to save me, yet each of them let me fall apart in their arms as they sent me to the slaughter. I said my final goodbyes, and they wiped my tears, promising that in another life we'd find each other again. Easton told me to be brave while Dalton put a ring on my finger, making me vow to think of his love in those final moments. And Sawyer? Fuck. He finally found the courage to open his heart and whisper the words I'd been so desperate to hear.

How the hell could they do that knowing what was coming? How could they let me walk into that tomb thinking I was going to die? I laid on the sacrificial altar in chains, and my body shook with fear as I watched each of The Circle members file into the tomb.

I made peace with my death and held onto Zade's hand as he pressed the tip of the dagger to my chest. I didn't want to, but I was ready to go, ready for Zade to tear right through my chest and rise as the leader of Empire. But it was all for nothing.

All the fear and pain, all the running. For what?

I swallow hard, anger boiling in my chest as my throat screams in protest, but damn it, I need to get this out now. I feel the fog starting to cloud my mind, pulling me back down into the darkness, and I push through it as my gaze scans the room, taking in each of the frustratingly impossible men before me.

I could say so many things. Tell them I'm alright, how much I love them, or thank them for putting their lives on the line just to save mine, but instead, I hit them right where it hurts.

"How the hell could you do that to me?"

Both Easton and Zade's heads whip toward me as Sawyer throws himself right out of his seat. Dalton on the other hand just gapes at me, his jaw hanging open.

"You're awake," Sawyer rushes out, springing toward me and

scooping my other hand into his, clutching on with everything he has. I can almost feel the vibration of his rapid heartbeat as relief surges through his stare and then, all at once, that stare turns hard, anger booming through his salty glare. "How the fuck could you just die in my arms like that? Do you have any fucking idea how that feels? You were supposed to fight, Oakley. But you just gave up."

I stare at him, my chest heaving as Zade shoves Sawyer away, pushing him back into his seat. "Give her some fucking space," he says. "It's not her fault we weren't good enough to protect her. That's on us. Not her. *We* failed her."

Dalton squeezes my hand, and I turn to look at him, taking in his concerned stare. "How are you feeling? Do you need water or anything? Painkillers?"

Betrayal and hurt settle into my heart, and I look at him as though he's the perfect stranger. I understand Easton and Sawyer keeping their mouths shut about it, but Dalton . . . now that one stings.

"You let me walk into that tomb thinking I was going to die," I murmur, pulling my hand free from him. "How could you do that to me?"

"Firefly," he says, completely deflated as regret shines through those bright blue eyes I love so much. "I'm sorry, but I did what I had to do to protect you. You know if I had any other choice, if there were another way, I would have done it."

A tear falls down my cheek, and he reaches for me, gently wiping it away as the heaviness fades in and out, my eyelids fluttering. I turn to meet Zade's haunted stare before continuing to Easton's, needing to get a read on him, needing to know where he's gone inside that dark and depraved mind of his.

"I . . ." I start, the heaviness weighing down on me, my eyelids growing heavier as the fog fights for dominance. "I need . . ."

My words fall away as Easton leans forward in his seat, those fiercely loving eyes locked on mine. "What do you need, Pretty?" he prompts and just as he gets to his feet and strides toward me, the fogginess claims me, sending me back into the dark pits of nothingness.

A sharp pain tears through my arm, and my eyes spring open to find Zade hovering over me, urgency flashing in his eyes. "What?" I rush out. "What's happening?"

He doesn't get a chance to respond before he grips my cannula and rips it from my arm, the machines around me furiously beeping. Blood spurts from my arm, but before I can even scream, the blanket flies off me and his strong arms scoop beneath me, pulling me into his chest.

"Fuck," Easton grunts, rushing toward the door, Dalton and Sawyer heavy on his heels as they reach for their guns. "We're out of time."

"Out of time for what?" I panic, trusting the boys blindly, fear pounding through my veins.

"Empire," Zade mutters, his jaw clenched. "They know what we did, and they're coming for us. It's a fucking manhunt, Lamb."

"Congratulations," Dalton says as a piercing scream sounds from down the hallway, gunshots echoing through the hospital. "You're officially a fugitive."

With that, Easton barges out of the room, taking a protective stance in the middle of the hallway, his gun held out as he quickly fires off a few rounds. "Go. Go. Go," he roars over the noise.

Zade wastes no time, shooting out into the hallway, Dalton in front while Sawyer takes the rear. Bullets whiz past my face, and I try to curl into Zade, not knowing who the hell they're after. Do they just want Zade or are they after all of us?

Easton holds down the fort, protecting each of our backs as he fearlessly fires back. Zade runs as Dalton leads the way, slamming through the fire exit and into the stairwell, taking the steps two at a time, my weight not slowing Zade down an inch.

Sawyer and Easton barge through to the stairwell, slamming the door behind them, and with Empire behind us, we shoot down to the ground floor before breaking out into the lobby, the rough jostling making my head spin as my chest aches.

I struggle to hold onto consciousness as I cling to Zade, trying to breathe through the pain, but the heaviness slams back. "Zade," I breathe, the movement too much for me to handle, the grogginess clouding my head.

"Hang in there, Lamb," Zade grunts. "We're almost there."

Gunshots tear through the hospital lobby as we race toward the main entrance, the bullets shattering the glass as people scream, ducking for safety.

"Fuck," Dalton grunts, pressing his hand to his side as he glances back over his shoulder, assessing the situation, his gun held firmly in his other hand. "I tore my fucking stitches."

"Stitches?" I rush out. "Why the fuck do you have stitches?"

Nobody responds, but then I remember the very moment in the bottom of that fucked-up tomb when the blade sunk into my chest. I screamed, distracting the boys and opening Dalton up to suffer a stab wound.

Shit. How could I have forgotten? They all suffered while trying to save me, just like they're suffering now.

We finally make it across the lobby as Sawyer fires back, giving us a chance to get through the door before making it out into the parking lot. My gaze shoots left and right, not knowing where the hell to go, when a familiar SUV screeches around the corner, Cara taking up residence in the driver's seat.

My eyes widen, and before the SUV has even come to a full stop before us, the doors are already open. The boys rush into the backseat, and Zade pushes me into Easton's arms before moving to the driver's seat. He takes one look at Cara and lets out a ferocious growl. "Move."

She scrambles through the car, crawling through to the back and uncomfortably settling between Dalton and Sawyer, her ass barely hitting the leather before Zade's foot slams down on the gas, propelling us through the parking lot.

I frantically grab Easton, my head spinning as my chest aches. "Easton," I breathe, feeling myself beginning to slip away.

"It's okay, Pretty. You're safe," he murmurs, his fingers brushing through my hair, gently soothing me as he holds me tight. "I've got you. You can sleep now."

The grogginess fades, the fog lifting as I finally open my eyes and find myself in a warm bed with Dalton's protective arms wrapped around me. I take a moment, breathing him in as I snuggle into his side, doing my best to ignore the pain radiating through my chest.

I take a deep breath, trembling at the pain that blasts through my left lung, and let out a heavy sigh. "You okay, Firefly?" Dalton murmurs, his thumb brushing over my waist.

"Yeah, it just really hurts."

"No shit," he chuckles. "You got stabbed right through the chest and suffered a collapsed lung. That wasn't supposed to be a walk through the fucking park."

Rolling my eyes, I rest my hand over his chest, feeling the steady thrum of his heart. "How long have I been out?"

"On and off for two days," he tells me, making my eyes widen. "I think the mix of anesthesia from surgery and your overall exhaustion have kept you out longer than expected, but on the plus side, it's given your body a chance to start healing."

"How bad was it?"

"It was bad, babe," he states. "Real fucking bad."

Shit.

The bed dips on my other side, and I roll onto my back to find Easton sitting on the edge. His soft gaze lingers on my face as he reaches toward the medications left haphazardly on the bedside table. "Here," he says, grabbing the painkillers and pouring a few into the palm of his hand as I sit up.

I quickly take them, hoping like hell they work fast. "Where are we?" I ask after swallowing the little pills, taking a look around and not recognizing the small home.

"One of Zade's safe houses. We all have a few scattered across the country, but this one was the closest," he tells me before grabbing the array of pills on the bedside table and dumping them into my lap. He gives me a rundown of what I need to take and why, but something tells me he'll be keeping me right on schedule.

"Is the safe house really necessary?" I ask, meeting his stare and trying to figure out just how dire this situation has become.

"Oh yeah," Sawyer says, walking into the cramped bedroom and dropping down into the armchair across the room. "Empire is out for blood. They're coming for us no matter what we do or say. We just slaughtered The Circle, we committed treason against our own, betrayed our vows, and broke some of our most sacred laws. It's a fucking manhunt, babe. A fucking war, and there's nowhere for us to run, nowhere to hide."

Shivers sail down my spine as I hold his stare. "So what now?"

"Now . . . I don't fucking know. It's in Zade's hands now. He's making the call," he says. "All I know is that we're not doing shit until you're healed enough. If we need to run, we need to know that you're going to be alright. So I suppose for now, all you need to do is sit in that fucking bed and get better."

I roll my eyes, not liking the idea of just sitting back and doing nothing. "You know, I'm still really angry with you guys," I remind them. "You should have told me that you were coming for me. You let me fear for my life."

Easton shakes his head, his hand dropping to my thigh. "To be honest, there was a good chance that we weren't going to see you again. You could have died in there. You almost fucking did, but what Dalton told you at the hospital still stands. We did what we had to do to protect you, and I'm not going to apologize for that."

"I don't understand," I say, willing the painkillers to work faster. "How is that protecting me?"

"Despite what you think, The Circle wasn't just made up of a bunch of old, random rich dudes. They were trained by their fathers, just as Sawyer was trained by his. A man who stands at the top of our organization can't be foolish. He needs to be switched on, and if you walked into the tomb knowing you were about to be freed, they would have sniffed out the deceit a mile away," he tells me. "Your fear needed to be real. They needed to see the terror in your eyes, the raw despair in your tone as you screamed. I know it sucked, and fuck, Pretty, if there were anything we could have done to be able to spare you that fear, we would have, but it needed to be this way."

I bow my head, tears welling in my eyes at the horrific memories that haunt me from that tomb. It's never going to be okay, but for now, I can at least understand why they did it. "Okay," I whisper, reaching out and taking his hand. "I can accept that."

Dalton lets out a heavy sigh of relief and hooks his arm over my shoulder before carefully pulling me into his side and pressing a kiss to my temple. "Thank fuck for that."

"Thank you, though," I murmur. "What you did . . . that couldn't have been an easy decision to make, and I don't take it lightly. I know what this means for you all and the positions you've now put yourselves in. Fighting for your lives . . . that was never a part of the deal, and the fact that you're still here, willing to put yourselves on the line to protect me—"

"Don't," Dalton says. "There was no question. There was a chance to save you and we all took it without hesitation. It was the easiest decision I've ever made, and I'd do it a million times over if I had to."

I glance up at him, warmth spreading through my chest as he presses a soft, lingering kiss to my lips. "I love you," I tell him. "But just so you know, that ring you shoved on my finger is going to be one hell of a conversation."

"The hell it is," he says, reading exactly where this is going. "I'm going to marry you whether you want me to or not, and there's not a damn thing you can do about it."

Rolling my eyes, I shove his heavy arm off me. "I don't know if you've realized this, but you're kinda not the only man I'm with, and I'd hate to burst your happy little bubble, but I've been screwing all your friends behind your back, and something tells me that they're not going to appreciate you stealing me away to keep all for yourself."

Dalton laughs. "Yeah, that's not going to be an issue."

"Huh?"

"Cross doesn't believe in the sanctity of marriage," Dalton explains, nodding toward Easton beside me. "He doesn't give a shit if you were in the middle of saying your vows, he's still going to fuck you until you scream. And Zade . . . same."

Easton smirks. "He ain't lying."

"What?" I sputter, glancing across at Sawyer. "And you?"

Sawyer shrugs his shoulders. "I've never been one to want the big white wedding bullshit," he says. "And besides, I don't need some piece of paper to know that you're mine, so if that bastard really wants to send you down the aisle and put on a big show just so he can call you his in front of a bunch of people who don't matter, then that's on him. But I'm not gonna lie, the idea of seeing you as a bride has me feeling some kind of way."

"What kind of way?" I question, my lips pulling into a wicked grin, liking the hungry gaze in his eyes.

"The kind of way that will have you up against the wall while I tear your wedding dress off with my teeth."

"Well damn," I breathe. "I guess I'm going to have to get married now."

"What?" Dalton rushes out, gaping at me in horror. "You're going to fuck him on our wedding day?"

"No, of course not," I say, a thrill shooting through me. "I'm going to fuck *all* of you, but relax. I'm too young to get married, and after all of that shit we've just gone through, I just want to focus on living and having a good time."

"Agreed," Easton says. "But before you can do that, you need to get better. Why don't you lay down for a bit and then we can grab you something to eat. You must be starving."

Fuck yeah, I could definitely eat, but first, there's something I need to do.

"Where's Zade?" I ask, sitting up straighter in bed.

"Out keeping watch," Easton says. "Did you want to talk to him?"

"Yeah, I just—"

"Hold up, I'll grab him."

"No," I say, throwing my blankets back and starting to get up. "I'll go to him."

"No, no, no," Easton rushes out as Dalton goes to grab me. "Don't get out of bed. You need to rest."

"If you assholes think for one second that I'm about to let you chain me to this bed for the next few days, you've got another thing coming. And besides, it's not like I'm going out there to start breakdancing for him. We just need to talk, and when we're done, I'll come right back."

Dalton mutters to himself as Easton quickly realizes that I'm going to do this with or without their approval, and he offers me his hand to help me to my feet. I give him a grateful smile as he walks me out of the bedroom. "So, just to clarify," he says as I stop by the bathroom door, busting to pee. "You don't want to be chained to the bed just this week, or is being chained to the bed a hard no in general?"

A grin pulls at my lips as I step into the bathroom and pause in the doorway, my hand resting on the small handle. "All I'm saying is if you chain me to your bed, you better make it worth my while." And with that, I close the door between us, loving the devilish smirk that tears across his face.

Quickly cleaning myself up in the bathroom, I splash water over my face and take care of business, my stomach desperate for something to eat, but it's going to have to wait a few minutes. I run my fingers through my hair and can't help but lift my shirt, needing to see the damage, and fuck, it's just as bad as Dalton said it was.

I quickly drop my shirt back into place, not wanting to think about it, because honestly, a nasty scar is better than a grave any day. I need to be thankful that I'm still breathing, that I've been given this chance to live a long and happy life with the four guys who have somehow fallen in love with me.

Knowing damn well I'm not going to be able to fix this train wreck until I have the energy to properly shower and wash my hair, I step out of the bathroom, taking it slow. I pass the bedroom door and find my way out to the living room where Zade sits back on the couch, his sharp gaze locked out the window, keeping us safe.

Hearing me in the room, Zade looks back at me, and his brows furrow. "What are you doing out of bed?" he questions, that deep tone rumbling right through my chest. "You should be resting."

I shake my head and keep making my way toward him before pressing my knee to the couch cushion beside his thigh and straddling his lap. His hands automatically fall to my waist as he watches me, my gaze locked on his, a seriousness falling between us. "You gave up everything you've worked for to save me," I whisper, still unable to believe the words coming out of my mouth. "Everything that you've done and sacrificed, all the work and the hours preparing yourself. You've dreamed about rising in power, you took your own father's life just to get one step closer, and you gave it all up just so I could live."

Zade nods, his hand curling around the side of my neck as his thumb strikes out, brushing across my jaw. "I don't want any of it if I can't have you," he murmurs, his eyes so full of love. "You don't know just how much I'm willing to sacrifice just to see you live another day. I love you, Lamb, and I'm done holding back from you."

I lean into him, dropping my forehead against his as my hands rest against his wide chest. "Zade?" I question. He lifts his chin, his lips barely a breath away from mine, silently asking what I need. "Hurry up and kiss me."

A soft groan rumbles through his chest and without hesitation, Zade closes the gap, fusing his lips to mine in the most passionate kiss he's ever given me. His lips move so perfectly with mine as his arm winds around me, holding me close while being so gentle. "I need to feel you inside me," I breathe into his mouth.

"No, Lamb. Not so soon after surgery," he says. "You're not ready, and I don't want to hurt you."

"You won't," I promise him, knowing there's not a thing Zade DeVil could ever do to hurt me. Not now. "Just take it slow. Just let me feel you."

With that, Zade reaches down between us, tearing my panties right off my body as my oversized T-shirt hangs low around my hips. Then with skilled ease, he releases his cock from the confines of his pants, and as his lips come back to mine, I rise up on my knees and he guides himself to my entrance.

Feeling his tip against me, I slowly sink down over him, needing that closeness like never before, loving him to extents I didn't even know were possible.

I suck in a soft gasp as my walls stretch around him, sinking all the way down and already feeling my body begin to tremble. Needing to feel that undeniable pleasure, I slowly rock my hips while keeping the rest of me as still as possible, terrified of hurting myself further, but Zade would never allow that to happen.

It's slow and sensual, our hungry kisses fueling the fire between us. His arms hold me secure and safe against him, and when we finally find our release, it's more than I could have ever needed.

The high rocks through me like the most sensual explosion, and I tip my head back as it works through my body. Zade's lips trail over my neck, the intensity growing, and as he empties himself inside of me, I've never felt more alive.

When we're finally done, Zade settles me down on the couch beside him, the boys appearing from deeper in the house with blankets and pillows. Then before I know it, they've made me a makeshift bed right beside him, my head in his lap and his fingers in my hair as the UberEats driver shows up at the door, more than ready to feed me for the first time in over two days.

CHAPTER 29

Oakley

Stepping out of the shower, my gaze sails over my body. We've been holed up in Zade's safe house for a few days now, and so far, it's driving me insane. We can't do anything, can't go anywhere, and with the boys determined to see me heal as fast as humanly possible, we can't even fuck.

Well, I mean . . . not in the way I usually prefer. I'm definitely getting dicked down as much as possible. Without a gym, these guys have too much energy to burn, and I'm more than happy to be that outlet for them, but I just wish they'd throw me up against the wall and fuck me into a coma.

I'm done with missionary. I'm not a missionary kind of girl, and I mean, sure, sometimes the good old one-on-one dance is exactly what

I need, but when I have four horny guys who are all holding back, it's hard to be satisfied when I know just how wild and wicked it can get.

With nothing to do but screw and binge-watch The Vampire Diaries with Cara, I've been quickly going out of my mind, and soon enough, I'm going to break. After scanning over my healing injuries and deciding another day of this bullshit will physically kill me, I tighten my towel around my body and step out of the bathroom, more than ready to declare we get out of here, when Easton strides in through the front door with a burner phone in his hand.

"It's go time," he says, the guys whipping their heads toward him as I just stare, suddenly not feeling so brave about going anywhere. I mean, sure, I'm happy to move onto the next safe house, possibly one that has a pool and some nightlife so Cara and I can sneak out and enjoy a few drinks. Not that we'll actually get very far. Hell, we won't even make it to the bedroom window before being sprung, but it'll still be better than living here. As for heading back to Faders Bay for round two? No thanks. Hard pass.

"What do you mean?" Zade questions, getting up, ready to spring right into action. "What's happening?"

"That was Benny," he says, Zade's right-hand man at the DeVil hotel and loyal member of Empire, though fortunately for us, Benny still believes that Zade is the only rightful leader and therefore, that loyalty belongs to us. "Matthias is making his move today."

"But it's the mass funeral today," Cara says.

"Exactly," Easton says, striding across the room and grabbing a heavy black bag and dumping it on the table, guns spilling out of it. "What better time to make his claim to leadership? The funeral is going to be the biggest turnout Empire has ever seen. If he wants to make a move and declare himself, then that's how he's going to do it."

"Shit," I mutter, watching the boys scurry around the room. "How's this going to work?"

"We go in and take him out," Zade says bluntly.

"The hell you are," Cara splutters, finding a backbone. "It's a mass funeral, and you're not about to go in there guns blazing and disrespect the families of our dead. Children will be there, Zade. If Matthias is going to make a stand during the funeral, then we'll deal with it and put the fires out, but I am not about to let you cause more bloodshed on today of all days. Besides, if you go in there and start shooting the place up, you'll be public enemy number one."

"I'm already public enemy number one," Zade throws back at her. "It doesn't get much worse than that."

"You're Zade DeVil," Cara mutters. "You have a gift for making matters worse."

"Would the both of you just knock it off?" Sawyer says, making his way toward the table and scanning over the selection of weapons. "What are our options?"

Dalton shakes his head, deep in thought. "We're outcasts. We don't have any."

"You might be outcasts," Cara says. "But I'm not. I'm the highest-ranking official Empire has. We've got to be able to use that in some way. They don't know that I had anything to do with what happened in the tomb."

"No offense," I say with a cringe, "but the fact that you were the only Circle member able to walk out of the tomb alive speaks volumes. They know you were with us. It might not have been voluntary and you might have been in the dark like I was, but they know whose side you're on."

"Honestly," Easton says with a shrug. "I say we just wing it. There's going to be hundreds if not thousands of people showing up to this. We play our part, keep our heads down and blend in with the crowd. No one even has to know we're there. Then, when the right time presents itself, we make our move."

"And what move is that exactly?" I ask, not liking where this is going.

"Who knows?" he says, a devilish grin pulling at his lips. "That's all part of the fun."

Ahh shit.

With the boys all in agreement, we quickly find ourselves back in Zade's SUV and flying back toward Faders Bay before making a pitstop at the mall to find appropriate funeral attire. Apparently, an oversized t-shirt that reads *Why is it always WYD and never DYWMTCOAEYPTYCOMF?* isn't going to hack it.

It's a long drive back into Faders Bay, and I find myself gazing out the window as I sit across Dalton's lap, my head resting against his wide chest, listening to the steady beat of his heart. Dalton is too good for this. He's got the biggest heart I've ever seen, and I can't stand the thought of him being an outcast like this.

My fingers lace through his as we listen to the soft music playing through the car speakers, and I find myself considering what could potentially come of today. If my father really does stand before the people of Empire and make his intentions known, and it somehow turns into a battle that claims his life, where does that leave me?

I'll officially be the only true blood heir of Empire, next in line to claim the throne, but do I actually want it? I don't know. I mean, sure. I've pictured myself stealing it out from under Zade with the intention of burning it to the ground, but to take it and lead? I can't say it's ever been something I've wanted for myself. But if that's what it comes down to, if that's the fate I am thrust into, can I actually go through with it? Will I be required to follow the archaic rituals and sacrifice the heart of an innocent life?

I couldn't. Nothing is worth that.

But the biggest question is, could I take the leadership if it meant selfishly taking the one thing Zade has ever wanted?

No. I don't think I could.

It's another hour before we reach the city limits of Faders Bay and another fifteen minutes before Zade brings the SUV to a stop in the backstreets behind the massive cathedral. Today has been planned as two separate events. It will start with the funeral in the cathedral with what I'm sure will be a beautiful ceremony, and then later tonight, after each individual family has taken the time for a private burial, there will be a mass celebration of life. A party to honor the victims of the explosion, a night their families and friends can always look back on.

The funeral is due to start in the next thirty minutes, and the streets are already packed with bodies. The boys scan the streets with their skilled stares, checking for possible threats and spotting each of my father's snipers within seconds.

We don't dare risk going in just yet. Instead, we remain in the car and watch our surroundings. Then as Zade cracks his window, we hear his name whispered on the lips of those walking by, calling him a traitor and a joke, and I've never wanted to drop a bitch so bad in my life. If only they knew.

The boys are not usually the type to make a late entrance. They like to have the upper hand, but that's not possible today, and as we slip out of the SUV and into the street, we do what we can to discreetly blend in with the crowd.

Dalton walks beside me, his hand on my lower back and his head down, much like many of the other men making their way into the cathedral. We spread out so we don't look like some kind of avenging pack storming through the gates of hell, and within minutes, we've entered the cathedral and are taking our seats.

Cara and Easton sit in the pew in front, Easton leaving enough space on either side of him in case he needs to move quickly, while Sawyer sits on my opposite side. Zade stays hidden at the back, not wanting to risk showing his face until it's completely necessary, but he keeps a watchful eye over everything, ready to have our backs at a moment's notice.

I don't see my father, but the chill in my veins tells me he's here.

The last time I saw him, he launched a knife right through my chest, and I can only assume that he thinks I'm dead. I hope at least. If he's expecting me, this isn't going to go well, but if we have the advantage of the shock factor working in our favor, that could potentially help.

With so many bodies trying to cram into the cathedral, it takes a little while for the service to get underway, and when it does, it's just as beautiful as I expected. The names are read out one by one—a role that was originally supposed to be performed by Zade—and a representative from each family rises and walks to the front of the church before lighting a candle in honor of their loved one.

I hear people weeping from every corner of the room, the emotions riding high, and as the service begins to wrap up, I start to wonder if my father is even planning on making his appearance.

When a noise sounds from the back of the room, all eyes turn to find the source, and I clench my jaw, seeing the one and only Matthias Quinn. My hand squeezes Dalton's, and my nails dig into his skin as I watch the old bastard stride down the aisle. I have to give him credit, I'm impressed that he managed to wait until the end of the service before making it all about him.

He walks right up to the dais, all but shoving the priest out of the way and waiting a moment as gasps are heard through the room. It's clear some of the older generation knows who this is and believe they're seeing the ghost of Matthias Quinn, having known him as a young man. But for the most part, these people don't have a fucking clue what's going on or why this man would be interrupting such an important service.

"Friends and family of our beloved Empire," he starts, his tone loud and full of pride as he stands before us in a well-fitting suit, looking like the father I always remembered from my childhood, not the scruffy prisoner I've come to know him as. "I thank you all for being here and making the trip out as we bid farewell to the victims of the tragic explosion that shook our great Empire. For those who don't know me, my name is Matthias Quinn, and I have spent the past thirteen years locked in Empire's underground prison, an innocent man, torn away from the loving arms of his eight-year-old daughter simply for being the real, biological son of the great Julius DeVil."

Gasps tear across the cathedral as I clench my jaw and go to stand, but Dalton pulls me back down. "Not yet," he says. "We need to play this smart."

Swallowing my pride, I try to relax, but my blood pulses furiously through my veins, the adrenaline having me ready to explode.

"How dare you," someone yells from the front.

"You're a liar," comes another.

My father holds up a piece of paper and slams it down on the dais. "My birth certificate," he says before producing another. "And a DNA test proving that Julius DeVil was my father. However, I am happy to have these tests confirmed."

There's more gasping that quickly turns into chatter before my father calls attention to the room. "I, Matthias Quinn, stand before you as the sole living blood heir of Empire, the true heir, and after having my legacy torn from my hands by none other than Lawson DeVil, a fraud who knowingly never possessed the blood of Empire, I have come to reclaim what is rightfully mine."

The room erupts into chaos, people yelling and demanding answers as others just stare in shock, not believing my father for even a second.

"QUIET," my father booms, the dead seemingly long forgotten. "I understand that you have many questions, and I will strive to answer them all. However, in light of the brutal slaying that took place four nights ago in our sacred tomb, that of which took the lives of eleven Circle members, I ask the congregation to have a little patience."

The murmurs from the crowd continue just as my father does, clearly not having the respect of the room. "During this time of grief, I stand before you as your future leader, offering you solace in this difficult time with a promise that I will find the culprit responsible for the explosion that took the lives of so many—"

"ZADE DEVIL IS OUR REAL LEADER," a voice booms from the back, earning a round of cheers.

"Zade DeVil is a fraud just like his father," Matthias spits. "He doesn't even possess the blood. Lawson was adopted into the family, and I was cast away, the true heir thrown to the side in order to protect my father's adulterous indiscretions. Zade should never have been in line for the crown. He is a spineless fraud, a leech who slaughtered The Circle for sport."

My jaw clenches as my hands ball into fists, rage blasting through my veins as my father turns Zade's people on him, exposing him in a filthy light.

My knees bounce, terrified of what's to come, terrified of the power my father is gaining by giving the congregation a common enemy, and I can't help but think back to what Easton said at the safe house, that sometimes not knowing how you're going to handle something is all part of the fun. And with that, I throw myself to my feet and stand up on the chair, making sure every eye in the cathedral can see me.

"My name is Oakley Quinn, the daughter of Matthias Quinn and a true blood heir of Empire," I declare, my voice unwavering as I stare directly at my father, watching as his face starts to fall. "And four nights ago, I laid bound in Empire's sacred tomb as The Circle knowingly committed treason to the highest extent—"

"Silence," my father booms as men from his army start rushing toward me, making Dalton and Sawyer flinch at my sides, more than ready to put these fuckers down.

Only another voice sails through the cathedral. "Let her speak," Cara says, holding her head high before turning her gaze to my father. "I am the sole surviving member of The Circle, and until your lineage can be confirmed, you have no jurisdiction here. Now, if this girl can shed some light on the tragedy that took place four nights ago, I have a duty to hear her out."

The congregation voices their agreement, and I swallow hard as I climb down from the pew and make my way out to the aisle, Easton, Sawyer, and Dalton all getting up and walking with me.

They form a protective circle around me as I shakily walk to the front of the cathedral, my father's jaw clenched, knowing damn well this is not about to go down well for him.

Easton walks right up toward my father, the ferocious look in his eyes forcing him to back up a step, and with Sawyer and Dalton hovering close by, I step in front of the dais, my hands growing clammy.

I find Zade hidden within the shadows at the back of the room, and when he nods, I allow the words to flow free, letting these grieving families know exactly what kind of men they have been putting their loyalty into.

"Like I said, my name is Oakley Quinn, and this," I say, indicating the bastard behind me, "is my father, the real blood heir of Empire, and while he was telling you the truth, that as a young father, he was torn away and thrown into Empire's prison for thirteen long years, he also forgot to mention how during that time, he has been plotting to overtake Empire and rise to power."

Murmurs ripple through the cathedral, the high ceilings making the sounds bounce around the room. "My father, this man insisting he deserves your loyalty, has betrayed Empire in every way. He has lied and cheated, secretly building an army while giving the order for his men to slaughter me, his only daughter, the next in line for the crown, in a disgraceful attempt to wipe out any threat who could potentially challenge his rise to power."

My father grunts, spitting hate at my back. "That's a lie," he roars as Easton springs forward, gripping my father's arm and forcing him to his knees before the church.

I stare at him, more than ready to hammer the final nail into the coffin. Then turning back to these people, watching the way they hang off my words, waiting to hear what more I have to say, I give it to them straight. "Not only was my father responsible for the brutal attacks on me, he was also the man responsible for the explosion that took the lives of so many."

With that, I nod to Dalton who pulls out his phone and strides over to the projector that's currently running through a slideshow of the men and women we lost in the explosion. He takes only a moment to connect his phone, and before I know it, surveillance footage of that night appears on the screen.

Silence fills the room as Dalton hits play on the video, and we watch as my father and his men infiltrate the ballroom and plant the explosives that destroyed so many lives.

The video comes to an end, and the room erupts into chaos, men pulling out guns and waving them around as mothers of the dead weep, this revelation too much to handle.

"TAKE YOUR SEATS," I command the room, power bursting from my chest and watching as they immediately react, putting their weapons down and paying attention. "We are not heathens," I tell them. "We do not lower ourselves to the standards of this scum. Now I know you are ready and prepared to watch this man be punished to the full extent of Empire's sacred law, and we will in due time. However, I was not brought up here to discuss the crimes of my father, but to share with you my experience in Empire's sacred tomb four nights ago."

My voice starts to break and a woman in the front stands, and I quickly recognize her as Sawyer and Cara's mom. "It's okay, honey. Take your time."

I give her a fond smile before trying to work out how the hell to put this all into words before deciding not to sugarcoat it and give it to them straight. "The Circle members were a bunch of over-privileged corrupt men who did not deserve your continued loyalty," I say bluntly. "As you are all well aware, two months ago, after the death of Lawson

DeVil, his son, Zade inherited the crown and then commenced Empire's preparations for a new leader. Zade, who at this time fully believed that he was the true blood heir of Empire, was to complete the leadership ritual, to sacrifice the heart of an innocent, a task that the leaders before him have all performed."

"I don't understand how this has anything to do with The Circle being slaughtered four nights ago," someone calls out.

My gaze settles on the asshole across the cathedral, and as I fix him with a heavy glare, he quickly shuts up and allows me to continue. "Zade was instructed on the hour before dawn on the sixtieth sun and sixtieth moon, that this ritual will be performed, and with that, he was given my name—a name which the corrupted members of The Circle had known for many years."

Whispers and gasps of shock start to sound around the room, but I continue. "Over the course of the following sixty days, Zade discovered that he was not the heir to Empire's greatest throne and that his father had fraudulently ruled before him. He learned that The Circle knew who I was and that they had planned to use my death as a means to cover their indiscretions. With my father long forgotten in Empire's prison and Lawson DeVil already dead and gone, their lies and manipulations would have died with me."

Zade steps out from the shadows, and I watch as people start to notice him, some looking terrified, some already piecing together what had happened. "Zade DeVil is one of the greatest men I have ever had the pleasure of knowing," I tell the world, watching as he slowly walks toward me, holding his head high, proud of his actions in that tomb.

"Four nights ago, he gallantly protected me, the true blood heir of Empire, as I was bound to an altar and sentenced to slaughter."

The words get stuck in my throat, and as Zade nods, I find the strength to continue. "Zade DeVil is my hero," I say, hating how I have to keep the other's names out of my mouth right now despite how they deserve the praise for what they did. "He put his life on the line to protect me, and he did so, fearlessly fighting off eleven trained men. Their actions against me, and their dishonesty to you, the people, in knowingly allowing Lawson DeVil to fraudulently rise in power and deceive you all is an act of the greatest treason, punishable to the greatest extent of Empire's laws."

Horror tears across the faces of the congregation, unable to believe how easily they'd been led astray. "I am not here to sway you in some kind of direction, to try and manipulate you into allowing me to lead you. It's not a position I want nor am I prepared for. I'm simply here so that you can have all the facts and know exactly what kind of corruption has overtaken the organization that you all love so dearly," I say, not even bothering to tell them about the dagger my father launched into my chest. They already have enough proof to convict him.

Zade moves up on the stage beside me, his hand on my lower back as I move away from the dais, allowing Cara to take over, the only person in this room with any true authority right now. She turns to face the people and takes a shaky breath before raising her chin. "I know that I am still new at this and there are many customs I have yet to learn, however, one thing is abundantly clear," she says, her gaze shifting back to my father. "Matthias Quinn does not have the best interests of our people at heart. A power-hungry leader who so willingly disregards the lives of his people is not a leader at all, and I vote, as your sole remaining member of The Circle, that he be punished to the full extent of Empire's laws."

The whole congregation gets to their feet, roaring their approval as my father gapes, looking at them in horror as though he truly believed that his blood alone could save him. And with that, Cara addresses the congregation one last time. "I ask that if there are any children within the cathedral or anyone who does not wish to witness this public execution, that you now be dismissed. Please exit your pew and in an orderly fashion, make your way through the main doors."

A moment passes and I watch as children are scurried through the exit and then when the congregation settles and everyone goes quiet, Cara glances at me, giving me the go-ahead.

A strange nervousness flutters through my chest as Zade presses a gun into my palm. "Are you sure?" he questions. "I can do it if you need me to."

"No," I tell him, moving into position in front of my father. "I shot Aunt Liv right between the eyes and didn't lose even a wink of sleep. I'm sure as hell not going to lose any over this." And with that, I raise the gun without a moment of hesitation, and I pull the trigger to truly reclaim my freedom.

CHAPTER 30

Oakley

I collapse onto the couch in Zade's penthouse before immediately regretting it, a sharp pain jolting through my chest, realizing way too late that I'm well behind on my painkiller schedule. "Fuck, that hurt," I mutter as Sawyer falls down beside me, a heavy weight lifted off each of our shoulders.

"What's wrong?" Easton asks from the kitchen. "Are you hurting?"

"No," I lie, watching as he rolls his eyes before practically diving on my medications and finding the strongest one. He fills a glass of water, and with the little pills in his hands, he walks right around the back of the couch as I scramble onto my knees and turn to face him.

"Open wide," he instructs, placing the pills into my mouth and getting a wicked enjoyment out of this before handing me the glass of water. He braces his hands on the back of the couch, his feral gaze lingering on my mouth. "Now swallow."

Yes, sir.

I do as I'm asked as Easton watches me swallow the pills right down before taking my chin and forcing it up, holding my stare. "What a good little whore you are."

A squeak tears through my lips, and he watches me curiously, fire blazing in his eyes and holding me captive. He takes the glass of water and goes to walk away when I shake my head and grab hold of his belt buckle, keeping him planted behind the couch. "Where the hell do you think you're going, big guy?" I question, my pussy clenching. "You don't get to say something like that without following through."

"Oh yeah?" he challenges, all but thrusting the glass into Sawyer's hands before dropping his hands to his belt. He pulls his shirt free before slowly unbuttoning it, showing off those perfect deep ridges of his abs and making my mouth water. The fabric falls to the ground, and my gaze scans over his inked chest and arms before following his movement back to his belt buckle. "You want to show me just how good of a little whore you really are?"

I nod like a fucking bobblehead and watch as he opens his pants and reaches in, fisting his glorious cock. My tongue rolls over my bottom lip, and as he pulls it free, so hard, thick and long, I know I'm about to blow his fucking mind.

He slowly pumps his fist up and down, and as the hunger gets stronger, my patience wears thin. "Don't make me wait, Easton," I growl. "I might be a good little whore for you, but I'm an impatient one, and if it's not your dick in my mouth, it'll be Sawyer's."

Hearing his name, Sawyer's head whips up, only just now realizing we're about to have a party without him, and he jumps to his feet. "Woah, Doll," he says, pulling his shirt over his head and playing catch up. "Who said you get to celebrate without me?"

I grin as Sawyer moves in behind me on the couch, his knees on either side of mine, but all I can focus on is Easton as he moves in closer, his cock only a breath away. Easton grabs my chin, his thumb rubbing across my bottom lip. "Don't you fucking tease me, Pretty," he growls, that authoritative tone making me wet. "Now open wide."

Good fucking God.

His tip presses to my lips and I greedily lap up the small bead of moisture like it was personally gifted to me, and without wasting another moment, I open wide and groan as he slowly pushes inside. My fingers close around his base, firmly squeezing as I feel him in the back of my throat, and only when he reaches around me and curls my hair around his hand do I truly settle in for a good time.

Easton slowly pulls back, taking control of my movements with his hold on my hair, and when I feel Sawyer's cock grinding against my ass, my eyes roll in the back of my head. His fingers pinch the small zipper at the top of my black dress, and as he drags it down and the fabric loosens around me, a shiver runs down my spine.

I have to release my hold on Easton's cock to allow the dress to fall right down my arms, but the moment I do, Sawyer is all too eager to pull the rest of the fabric away. His fingers slip into the sides of my black lace panties, dragging them over my ass and right down my thighs. Then as he grinds against my ass, he reaches around me, flicking his fingers over my clit and pushing down to my entrance.

I'm soaking wet for them, and he slowly pushes his fingers inside me before returning to my clit, making my body jolt with pleasure. I groan against Easton's cock, and I know he feels the vibration from my throat by the way his eyes flutter, and it only makes me want it more.

His intense stare remains locked on my mouth, watching the way I take him, and knowing how much he loves it, I make sure to put on a good show.

Sawyer's fingers are like magic, rolling over my clit before dipping inside me and repeating the process, but knowing all about that lack of patience I so willingly possess, he doesn't make me wait before taking my hips and pulling me back. The move puts a hot-as-fuck arch in my back that makes me feel like their personal little sex goddess.

Then with his fingers rolling over my clit, he presses his tip to my entrance and slowly pushes inside me, filling me inch by inch as my walls clench around him. My eyes roll in the back of my head, loving the way he fills me, but damn, there's nothing quite like the feeling when he starts to move.

He's still careful with me, still taking it easy after my surgery, and for once, I don't mind.

My tongue rolls over Easton's tip, and he groans, pulling back just an inch. "You're gonna need to slow down, Pretty," he warns me as Sawyer's soft grunt fills the air behind me. "I intend on fucking you all night, and you're not about to make me come just yet."

Fuck, it's like setting down a challenge and expecting me not to rise to the occasion; it's, almost impossible. The idea of having them inside me for hours on end is just too good to pass up.

Sawyer takes slow, sensual thrusts that make my pussy shake with need, and I push back against him, feeling him go deeper, when I hear a door opening from down the hall. "Aww, what?" Dalton grunts, betrayal thick in his tone. "I told you assholes not to start without me."

Then not a second later, I hear whatever is in his hands being launched over his shoulder, and he bolts through the penthouse, grabbing at his clothes and yanking them off. A laugh bubbles up my throat, ruining the rhythm I've got going on Easton's cock, but as Dalton clambers onto the couch and gives me a cheesy-as-fuck grin, nothing else matters.

"Well hey there, you sexy little minx," he says, his gaze sailing over my naked body, taking in the way Easton fucks my mouth before sailing down over my tits and to Sawyer's fingers against my clit. "Got some room for me?"

He doesn't wait for a response as he slides in between me and the couch, and we have to jostle around to make it work, but the second I'm straddled over his lap, it's time to get back to it. Dalton is careful not to touch my wounds as Easton's cock practically ends up on his shoulder, and for a brief moment, I wonder how the boys would feel about helping each other out, but to be honest, as much as I'd love to see them enjoying one another, I think I'm too greedy to share, even with them.

Reaching down between us, I fist Dalton's cock and start working him as Sawyer slowly moves in and out of me, adding his fingers to the mix and spreading my arousal to my ass. He teases me there, applying just enough pressure to make my eyes flutter, and Dalton closes his lips over my nipple as his hands skim across my waist.

"Fucking hell, Firefly," Dalton murmurs against my nipple as it pebbles under his tongue.

His cock strains in his hand, and knowing just how desperate he is, I rise a little higher on my knees, guiding him to my entrance, but when Sawyer goes to pull out of me to make way for Dalton, I shake my head. "Both," I murmur around Easton's cock before noticing the way Dalton grins at Sawyer over my shoulder.

Fucking boys. I bet the second we're done and their hands are free, they'll be high fiving each other.

Not wanting to hurt me, Dalton takes his time, pressing against my entrance and allowing me to slowly lower myself onto him, his cock stretching me wider than ever as he situates himself beside Sawyer.

I suck in a gasp, needing a moment to relax around them, my eyes closing with intense pleasure. Easton eases up in my mouth, pulling free from my lips and giving me just a moment before taking my chin and lifting my gaze to his. "Breathe, Pretty," he murmurs, coaching me through it as he grasps his cock, giving it a firm squeeze.

I do as he says, taking a slow, deep breath before blowing it out and relaxing around them both.

"That's my girl," Easton says in that same authoritative tone as he sees the tightness in my eyes begin to fade. And with that, I test the waters, slowly moving up and down, my eyes fluttering with intense pleasure.

"Oh fuck," I breathe, immediately doing it again as Sawyer's fingers roll over my clit, making my body jolt with need. I move again slowly, this time not stopping before reaching for Easton again and guiding him back to my mouth.

I take them all deep, the pleasure too much to handle when a shadow across the room catches my eye, and I find Zade leaning against the closed door of his bedroom, his gaze focused heavily on me.

I grin against Easton's cock, knowing damn well what he's thinking, and I don't miss the way Easton glances over at him, noticing what's caught my attention. "What the fuck are you waiting for, man? Can't you see she wants you too?"

Zade's gaze drops back to mine, the desire thick in his eyes, and for a moment, I think he's going to walk away, assuming three is a party but four is a crowd, but when he pushes off the door and strides toward me, my excitement becomes almost unbearable.

Zade walks right around the couch, slowly peeling off his shirt as he goes, his intense stare roaming over my body, watching the way I take his friends. "Look at you," he commends, the kind of pride in his eyes that has a wide grin stretching across my face.

"Fuck, Zade," Sawyer grunts. "If you're gonna get in on this and have any intention of finishing at the same time as her, you're gonna have to hurry the fuck up and get your cock out."

Excitement fires through my veins. Even in my wildest dreams, I never thought I'd ever have them all at once. Zade kneels on the couch beside me, and his intense stare is like nothing I've ever felt.

Sawyer eases up on my clit, knowing I'm going to want to make this moment last, and as Zade reaches for his belt buckle, I nearly come just thinking about it. He frees that deliciously thick cock, and as I reach for him, curling my hand around his already straining base, Dalton's fingers dig into my hip.

"Fuck, Firefly," he says as I drop down further. "That's the way. Take it all."

Dalton's filthy mouth is like a fucking drug to me, and I can't help but clench around them both as my tight fist works up and down Zade's cock, only my brows furrow when Easton pulls free from my mouth.

I glance up at him, a little unsure as he still clutches my hair, taking control of my neck. "I want to watch you take Zade, Pretty. Open wide and show me how you fuck him with your mouth."

The filthiest little thrill sails through me, and I can't resist bringing Zade to my lips, never having gotten the chance to taste him like this before. But if I get to do it with Easton's eyes on me as well, that's even better.

I take Zade right to the back of my throat, showing him just how good I can work him with my tongue as Easton pulls back on my hair, forcing my stare up at Zade, the heat between us too much to bear. I see Easton out of the corner of my eye, his other hand stroking his cock, and I reach right over Dalton's shoulder and close my hand over his, working them together as my other hand closes around Zade's base.

The movement becomes too much as my eyes start rolling in my head and Sawyer quickly takes over for me, slowly thrusting in and out, his cock rubbing up against Dalton's as his fingers tease my ass.

Dalton takes over for Sawyer at my clit, rubbing just a little bit faster and sending me into overdrive as I feel myself flying right toward the edge. I can't hold on much longer, and I give the boys my all as my tongue rolls over Zade's tip before working down his length and taking him deeper. I suck hard, and when Sawyer groans I know this is it.

"Ahh, fuck, Doll." He comes hard, shooting hot spurts of cum deep inside my pussy, and just the thought of him spilling inside me with Dalton in there too is too much for me to handle, and I fly right over the edge, an intense, raging orgasm exploding through me.

I cry out, the sound muffled around Zade's cock, but not one of them stops, all of them watching me as I come, my pussy shattering around the boys. My whole body jolts and shakes, my eyes clenching as my toes curl, then as Dalton's tongue flicks over my nipple, he comes undone, emptying himself inside me.

My high rocks through me, every touch only making it more intense, and when Easton pulls back on my hair and turns me to face him, I know exactly what he's asking for.

Releasing Zade's cock, I open wide for Easton, and not a second later, he comes on my tongue, hot spurts sinking to the back of my throat before he uses the same authoritative tone. "Swallow it, baby," he tells me. "Take it now."

I put on a fucking show for him, loving how it gets him off, and once I've taken him all, he releases his hold in my hair and allows me to focus my attention on Zade. Only as I come down from my high and Sawyer and Dalton pull free, Zade decides he needs so much more.

He locks his strong arm around my waist and lays me down across his couch.

He comes down on top of me, taking my thigh and hitching it up high before thrusting that glorious cock deep inside my pussy. He fucks me hard, rolling his hips and taking long, deep thrusts, and I tip my head back over the armrest of the couch, the intensity making me dizzy.

"Oh fuck, Zade," I groan, reaching up and clutching his shoulder, my nails digging into his warm skin.

"That's right, Lamb," he says. "From now on, when we fuck, I'm always the last to take you, always the last to touch you. That way when your sweet little cunt is hurting, it'll be me you feel there. You understand me?"

God, do I ever!

Then shifting my hand to his chin, I force those dark, deadly eyes to come back to mine. "Make it worth my while and you've got yourself a deal," I tell him. "I'm not fucking fragile, Zade. Fuck me like you really mean it."

And with that, he rises to the challenge and has me screaming within seconds, and barely a moment later, an even more intense orgasm tears through me. Then only when my pussy is convulsing around him does he finally empty himself inside of me as a dark, wicked grin pulls at the corner of his lips—a silent warning that I just unleashed the kind of sexual beast that only a woman with one hell of an appetite could take. And lucky for me, I've never been so hungry.

CHAPTER 31

Oakley

Standing in the center of the function hall in the bottom of the DeVil Hotel with Sawyer's arm locked tightly around my waist, I stare up at the incredible display. This place is breathtaking and leaves me wondering how the hell I never knew this was down here. Actually, there's a shitload of things I'm only just discovering about this hotel. Like the fact there's an indoor pool on the thirty-eighth floor with a swim-up bar. Though to be fair, I think someone mentioned a pool at one point, but it's not like my horny kidnappers thought to actually show it to me.

The function hall is filled with bodies, the room overflowing as Empire puts on one of the greatest celebrations of life this world will ever see.

The music flows with just the right amount of champagne, and while this party would have been incredible in the marvelous setup of the ballroom, Zade's function hall is the next best thing. Though in hindsight, perhaps Empire should steer clear of the ballroom from now on, you know . . . when it's rebuilt of course. It couldn't be healthy for us to return there after everything that went down.

Empire needs a fresh start, and that's exactly what this is . . . kind of.

"Have I told you how fucking delicious you look?" Sawyer murmurs in my ear.

"You did," I say with a sultry smile. "You told me when I was putting the dress on and then you told me again in the elevator right before you took the dress off."

A smirk pulls at his lips, his eyes sparkling with mirth. "I don't know what the hell you're talking about," he lies just as he spins me out before pulling me back in, his hand falling into place on my lower back and making me feel like an absolute princess.

I've never had a man dance with me like this before. Don't get me wrong, my prom date definitely tried, but when his hand disappeared up my skirt, I realized maybe he was thinking about the wrong kind of tango. But Sawyer Thorne has me here blushing like a little schoolgirl, completely swept off my feet.

I soak up every second of the dance, and when the music stops, my heart breaks just a little. But Sawyer is a pushover, and I know without a doubt that I will have a few more dances before the night is through.

Easton catches our attention from across the room, holding up a glass for me, and I smile as we walk over to the guys. I gingerly take the drink from his hand and take a greedy sip before realizing it's just water and give him a hard stare.

"What?" he mutters as the boys talk among themselves. "You're on strong painkillers and medication. You can't drink."

"I just had your cock so far down my throat I could feel you in my stomach, and you have the nerve to tell me that I can't have a drink?" I question.

"Damn straight."

"Well, in that case, the next time you feel like putting that thick cock of yours down said throat, I might remember just how parched I was and decline the offer."

Easton gives me a hard stare, his dark eyes tightening with fear as Venom peeks her head out from around his neck. "You wouldn't," he says, trying to call my bluff.

"Wouldn't I?" I say, knowing damn well if the opportunity presented itself to show this man the time of his life that I'd be down on my knees before he could even call me his good little whore. But hell, he doesn't need to know that.

I'm pulled in between Dalton and Zade, and I glance up at Zade. "Any sign of Santos?" I murmur, wanting to keep it private.

He shakes his head and disappointment fires through me, having hoped that he might have made one last ditch effort to prove himself, but like the boys have always said, Santos is a ghost with a gift of slipping away when it matters most. "Don't worry," Zade tells me, his hand lingering on my lower back. "He can't hide forever. He'll slip up at some point, and when he does, we'll be waiting."

Letting out a heavy sigh, I sip my water and consider finding someone to spike it when the music begins to fade. I look out at the impressive party, catching Cara's eye across the dance floor and offering her a small smile. Things are still strained and a little weird, but I feel as though that bridge is starting to mend, and I hope one of these days we can find that easy, relaxed friendship we used to have.

Shifting my gaze away, I notice somebody watching me before noticing another and then another, and as my brows start to furrow, I realize it's not just a handful of people, but that I have the eyes of the whole room on me. My heart starts to pound, and for a moment, I wonder if I've accidentally tucked the back of my dress up into my thong when I find myself looking up at Zade. "What's going on?" I question, unease beginning to rattle me to my core. "Why's everybody looking at me?"

Pride shines in his eyes as he stares out at the people he once yearned to call his own. "They're looking to you for guidance," he tells me. "They're lost. Empire as a whole functions through leadership, and while these people as individuals in their personal lives are extremely powerful in their own right, in here, they're motivated by a strong leader, and you, Oakley Quinn," he says, pressing his lips into a forced smile. "You're their rightful leader."

I hold his stare a while longer, shaking my head. "I never asked for this," I tell him. "I can't lead these people."

"You can," he says, gently taking my shoulders and spinning me to face the crowd, encouragement thick in his proud tone. "I'll teach you how."

Oh, God. This is going to be a disaster.

Nerves pound through my veins as I make my way through the crowded bodies and toward the impressive stage, certain that I'm about to humiliate myself. I wasn't a public speaker in school. I never tried out for the debate team and always made sure I had an excuse for why I couldn't go to school on speech days.

Speaking in front of everyone during the service this afternoon was different. I was defending Zade, earning his freedom, and prosecuting my father. This right here? This is a fresh pile of steaming bullshit. If there were ever a time when I would end up humiliating myself, I'm sure it's bound to happen in the next few seconds.

Making it across the stage to the dais, I hide my hands behind it as they violently shake, and I try to remember who the hell I am. Then raising my chin, I focus my stare on the four loves of my life, and something just clicks inside of me, a newfound confidence telling me that I can do this.

"Today, as we came together as a congregation, lending one another our love and support, we farewelled the many lives that were tragically lost fourteen days ago. We grieved as a whole and we buried the loved ones who have so generously impacted our lives for the better. We will miss them, we will love them, we will never forget them."

With that, I hold up my glass of water toward the crowd and watch as they follow my lead before taking a sip. As I place my glass down on the dais, I continue. "Tonight we welcome a fresh beginning, we rebuild and rise as one, reborn out of the ashes. We celebrate those we have lost while vowing to make them proud with every step we take."

"Here, here," someone calls from the crowd, prompting another rise of everyone's glasses.

I go along with it before taking a moment, letting a hush fall over the crowd.

"My name is Oakley Quinn," I say proudly, holding my head up high and noticing the way Cara creeps toward me, realizing exactly what I'm about to do. "Many of you were introduced to me this afternoon at the Faders Bay cathedral. However, for those who were not in attendance, allow me to do it again." I pause, trying to enjoy this moment. "My name is Oakley Quinn, and I am the rightful heir of Empire—*the only living blood heir of Empire*, and as I stand before you, I state my intention to claim what is rightfully mine. I ask your approval, that you as a people, will allow me to stand at the head of this great organization and return it to its former glory, a united people, free of corruption."

Cheers boom through the room when Cara appears on the stage to my right, her strong tone easily flowing through the room. "I, Cara Thorne, stand before you as a representative of The Circle, the sole living member, acting as a voice for the people. I acknowledge your intention to command the leadership of Empire, and as both representative of The Circle and the people, we accept you, Miss Oakley Quinn, the rightful blood heir of our great organization, to rise as our loyal leader. And we, as a people, vow loyalty to you."

Then as one, every head bows to me, the boys included. "We vow our loyalty," every voice in the room declares.

And with that, I stare out at the function hall at the people watching me eagerly, having no idea where to go from here. Then as if on cue, they break into loud hollers and cheers, madly celebrating the birth of a new reign, a legacy free of corruption and fear.

I can't help but watch them as I stand here, a forced smile across my lips and an uneasiness in my heart. This was never anything I wanted. Empire has been thrust into my hands, and if I had my way, it would all be Zade's, and yet here we are.

Cara comes racing into me, throwing her arms around my shoulders and squeezing me tight. "Congratulations," she smiles. "This is so amazing. I can't believe that just happened."

"Yeah, me either," I scoff, in a world of disbelief, watching from the corner of my eye as the boys make their way up here. "So, what happens now? Am I going to have to perform some kind of cult-like ritual, drink the blood of a goat, or start chanting something ridiculous?"

Cara shakes her head as the boys finally reach us, Dalton's hands slipping around my waist, intently listening to what's being said. "I, uhh . . . I don't think so," Cara says. "The leadership ritual is typically something which is done prior to The Circle and the people declaring their acceptance of their new leader. That's been done, so you shouldn't be required to do anything."

"And I have the power to eradicate that kind of bullshit now?"

Zade nods. "Yes," he says. "There are some technical hoops that come along with every change to the bylaws but with only Cara holding a seat on The Circle, there shouldn't be any issues revising these laws."

"Okay," I say, my mind working overtime. "So anything I say goes?"

"One of the many perks of rising in power," Easton tells me. "These people are now your subjects. Your laws are their laws."

I nod, feeling everything starting to come together when I turn back to the dais, looking out at the celebrating crowd. I raise my chin, and as I prepare to address them again, I watch in amazement as they simply fall into place, not needing to say a word.

The room falls silent again, and I will myself to find that same confidence that burned through my chest only a moment ago. "I am unsure of when I will get the chance to address you all like this again, so I would like to take this moment to tell you that I strongly believe that every leader is stronger due to the team they have supporting them. And with that being said, as my first act as your new reigning leader, I will be reducing The Circle to only five of our most trusted members."

The boys glance at me, unsure what the hell I'm doing, and honestly, I think I'm a little unsure too.

"Cara Thorne," I start, prompting her to step forward before going on, indicating to the boys. "Dalton Eros." He steps forward, his hands clenched in front of him, his face like stone as I move on. "Easton Cross." Falling in line, Easton moves in beside Dalton before I indicate Sawyer, watching him move before I've even said a word. "Sawyer Thorne."

There's a round of applause after each name, and as I go to say the last name, I raise my chin a little higher. "And your fifth and final member of The Circle is myself, Oakley Quinn."

"What?" Cara grunts as confused murmurs begin to fill the room.

"The fuck are you doing?" Zade says, taking my elbow and trying to lead me away, only I resist, determined to see this through.

"I understand that many of you are confused by this move," I tell them, ready for a little raw honesty. "However if you knew me, if you knew my heart, you would understand that this is where I need to be, and as your leader, I am requesting that this decision be final and respected."

My gaze shifts around the room, really wishing I had that drink right about now. "I am very aware of my limits," I tell the people of Empire. "I know what I want and I understand my greatest desires, and this, standing before you as the leader of an organization I only learned about two months ago was never part of my plan. On the outside, I may appear to be a good leader, but I was not trained for this. Empire deserves a great leader, someone who will lead with honor, and while I believe I would do that, what kind of leader would it make me if I knew someone else could do it better and I held that back from you?"

The murmurs get louder as Zade's hand tightens on my elbow, more than ready to yank me away from the dais if something absurd decides to come flying out of my mouth.

Then raising my chin and declaring in a strong tone, I make my final declaration, writing it in stone and allowing the masses to hear the undeniable pride in my tone. "The real leader here is this man standing right beside me, and effective immediately, I renounce my leadership and hand it to Zade Alexander DeVil."

Gasps fill the room, hands flying to people's hearts as the boys gape at me in shock, never having expected that in a million years. A weight falls from my shoulders as everything settles into place, right where it was always meant to be, when Zade pulls me away, clutching my shoulder. "What the fuck are you doing?" he demands.

I look up into the dark, stormy eyes, seeing my whole world before me. "I may be the true blood heir, Zade, but you're the rightful leader. You always have been, and you don't need the same blood that runs through my veins to pulse through yours to know that you are exactly what Empire needs to rebuild and stand tall. You can breathe life back into this, Zade. I would have been good, but you . . . you are going to be amazing."

A wide smile pulls at the corner of his lips, and without even a moment of hesitation, he pulls me into him, those warm lips crushing down on mine as he kisses me deeply. His arms wrap around me, and for just a moment, the world fades around us and all that exists is us.

I feel his smile against my lips, and it's everything I knew it would be, but nothing will ever compare to watching the way that Zade steps up in front of his people, right where he's always belonged, his arms stretched out wide, welcoming a new DeVil legacy.

EPILOGUE

Oakley

THREE YEARS LATER

A soft groan rumbles through my chest as the small rose-shaped vibrator goes to town on my clit, my body arching off my bed. God, this thing is a little slice of forbidden heaven. But when the boys use it on me, it's so much better.

Unfortunately for them, this is a solo performance.

My hand skims across my breast, my nipple pebbled beneath my touch, and just as I feel my orgasm building deep within me, my world thoroughly about to be rocked by this magical little device, my phone sounds through the room, Dalton's ridiculous Rocky ringtone blasting in my ears.

My arm stretches out across my bed, feeling for the phone, and when I see a video call on the screen, a wicked grin tears across my face as I gingerly accept it.

"Where the fuck are ya, Firefly?" Dalton demands as I hold the phone back enough so that he can see my perfectly flushed cheeks and the way my bare body arches off my bed.

A satisfied groan tears through me as I see Dalton's handsome face, the boys all peering into the screen in their matching suits that have my mouth watering with need. God, there's nothing better than these men in suits. They are not the type of guys to just pick up the typical ninety-nine dollar special. No, when my guys pick out a suit, it's always flawless and well-fitted. The type of suits that have me coming undone. There's simply nothing better . . . apart from when they take those suits off, of course.

"I swear," I pant, the vibrator practically sucking my soul right out of my body. "I'm around the corner. Practically there already."

"Are you—" Sawyer says, leaning in closer to the screen before snatching it right out of Dalton's hand. "What's that noise?"

"Only the best thing that's ever happened to me," I tell him, a smug grin on my lips as I scooch up the bed and lean right down between my legs, fixing my phone at the end so they can watch the whole show.

"Goddamn," Dalton breathes. "Baby, come on! Without me?"

I grin wide. "And risk having you know just how much of a filthy whore I am when you're not around? No way."

Easton watches closely, his eyes flaming with need as his lips pull up at the corners. "Look how fucking close she is," he praises. "You got this, Pretty. That's right."

My eyes flutter, and I tip my head back before falling in love with the way they coach me through it, though there's no doubt that the moment they get me alone, I'll be punished for flying solo.

The heat kicks up a notch, and with their eyes on me, I feel like a fucking goddess, and as the little rose vibrates against my clit, my orgasm builds until it's finally set free, booming through my body and making me scream.

My head flies back as my thumb roams over my nipple, the intensity rocking through me and making my toes curl. "Awww fuck, Firefly. I need to be inside you."

God, what I wouldn't give to feel that too.

I start coming down from my high, collapsing against my bed, and I try to catch my breath, and the second the last remnant of my orgasm fades away, I close my eyes and reach for my phone, bringing it right up to my face. I kiss the screen, a smile pulling at my lips. "Okay, now I'm ready to leave," I tell them. "I'll see you in a minute."

And with that, I end the call and scramble out of bed before moving across to my closet and staring up at the most elegant wedding dress I've ever seen.

Shivers sail across my skin, and as I reach for the gown, butterflies stir in the pit of my stomach. Pride swells in my chest, the excitement pulsing through my veins. I never pictured myself as the blushing bride type, but every facet of my life has been an unpredictable, wild ride since the moment these boys came into my life.

Not wanting to be that bride who keeps her man waiting, despite very much already being that, I quickly pull the flawless gown on, needing a moment to get everything sitting just right. Then peering at my reflection in the full-length mirror, I fluff out my hair before checking my makeup and deciding that it doesn't get better than this.

After stepping into my heels, I blow out a breath, trying to expel the butterflies before finally stepping into the penthouse's private elevator. I press the button for the lobby, and it zooms right down to the bottom, and as I step out, I find Benny waiting for me, his hand already outstretched.

"Miss," he says, bowing his head. "Your chariot awaits."

I grin at my friend, rolling my eyes as I take his hand, feeling like an idiot for being so formal with him, when in reality, this man has watched me annihilate three juicy hamburgers, two super-sized Diet Cokes, and a serving of curly fries in the space of seven minutes, only to projectile vomit it back up across the living room. But what can I say? Shit happens, and on that day, my eyes were definitely bigger than my stomach.

Benny leads me out to the street, and a wide grin stretches across my face, finding one of Zade's most prized cars, the only one he'll refuse to allow me to drive—his Lamborghini Veneno, worth almost ten million dollars.

"Noooo," I grin, gaping at Benny. "Really?"

"Happy wedding day," he says before tossing me the keys.

I'm in the car and revving the engine within seconds, watching the way Benny cringes from the hotel valet stand. "Don't hurt her," he calls through the open window, but all I can do is crank up the music, feeling it vibrate right through my chest before miming to Benny, putting on a show of not being able to hear him. And with that, I hit the gas, taking off like a rocket toward my men.

Pulling up right at the cathedral doors, I cut the engine and smile as I see Zade stepping out into the early evening moonlight. He walks right over to the door before offering his hand and helping me out. His gaze sails over my body, taking in every inch of me. "Fuck, Lamb. You're radiant," he murmurs, leading me toward the cathedral doors. "Are you sure about this? I could steal you away."

"I've never been so sure," I tell him, scooping my arm through his as I hear the music from inside. I hold onto him tighter as he prepares to give me away, and not a moment later, the big double doors open and I see them at the end of the aisle, my three men waiting just for me.

Dalton, Sawyer, and Easton look at me as though I'm an angel sent here from the heavens, and the second I take my first step toward them, the butterflies fade away, leaving me with nothing but pure happiness.

The pews are packed, leaving people to stand around the edges, but all that matters right now is the man standing at the end, the one I will call my husband.

Zade walks me right to the end and I step right into Sawyer's arms, his lips coming down on mine in a gentle kiss. "You're fucking beautiful, Doll," he murmurs, those deadly green eyes lingering on mine. "Not gonna lie, seeing you like this, I'm kinda regretting letting this asshole beat me to the punch."

I laugh and kiss him again. "I thought you didn't care for big white weddings?"

"I don't," he tells me. "But I'd fucking do it just to be able to be the one you're walking toward."

"I mean, bigamy has got to be legal somewhere, right?"

Sawyer laughs and hands me off to Easton, who pulls me right against his chest, his hand dropping to my ass. "Let's make this quick, alright?" he says, his eyes sparkling with a wicked secret, and I know he only wants this done and out of the way because he vowed he would consummate my marriage before my new husband ever got the chance to. Though to be honest, I think he just wants to be able to claim he fucked another man's wife.

He can try all he wants, but nothing is keeping me from my husband tonight. Not even the promise of four delicious men all taking me at once.

I laugh and push up onto my tippy toes, gently kissing him. "Play nice," I warn as Zade steps up in the center of the stage, facing the congregation, more than ready to bind me in holy matrimony to one of the four loves of my life.

And as Easton releases me into Dalton's strong arms, I take his hands, the undeniable joy spreading across my face and making his eyes sparkle with unconditional love. "Are you ready for this?" he murmurs, his thumbs moving back and forth over my knuckles.

"I've never been so ready," I whisper, inching in a little closer. "Make me your wife, Dalton. Make me the happiest girl in the world."

And with that, Zade raises his chin, officially welcoming the people of Empire to the most extravagant wedding of the year.

THANKS FOR READING

If you enjoyed reading this book as much as I enjoyed writing it, please consider leaving an Amazon review to let me know. https://www.amazon.com/gp/product/B0BXQPKFR7

EMPIRE EXTRAS

Empire Pinterest Board

https://pin.it/6DZLmZN

Cara's Smut_XPERT Bookstagram

https://www.instagram.com/smut_xpert/

Playlist

https://open.spotify.com/playlist/1NBPuMI15YFObcqC-716Qf0?si=fcb9db9b46084fa1

STALK ME!

Join me online with the rest of the stalkers!!
I swear, I don't bite. Not unless you say please!

Facebook Reader Group

www.facebook.com/SheridansBookishBabes

Facebook Page

www.facebook.com/sheridan.anne.author1

Instagram

www.instagram.com/Sheridan.Anne.Author

TikTok

www.tiktok.com/@Sheridan.Anne.Author

Subscribe to my Newsletter

https://landing.mailerlite.com/webforms/landing/a8q0y0

Hive Social!

@SheridanAnne

MORE BY SHERIDAN ANNE

www.amazon.com/Sheridan-Anne/e/B079TLXN6K

YOUNG ADULT / NEW ADULT DARK ROMANCE

Broken Hill High | Haven Falls | Broken Hill Boys
Aston Creek High | Rejects Paradise | Boys of Winter
Depraved Sinners | Bradford Bastard | Empire

NEW ADULT SPORTS ROMANCE

Kings of Denver | Denver Royalty | Rebels Advocate

CONTEMPORARY ROMANCE (standalones)

Play With Fire | Until Autumn (Happily Eva Alpha World)

PARANORMAL ROMANCE

Slayer Academy [Pen name - Cassidy Summers]

Printed in Great Britain
by Amazon

25766773R00227